Sleeping
by Sheri

'I can't wait until this phoney affair is over.'

'You and me both.' But that didn't stop him from wanting her.

She gave him a haughty look. 'What are you doing?'

'Walking you to your door.'

'Don't bother. I can manage just fine without you.'

'Too bad.' He strolled beside her. The brownstone was at the other end of the street, and he was determined to get her there. And, he supposed, to annoy her on the way. When they reached the brownstone, he grabbed her and pushed her against the door.

'Don't you dare—'

He cut her off with a kiss. A brutal, desperate, open-mouthed kiss.

She didn't fight him. She took his tongue with the same fury, the same passion, the same angry heat that welled inside him. And then she shoved him away.

'I hate you,' she said.

'I hate you, too.' He shot the words back, aching to make love to her.

Without another word, he turned and walked away.

Taming the Beastly MD
by Elizabeth Bevarly

ဢ ✺ ဢ

'Guess I'll be the one to bring it up then,' he said dryly.

'Bring what up?' she tried again. Futilely, she soon learned.

'What happened out on the terrace tonight,' he said plainly. 'You…kissing me.'

'I'm not sure what happened,' she told him honestly. 'I just…' She gave a half-hearted shrug. 'It seemed like the thing to do at the time.'

'So if I kissed *you* this time, what would happen?'

A splash of heat spilled through Rita's mid-section, not just because of the question itself, but because of the way he uttered it—as if he fully intended to find out.

She swallowed with some difficulty. 'Why, um, why would you want to do that?'

'It just seems like the right thing to do,' he told her. And then he was kissing her, and she was kissing him back, and a swirl of tempestuous hunger was eddying up inside her.

Oh, dear heaven, she thought. What was happening? And why couldn't she make it stop? Why didn't she *want* it to stop?

Sleeping with Her Rival
SHERI WHITEFEATHER

Taming the Beastly MD
ELIZABETH BEVARLY

SILHOUETTE®
DESIRE™

*Silhouette, Silhouette Desire and Colophon
are registered trademarks of Harlequin Books S.A.,
used under licence.*

*First published in Great Britain 2004
Silhouette Books, Eton House, 18-24 Paradise Road,
Richmond, Surrey TW9 1SR*

The publisher acknowledges the copyright holders of the
individual works as follows:

Sleeping with Her Rival © Harlequin Books S.A. 2003
Taming the Beastly MD © Harlequin Books S.A. 2003

*Special thanks and acknowledgement are given to
Sheri Whitefeather and Elizabeth Bevarly for their contribution to
the Dynasties: The Barones series.*

ISBN 0 373 04977 3

51-0304

*Printed and bound in Spain
by Litografia Rosés S.A., Barcelona*

♥ SILHOUETTE®
DESIRE™

are proud to introduce

DYNASTIES:
THE BARONES

*Meet the wealthy Barones—caught in a
web of danger, deceit and…desire!*

Twelve exciting stories in six 2in1 volumes:

SLEEPING WITH HER RIVAL
by
Sheri WhiteFeather

SHERI WHITEFEATHER

lives in Southern California and enjoys ethnic dining, American Indian powwows and visiting art galleries and vintage clothing stores near the beach. Since her one true passion is writing, she is thrilled to be a part of the Silhouette Desire line. When she isn't writing, she often reads until the small hours of the morning.

Sheri is married to a Muscogee Creek silversmith. They have a son, a daughter and a trio of cats—domestic and wild. She loves to hear from her readers. You may write to her at: PO Box 17146, Anahaim, California 92817, USA.

To Silhouette, for inviting me to do this project.
To the other DYNASTIES authors and our editor,
Mavis Allen, for being such a joy to work with.
To Frank Cardinal, my *primo* dad, for introducing me
to Italian delis, Italian words and Italian humour.
To Rick Bundy, my very special second dad, for
inspiring the classic Corvette and the *Caine Mutiny* in
this book. To Joanne Rice, my cousin, and Flora and
Mary Yacabucci, my great aunts, for their unwavering
support. And, finally, I would like to acknowledge two
remarkable teenagers—Brenna, my beautiful 'new'
daughter, and Nikki, my 'old-soul' son.
I love you both.

One

Gina Barone wasn't in the mood to party, but she sipped a glass of chardonnay—praying it wouldn't irritate her stomach—and worked her way through the charity mixer, feigning an I'm-in-control smile.

She knew it was important to be seen, to hold her head high, especially now. Gina was the vice president of marketing and public relations for Baronessa Gelati, a family-owned Italian ice cream empire—a company being shredded by the media.

Something Gina felt responsible for.

Moving through the crowd, she nodded to familiar faces. Although she'd come here to make her presence known, she thought it best to avoid lengthy conversations. A polite greeting was about all she could handle. And with that in mind, she would sample the food, sip a tiny bit of wine and then wait until an appropriate amount of time passed before she said her goodbyes and made a gracious exit.

"Gina?"

She stopped to acknowledge Morgan Chancellor, a business associate who flitted around the social scene like a butterfly, fluttering from one partygoer to the next.

"Oh, hello. You look lovely, Morgan. That's a beautiful dress."

"Why, thank you." The other woman batted her lashes, then leaned in close. "Do you know who asked about you?"

Gina suspected plenty of people were talking about her, about the fiasco she'd arranged last month, the Valentine's Day publicity event that had ended in disaster.

Baronessa had been launching a new flavor called passionfruit, offering a free tasting at their corporate headquarters. But pandemonium erupted when people tasted the gelato.

An unknown culprit had spiked the ice cream with a mouth-burning substance, which they'd soon discovered was habanero peppers—the hottest chilies in the world.

And worse yet, a friend of Gina's who'd stopped by the event at her invitation had suffered from an attack of anaphylaxis, a serious and rapid allergic reaction to the peppers.

She'd nearly killed someone. Inadvertently, maybe, but the shame and the guilt were still hers to bear.

Gina gazed at Morgan, forcing herself to smile. "So, who asked about me?"

"Flint Kingman."

Her smile cracked and fell. "He's here?"

"Yes. He asked me to point you out."

"Did he?" Gina glanced around the room. The crème de la crème of Boston society mingled freely, but somewhere, lurking amid black cocktail dresses and designer suits, was her newly acquired rival.

Anxious, she fingered the diamond-and-pearl choker around her neck, wishing she hadn't worn it. Flint's reputation strangled her like a noose.

The wonder boy. The renowned spin doctor. The prince of the PR world.

Her family expected her to work with him, to take his advice. Why couldn't they allow her the dignity of repairing the media damage on her own? Why did they have to force Flint Kingman on her?

He'd left a slew of messages at the office, insisting she return his calls. So finally she'd summoned the strength to do just that. But their professional conversation had turned heated, and she'd told him to go to hell.

And now he was here.

"Would you mind pointing him out to me?" she asked Morgan.

"Certainly." The redhead turned to glance over her shoulder, then frowned. "He was over there, with that group of men, but he's gone now."

Gina shrugged, hoping to appear calm and refined—a far cry from the turmoil churning inside.

"I'm sure he'll catch up with me later," she said, wondering if he'd attended this party just to intimidate her.

If he didn't crawl out of the woodwork and introduce himself, then he would probably continue to spy on her from afar, making her ulcer act up. It was a nervous condition she hid from her family.

"If you'll excuse me, Morgan, I'm going to check out the buffet."

"Go right ahead. If I see Flint, I'll let you know."

"Thanks." Gina headed to the buffet table to indulge in hors d'oeuvres, to nibble daintily on party foods, to pretend that she felt secure enough to eat in public. No way would she let Flint run her off, even if she wanted to dart out the door.

As she studied the festive spread, her stomach tightened. This wasn't the bland diet her doctor recommended, but what choice did she have?

The shrimp dumplings would probably hit her digestive

system like lead balls, but she placed them on her plate next to a scatter of crab-stuffed mushrooms and a small helping of artichoke dip.

Balancing her food and a full glass of wine, she searched for a sheltered spot. The posh hotel banquet room had been decorated for a cocktail gathering with a small grouping of tables and lots of standing room.

Gina snuggled up to a floor-to-ceiling window, set her drink on a nearby planter ledge and turned to gaze at the city. Rain fell from the sky, and lights twinkled like pinwheels, casting sparks in the brisk March air.

She stood, with her plate in hand, admiring the rain-dampened view. And then she heard a man speak her name.

The low, vodka-on-the-rocks voice crept up her spine and sent her heartbeat racing. She recognized Flint Kingman's tone instantly.

Preparing to face him, she turned.

He gazed directly into her eyes, and she did her damnedest to maintain her composure.

She'd expected tall and handsome, but he was more than that. So much more.

In an Armani suit and Gucci loafers, he stood perfectly groomed, as cocky and debonair as his reputation. Yet beneath the Boston polish was an edge as hard as his name, as sharp and dangerous as the tip of a flint.

He exuded sexuality. Pure, raw, primal heat.

She steadied her plate with both hands to keep her food from spilling onto the floor. Men didn't make her nervous. But this one did.

He didn't speak; he just watched her through a pair of amber-flecked eyes.

"Aren't you going to introduce yourself?" she said, her posture stiff, her fingers suddenly numb.

A cynical smile tugged at the corner of his lips, and a strand of chocolate-brown hair fell rebelliously across his forehead.

"Nice try. But you know exactly who I am."

"Oh, forgive me. You must be that Bowie guy."

He smoothed his hair into place, his mouth still set in a sardonic curl. "Flint. Bowie is a different kind of knife."

And both would cut just as sharp, she thought, just as brutal.

Like a self-assured predator, he moved a little closer, just enough to put his pheromones between them. She took a deep breath, and the sore in her stomach ignited into a red-hot flame.

Damn her nerves, she thought. And damn him.

"I'll stop by your office on Tuesday," he said. "At two."

"I'll check my calendar and get back to you," she countered, wishing she could dig through her purse for an antacid.

He shook his head. "Tuesday at two. This isn't up for negotiation."

Gina bristled, hating Flint Kingman and everything he represented. Would the stress ever end? The guilt? The professional humiliation? "Are you always this pushy?"

"I'm aggressive, not pushy."

"You could have fooled me."

She lifted her chin a notch, and Flint studied the stubborn gesture. Gina Barone was a feminine force to be reckoned with—a long, elegant body, a mass of wavy brown hair swept into a proper chignon and eyes the color of violets.

A cold shoulder and a hot temper. He'd heard she was an ice princess. A woman much too defensive. A woman who competed with men. And now she would be competing with him.

She gave him an annoyed look, and he glanced at her untouched hors d'oeuvres. "Don't you like the food?"

"I haven't had the chance to eat it."

"Why? Because I interrupted you?" He reached out, snagged a mushroom off her plate and popped it into his mouth, knowing damn well his blatant behavior would rile her even further.

Those violet eyes turned a little violent, and he suspected she was contemplating a childish act, like flinging the rest of the mushrooms at him. He pictured them hitting his chest like crab-stuffed bullets. "I don't have cooties, Miss Barone."

"You don't have any manners, either."

"Of course I do." He went after a dumpling this time, ate it with relish, then reached into his jacket for a monogrammed handkerchief and wiped his hands with casual elegance. This party was too damn prissy, he thought. And so was Gina Barone. Flint was sick to death of the superficial society in which he lived. He used to thrive on this world, but now it seemed like a lie.

Then again, why wouldn't it? After all, he'd just uncovered a family secret, a skeleton in his closet that made his entire life seem like a lie.

Still eyeing him with disdain, Gina set her plate on the planter ledge. "Thanks to you, I lost my appetite."

She didn't have one to begin with, he thought. The trouble at Baronessa Gelati must be weighing heavily on her inexperienced shoulders. She'd never outfoxed a public scandal, particularly something of this magnitude.

Flint had, of course. Scandals were his specialty. But not family secrets. He couldn't outfox the lie in which he'd been raised.

He dragged a hand through his hair and then realized that he'd zoned out, losing sight of his priority. Nothing, not even the turmoil in his life, should interfere with business.

Pulling himself into the moment, he stared at Gina.

Did she resent his take-charge attitude? Or did the truth upset her? The fact that he was more qualified for the job?

Truthfully, he didn't care. He was damn good at what he did and he'd worked hard to prove his worth.

"Stop looking at me like that," she said.

"Like what?"

"Like you're superior."

"Men are superior," he responded, deliberately baiting her.

"And that's why Adam ate the apple?" she asked. "Because he had brains?"

"What kind of question is that?"

She rolled her eyes. "A rhetorical one. Everyone knows Adam ate the apple because of Eve."

Which meant what? That she thought the male brain hinged on what was behind his zipper? Or in Adam's case, a fig leaf?

Flint assessed his companion. The lights from the city shimmered behind her, as white and bright as the diamond brooch on the front of her choker. It was an exceptional piece, but he would have preferred an unadorned view of her neck. She had smooth, touchable skin, kissed by the sun and boasting her Sicilian roots.

His gaze slipped slower, to the swell of her breasts. No matter how high a man's IQ was, his brain did get scrambled now and then. Flint was no exception.

He lifted his gaze. "I'm not offended, Miss Barone."

"About what?"

"About you thinking my brain is in my pants."

"Well, you should be."

"And you should offer me a shiny red apple." He paused for effect. "I'll take a big, juicy bite if you will."

Gina glared at him.

Enjoying the game, he flashed a flirtatious smile. Sparring with her was actually kind of fun. And it certainly beat crying into his beer.

"I'll be damned if I'm going to work with you," she said.

He tilted his head, wondering what she would look like

with her hair rioting around her face, framing her in untamed glory. "As I understand it, you don't have a choice."

"Don't bet on it," she quipped.

"I'll see you on Tuesday. At two o'clock," he reminded her before he walked away.

His lovely nemesis was quite a challenge. But he wasn't worried about it. Sooner or later, she'd give in and let him fix the disaster in her life.

Even if he couldn't fix his own.

Gina awakened with a start the following morning. She sat up and squinted, then hugged a pillow to her chest.

She'd actually dreamed about Flint Kingman.

And erotic dream. An illusion of mist and midnight, of his long, lean, muscled torso gleaming in the rain.

While she'd slept through a stormy night, he'd invaded her bedroom, her private sanctuary.

Gina reached for her robe and wrapped herself in terry cloth. Everything seemed different now. The cherry armoire and big brass bed. The hardwood floors and Turkish rugs.

With a deep breath, she turned and peered out the blinds. Thank God, it wasn't raining anymore. She never wanted it to rain again. Not if it meant revisiting that half-naked image of Flint, his head tipped back, water running in rivulets down his stomach and into the waistband of slim black trousers.

Gina tightened her robe. She'd dreamed of him in the clothes he'd worn last night, only he'd been standing on the rooftop of the hotel, allowing her to undress him.

Damn that sexy smile of his. And damn that cocky attitude.

She had two days before their meeting, two days to arm herself with information. She knew virtually nothing about Flint, but she suspected he knew plenty about her.

He'd probably done his homework weeks ago, analyzing

his opponent, charting her strengths and weaknesses, her successes, her failures.

Well, at least her dreams were her own. And so was her ulcer. She doubted Flint had pried into her medical records.

She crossed the living room, entered the kitchen and eyed the coffeepot. It sat on a bright, white counter, luring her with the temptation of a hard, strong dose of caffeine.

With a practical sigh, she poured herself a glass of milk instead, then reached for the phone.

Seated at the breakfast nook, she looked up Morgan Chancellor's number, hoping the socialite was available. Morgan wasn't a vicious gossip. She didn't spread unholy rumors, but she seemed to know everybody's business. And Gina intended to discuss Flint with someone willing to answer questions about him.

Morgan picked up on the fifth ring. Gina started a friendly conversation, asking the other woman if she'd enjoyed the charity mixer.

Morgan babbled for a while, and Gina pictured the redhead's no-nonsense husband scanning the *Boston Globe* at their elegant dining room table, shutting out his wife's perky voice.

Weaving her way toward the man of the hour, Gina said, "By the way, Flint Kingman finally caught up with me."

"Really? So, what do you think of him?"

Gina shoved away the image of his dream-induced, rain-shrouded body. "I'm not sure. I can't quite figure him out." When the other woman breathed into the receiver, she asked, "What do you know about him, Morgan?"

"Hmm. Let's see. His father is an advertising mogul, and his stepmother is absolutely riveting. Of course his real mother was equally stunning. She was a Hollywood starlet, but she died when Flint was a baby."

Intrigued, Gina adjusted the phone. "Was she famous?"

"No, but she should have been. Supposedly she was really talented."

Gina tried to picture the woman who'd given Flint Kingman life. "What was her name?"

"Danielle Wolf. But there isn't a lot of old press about her. If you're really curious about Flint, you should read up on Tara Shaw."

"The movie star?" The aging bombshell? The world-famous blonde? "Why? Was she friends with his mother?"

Morgan made a crunching sound, as if she were eating breakfast while she talked. "Oh, no. It's nothing like that. Flint used to work for Tara."

"So? He's a PR consultant. That's perfectly understandable."

The crunching sound stopped. "He had an affair with her, Gina."

"Oh, my goodness." Flint and Tara Shaw? The screen goddess of the 1970s? She had to be twice his age.

Morgan resumed eating. "Some reports say she broke his heart. Others say he broke hers. And some say they were both just playing around, tearing up the sheets for the fun of it."

Gina shifted in her seat, nearly spilling her milk. She grabbed the glass before it tipped over. "When did this happen?"

"When he was fresh out of college. I'm surprised you didn't hear about it."

"Normally, I don't pay attention to things like that. I've never really followed the Hollywood scene."

"Well, I do," Morgan said. "Their affair didn't last long, but it created quite a scandal."

"Bigger than the one going on in my life?"

"Much bigger."

That was all it took. Gina spent the rest of the morning on the Internet, pulling up old articles on Tara Shaw and her wild, young lover.

While driving past the prestigious homes in Beacon Hill, Flint got the sudden urge to call Tara, to tell her what was going on.

He glanced at his car phone and realized foolishly that he didn't have her number. He hadn't spoken to Tara Shaw in over eight years. Flint had left Hollywood without looking back.

Besides, what the hell would he say to her? And what would her new husband think if her old lover just happened to ring her up?

With a squeal of his tires, he turned onto a familiar street and pulled into his parents' driveway, knowing his dad would be home on a Sunday afternoon.

Flint and his father saw each other often. They worked in the same bustling high-rise, but these days they rarely spoke, at least not about important issues.

He unlocked the door with his key, the same key he'd had since he was a teenager. For eighteen years, this elegant mansion had been his home.

He stood in the marbled foyer for a moment, catching his reflection in a beveled mirror. It wasn't a cold house, completely void of emotion, but it didn't present a warm, fuzzy feeling, either.

But then how could it? Especially now?

He crossed the salon, passing Chippendale settees, ornate tables and gilded statues. The Kingmans were a successful family, but money didn't necessarily make people happy.

He located his dad in the garden room, a timber-and-glass structure flourishing with greenery. Shimmering vines twined around redwood trellises, and colorful buds bloomed in a shower of floral abundance, thriving in the controlled environment.

James Kingman, a tall, serious man, with a square jaw

and wide shoulders, enjoyed growing flowers, and he tended them with a gentle hand.

Today he hovered over a cluster of lady's slippers, orchids as beautiful and beguiling as their fairy-tale name.

Flint shed his jacket, and the older man looked up.

"Well, hello," he said, acknowledging his son's presence. "What brings you by?"

You, me and my mom, he thought. *The past, the present, the pain.* "I was hoping we could talk."

"About what?"

"My mother."

James shook head. "I don't want to rehash all of that again."

"But I want to talk about it."

"There's nothing more to talk about. I told you everything. Just forget about it, let it go."

Let it go? Forget about it?

Two weeks ago Flint had stumbled upon a horrible secret, and now the truth haunted him like a ghost. "You lied to me all those years, Dad."

James shifted his stance. He wore jeans and a denim shirt, but he was impeccably groomed—a man of wealth and taste. "I did it to protect you. Why won't you accept that?"

"Just tell me this much. Does *Nĭsh'kĭ* know the truth?" he asked, thinking about his Cheyenne grandmother.

"Yes, she knew when it happened. It broke her heart."

And now it's breaking mine, Flint thought.

"You can't bring this up to your grandmother," his dad said. "It wouldn't be right."

Flint nodded. As a rule, the Cheyenne didn't speak freely of the dead, and *Nĭsh'kĭ* adhered to the old way. "Is she aware that I came upon the truth?"

"Yes, I told her. But she didn't want to discuss it."

No one wanted to discuss it, no one but Flint. Didn't they understand that he needed to grieve? To come to terms with his role in all of this?

"It isn't fair," he said.

"Life isn't fair," James replied, using a cliché that only made Flint feel worse.

In the next instant they both fell silent. Water trickled from an ornamental fountain, mimicking the patter of rain.

Flint glanced at the glass ceiling and noticed dark clouds floating across a hazy blue sky.

He shrugged into his jacket. "I better go. I've got things to do."

James met his troubled gaze. "Don't be angry, son."

Flint looked at his dad, at the blond hair turning a silvery shade of gray. He'd inherited his dad's hazel eyes, but his dark hair and copper skin had come from his mother. The woman he wasn't allowed to talk about.

"I'm not," he said. It wasn't anger eating away at his soul. It was pain. "I'll see you tomorrow at the office. Give Faith a kiss for me," he added, referring to his stepmother.

"She'll be sorry she missed you."

"I know." He loved Faith Kingman. She'd raised him since he was ten years old, but she wasn't willing to talk about this, either. Not if it meant betraying her husband.

Flint left his parents' house, and James went back to his flowers, hiding behind their vibrant colors and velvet petals.

On Tuesday, Gina wore what she considered a power suit to the office. The blouse matched her eyes, the tailored black jacket nipped at her waist and the slim-fitting skirt rode just above her knees. But her pumps, bless them, were her secret weapon. When she strode through Baronessa's corporate halls, they made a determined, confident click, giving her an air of feminine authority.

The fourth floor of the chrome-and-glass structure was Gina's domain, and she often gazed out the windows, drawing strength from the city.

Today she needed all she could get.

She glanced at the clock on the wall. Flint would be here any minute.

Gina moved in front of her desk and remained standing, waiting anxiously for his arrival. She'd been rehearsing this moment in her mind for two days, practicing her lines, her gestures.

She knew plenty about Flint Kingman now. She'd even uncovered a few facts about his mother. Danielle Wolf, a half-Indian beauty from the Cheyenne reservation, had left home to pursue an acting career. Five years later she'd abandoned Hollywood to become a wife and mother and then died in a car accident a month after her son was born.

Gina intended to rent the B movies Danielle had co-starred in. She suspected Flint had inherited his mother's adventurous spirit. It wouldn't hurt to analyze every aspect of her opponent's personality, particularly if she was going to kick him off this harrowing project.

Gina's secretary buzzed. She pressed the intercom. "Yes?"

"Mr. Kingman is here."

She let out the breath she'd been holding. "Send him in."

A minute later he strode through the door in a gray suit and silver-gray tie, his thick dark hair combed away from his face. Suddenly Gina could see the Native American in him—the rich color of his skin, the killer cheekbones, the deep-set eyes. They looked more brown than gold today, and she realized they were actually a stunning, ever-changing shade of hazel.

He flashed a cocky grin, and she reached for the apple

on her desk and tossed it to him. Or at him, she supposed, since she'd heaved it like a shiny red baseball.

Caught off guard, he fumbled, dropped his briefcase and retrieved the apple in the nick of time.

The grin returned to his lips. "The forbidden fruit, Miss Barone?"

"Consider it a parting gift."

He arched an eyebrow. "Am I going somewhere?"

"Anywhere but here," she said, leaning against her desk like a corporate vamp. "I told you before that I'm not working with you."

He picked up his briefcase and came forward. As self-assured as ever, he pulled up a chair and sat down, studying the apple.

"What are you doing?" she asked.

"Checking for worms."

She smiled in spite of herself. "I'm not that evil."

He lifted his gaze, and her smile fell. Why did he have to look at her like that? So sly, so sexy. She could almost feel his rain-slicked, dream-induced skin.

"All women are evil. And beautiful and clever in their own way," he said. "I enjoy females."

"So I've heard." She walked around to the other side of her desk and sank into her leather chair, hoping to appear more powerful than she felt.

"You're holding my dating record against me?" he asked.

"You mean your scorecard? Let's face it, Mr. Kingman. You're a player. You drive a fast, ferocious, racy red Corvette, keep company with bimbos and then notch your bedpost after each insensitive conquest."

He gave her a level stare. "Nice try, but that's not quite accurate. You see, I have a brass bed, and the metal is a little hard to notch."

Gina steeled her nerves. She had a brass bed, too. The one he'd invaded. "You indulged in an affair with a movie star twice your age."

Something flashed in his eyes. Pain? Anger? Male pride? She couldn't be sure.

"Aren't you going to defend yourself?" she asked, confused by his silence.

Suddenly Flint Kingman, the confident, carefree spin doctor, was impossible to read.

Two

Gina waited for him to respond, but he just sat there, staring at her.

"Well?" she asked, unnerved by those unwavering eyes.

Finally he blinked, sending sparks of amber shooting through his irises. "What do you want me to say? I was only twenty-two at the time."

Which meant what? That he'd actually bccn in love? Or that he'd been too young and too wild to control his sexual urges?

"How are you going to polish Baronessa's reputation when your own reputation isn't exactly glowing?" she asked, refusing to let it go. Flint had been a virile twenty-two-year-old, and Tara had been a dazzling role model for forty-three-year-olds everywhere, proving women could be desirable at any age. But their relationship still bothered Gina.

He squared his shoulders. "I'm more than qualified to pull Baronessa out of this mess."

"And so am I." Even if she had been the one who'd unwittingly dragged Baronessa into it.

"Really?" He placed his briefcase on his lap and opened it, and with the flick of his wrists he scattered a stack of supermarket tabloids across Gina's desk.

The headlines hit her square in the chest.

Mysterious Curse Destroys Ice Cream Empire.

Mafia Mayhem in Boston. Will the Sicilian-Born Barones Survive?

Passion Fruit Versus Passion Death. Who Tried to Murder an Innocent Man?

"I've read these," she said. "And they're filled with lies. That curse is nonsense. My family isn't connected to the mob. And the man who suffered an allergic reaction to the peppers recovered with no ill effects."

"Maybe so, but just stating the facts isn't enough. What's your plan to counter the negative press, Miss Barone? This is some pretty heavy-duty stuff."

She shoved the tabloids aside, and her ulcer sprang to life, her stomach acids eating a hole right through her, creating a familiar pain.

"I intend to hold a contest," she said. "Something that will get the public involved."

"Like what? Name That Curse?"

Smart-ass, she thought, narrowing her eyes at him. "More like create a new gelato flavor. Baronessa will invite the public to come up with a flavor to replace passionfruit. The winner of the contest and the new flavor will get lots of press, plenty of positive media attention."

He sat quietly, mulling over her idea. Finally he said, "That's a great marketing tool, but it's too soon for a contest. First we need something juicier. A bigger scandal, something that will make the press forget all about that pepper fiasco."

"And I suppose you've already cooked up the perfect scandal."

He smoothed his hair, a gesture she'd seen more than once. But he did have that rebellious strand, the Elvis lock that repeatedly fell forward.

"Truthfully," he admitted, "I haven't zeroed in on the perfect scandal, but when I do, you'll be the first to know."

"I don't like the idea," she told him. "All we'll be doing is replacing one set of lies for another. That doesn't cut it for me."

"Too bad. It's the way to go. Believe me, I've worked this angle before." He reached for one of the tabloids. "So what's the deal on this curse?"

Gina pressed against the pain, the gnawing, burning sensation in her stomach. "Aren't you supposed to know all of this already?"

"I want to hear it in your words. I want your take on the curse."

"I already told you, it's nonsense." She rose and walked to the bar. Not because she was a gracious hostess, but because she needed to coat the burn. "Would you like something to drink?" she asked.

He shook his head, and she poured herself a glass of milk. "It does a body good," she said, when he eyed the white liquid curiously.

He roamed his gaze over her, sweeping her curves with masculine appreciation. "So I see."

Her pulse shot up her arm. *Don't flirt with me,* she thought. *Don't look at me with those bedroom eyes.*

But he did. He watched her. Closely. They way he'd watched her in that dream, just seconds before she'd undressed him.

Neither spoke. They stared at each other, caught in one those awkward, sexually stirring moments.

Finally, he broke eye contact, and she brought the milk to her lips. The thick, creamy drink slid down her throat.

"The curse," Flint reminded her, his voice a little too rough.

Gina took her seat, struggling for composure. This felt like a curse, she thought. This impossible attraction.

"It started with my grandfather," she said. "He jilted a girl who'd wanted to marry him, and on Valentine's Day, he eloped with my grandmother instead. So the other girl put a curse on my grandparents and their descendants. She vowed that misery would strike on their anniversary, marking Valentine's Day a holiday of disaster."

"Then why did you schedule the passionfruit tasting on February fourteenth?" he asked. "That seems a little risky to me."

"Because I was determined to prove that curse wrong. Besides, a flavor called passionfruit made a nice Valentine's Day promotion." She drank some more milk. "Or it should have."

He gathered the tabloids and put them into his briefcase. "You lied to me, Miss Barone. You don't think the curse is nonsense. You believe in it now."

Steeped in guilt, she defended herself. "I'm not a superstitious woman, but I should have been more cautious. Some unfortunate things have happened to my family on Valentine's Day over the years, but those events seemed like coincidence. A fluke here and there."

"Don't worry about it," he said. "I'll repair the damage."

"No, I will," she countered.

He shrugged, then taunted her with that slow, sensual smile, reminding her that she'd dreamed about him.

When he stood to leave, she heard a sudden burst of rain hit the windows behind her.

A cool, hard, male-driven rain.

After Flint departed, Gina went straight to her brother's office. Nicholas held the prestigious COO title, the chief operations officer, at Baronessa Gelati.

He stood well over six feet, with a strong, athletic build,

jet-black hair and blue eyes. Women, including his new wife and daughter, found him irresistible. Gina, however, considered herself immune to his charm. He'd abandoned his playboy ways for a blissful marriage, but he still had a high dose of testosterone running through his veins, which made him difficult to manipulate.

"I want you to fire Flint Kingman," she said.

Nicholas sat behind his desk and rolled his impressive shoulders, looking like the powerful corporate male he was. "Why?"

Because I dreamed about him, she wanted to say. *He invaded my mind, my bed.* "Because he's going to do this company more harm than good."

"How so?"

"He intends to cook up a phony scandal to divert the press."

"That's what he does, Gina. He's a spin doctor and a damn good one. I trust his instincts."

"What about my instincts?"

"You're a bright, capable woman, but this is his area of expertise."

She sat across from her brother and picked up a rubber band off his desk, wishing she could flick it at him. He was eight years her senior, and he'd always treated her like a child. He used to call her noodle head because curls sprang from her scalp like spiral pasta.

Gina glared at Nicholas and smoothed her hair. These days she tamed her curls in a professional chignon. "So you're taking Flint's side?"

He leaned forward, trapping her gaze. "His side? You're not turning this into a gender war, are you?"

She thought about the apple, the forbidden fruit, she'd tossed at Flint this afternoon. "He bosses me around."

"Probably because you're fighting him every step of the way. You've got to curb your temper, Gina."

She stretched the rubber band, wishing she had the courage to let it fly.

"We brought Flint in as a consultant." Nicholas went on. "The idea is for the two of you to work together."

"Fine." She could see this was going nowhere. Coming to her feet, she blew a frustrated breath. Rain still pounded against the windows, reminding her that Flint controlled the weather, too.

Would she ever get that image out of her mind? That long, lean, water-slicked body?

"And don't go running to Dad about this," Nicholas warned.

"I don't intend to," she responded, trying to sound more grown-up than she felt. "I'll work with Flint if I have to. But I won't let him call all the shots."

Nicholas grinned. "Spoken like a true woman."

"And don't you forget it." She turned to march out of his office, her feminine armor—the tailored suit and high-heeled pumps—securely in place.

"I love you, noodle head," he said before she reached the door.

She stopped and smiled. She loved Nicholas Barone, too. Even if he was her big, brawny, know-it-all brother.

Hours later Gina drove home, her windshield wipers clapping to the rhythm of the rain. She lived in a brownstone in the North End, a family-owned, renovated building she shared with two of her sisters. They each had their own sprawling apartment, but they often gathered in the community living room on the first floor to curl up with a bowl of extra-buttered popcorn and talk.

She parked her car and walked to the front of the brownstone, only to find Flint sitting on the stoop, his overcoat flapping in the wind.

She stopped dead in her tracks and stared at him. He looked up, his face speckled with rain, his waterlogged hair slick and shiny.

"It didn't work, did it?" he said.

"Excuse me?"

"Your brother wouldn't fire me, would he?"

She moved forward, taking shelter from the storm. How did he know that she'd complained to Nicholas? Was she that predictable?

He rose, attacking her with that insufferable smile. "I want you to have dinner with me tonight."

Her heart pole-vaulted its way to her throat. "What? Why?"

"So we can get used to each other. We've got a lot of work ahead of us. And there's no point in wasting time."

She snuggled deeper into her coat. "But it's raining."

He gave her an odd look. "You don't eat when it rains?"

Of course, she did. She just didn't relish the idea of spending time in his company, particularly with water falling from the sky.

Then again, maybe a business dinner would take the edge off. Maybe it would help her forget that other image. "Fine. I'll have a meal with you." But he'd better not steal food from her plate, she thought.

"Meet me at the Beef and Bull around seven," he said. It's a steak house on—"

"I know where it is," she interrupted. "And I'll be there at eight."

"Seven-thirty," he challenged.

"Eight," she countered in a firm tone. She needed time to bathe, to change, to fix her rain-drizzled hair.

"All right," he said, giving in with a grumble. "But don't be late."

Gina reached for her keys and sent him a triumphant smile. She'd finally gotten her way. On a small scale, maybe, but it was a start.

At precisely eight o'clock, Flint arrived at the Beef and Bull, a quiet, dimly lit steak house decorated with knotty-pine walls and Western antiques.

He approached the hostess and gave her his name. "I'm expecting a companion," he said. "Has she arrived yet?"

The young woman shook her head. "No, Mr. Kingman, she hasn't."

He gestured to a shadowy corner in the waiting room. "I'll just kick back over there until she gets here."

The hostess nodded and smiled. He returned her polite smile and moved out of the way, giving the people behind him a chance to check their reservation.

Settling onto a leather cushion, he stretched his legs out in front of him.

Impatient, he checked his watch, and suddenly the diamond-and-gold timepiece glinted like a superficial jewel, a reminder of who he was and where he'd come from.

Damn it, he thought. Why couldn't he accept the way things were? The way he'd been raised?

Because his charmed life had changed. Flint Kingman wasn't the same man anymore. The truth about his mother had altered his heart, his soul, the very core of his existence.

Gina entered the restaurant, and he steadied his emotions.

No matter how troubled he was, he wouldn't let it affect his career. The Barones had hired him to defuse the crisis in their company. And come hell or high water, that was what he intended to do.

He remained seated and assessed Gina for a moment. After he'd left her office this afternoon, he'd come up with a plan. A damn good one. But it meant getting close to Gina, not close enough to infringe on the confused order of his life, but close enough to fool the public.

And with that in mind, he'd invited her to dinner. He needed to see her in a romantic setting, to explore the energy between them.

The sexual energy, he thought. The unexpected heat.

Gina Barone couldn't stand his dominating personality,

and her high-and-mighty attitude annoyed the hell out of him. But that didn't matter. This was strictly business, a teeth-gnashing, tough-to-temper attraction that could work in their favor.

Besides, he'd already fantasized about her. Earlier this evening, when he'd taken a stress-relieving shower, she'd slipped right into the steam.

He hadn't meant to think about her and certainly not in a state of undress, but he'd lost the battle. With a sizzling, soap-scented mirage of her in his mind, he couldn't seem to control the yearning, the I'm-too-old-for-wet-dreams hunger. Trapped beneath a spray of warm water, he'd closed his eyes and imagined her—

She turned and saw him, and Flint gulped a gust of air.

How tall was she? he wondered. Five-nine? Five-ten? In his mind's eye, she'd fit him perfectly in the shower, that sweet, slim, incredibly moist body—

She moved closer, and he came to his feet, his six-foot-three frame still draped in a knee-length raincoat. Beneath it, he wore a suit with a Western flair, but if he didn't get his hormones in check, he would be sporting a big, boyish bulge in the vicinity of his zipper.

"You're late," he told her, when they were eye to eye.

"And you're acting like a jerk, as usual," she responded.

He couldn't help but smile. They had the weirdest chemistry, but somehow it worked.

Of course that ice-princess act of hers wouldn't charm the media, and it wouldn't seduce the public, either. Which meant he would have to revamp her image a little.

She removed her coat, and he slid his gaze up and down the luscious length of her body. Oh, yeah, he thought. He could mold her into a nice yet naughty girl—a kitten with a whip.

"What are you doing?" she asked.

"Just looking," he responded, shooting a smile straight

into her eyes. Her dress wasn't quite short enough, but the creamy beige color complemented her skin.

He reached out to loosen one of her curls, but she backed away, refusing to let him touch her. "Keep your hands to yourself, Kingman."

"But the rain messed up your hair," he lied. "I was just going to fix it."

She huffed out a shallow breath, and he knew he'd made her nervous. A good kind of nervous. The sexy kind.

"My hair's fine," she said.

No, it wasn't, he thought, itching to tousle it. The lady-of-the-manor style was too damn proper, too coiffed.

"Are you going to buy me dinner or not?" she asked.

"Sure. Let's get our table."

The hostess seated them in a fairly secluded booth. A snow-white candle dripped wax, and a single red rose bloomed in a bud vase, giving the rustic tabletop a touch of date-night ambience.

The waiter came by, offering cocktails. Gina declined a glass of wine, opting for iced tea instead. Flint went for an imported beer.

Silent, they studied their menus. Five minutes later, when the waiter returned with their drinks, Flint and Gina ordered the same meal. Or nearly the same meal, with the exception of a rare steak for him and a well-done cut for her.

Soon a basket of warm bread arrived. He reached out to offer her a slice at the same time she chose to get one for herself. But before their hands collided, she pulled back.

He took the lead, following his original plan. Tilting the basket toward her, he said, "Go ahead, Miss Barone. Or would it be all right if I called you Gina?"

She made her selection, then proceeded to lather it with whipped butter. "Gina is fine."

He watched her take a bite. "And so is Flint," he told her.

She swallowed and then made a pleasured sound, like a soft, sweet, bedroom murmur.

Amused, he reached for his beer. "Say it," he said.

She glanced up. "Excuse me?"

"My name. Say my name."

She gave him a curious look. "Flint."

Enjoying himself, he bit back a grin. "That was pretty good, but it wasn't quite right. You need to moan after you say my name, like you did after you ate the bread."

Finally aware of his little joke, she shoved the basket toward him. "Stuff it, *Flint.*"

He flashed the grin he'd been hiding. "I couldn't help it. I mean, here's a woman who gets orgasmic over bread and butter."

"I wasn't orgasmic."

"Yes, you were."

"I was not."

She glared at him from across the table, but her haughty expression fell short. When he stared at her, she became flustered, toying with the napkin on her lap.

"Don't," she said.

"Don't what?"

"Look at me like that."

He studied her features, struck by those violet eyes and that full, lush mouth. "But you're beautiful, Gina." And he couldn't stop the attraction, the heat, the sexual spontaneity rising in his blood.

She drew a ragged breath, and a shimmer of silence ensued.

Rain pounded against the building, and the flame on the candle danced between them, intensifying the moment.

Flint sent her a small, sensual smile. She was perfect for the scandal he had in mind.

Three

Two days later Gina entered the impressive high-rise that housed Kingman Marketing, a global advertising, public-relations and marketing agency.

Flint had called her this morning, demanding a meeting. Gina had tried to talk him into coming to her office, but he'd refused. For some unexplained reason, he wanted her on his turf.

She suspected that he'd devised a scandal and intended to make a presentation of some sort.

Standing in front of the elevator, she waited for the doors to open. She'd done some research on Kingman Marketing and learned that the company had built its stellar reputation on a high-profile clientele, which included well-known corporations, politicians and celebrities.

Like Tara Shaw, she thought. The actress Flint had bedded all those years ago.

The elevator opened, and Gina entered the confined space. Alone with her thoughts, she pressed the appropriate button and released an edgy breath. She wasn't comfortable seeing Flint again, especially after that awkward "business" dinner.

They'd stared at each other half the night like sex-starved teenagers on a first date. She'd hated every minute of that warm, woozy, he's-so-gorgeous feeling. She'd struggled through the meal, the food melting in her mouth like an unwelcome aphrodisiac. And he kept smiling at her, teasing her in that playful manner of his, which had only managed to make her more nervous.

The elevator stopped, and Gina stepped into the hallway and faced a set of smoked-glass doors, knowing it was the entrance to Flint's domain.

The sixth floor was dedicated to the public-relations department, and she'd heard that he ran his division with strength, strategy and creativity.

She stalled for a moment, battling a bout of anxiety. Smoothing her jacket, she told herself to relax. She didn't intend to let Flint eye her the way he'd done at the restaurant. Today she wore a camel-colored pantsuit, a ribbed turtleneck and conservative boots. Aside from her hands and face, she was completely covered. This outfit couldn't possibly turn him on.

Ready to do battle, she went inside, and then she stood and gazed around the massive reception area.

Antiques from every corner of the world made an incredible display, and so did modern works of art. She knew instantly that Flint had worked closely with the decorator.

"Are you Gina Barone?"

She turned to see a slim, chic woman rise from a birch desk—a unique piece of furniture that fit her vogue style. Alabaster skin showcased cropped black hair and trendy black glasses, making her look fashionably efficient.

"Yes, I am."

The woman came forward and extended her hand. "I'm Kerry Landau, Flint's assistant."

Gina smiled. "It's nice to meet you."

Kerry lowered her glasses and peered at Gina with exotically lined eyes. "I couldn't help but notice that you were admiring the decor." She pointed to a table-high statue—a depiction of a long, lean, naked lady. "That's my husband's work. He's still a struggling artist. But he's exceptional."

"Yes, he is." Gina studied the piece. The marble lady stood there, one hand draped between her thighs, her other arm barely shielding her aroused nipples. She seemed sensuously vulnerable, innocent yet erotic.

Gina turned to speak to Kerry and caught sight of Flint. He'd appeared out of nowhere, and he leaned against the doorjamb that led to his office, his head tilted at a curious angle.

"Ms. Barone is here," Kerry announced.

"So I see."

Flint's gaze roamed over Gina's carefully clothed body, and suddenly she felt as naked as the statue. And just as vulnerable.

"Are you ready?" he asked.

To enter the wolf's private den? No, she wasn't the least bit ready. "Of course."

"Good." He escorted her down a brightly lit hallway and into his office.

Offering her a seat, he gestured to a comfortable yet elegant sitting area. He'd spared no expense in decorating his domain, and she suspected his family was as wealthy as hers. But that was where the similarity ended.

Flint was an only child—the prince, the heir to the Kingman throne. Gina, on the other hand, struggled with being a middle child, the one her parents overlooked, the one who had to work twice as hard to get noticed.

Gina sighed, then glanced up and caught Flint watching her.

Uncomfortable, she folded her hands on her lap.

He moved to stand in front of his desk—a rich, intricately carved block of mahogany.

"You have exceptional taste," she said, struggling to fill the silence.

A small smile curved his lips. "In women?"

She shifted on the sofa. "In furniture."

"Thank you." The teasing smile remained. "Would you like a drink? Coffee, tea, a soft drink?" He walked to the bar. "A glass of milk?"

"A cup of hot tea would be nice," she responded, wishing he would stop flirting.

"Coming right up."

Within minutes he placed a silver tea set on the table beside her. It looked much too refined to be served by a tall, broad-shouldered man.

He sat across from her, looking wildly attractive, his rebellious hair falling onto his forehead.

She prepared her tea, adding cream and sugar. "So, what's the purpose of this meeting? Did you mastermind a scandal?"

"Yes."

She tasted the hot brew, sipping delicately. "And?"

"And I think we should have an affair."

Gina nearly spilled her tea, and Flint laughed.

"Not a real affair," he clarified.

"Let me get this straight." She set her cup on the table, knowing she wasn't steady enough to balance it. Apparently he'd meant to knock her for a loop, to heave his proposal at her, much in the way she'd tossed that apple at him. "You're suggesting we fake an affair?"

"That's right. A whirlwind romance and a stormy breakup."

She released a choppy breath. "You can't be serious."

"Of course, I am. Your family is already being targeted in the tabloids, so you'll draw plenty of attention. And so will I, considering I've been in the spotlight before."

Yes, he'd been in the spotlight before, playing around with a movie star.

"I'm telling you. This will work. Just picture the head-lines. 'PR prince melts Italian ice-cream princess.' It'll make great copy."

She shook her head, still trying to fathom the idea. "We don't even like each other."

"So what? It's just a phony affair. Three weeks of prom-inent dating, then a public breakup, and I'll be out of your hair." He removed his jacket and loosened his tie, giving himself a rakish look. "By the time we're done with the media, they won't care about pepper-spiced gelato or fam-ily curses. All they'll care about is the hip-grinding, mind-blowing displays of affection we'll be tossing their way." He gazed directly into her eyes. "Come on, what do you have to lose?"

My sanity, she thought.

"We've got great chemistry, Gina." He moved onto the sofa and reached for her hand. And when he linked his fingers with hers, a jolt of electricity shot up her arm.

"You can't deny our chemistry. I know you can feel it." He brought her hand to his mouth and brushed her knuckles with his lips. And then he teased her with a quick, playful bite.

Gina's blood rushed from her head to her toes. Heat pooled between her legs. Her nipples went hard.

But when he sent her that sly, sexy smile, she jerked her hand back.

Damn him, she thought, as her pulse jumped and jittered. *Damn him to hell.*

He was right, of course. His ploy would work. The tab-loids would feed on the sexual frenzy he intended to create. The press would sensationalize her affair with him instead of trashing Baronessa.

But could she actually paw him in public? Or let him run those spine-tingling hands all over her body?

"So, what do you say?" Flint asked. "Are we on?"

Yes. No. Maybe. Her mind spun. Her heart raced. "I don't know. I—"

"Hey, if you're worried about your image, relax. I've got that covered."

She blinked. "What are you talking about?"

He crossed to the bar. "That stiff nature of yours. You know as well as I do that it won't fly, Gina. It'll make you seem unlikable."

She eyed him with annoyance. "Oh, really?"

"Yeah." He popped the top on a soda and took a swig. "But I've dealt with this sort of thing before. I'm just the guy who can give you an image that will dazzle the media, charm the public and make men fall at your feet."

Offended, she lifted her chin. "I don't need you to run my social life."

He set his drink on the table. "The hell you don't. You've got incredible sex appeal, but you don't know how to use it."

"And a phony affair with you is going to turn me into a femme fatale?"

He slanted her his signature grin. "You bet is it."

"Go to hell, Flint."

"Hey, come on. Don't be that way. This is business."

At the moment she didn't care. Refusing to listen to any more of his spin-doctor spiel, she rose and headed for the door, leaving him cursing behind her.

The community living room at the brownstone was cozy yet elegant, with tall, leafy plants, beige furniture and an array of pale blue pillows, but the familiar atmosphere didn't lighten Gina's mood.

Eight hours after her meeting with Flint, she sat on a big, comfy sofa, venting her frustration to her younger sisters.

Rita, an almost twenty-five-year-old nurse at Boston General, listened with a sympathetic ear.

Twenty-three-year-old Maria, on the other hand, seemed preoccupied. She stood beside the window, gazing at the setting sun. Gina admired her sister's business savvy, and tonight she needed the other woman's undivided attention.

"Don't you care about what's going on?" Gina asked, unable to temper her irritation.

Maria turned instantly. She stared at Gina with dark eyes, her chiseled features a mask of composure. In spite of her petite frame, she exuded strength. "That isn't fair. You know how important the Valentine's Day promotion was to me. I'm as concerned as you are about the company our grandparents built."

Of course she was, Gina thought guiltily. Maria managed Baronessa Gelateria, a family-owned, old-fashioned ice-cream parlor—a Hanover Street location overflowing with charm and an emotional cloud of memories.

Still, Gina couldn't help but wonder if there was something else going on in Maria's life. Her sister had been slipping off lately, almost as if she were meeting someone on the sly.

Startled by her imagination, Gina shook her head. The phony affair Flint had proposed had warped her mind. Now she was conjuring a secret lover for Maria.

"I feel like I'm trapped between a rock and a hard place," Gina said, drawing the conversation to her rival. "Baronessa's reputation is floundering, and I just locked horns with the spin doctor who's supposed to pull us out of this mess."

Maria moved away from the window. "I'm sorry, Gina. I know this isn't easy on you."

Rita, seated in one of the overstuffed chairs, tucked her legs beneath her. She still wore her uniform, but she'd removed the white, crepe-soled shoes. "There has to be a solution."

"Yes, but what?" Gina asked. "I'm willing to do whatever it takes to restore Baronessa's reputation, but I can't stand the thought of snuggling up to that macho, arrogant man.'' She dragged a hand through her hair, tugging her fingers through the loosened, unruly curls. ''He doesn't think I can dazzle the media on my own. He thinks I need him to coach me.''

''Then prove him wrong,'' Maria suggested. ''Show him that you can handle the press.''

Rita perked up. ''That's a great idea. After all, Gina, you have your own brand of charm. There's nothing wrong with your image.''

''That's right.'' Maria sent her a warm smile. ''You're a beautiful, powerful, successful woman. What can a spin doctor teach you that you don't already know?''

''Nothing,'' Gina said, her confidence budding. But she could teach Flint Kingman plenty.

After an exhausting ten hours at the office, Flint unlocked his front door, then dropped his keys and spewed a vile curse.

His day had gone from bad to worse, and it was all Gina's fault.

How could she have turned him down? His plan was brilliant. But she was too stubborn to admit it, to thank him the way she should have. He wasn't just offering to repair the damage at Baronessa, he was offering to glamorize her image.

What female in her right mind wouldn't want that?

Didn't she know whom she was dealing with? Flint was an expert. Even his house was a work of art, a renovation with bold lines and stunning curves.

He glanced around, proud of the changes he'd made. His entryway featured hardwood floors instead of cool, marble tiles, and a fluid archway led to a collection of carefully chosen antiques, erotic paintings and a spiral staircase as smooth and sleek as a woman's body. He liked to run his hands along the banister, to feel the architectural beauty it possessed.

After all, he thought, everything, even inanimate objects, represented life.

Suddenly craving a warm shower and a cold beer, he headed to a large, custom-designed kitchen, grabbed a long-neck bottle and started stripping off his clothes.

By the time he climbed the stairs to the master bedroom, he'd left a careless stream of garments strewn along the way.

Standing beside the bed in a pair of pin-striped boxers, he twisted the cap on the beer and took a swig.

And then the damned phone rang.

Still feeling surly about Gina walking out on him, he grabbed the receiver. "What?" he said in place of a proper hello.

"It's me," a feminine voice announced.

"Who's me?" he asked, even though he knew it was the ice princess herself.

"It's Gina. And I changed my mind."

"Did you, now?"

"Yes, I did. After all, it is a woman's prerogative."

"So you'll have that phony affair with me?"

"Yes," she said primly. "But I won't allow you to alter my image."

He glared at the phone for a second. She would take his advice whether she liked it or not. But he wasn't about to argue the point. For now he would let her think she'd won. "Fine, but you can't back out if things get a little rough. So you better be damned sure you're committed to this project."

"I intend to combat the trouble at Baronessa," she retorted. "Even if it means faking a relationship with you."

"All right, then. I'm coming over."

"What for?" she asked suspiciously.

"To work out the details. I'll be there in about an hour."

He hung up before she could protest, then proceeded to peel off his boxers and climb in the shower, hoping to hell she didn't invade his mind. The last thing he needed was to fantasize about Gina Barone again.

To make sure he didn't falter, he turned the water to cold and then cursed when the frigid droplets sprayed him.

Why was he so attracted to her? She was as stiff and corporate-minded as a woman could be. She didn't have a warm, nurturing bone in her body.

And these days Flint wanted someone to care. He wanted a woman who would do anything for him—even give up a thriving career.

It was a selfish thought, but he didn't give a damn. The news about his mother had changed him, and he couldn't help but long for what he'd been denied.

He shut off the icy water and dried vigorously. Then he reached for the abalone shell on his dresser and lit the bundle of sage contained within it. When he was just a boy, his grandmother had taught him to smudge, to purify himself and his surroundings.

Flint walked a somewhat shaky line between the white and Indian worlds, and he supposed he always would. It came with the territory, with being a mixed-blood living in the brain-jarring, fast, furious, ever-stimulating pace of the city.

He wanted to raise his future children within the pow-wow circle, to teach them to dance, but he wondered if that time would ever come. Or if it was meant to be.

With the scent of sage on his skin, he dressed in a pair of black trousers and a gray sweater, preparing to see Gina.

As promised, he arrived at her door within the hour and pressed the intercom to the fourth-floor apartment.

She buzzed him into the building, and he waited for her in the foyer. The brownstone presented a polished-wood staircase, a modern elevator with an old-fashioned gate and a reception area decorated like a living room.

Suddenly Flint could feel a gust of feminine energy swirling around him like a perfumed ghost. He jammed his hands in his pockets, then glanced at the staircase.

Gina descended the steps, looking like a siren from the Italian sea. Her hair fell in a wild mass over her shoulders, each strand rioting in disarray.

Instantly, a surge of sexual heat blasted through his veins.

She reached the foyer, and they stood for a moment, staring at each other.

"I like your hair that way," he said casually, digging his hands deeper into his pockets, where his body had gone hard.

"Thank you," she responded in that cool tone of hers. "But I prefer it up."

Little witch, he thought. She couldn't even take a compliment graciously. He imagined tangling his hands in all those bohemian curls and tugging until she yelped—in pain and in pleasure. "I want you to wear it down when you're with me."

Her chin lifted. "Don't start, Flint."

He flashed a rakish smile, knowing his devil-may-care grin would annoy her. "Don't start what?"

"Telling me what to do."

He shrugged, and she gestured to the reception area. "Have a seat, and I'll pour you a drink."

"Thanks, but I'll have it in your apartment."

She gave him a haughty look. "I'm not inviting you upstairs."

He moved a little closer, crowding her. "Yes, you are. In a few days you and I are going to start dating. That gives me the right to see your place."

She backed away. "Yeah, well, just remember that in a few weeks I'm going to kick you to the curb."

"That's right, you are. And I'm sure you'll enjoy every

minute of it." Flint started up the stairs without her. "But for now you're stuck with me."

She blew out a windy breath and followed, catching up to him. They reached her apartment at the same time, and she opened the door.

"Nice," he said. Very nice. Hardwood floors led to an enticing display of international furnishings. An English writing table sat below a leaded-glass window, and a Chinese vase decorated a stark and stately fireplace mantel. The walls were painted a soft shade of cream and accented with a touch of wine. The sofas, he noticed, were covered in Italian silk.

The lady had taste.

"What would you like to drink?" she asked.

"Coffee," he decided, heading for the kitchen.

He nosed around while she brewed a European blend. "You can tell a lot about a person by what's in their refrigerator," he said. He opened hers and took inventory. She liked to cook, he realized, as he poked through containers of leftovers and a crisper filled with fresh greens.

She leaned against the counter while the coffee brewed. Her kitchen was white, with vintage-style fixtures and a hand-painted porcelain sink. A garden window held a variety of potted herbs, and French doors led to a terrace that overlooked the city.

"What's in your fridge?" she asked.

"Bachelor stuff."

She tilted her head. "Spoiled milk? Pizza growing mold?"

He helped himself to the coffee. "I'm not that bad." Sipping the hot drink, he studied her over the rim of his cup. Her hair was still driving him crazy. She looked as if she'd gone for a quick, hard ride—on a man's lap.

"I want to see your bedroom," he said, placing his coffee beside an ornamental decanter.

"No dice, Kingman. My bedroom is off-limits."

"Not to me. I'm about to become your lover."

"My fake lover," she corrected.

He ignored her and proceeded down the hall, where he assumed her room was. She stalked after him, grumbling about his manners. Or lack of them, he supposed.

He opened her door and stared in shocked silence.

"What's wrong?" she asked from behind him.

"This is my room," he responded, feeling as if she'd invaded his sanctuary. His soul. The emotions driving him.

"What are you talking about?"

He turned to look at her, this woman he barely knew. "I have a cherry armoire that was probably built by the same cabinetmaker. And my bed is almost identical. Even my quilt is the same color." A deep, sensual burgundy, he thought. Like the shade of her lips, the blush on her cheeks.

Gina glanced at the bed, then at him. "Something has to be different."

He walked to her dresser, an eighteenth-century piece similar to the one he'd found in a dusty little antique shop on the West Coast. Somehow they'd chosen nearly the same furniture.

"Did you use a decorator?" he asked.

She shook her head. "No. Did you?"

"No."

They stared at each other from across the room, trapped in an awkward gaze. It almost seemed as if they'd been sleeping in a parallel universe, as if their spirits knew each other from another time or another place.

Searching for a diversion, for an escape from the unwelcome bond, he shifted his attention to the top of her dresser.

And then he noticed the figurines. Some were whimsical and cherubic and others shone like jewels, their wings tipped in gold.

The ice princess collected angels.

Flint looked up and caught a confusing image of Gina.

As she moved toward him, the glow from an amber bulb illuminated her skin and sent highlights dancing through her tousled hair, giving her a heavenly aura.

"They're beautiful, aren't they?" She picked up a gilded figure and held it up to the light, to the halo surrounding her.

For a long, drawn-out moment he couldn't take his eyes off her. He just stood, awed by her beauty, by the sheer radiance of her magic. The tiny statue shimmered gloriously in her hand.

Before he did something stupid, like telling her how exquisite she was, Flint broke the spell.

"I don't believe in angels," he said. It was bad enough she'd stolen his bedroom. He wasn't about to let her con him into thinking she was some sort of celestial being.

A disapproving scowl appeared on Gina's face, and he headed to her walk-in closet and opened the door, determined to get back to work.

She spun, clutching the gold-leafed figurine to her chest. "What are you doing?"

"Checking out your clothes."

"Why? Are you afraid we have the same wardrobe?"

"No, smart aleck. I'm looking for something for you to wear on our first date. Something long and slinky. Maybe a little glittery."

"I don't do slinky."

"You will when you're with me," he told her. One way or another, he intended to turn Gina Barone into a femme fatale. Not an angel, he reminded himself. But a sizzling, sultry she-devil.

A woman who would stir his blood without stirring his heart.

Four

Gina wondered what Flint was up to. He'd gone to her apartment last night, and this afternoon he insisted she come to his office. Supposedly he had a surprise in store.

Although she didn't trust him, she was just curious enough to show up.

When she entered the reception area, Kerry, Flint's loyal assistant, looked up and smiled. The young woman sat at her trendy desk, studying the monitor on her computer.

"He's expecting you," Kerry said. "So you can go right in."

"Thanks." Gina drew a breath and headed down the hall.

She found Flint waiting casually for her arrival with three rolling racks of clothes, shoeboxes stacked a mile high and a full-length, portable mirror at his disposal.

"What's all this?" she asked.

He sent her his spin-doctor smile. "Your wardrobe selection for the next two weeks. I told a stylist what you needed, and she sent them over. She shops for some of the most famous women in the world.''

Gina scanned the racks and took in an eyeful. Evening gowns, bodysuits, skirts that would barely cover her rear.

He reached for a long silver gown. ''Try this one on. You can change in my bathroom. And if it fits, you can wear it tomorrow night.''

She studied the sparkling garment. The neckline plunged in front, in what she assumed would be from her breasts to her navel. ''You've got to be kidding.''

''You'll look hot in this, baby.''

Her full Cs would fall right out of that flimsy contraption. ''If you like it so much, you wear it.''

Not easily deterred, he reached for another gown, a cherry-red, skintight number slit to the hip. ''How about this one? It's got a G-string to match.''

A G-string she was going to use as a slingshot if he foisted one more skimpy dress on her. ''You're not turning me into a bimbo, Flint. So knock it off.''

He jammed the red gown onto the rack. ''You're a prude, Gina.''

She crossed her arms. ''I am not.''

''Oh, yeah?'' He sat on the edge of his desk, his hair falling onto his forehead. ''I'll bet you've never made love on an airplane. Or in an elevator. Or even beneath a big shady tree at the park.''

She tried to act as if his accusation hadn't embarrassed her. Or made her skin warm. ''It's illegal to mess around in public places.''

''True, but that's what makes it so exciting.''

Gina did her damnedest to avoid his gaze, but she could feel those hot amber-flecked eyes shooting sexual sparks right at her.

''I'm a lady,'' she said. ''I behave properly in public.''

''Yeah, but don't you ever want to live out your fantasies?''

"I don't have airplane fantasies."

He cocked his head. "What about elevators?"

Okay, so maybe he had her there, but she wasn't about to admit it. Gina wasn't brave enough to pursue her fantasies, to live on the edge. She drove a luxury sedan instead of a sports car, took practical vacations rather than slip away to unpredictable locations and battled an ulcer that flared up whenever her stress level hit the Richter scale. Which meant sex in an elevator wasn't very likely.

She'd slept with two men her entire life, and both relationships had fallen flat. Her first lover, a striving-for-success executive in a Fortune 500 conglomerate, had been envious of her inheritance, claiming that she didn't work nearly as hard as he did. So she'd gone for a doting, less ambitious partner the next time, but he'd bored her to tears with his hand-patting, milquetoast ways.

"What about in private?" Flint asked.

She glanced up. "I'm sorry? What?"

He reached for a short black dress and gave it a masculine study. Gina thought the leather garment looked like something a dominatrix might wear. She couldn't help but wonder if the stylist had sent over a pair of thigh-high boots, as well.

"Do you behave properly in private?"

Her mouth went dry. She'd never torn off a man's clothes or clawed his back. But she wasn't a Puritan, either. "I behave just fine."

He tossed the minidress at her. "Go put this on. I want to see your legs. All of them, all the way to your thighs."

She caught the leather garment, then felt the smooth texture slide against her skin. "No."

He watched her through those whiskey-flecked eyes. "We're supposed to fool the world into believing we're lovers. You realize that, don't you?"

"Of course, I do. But can't we pretend our first date is

actually our first date instead of posing as lovers right away?"

"Yes, we can do that. But we've only got a few weeks to pull this off, so you're going to have to fall for my charms pretty damn quick."

Trust Mr. Macho to word it like that. "Why can't you fall for my charms?"

"Because you'll be dressed like a prude, that's why."

"Fine, I'll wear something provocative. But I'll shop for myself." She hung the whips-and-chains dress on the rack. "Where are we going, anyway?"

"To the opening of a new play. An erotic play," he added. "So be prepared for a hot, sultry night."

Gina's heart clamored against her breast. An X-rated production? A hot, sultry night?

"I can handle anything you dish out," she told him, even though she was suddenly scared out of her properly behaved wits.

Gina gazed at herself in the mirror. Could she pull this off? Could she actually wear this gown in public?

The seventies style looked like something Tara Shaw would have donned in her heyday. The white fabric clung to Gina's body in a slim, simple line. But that wasn't the problem. The halter dress left her back completely bare. Which meant that she'd forgone a bra—something she'd never done before.

What was wrong with her? Was she trying to compete with a young Tara Shaw? Prove to Flint that she was as daring as his former lover?

Gina checked the clock, and her heart did a somersault. Flint would be here any minute.

She scrambled around the apartment for her shoes and her wrap. And the evening bag containing her stomach medicine.

She nearly tripped putting on her heels, then ran to the mirror for a final inspection.

And that was when she saw one nipple staring at her. Good grief. She looked like a car with a burned out headlight.

Should she arouse the other nipple? Or try to make the erect one recede?

Tilting her head, she frowned. She had no idea how to turn off the shining headlight, so she closed her eyes and rubbed her thumb against the shy breast.

And suddenly an image of Flint invaded her mind—that wild, dream-induced image.

Moonlight bathed him in a hazy glow. Water fell from the sky. The wind blew rain against his face, his arms, his naked chest.

As he moaned his pleasure, she toyed with his fly, working the damp zipper, brushing the hardness—

And then the intercom sounded.

Gina's eyes flew open. She rushed to the door and pressed the button. "Yes?"

Flint's voice came over the speaker. "Are you ready?"

"No. I mean, sort of. Not quite." She needed a moment to breathe, to gain the confidence to face him. Both nipples were painfully aroused. "Wait for me on the first floor, and I'll meet you there."

She buzzed him into the building then raced to the mirror and slipped on a wrap that complemented her dress.

A quick glass of wine would take the edge off, but she feared it would irritate her ulcer. Abandoning the idea, she gave herself a few minutes to calm down.

When she opened the front door, she nearly bumped into Flint.

Cool and collected, he wore a classic black suit, a crisp white shirt and a slim black tie. She detected European cologne and a dash of peppermint, and she assumed he sucked on a breath mint.

She closed the door behind her. "You were supposed to wait for me downstairs."

He flashed a rebellious grin. "Since when do I listen to what you tell me to do? Now take off your jacket and let me see your dress."

"It's a provocative gown," she told him, trying to sound casual. "It'll get me noticed."

"Let me be the judge of that." He reached for the jeweled buttons on her wrap.

"I'll do it." Fidgeting with the sequined jacket, she removed it, did a quick twirl to show him her exposed back and tried to cover up again.

"Hold on. Wait." He snagged the wrap, leaving her vulnerable to his eyes.

Those hot, amber-flecked eyes.

She put her arms at her sides, wishing she hadn't worn a braless-style gown. As he zeroed in on her protruding nipples, she clutched her handbag.

Say something, she thought. *Don't just stand there and stare. Don't remind me that I fantasized about you in front of the mirror.*

He moved closer, and she fought for her next breath. "May I have my jacket back now?"

"No." He draped the sequined wrap over the banister. "I want to look at you some more."

"You're making me nervous, Flint."

"I know."

He moved even closer, and she shuddered.

"Relax. We're supposed to be on the verge of becoming lovers. You can't jump every time I touch you."

He slid his hands into her hair, and she battled a bout of dizziness. "What are you doing?"

"Loosening a few pins." Strands of hair fell, curling around his fingers. "There," he said. "Now you're perfect."

She couldn't imagine how she looked with half her chignon falling down. Tousled, she imagined. As if she'd just tumbled out of bed.

He stepped back and gave Gina her wrap. They took the elevator, and the ride to the first floor seemed to take forever.

"Do you think anyone has ever made love in here?" he asked.

"I doubt it. I mean, no." Her sisters wouldn't do something that like that. Would they? Of course not. Rita and Maria were proper girls, like her.

"We should fake it sometime." A boyish grin tilted his lips. "Pretend we're making out in here."

"That isn't funny." The automatic gate opened, and she bolted out of the elevator, her nipples still protruding like bullets.

Flint and Gina walked to his car. He opened the passenger door and watched her slide into the Corvette.

A moment later, he climbed behind the wheel and latched his seat belt. Gina sat beside him, her hair tumbling around her face. She turned to look at him, and his blood went hot.

Her lips were painted red, just like his car.

The 1963 Sting Ray offered sleek, smooth lines, a split-window design and a fast, fuel-injected ride. The lady, he thought, gave him an even bigger thrill.

He wanted to kiss her, to taste that luscious mouth. But he couldn't, not until they were in a public forum. The seduction was supposed to be for the press.

Flint started the engine, shifted into gear and pulled into traffic. Soon he sped through a yellow light, making it across the intersection before it changed to red. Red meant stop. But tonight, he decided, thinking about Gina's lips, it meant go.

"Have you heard about this play?" he asked.

She nodded. "Yes, but I hadn't planned on seeing it."

"Why not?" He stole a glance at his date and noticed her hands were folded anxiously on her lap. "Because of the nudity?"

"I suppose. I mean, I don't know. I prefer musicals."

He grinned. She was so damn proper. In some ways that turned him on. He liked the idea of corrupting her, even if it was for show. "*Hair* is a musical, and in the production I saw, the cast took off their clothes. Of course, that wasn't exactly erotica." He ran another yellow light and tossed an important detail of their scandal at her. "Speaking of erotica, I arranged for us to pose for a portrait."

Her voice jumped. "What?"

"Kerry's husband is an artist, and he agreed to do this. It'll be great publicity for him. And for us, of course. He'll take some sexy photographs to sketch from. But before he gets a chance to decide which shot to use for the painting, the pictures will be stolen from his studio and sold to the tabloids." Flint kept his eyes on the road. "We'll be the talk of the town."

Gina's breath rushed out. "Sexy photos? You can't mean that."

"It's part of the scandal. A big part of it."

"Why didn't you tell me this before now?"

Because she wouldn't have agreed if she'd known about it in the beginning. "I didn't want to spring everything on you at once."

She crossed her arms. "I'm not doing it. No way am I going to allow you to circulate those kind of pictures of me."

"They'll be pictures of us, not just you."

"I'm not taking off my clothes in front of you or Kerry's husband. So forget it."

"You won't be naked. You'll be wearing lingerie. And Kerry will be there to help you style your hair and touch up your makeup." He pulled into the theater's parking lot. "You don't have a choice, Gina. You've got to do this. It's an important part of the scandal. It will generate all sorts of press.''

"I don't care. I'm still not doing it."

"The hell you aren't." He stopped for valet service, waiting behind other cars. "You promised you wouldn't back out, even if things got a little rough. And I'm holding you to that promise."

"You tricked me."

"I did what I had to do." He met her riled gaze. "This is supposed to be one of those impulsive, whirlwind romances. So it's only natural that I would commission a portrait."

"Why? Just because Kerry's husband is an artist?"

"No. Because I collect erotic art, and you're my obsession. We're supposed to be falling in love. Even if we're not right for each other."

She shook her head. "People don't fall in love in two weeks."

"People in lust do. Sometimes they don't know the difference."

Suddenly Gina seemed shy. She glanced down and toyed with her handbag, fingering the jeweled clasp. "I don't think I can pose like that."

"Yes, you can. We both can." Flint couldn't help himself. He had to touch her.

When he reached out to smooth one of the stray curls from her face, she looked up, and they got caught in a quiet stare.

He brushed her cheek, absorbing the soft, satiny texture of her skin. How could an ice princess feel so warm? So sensual? So sweet and angelic?

"What will be you be wearing?" she asked.

He withdrew his hand. "In the pictures?"

She nodded.

"Jeans, no shirt and no underwear, I guess. Kerry's husband said something about me unbuttoning my pants. You know, kind of far down.''

She chewed her bottom lip. ''When are we supposed to do the shoot?''

He studied her mouth, her teeth, the way she nibbled her lip. ''In two days. So we'll be sleeping together by then. Or pretending to,'' he clarified.

''I guess it could happen tonight. I've never made love on a first date, but this is different. Since we won't really be…doing it.''

''I should probably hang out at your apartment after the play. Just for a few hours, so it seems like we couldn't resist each other. Is that all right with you?''

''Yes,'' she said, as their eyes met again.

A horn honked, and Flint realized he hadn't moved up in line to take his turn. A uniformed valet waved him forward, urging him to pay attention to something other than the beautiful woman with whom he was faking an affair.

The theater was built in Romanesque architecture, with stone columns, a mosaic ceiling and ornamented walls.

The lobby featured plush carpeting and several crowded bars. As Gina and Flint milled through the grand room, her stomach flipped and flopped, and the evening had just begun.

He leaned into her. ''Let me help you with your wrap.''

''All right,'' she said, knowing he expected her to remove the only protection she had.

She unbuttoned the sequined jacket, and he stood behind her. His breath stirred against the nape of her neck, making her much too warm. The instant she was free of the wrap, her nipples brushed the clingy fabric of the halter dress.

''You're so beautiful.'' Flint still stood behind her, only now he touched her skin, sliding a finger down her spine, teasing bare flesh.

This was part of the game, she thought. Part of the public

scandal. But his caress was real. And so was her reaction. Every nerve ending in her body came alive, tingling with sensations she hadn't known she possessed.

He put his arms around her and pulled her tight against him. Her rear bumped his fly, and he tugged at her earlobe with his teeth.

Hundreds of people filtered through the lobby, talking and drinking, enjoying the cocktail hour before the show, and all the while Flint had his hands and his mouth all over her. His fingers, she noticed, were dangerously close to her aroused nipples.

"Would you like a drink?" he asked against her ear.

She managed a shaky yes and told him to get her a glass of white wine. Not because she wanted to ply her ulcer with alcohol, but because she needed something to calm her nerves.

"I'll be right back." He headed to the bar, and she smoothed her dress and clutched her jacket, wishing she could cover herself.

In two days she and Flint would pose for pictures. Erotic photographs.

Dear God. What had she gotten herself into?

"Gina?" A familiar, feminine voice spoke her name. "Is that you?"

She glanced up and saw Morgan Chancellor, the business associate who'd given her the scoop on Flint and Tara Shaw. "Hello, Morgan. Of course, it's me."

"Oh, my. You look simply ravishing."

"Thank you. I'm on a date."

"Yes, I saw your escort. You're with Flint." Morgan glanced in the direction of the closest bar. "I guess you two are hitting it off."

Gina fidgeted with her wrap. "He's an intriguing man."

"Yes, he is." The socialite lowered her voice to a discreet whisper. "And I can tell you've been kissing him.

Darling, you need to fix your lipstick. It's terribly obvious.''

"Is it?" Struggling to play her part, Gina reached into her purse and removed a compact. She hadn't been kissing Flint. She'd been fretting about those upcoming photos, chewing anxiously on her lips, then licking the lipstick from her teeth.

She reapplied the racy red color and smiled at Morgan. "I couldn't help myself."

"I don't blame you a bit. But be careful. He'll take you for a walk on the wild side."

"That's the idea. To be quite honest, I'm tired of being a good girl. And I need a diversion, something to help me forget about the trouble at Baronessa."

"Then you found the right guy. And he chose the perfect event. I've heard this production is absolutely decadent. Which is why I couldn't stay away. Of course, I'm here with some girlfriends. My husband isn't comfortable around this sort of thing."

Neither am I, Gina thought.

Flint returned with her wine. He greeted Morgan and slid his arms around Gina's waist.

"I should get back to my friends," the redhead said. "You two enjoy your evening."

Flint smiled. "Thanks. We will."

As Morgan walked away, he nuzzled Gina's neck. "Did you miss me?" he whispered.

She took a gulp of wine, then turned in his arms. "Maybe we should find our seats." Her knees had gone weak, and she needed to sit.

"Okay, baby."

He stroked her cheek, brushing it tenderly with the back of his hand, and for a moment, she almost wished the affection was real.

Flint Kingman was a damn fine actor. But his mother had been a Hollywood starlet, so acting was in his blood.

As they located their seats, Gina wondered if she should tell him she'd purchased a movie his mother had costarred in. She'd watched the film three times, awed by the young woman's beauty. Flint had inherited his mother's stunning cheekbones, her natural sex appeal, her sly, flirtatious smile. He was, without a doubt, Danielle Wolf's son.

And then, of course, there was his scandalous affair with Tara Shaw. She imagined that had shaped Flint into who and what he was, as well.

Gina turned to look at him, and suddenly a strange thought hit her. Had he truly made love to Tara? Or had their relationship been a publicity stunt? Something to boost the aging actress's career?

"What are you thinking about?" he asked.

"Nothing," she said. Nothing but his ex-lover. Or his fake ex-lover. With Flint, anything could be a lie.

Within thirty minutes, the theater was full. As the lights dimmed and the curtain opened, Gina stared at the stage.

The opening scene stunned the audience. A young woman began to undress in front of a mirror. When she was completely naked, she closed her eyes and touched her nipples, slowly, seductively, whispering a man's name.

Gina nearly gasped. She'd done the same thing this evening. She'd stood in front of a mirror, thinking about Flint.

Smoke filled the stage, and a man appeared. It was a dream sequence, Gina realized. But that didn't stop the dream man from taking the flesh-and-blood woman into his arms.

And teasing her with foreplay.

Gina knew they were only acting. But their performances affected her nonetheless.

Heat pooled between her legs. An erotic chill raced up her spine. She felt what the actress was feeling—fire, moisture, a prelude to sex.

And when Flint moved closer, she knew the scene aroused him, too.

Suddenly the stage went dark. There was no light, only the sighs of lovemaking, the whispers of a dream.

In the blackness, Flint ran his hand along the side of Gina's dress, pressing against her rib cage, the fullness of her breast, her bare arm.

She turned her head, and he kissed her.

Hard.

So hard, her breath rushed into his.

The woman on stage was climaxing, making throaty little sounds. Lights flickered on and off, flashing naked images of the actors, but Flint kept kissing Gina.

As he delved into her hair, he wrapped his hands around the curls that fell and tugged her closer.

His tongue took hers over and over. He was hot and demanding, rough and insistent. He made her want; he made her ache. Yet somehow, he made her part of him.

Overwhelmed with pleasure, she kissed him back, uncovering a flavor so rich and forbidden, she hungered for more.

In the next instant, light flooded the stage, and the woman was alone.

Gina pulled away and stared at Flint. She could see the shadowy outline of his face, and she knew he was her dream man. Her fantasy. The actor who would disappear when their scandal ended.

Heaven help her, she thought. She was trapped in a torrid affair that wasn't even real.

Five

Flint stood in front of Gina's living room window, staring out at Boston's North End. They'd just returned from the theater, and he couldn't get his emotions in check.

"What should we do now?" she asked.

Kiss, he thought. *Touch. Make love.* Suddenly he wanted the affair to be real. He wanted to sleep with Gina, to have a wild, passionate, fire-induced fling with the ice princess and get her out of his system.

"Nothing," he said. "We don't have to do anything."

"Should I make some tea? It's late, so maybe we should have a herbal brew. How about chamomile? I have home-made muffins, too."

He turned to look at her. She still wore the backless white dress, and her hair still tumbled from its confinement. They'd kissed over and over during the play and during the brightly lit intermission, creating a public scene. And now she was suggesting a spot of chamomile and a plate of leftover muffins. Hell, it might as well be tea and crumpets with the queen.

"We're supposed to be bumping and grinding, Gina. Screwing each other's brains out."

Her face flushed. "Don't think you'll be taking your sexual frustration out on me."

He held her gaze. He knew her mouth tasted as luscious as it appeared, and somehow that only made him angrier. "Why not? You caused it."

"And you're a crude, unfeeling man."

Unfeeling? He ached for her. He hurt so badly, he could barely breathe. "I have plenty of feelings." *Too many,* he thought.

"This isn't easy on me, either." She tried to smooth her hair and gave up when she encountered a handful of disheveled curls. "I'm attracted to you, Flint. But I'm not going to sleep with you. I'm not going turn this into a real affair."

Defensive, he jammed his hands in his pockets. "Did I say that's what I wanted?"

"No, but I thought some tea would take the edge off. You know, to keep our minds from straying in that direction." She dropped her gaze to the floor. "Maybe you should just go home."

Damn her. Why did she have to look so vulnerable? "I'm sorry. I didn't mean to offend you. It's just been a weird night." First the show at the theater, and now he was in her apartment trying to establish a cover in case anyone in the neighborhood was watching. "If I leave now, it won't seem as if we made love. I've only been here for ten minutes."

She didn't respond. She seemed shy, her gaze riveted to the floor.

Unsure what to do, he shifted his stance. Part of him wanted to go home and never see her again, while another part imagined carrying her to bed.

"So, is it all right if I stay for a while?" he asked, his voice a bit too rough.

She glanced up, and they stared at each other. The energy between them remained thick, and so did the air in his lungs.

Finally she nodded, and Flint forced a breath. He hadn't expected this to happen, at least not to this degree. He was so damn sure he could handle his attraction to her. But here he was, stuck in a state of arousal.

"Maybe you should brew that tea," he said.

"Will you drink some?"

"Sure." He didn't particularly care for tea, but he knew she needed to refine the rest of their evening, to make it seem proper somehow.

She turned away, and he sat on the couch and stared at the blank TV screen.

When she returned, he noticed she'd laced the tray with heated muffins, sugar, cream, lemon wedges and honey. He wondered what she would do if he revealed that he had a honey fetish. That one of his fantasies was drizzling the sticky substance all over a woman's body and licking her until she—

"Do you want a muffin?" Gina gestured to a flowered plate. "These are blueberry and those are bran."

Guilty, Flint froze. "No, thanks." He kept his eyes away from the honey, especially when she spread some onto a muffin and nibbled daintily.

If she moaned, he was going to lose it. He would jump right out of his skin.

She sat next to him, picked up the remote control and turned on the TV. He tasted the unappealing tea and studied the flickering images.

She changed the channel repeatedly, the way he did at home when he was bored. But he knew Gina wasn't bored. She was nervous.

"Maybe we should watch a movie," she said. "I have a fairly large selection."

She rifled through her videos and DVDs, and he figured she would offer a girly movie, a chick flick that would calm her down. He would rather get absorbed in guts and glory, in a good, old-fashioned war picture, but he decided to be polite and keep his mouth shut, something he rarely did around her.

"How about this?" She held up *The Caine Mutiny,* and he stared at her in stunned silence. That was one of his all-time favorite films, a Humphrey Bogart vehicle about a crazed captain and his crew.

"What's the matter?" she asked.

"Nothing. I like that movie."

"Me, too. I had a pug named Captain Queeg, but he died a few years ago."

Again, Flint could only stare. "That's not my dog's name, but that's what I call him when he goes nuts and digs up the yard." Flint owned a Jack Russell terrier that kept his gardeners cursing into their shovels.

"Oh, my God. That's so strange. My Captain Queeg wasn't crazy, but he loved strawberries."

"Really?" They looked at each other and laughed. The strawberry scene in *The Caine Mutiny* was a classic.

Without another word, they settled into the evening and watched an old movie, even though they were trying to fool the world into believing they were making long, hard, passionate love.

What had she gotten herself into? Gina sat in front of a lighted mirror, taking deep, anxious breaths.

Kerry stood behind her, putting the final touches on her hair. Flint's assistant had decided that Gina should wear her hair loose for the photo shoot. But that wasn't the problem.

The wardrobe selection troubled her. A red silk nightgown clung to her curves, outlining her breasts and show-casing a pair of skimpy lace panties.

"You're ready," Kerry said.

Gina gazed at the other woman in the mirror, catching both their reflections. She wanted to back out, to say she couldn't go through with this, but she put on a brave front instead.

She came to her feet and accepted the matching robe Kerry offered. She belted it with shaky fingers, and they left the tiny makeup room and entered the studio.

The first thing Gina noticed was the prop that had been brought in for the shoot—a king-size bed, draped in red and white satin.

She scanned the rest of the room and zeroed in on Flint. He leaned against a small table, chatting with Lewis, Kerry's slightly eccentric husband.

Flint glanced over and spotted her. When their eyes met, her heart leaped to her throat. He wore a pair of faded Levi's and little else. His feet and chest were bare. His stomach corded in a six-pack of hard-earned muscle.

Lewis turned, as well. "I see our lady has arrived on the set." He came toward her, but Flint remained where he was.

"Would you like a glass of wine?" Lewis asked. "It'll help you relax."

"Thanks, but I'm okay."

He tilted his head, looking like the artist he was. He wore his bleached hair short and spiked, and both ears possessed multiple piercings. "Are you sure? This is a pretty heavy shoot."

"I can handle it," she lied. "I don't need a drink." She wanted to down an entire bottle of wine, but her ulcer had been acting up for the past few days, and alcohol would only irritate her condition.

"Then let's get started." Lewis instructed Gina and Flint to stand at the foot of the bed while he fiddled with his camera. Kerry adjusted the lights, leaving Flint and Gina to their own devices.

Was Flint nervous, too? She'd never seen him so quiet.

"This is strange, isn't it?" she said, struggling to make conversation.

He nodded. "Yeah, it is."

They both lapsed into silence. Gina glanced at the bed and noticed the lace-edged pillows. The stage was beautifully set, with two tall, wrought-iron candelabras on either side of the bed. Burning candles filled the room with scented wax, giving it a romantic ambience.

"Okay," Lewis called from behind the camera lens. "It's show time."

Flint took a step toward Gina, then skimmed her cheek, brushing her skin with the back of his hand. She liked the sweet, butterfly sensation, but the photographer wasn't impressed.

"Come on, Flint," he coaxed. "You can do better than that. You collect erotic art. You know what this is all about."

Gina lowered her gaze and stared at Flint's naked chest. She knew he collected erotic art, but somehow she hadn't let herself think too deeply about it. Now that seemed impossible.

He reached for the belt on her robe, and she gulped the air in her lungs. What kind of erotic art did he favor? Slim, sultry women in provocative poses? Or hot, hungry couples engaged in illicit acts?

He pushed the robe from her shoulders, and the garment fell to the floor. She stood before him, dressed in the clingy red nightgown, her nipples brushing the fire-tinged silk.

Somewhere in the back of her whirling mind, she heard a clicking sound. Lewis must be taking pictures, capturing the moment.

Flint leaned in close and kissed her, and she ignored the camera. His mouth proved warm and wet, gentle yet demanding. He tasted of breath mints and beer, of masculine beauty and spring lust.

"Take off his belt," she heard Lewis say.

Yes, Gina thought. She wanted to touch Flint, and she hardly cared that Lewis and Kerry watched.

She reached for Flint's belt and felt a shiver rack his body. They stopped kissing and stared at each other. She unhooked the silver buckle. The metal was cold, but his skin, that bronzed flesh, radiated heat.

She pulled the leather through his pant loops, and Lewis instructed her to toss the belt onto the bed and undo Flint's jeans.

Okay, she told herself. She could do this. But after releasing the first two buttons, she bumped a slight hardness beneath Flint's fly, and her fingers froze. He was partially aroused, turned on by her touch.

"Keep going," Lewis prodded.

She bit her lip and went after the third button.

"Good," the artist crooned. "Now drop to your knees."

Stunned, Gina gazed at Flint. He sent her a boyish smile, and her heartbeat skittered.

This wasn't real, she reminded herself. This photo session was as phony as their affair.

Sliding down his body, she landed on her knees and looked at him. She noticed a line of hair that started just below his navel and disappeared into the open waistband of his jeans.

Gina wanted to trace it with her nail, but she didn't dare. Flint couldn't take his eyes off her, and she could barely breathe. This position left her dizzy.

"That's perfect," Lewis said, pleased by what he assumed was their professionalism. "Okay, now, Flint, twist your hands in her hair. Yeah, just like that. And, Gina, play with his jeans. Tug at them a little."

She did as she was told, and after the shoot ended, she came to her feet and teetered on a pair of stiletto heels.

No one spoke, not even Lewis. He gathered his equipment, and Kerry reached for Gina's robe and handed it to her.

The fading sun shone through the skylight, sending streams of gold across a stark white floor. Although the satin-draped bed remained unused, Flint's belt lay across it, reminding Gina of what they'd done.

He turned away to fasten his jeans, and when he spun around, she glanced at his fly and felt her skin warm. She'd seen just enough to trigger her imagination.

He cleared his throat, and she tightened her robe, wondering how they were going to face each other over the casual, late-day lunch they'd agreed upon earlier.

Flint stared at the road. Gina sat beside him, looking prim and proper, but he couldn't get the other image of her off his mind.

The one of her on her knees. That tousled hair, those violet-colored eyes, the slim, silky nightgown displaying every curve.

He would never be the same.

Flint shifted in his seat. He was still aroused, still battling the body part that refused to behave.

"I'm not really in the mood to deal with the public," he said. "So maybe we should skip the diner."

"Do you want to get take-out?" she asked.

Did he? Going to her house didn't seem like a good idea. And he wasn't about to bring her to his place, not when all he could think about was getting her on her knees.

"Why don't we just eat in the car?" He motioned to a hamburger stand across the street. "Is that all right with you?"

She nodded. "Sure. I could go for a milk shake."

"Yeah. Me, too." Something cold, he thought. Something to douse the fire burning inside him.

He headed for the drive-up menu, and they ordered the

same meal. They did that fairly often, he noticed. They liked the same kind of food, the same movies, the same type of furniture.

He parked in a shady spot, and they divided their lunch. When she ate a French fry and licked the salt from her fingers, he nearly groaned.

Was she still wearing those wispy red panties she'd had on under the nightgown? Flint still wore the same jeans, the old, threadbare Levi's she'd had her hands all over.

She glanced at him, and their eyes met. In the next instant they stared at each other in silence. He unwrapped his burger, but the sound of paper rattling made their discomfort even more obvious.

Damn it. Say something. Break the tension.

"It was weird, wasn't it?" he asked.

"The photo shoot?" She toyed with a French fry. "Yes, it was."

"But you did well, Gina." Really well, he thought, recalling the feel of her fingers against his fly.

She dropped her gaze, and he realized how truly shy she was. The ice princess never failed to confuse him.

"Thank you. You did well, too, Flint."

He took a bite of his burger. "Thanks."

"When will the pictures hit the tabloids?" she asked.

"If everything goes according to schedule, they'll be in the next issue."

"That soon?"

"Yep. That soon." He squirted ketchup onto a napkin. "And the media attention we've been getting is nothing compared to the frenzy those pictures are going to generate."

"So we better value our privacy while we've got the chance?"

"Exactly."

She dipped into the ketchup, and their gazes locked again. He wanted to kiss her, but he knew better. Their affair had been created for public display, not for quiet, breathless moments.

She finally ate the fry, leaving him fixated on her mouth. "Do you have an extra set of keys to the brownstone?" he asked.

She blinked. "Yes. Why?"

"Because I need a set."

She blinked again. "Why?"

"So I don't have to wait for you to let me in. Once the media frenzy starts, the reporters are going to follow us. I don't want to be stuck on your stoop with cameras flashing in my face."

"I've never given a man keys to my house before."

"I'll give them back once this is over." He took another bite of his burger, then paused to swallow his food. "I've never given anyone keys to my place, either."

Gina tilted her head. "Not even Tara Shaw?"

Flint didn't want to talk about the past. "That was ages ago. And I was staying in Hollywood at the time."

"Which means what?" She righted her posture. "I can't figure you and Tara out. I'm not even sure that your affair with her was real."

Suddenly irritated, he tapped his fingers on the steering wheel. "My relationship with Tara is none of your business."

"Why? Because you were faking it? Just like you're faking it with me? You're probably not capable of a real relationship."

Flint snarled. As usual, the ice princess had tossed his attitude in his face. "Me?" he retorted. "What about you? You probably fake orgasms."

"I do not, you big jerk."

Then prove it, he wanted to say. *Climb onto my lap and—*

"I can't wait until this phony affair is over." She moved

closer to the window, as far away from him as she could get.

"You and me both." But that didn't stop him from wanting her. "Hurry up and finish your food. I'm taking you home." He didn't need the aggravation of being near her, of fighting the pressure in his loins.

"Fine. I'm done." She jammed her half-eaten meal into the bag.

He followed suit and peeled out of the parking lot, barely giving her time to latch her seat belt. Speeding through traffic, he cursed to himself.

Women were nothing but trouble.

"You drive like an idiot," she complained.

"So sue me." He had a fast car and raging hormones. That gave him the right to be an idiot.

He turned onto Paul Revere Way and shoehorned his way into a parking spot. They both exited the Vette at the same time.

She gave him a haughty look. "What are you doing?"

"Walking you to your door."

"Don't bother. I can manage just fine without you."

"Too bad." He strolled beside her. The brownstone was at the other end of the street, and he was determined to get her there. And, he supposed, to annoy her on the way.

He reached for her hand, and when she tried to pull away, he held it tighter. "We're on a public street, Gina. So be a good girl and play your part."

She bit her nails into his skin.

"Are you one of those women who claws a man's back, too?" he asked, giving her a smug smile.

"Wouldn't you like to know?" She tossed her head and dug her nails deeper into his hand.

At this point he would take what he could get. Pain, pleasure. He didn't give a damn, as long as it gave him a forbidden thrill.

When they reached the brownstone, he grabbed her and pushed her against the door.

"Don't you dare—"

He cut her off with a kiss. A brutal, desperate, open-mouthed kiss.

She didn't fight him. She took his tongue with the same fury, the same passion, the same angry heat that welled inside him.

He rubbed against her, showing her how hard he was. She slid her hands around his waist and pulled him even closer.

They practically ate each other alive, sucking and licking and hissing like a couple of alley cats.

And then she shoved him away.

"I hate you," she said.

"I hate you, too." He shot the words back, aching to make love to her.

Without another word, he turned and walked away. Did he hate Gina, or hate what she did to him? Somehow, they seemed like the same thing.

Six

Three days later, Gina sat in the community living room at the brownstone, waiting for Flint to arrive.

Another date.

She didn't know how much more of this she could take. They'd avoided each other since their last heated encounter, but he'd finally called and insisted it was time for another public appearance. So here she was, attired in a short, body-hugging dress and a pair of spiky-heeled pumps that added three inches to her already towering height.

She'd purchased the outfit to get back at Flint. She knew the show of legs would drive him crazy. And the push-up bra she'd chosen shoved her breasts up and almost out of her dress, giving her an extra boost of cleavage. Flint would be lusting after what he couldn't have.

And that served the jerk right.

She checked her watch. Where was he, anyway? Of all nights to keep her waiting. She was already on edge, the anger inside her building to a raging inferno.

Why was he so damn secretive about Tara Shaw? Why wouldn't he admit if their relationship had been real or not?

Gina stood and pushed back her hair. She'd whipped her curly mane into a long, tousled mass, scrunching it with a mega-hold hair spray.

Tara Shaw had nothing on her.

Footsteps sounded on the stairs, and she turned to see Rita descending.

"Wow." Her sister stopped to stare. "What a transformation. You're as slinky as a black cat on Halloween."

And just as dangerous, Gina hoped. "Thanks. I intend to make him suffer."

"So I see."

Rita moved forward. And then she flashed a coy, feminine smile. She had a caring, loving nature, but her smile was often laced with mischief. Gina supposed it came with the territory. Rita was a serious woman, dedicated to her career, but the nurse, like many others in her profession, possessed a wry, sometimes playful sense of humor.

Rita went into the kitchen and started a pot of tea. Gina followed her, her high heels clicking on the tiled floor.

"Are you any closer to figuring out who your secret admirer is?" Gina asked.

Rita shook her head and sighed. "No."

On Valentine's Day, her sister had received a small white box tied with a gold ribbon. Inside, she'd found a pin—a small pewter heart with a gold-toned Band-Aid wrapped around it. The gift had been left at the hospital, which led her to believe her secret admirer was affiliated with Boston General.

"I wear the pin on my uniform every day," Rita said. "I keep hoping whoever gave it to me will notice and come forward and identify himself."

He could be an orderly, Gina thought. Or a male nurse. Or maybe even a patient who'd been released by now. "You may never find out."

"I can't imagine someone giving me a gift, then just disappearing."

"Men are hard to fathom," Gina said, thinking about Flint. And they were darn good at keeping secrets. Flint hadn't revealed a thing about himself, particularly his mysterious so-called fling with that Hollywood bombshell.

Maybe he really did have an affair with Tara. Or maybe he'd been in love with her.

Then again, he didn't seem capable of deep emotion.

After a cup of tea, Rita went to her apartment, leaving Gina waiting for Flint.

Where was he?

Finally, the buzzer sounded, announcing his late arrival. She let him into the building and gauged his reaction while he simply stared at her.

For the longest time he didn't speak, but his Adam's apple bobbed with each rough, masculine swallow.

Was he having trouble breathing?

Gina sent him an innocent smile. "Is something wrong?"

"What? No. Everything's just fine. I'm just peachy keen." He loosened the tie around his neck.

"You don't look fine." He looked flushed. And aroused. And gorgeous as ever. He wore an impeccably tailored suit and a shirt that matched the gold flecks in his eyes.

Her dress was gold, too, with just a hint of shimmer. For once she refused to let him intimidate her. He deserved to drool over her. This evening she would tease him into a sexual frenzy, then punish him by making him sleep alone.

He held out his hand.

Confused, she gazed at his palm.

"Give me the keys," he said. "I told you on the phone to have them ready."

"Oh, of course. It nearly slipped my mind." She opened her purse and removed an extra set of keys to the brownstone.

He snatched them and jammed them into his pocket. And then he stared at her again, like a man craving the forbidden. A muscle ticked in his jaw, and his chest heaved with a laden breath.

No doubt, he wanted to shove her against the wall and take what he wanted. But he wouldn't, of course. Stealing a kiss wasn't the same as stealing a woman's entire body.

Revenge was sweet, she thought, feeling like the femme fatale he'd claimed he could turn her into. Only she'd done it without his help. "We're going dancing, right?"

"That's right. To a hot spot downtown."

"That's perfect. Because I'm in the mood to party." She intended to get downright tipsy. How else could she parade around in public with her dress hiked to her rear and her breasts pushed up to her chin? Staying sober was out of the question.

"Let's go," she said, grabbing her jacket. Tonight she wasn't in the mood to worry about what the alcohol would do to her ulcer.

Tonight she would throw caution to the wind and drive Flint Kingman half mad.

Gina was driving him crazy. The hair, the dress, the cleavage he couldn't stop staring at. And if one more guy approached her to dance, Flint was going to kick some serious ass.

Nobody, but nobody put moves on his woman.

Okay, so maybe she didn't exactly belong to him. But they'd been linked together in the society pages, and the tabloids had already picked up on their affair, even though those sexy pictures hadn't surfaced yet.

As far as the world knew, Gina Barone was his.

She sat across from him at the trendy club, sucking on a maraschino cherry.

"I think I'd like to try a pink lady next," she said.

He watched her mouth form a pretty little O around the

cherry. He'd like to try a pink lady, too. But not the kind she referred to.

She'd been sipping one fruity concoction after the other, crunching ice cubes and toying with swizzle sticks and tiny umbrellas. She'd started off with a Midori sour, switched to a blue Hawaii, then went for a tequila sunrise.

"You're not supposed to mix drinks, Gina."

"I'm experimenting tonight."

Yeah, with his hormones. "You're half drunk already."

She tossed her head and sent that wild hair flying. "We're supposed to be out on the town, causing a scene, aren't we?"

I created a monster, he thought. *A tall, slim, high-heeled monster.* "Maybe you should eat something." He pushed a plate toward her.

She dropped the cherry in her glass and picked up a potato skin. After she tasted it, she made a surprised face. "It's spicy."

He shifted in his seat and watched her eat. The potato skins were flavored with cheddar cheese, sour cream and jalapeño peppers. Apparently she hadn't realized he'd ordered an array of spicy appetizers.

She swallowed the bite in her mouth, took a drink and then came to her feet.

"What are you doing?" he asked.

"I'm going to show you how hot it was."

Within a heartbeat, she stood in front of him, wedged herself between his legs and flung her arms around his neck. They were face to face but not quite mouth to luscious mouth.

The air in his lungs shot out. His blood sizzled. The muscles in his stomach flexed in anticipation.

She ran her tongue over her lips, sending his entire body into overdrive.

"Are you going to kiss me or not?" he asked, cursing his weakness, his desperate, all-consuming need for her.

She brushed his mouth in a gentle tease. He suspected half the people in the club were watching. And that aroused him even more. He wanted everyone to know the ice princess was his lady.

His pink lady.

"First you have to tell me your deepest, darkest fantasy," she said.

He caught his breath. Would she be this naughty in bed? "I have a honey fetish."

"Oh, my." She lowered her chin and gave him a sultry stare. "What else?"

He ran his hands along her waist, then down her hips, mesmerized by each rounded curve. "Women in short skirts." He raised her dress just a little. "With no panties."

"Do you want me to take my panties off for you, Flint?"

Yes. Oh, yes. He did. "Right now? Right here?"

She laughed and nipped his ear. "Only if you unzip your trousers for me."

This was insane. This incredible, heart-stopping, thrill-seeking attraction. They were good together. So damn good.

She finally kissed him, putting her mouth over his and sucking his tongue with a vengeance. He sucked back, over and over again. She tasted like tequila, rum and melon liqueur.

And peppers. He could taste the jalapeños.

She pulled back. "Hot, isn't it?"

Like a fever, he thought. "Will you get on your knees for me again, Gina?"

She raised her eyebrows. "Here? Now?"

No. When they were alone. When the public wasn't watching. When he could have her all to himself.

Struck by a jolt of fear, Flint gazed into Gina's eyes.

Heaven help him, he wanted her all to himself. But not just for mindless sex. Suddenly he craved something deeper, something substantial, something to fill the ache.

And that scared the hell out of him.

She wasn't just stirring his libido; she was tapping into his need for emotional security.

"So, do you want me on my knees?" she asked.

"Why not?" He tried to sound casual, to keep his voice even, his breathing steady. "I'll bet it would make the papers."

She tossed a flirtatious smile at him. "I think we'd get arrested instead."

"Yeah, but being hauled off to jail would get us some extra publicity." He hugged her a little closer, not quite able to let go.

"This is fun," she said.

"What? Messing around in public?"

"No. Torturing you."

The ache came back. Tenfold. Damn her, anyway.

He should have known. The little witch only wanted to make him suffer. She'd turned their attraction into a heartless game. Maybe she really did have ice flowing through her veins.

She wrestled out of his arms. "I think I'm ready for that pink lady now."

Fine. He'd let her get drunk. What the hell did he care? This phony affair would be over soon. And then he could find another woman to replace her. Someone sincere. Someone kind. Someone to get Gina Barone out of his system.

On Thursday afternoon, the telephone jangled in Gina's ear. She moaned and reached for the receiver.

"Hello?"

"Why aren't you at work today?"

She recognized Flint's hard-edged voice. "Because I'm sick."

"You've been sick for days. You're blowing our scandal. Get out of bed and get yourself together. I'm taking you out.''

''Leave me alone.'' She drew her knees to her chest. Her stomach burned like a furnace.

''No one has a hangover for that long.''

''I do.''

''Bull. You're just too chicken to face the press.''

''I am not.'' She squinted at the tabloids on her nightstand. At her request, her secretary had brought them by. Those racy pictures had come out yesterday, and they were causing quite a stir. Her reputation would never be the same. ''I just need some recovery time. I told you. I'm sick.''

''And I told you to get your butt out of bed.''

Gina glared at the phone. Flint had been calling her every day, making her illness worse. His constant badgering only heightened the stress.

She had enough to worry about. When those photos had hit the newsstand, she'd heard from everyone in her family, everyone but her dad. Of course, her mother had relayed a message. Her father wasn't pleased. He thought she'd gone too far.

Never mind that she'd done it for Baronessa Gelati. That she'd sacrificed her personal reputation to save the company. Her dad never awarded her with professional credit. He never treated her like a business equal.

''Are you still there?'' Flint asked.

''Yes.''

''Then get up and get ready. We need to be seen, Gina. To make a public appearance.''

''Back off, Flint.''

''Damn it, woman.''

She snarled at the receiver again. ''I'm hanging up on you.''

''You better not—''

Making good on her threat, she pushed the Talk button

and cut him off. And when the phone rang again, she refused to answer it.

Exhausted, she rolled over and went back to sleep.

An hour later she awakened in a stupor. Peering through hazy vision, she squinted.

Flint stood over her bed like the grim reaper. He wore a long black raincoat, and his features hardened around a snarl. His cheekbones were as sharp as knives, his hair ravaged by the wind.

Dear God. A nightmare. She closed her eyes again until his voice jumped out at her.

"You look like hell, Gina."

She sat up and grabbed her pillow. He was real. Much too real. "What are you doing here?"

"I have a key, remember?"

"That doesn't give you the right to invade my privacy."

"I have the right to check up on you. To make sure you're all right."

Trust a spin doctor to act as if he cared, to put a spin on his actions. "That's all fine and dandy, but I can't deal with you right now."

He sat on the edge of the bed and gave her a level stare. She pushed the covers away, wishing she had the strength to push him away. Why couldn't he let her suffer in peace?

He raised an eyebrow at her. "Charming outfit. It's so slinky. So seductive. So perfect for your new image."

She glanced at her baggy sweats. "I told you, I'm sick."

"What exactly is the nature of your illness? And don't toss that hangover crap at me. You can hold your liquor better than that."

Wanna bet? she thought. "I have a stomachache."

He made a face. "Why? Is it your moon time?"

Her moon—? Good grief. "Are you asking about my period?"

He made another face. "Women get cramps, don't they? And PMS and all that."

She rolled her eyes. "If I told you that was my problem, would you go away?"

"No. But a more conventional man would, I suppose. So, is that your problem?"

Hell's bells. She knew he wouldn't let the subject go until she admitted why she'd been holed up in bed for half the week.

"I have an ulcer, Flint. But keep your mouth shut about it. I don't want my family to know."

His eyebrows furrowed. "Is it bleeding?"

"No. I'm just suffering from the aftereffects of all that alcohol. And the spicy food." Jalapeño potato skins, Cajun chicken wings, curry-seasoned rice balls.

He removed his coat and tossed it over the back of a chair. "How long have you had this condition?"

"For years. But it tends to heal and then recur when I'm under stress. Or when I eat or drink something that doesn't agree with me."

Flint shook his head. "Where does it hurt?"

"Here." She placed her hand under her breastbone.

"I wish you would have told me earlier. I never would have let you eat all that stuff. Or get drunk."

"I don't need a nursemaid."

"The hell you don't." He stood and blew a frustrated breath. "I'm going to get you some milk. That helps, doesn't it?"

"Yes." She almost smiled. The big, gorgeous oaf was acting as if this was his fault. Of course, in a way, it was. He was a major stress factor.

"Should I warm it?"

"Sure." That sounded cozy. And deep down, she liked the idea of Flint waiting on her.

"I'll be right back."

She curled up again, and he returned with a coffee mug filled with warm milk. She accepted the drink and sipped gratefully.

He scooted into bed next to her. "Have you seen a doctor?"

"Yes, and I already took my medicine."

They sat in silence for a while. Her stomach still hurt, but the milk managed to coat the burn. Finally she finished the last of the soothing liquid and handed him the empty cup.

He put it on her nightstand. "You can go back to sleep if you want."

"That's okay. Maybe later." She turned to study his windblown appearance, his tousled hair and rumpled shirt. "Why do you look so beat?"

"I had to fight my way into the building. The vultures are hanging out at your front door."

She tried not to groan. "The press?"

"Yep." He smoothed a curl from her cheek. "We should probably spend our free time at my house in the future. All that ruckus isn't fair to your sisters."

"Will going to your house really make a difference?"

"Sure. If the reporters follow us to my place after a date, they won't be hanging out here."

"That makes sense." She grimaced. "So, what do you think of our photo debut?"

He reached for one of the tabloids. "I think we look pretty damn sexy."

To say the least. The picture on the cover portrayed them as they'd felt that day. Consumed with lust. Gina was on her knees, tugging at his pants. His fly was partially open, revealing rock-hard abs, a masculine navel and a slight shadow of hair that led to a part of him that wasn't visible but was still apparent through his jeans.

Gina leaned forward to assess her printed image. The red nightgown revealed the outline of her breasts and the blatant peaks of her nipples. Desire, she noticed, still studying the photo, burst onto the page, like a ravenous, powerfully winged raptor.

"If they could see us now," she said, nudging his arm.

"Yeah." He grinned, and they both laughed.

When their laughter faded, he said, "We're going to have to carry on this affair a bit longer than we'd originally planned. But I'm not pushing you. Take as much time as you need to feel better."

"Promise not to tell my family?"

"They must know you're sick. And besides, isn't your sister a nurse?"

"My family thinks I have the flu." Whenever her ulcer flared to this degree, she did her best to fool everyone, particularly Rita. It wasn't easy, but she'd gotten away with it so far. "Promise me, Flint."

He frowned at her.

"Please," she implored.

"Okay. I promise."

"Thank you." She closed her eyes and snuggled against him. He felt big and strong. And for now she needed him. "Will you stay for a while?"

He nuzzled the top of her head. "If that's what you want."

"It is."

Within no time Gina dozed off, content to be in her rival's protective arms.

Flint awakened later that evening, realizing he'd fallen asleep on Gina's bed. He flipped on a night-light and blinked to clear his vision.

Gina lay beside him, her eyes closed and her hair tangled around her face. She looked so vulnerable, so pale, so different from the woman who'd teased him at the dance club.

Tempted to hold her again, he reached out, then drew back, suddenly confused. As usual, she played havoc with his emotions.

He needed to get out of here, to go home and get his head straight.

Rising, he took care not to stir the mattress. But when his booted feet sounded against the hardwood floor, Gina woke up.

"Flint?" She gazed at him through shadowed eyes. "Don't leave. Not yet."

He stopped, struck by the quaver in her voice. "I wasn't," he lied. "I was just getting out of bed."

She sat up and pushed her hair away from her face, but several curls refused to comply. "Did you fall asleep, too?"

"Yeah." And he felt awkward about it. Somehow, sleeping in the same bed seemed more intimate than all the kissing and touching they'd done. And he wasn't comfortable feeling that close to her.

True, she was far more vulnerable than he'd ever imagined. She had an angelic side to go along with the devil in her, but she was still a career-minded woman.

Like his mother. And Tara, of course.

But at the time he'd been seeing Tara, he hadn't known the truth about his mom. Things were different now. What his mom had done had changed him.

"You were going home, weren't you?" Gina hugged a pillow to her chest. "Without saying goodbye?"

"No, I wasn't." Another lie. Another mark on his soul.

"Yes, you were. And just when I thought we were actually becoming friends."

Damn it, he thought. She looked mortally wounded, and that made him feel like a heel. He wanted to protect her, yet he wanted to push her away, to keep her at arm's length. Nothing was simple where Gina was concerned. Nothing at all.

"Friends?" He crossed his arms and heaved a rough breath. "Does that mean you don't hate me anymore?"

"Do you still hate me?"

He gave her a suspicious look. "You first."

She gnawed on her lip. "I never really did, I guess. I was just mad at you."

"Dogs get mad. People get angry," he responded, skirting around the subject.

"Don't correct my grammar. And answer the stupid question."

"Okay. I don't hate you, either." He liked her. Too damn much. But as to why, he wasn't quite sure.

"Will you fix me dinner?" she asked. "And serve it to me in bed?"

He almost laughed. She was a clever one, all right. "I suppose I could do that. But you have to return the favor sometime."

She smiled at him, and like an idiot, he wished he could kiss her.

"Thanks," she said.

"Don't thank me yet. You haven't tasted my cooking."

"I was thanking you for letting me confide in you. And for promising to keep quiet about it."

"Your family would understand, Gina."

"No, they wouldn't."

"I thought you were close to your sisters."

"I am. But they might slip up and tell my mom, and then she'd tell my dad. And if he knew I had an ulcer, he'd think I couldn't handle my job." She sat up a little straighter. "And I can. I'm darn good at what I do."

He didn't doubt that for a minute. "What are you in the mood to eat?"

"Something easy on the stomach."

"Which is?"

"How about chicken soup?"

He inclined his head. "I hope you mean the canned kind." Because he didn't have the slightest idea how to prepare soup from scratch.

"Of course not. I was talking about the real stuff."

"Sorry. That's not possible. How about just plain old

boiled chicken instead? And maybe a few bland vegetables?''

''Okay.'' She snuggled under the covers, wiggling her toes. ''I'm sure I'll be feeling better soon. And then we can face the vultures together.''

''Just take care of yourself.'' He turned away, knowing the media frenzy wouldn't be easy to bear, not for either of them.

The following afternoon, Flint needed to get away, so he drove to the country to see his grandmother.

He sat next to her on a floral-printed sofa, watching her repair a section of damaged beads on his regalia vest, an intricate garment she'd made for him several years before. Her hands, marred with liver spots, spoke of her age, even though she worked with deft precision.

Nĭsh'kĭ was a handsome lady, graced with exotic features and salt-and-pepper hair, which she routinely wore in a single braid down the center of her back.

Her home represented the beauty and simplicity of her lifestyle. She didn't fill the old farmhouse with Indian artifacts like some Native people did, but Flint saw traces of her ancestry scattered about. She took pride in being *Tsistsistas*—a term the traditional Cheyenne often used to refer to themselves rather than the tribal name history had given them.

''I saw those pictures,'' she said, slanting him a hawkish look.

Flint blew a windy breath. He knew *Nĭsh'kĭ* would disapprove of the tabloid photos, but she was a conservative woman who didn't understand the spin doctor in him.

''They weren't real,'' he explained. ''It was a publicity stunt.''

''They certainly looked real to me.''

''Well, they weren't. The whole thing was a scam. Gina's family hired me to divert the press.''

Nĭsh'kĭ adjusted the vest on her lap. "They hired you to pose half-naked with their daughter?"

"No. That was my idea." He gazed at his grandmother and saw her lips twitch. Suddenly he realized she was teasing him, making him pay for his public display.

Crafty old woman, he thought.

"That's what I figured," she said. "You like this girl."

He nearly squirmed, feeling like a kid who'd gotten caught with his hand in the cookie jar. "I'm attracted to her. But it's no big deal."

She threaded another bead onto the needle. "It must be a big deal. Or why else would you do that to yourself? Especially after the last one."

The last one. He knew *Nĭsh'kĭ* referred to Tara. His grandmother hadn't been pleased that he'd taken up with a Hollywood actress all those years ago. But she hadn't been pleased when her daughter had left the reservation to pursue an acting career, either.

Of course, they never talked about Flint's mother. Danielle was gone, and that was that. The Cheyenne, the *Tsistsistas,* didn't speak of the dead. What Flint knew about his mom, he'd learned from his father.

"So tell me about Gina," she said.

"I don't know what to say. She confuses me."

"You didn't look confused in those pictures."

"*Nĭsh'kĭ,* knock it off. I'm a grown man. I don't need this."

She chuckled under her breath. "So, when do I get to meet her? This Gina who confuses you?"

"You won't. Our scandal will be over soon."

"How soon?"

"I'm not sure." It depended on Gina's health, but he wasn't at liberty to say. He'd promised to keep her secret.

"Then why can't I meet her next week?"

Was his grandmother playing matchmaker? Or was she

simply curious about the woman he'd been photographed with? "I don't know what I'll be doing next week."

"You'll be at the church powwow with me."

Damn. He'd forgotten all about the one-day event *Nĭsh'kĭ* church sponsored. "I'm not sure I can go."

"Then why did you bring me your vest?" She shoved the beadwork under his nose.

"Because it was damaged, and you always repair my regalia."

She put her hand on his knee. "When's the last time you danced, Flint?"

"It's been months. But you know how busy I am." He sat for a moment, missing the powwow circle in which he'd been raised. His grandmother had moved to Massachusetts after his mother had died, and she'd taught him to honor the Drum. "Okay, I'll be there. But I'm not bringing Gina."

He wasn't prepared to invite her into his scared circle. Because that would be like inviting Gina Barone straight into his heart.

Seven

Gina's life spun out of control in the next two days. Private citizens asked for her autograph, and reporters dogged her every move. They waited outside the brownstone every morning to catch her on the way to work. They snapped candid photos, shoved microphones in her face and asked intrusive questions.

Questions about Flint. And Tara Shaw. Supposedly Tara and her current husband were having problems, which, according to the press, meant that Tara would probably seek out Flint. For comfort. And for sex.

The reporters wanted to know what Gina intended to do about it. Would she battle Tara for Flint? Would there be a catfight?

Gina turned to look at Flint. They walked hand-in-hand through an antique show, giving Boston and the rest of the world plenty to talk about.

He nuzzled her neck every time they stopped to view a

rare table or an ornate cabinet. And she, of course, returned his outward affection.

Gina played her part, even though she wanted to scream. The Tara Shaw mystery was driving her crazy, and the media fueled the fire, making her wonder what Flint was hiding.

"Let's check this out." Flint steered Gina toward a vintage jewelry display, then glanced over his shoulder.

"Is our shadow there?" she asked, knowing he was checking to see if a local cameraman still followed them. "Yep."

She sighed. The photographer had been a constant tag, an annoying tail. "What kind of pictures does he expect to get? After all, we're in a public setting."

Flint grinned. "Maybe he thinks we're going to do it, right in front of everyone."

"Very funny." She tried to keep her tone light, but she couldn't get Tara off her mind. What if the other woman really did come looking for Flint? What if she pressed those massive breasts against his chest and cried on his shoulder? The actress might be twenty-one years his senior, but she'd aged like a fine wine. Then again, she'd probably gotten a little help. A tuck here, a nip there. Beverly Hills overflowed with cosmetic surgeons, and Tara could afford the best.

Gina moved closer to Flint, making sure no one else was within earshot. "Did I tell you I was solicited by a men's magazine?"

"Really? Did they want an interview?"

"No. They asked if I was interested in doing a celebrity layout. A nude pictorial." They'd also informed her that Tara Shaw had appeared in their July, 1975 issue, posing in a feather boa and platforms.

For a moment Flint fell silent. And then he simply said, "Wow."

Wow? What was that supposed to mean? That she wasn't

sexy enough to make the grade? "I told them I would think about it."

His mouth snaked into a grin. "You're kidding?"

Gina wanted to kick him, but instead she tossed a stray curl over her shoulder. She'd taken to wearing her hair loose, at least during their public outings. And why not? The media had dubbed her a "bohemian-haired beauty," and she'd decided not to spoil her new, dangerous image. "I could pull it off if I wanted to."

His grin widened. "I don't doubt that for a second."

Surprised by his reaction, she met his gaze. "So you think I'd make a good nude model?" *As good as Tara Shaw?* she wanted to add.

"Hell, yes."

He brushed his body against hers, making her warm. When she brushed back, he kissed her.

The lady manning the jewelry counter gasped, but Gina didn't care. She slipped her tongue into Flint's mouth and tasted his desire.

A hunger that seemed much too real to be staged.

When the kiss ended, Gina kept her arms around him, even though an elderly couple walked by and gave her a disgusted look and a biker-type guy flashed a thumbs-up. The photographer lurked at the next booth, framing the entire scene for another shot.

"Do you know what the current gossip is?" Flint asked. "Hot off today's presses?"

"No. What?"

"That we made a sex tape."

Gina's breath rushed out. "A porno?"

"A private tape of us making love," he clarified.

That sounded like the same thing to her. "How do you know that's what they're saying?"

He flashed his spin-doctor smile. "I have connections."

She studied his smile, keeping her voice to a whisper. The cameraman probably thought she was begging Flint to take her home and have his wicked way with her. On film. "You didn't start that story, did you?"

"Me? No way. I just heard about it, that's all."

Gina tilted her head. Where Flint was concerned, she didn't know what to believe. "Are you telling me the truth?"

Suddenly evasive, he let her go and turned toward the jewelry display.

The woman behind the counter, the stunned female who'd gasped earlier, watched him in awe.

As he scanned the colorful gems behind the glass, Gina slipped her hands in her pockets and tried not to focus on how this scandal would affect the rest of her life. She wasn't a movie star, like Tara Shaw. She was just an Italian girl from Boston lucky enough to be born into a wealthy family. A rich girl with an ulcer and unruly hair. How glamorous could that be?

She turned and found herself besieged by at least a hundred pairs of curious eyes. About fifty people gathered near the jewelry booth, watching and waiting for something exciting to happen.

Flint pointed to an item in the case. "May I see that?"

"Certainly." The saleswoman removed a pendant and handed it to him. She was a mousy-looking brunette with wire-rimmed glasses and fading makeup, but she made a point of smiling at him. When he smiled back at her, she all but swooned.

"I'll take it," he said a moment later. "The necklace," he added, when the woman merely stared.

"Oh, of course." She rang up the sale, quoting an astronomical price.

He paid with a credit card and walked over to Gina. "For you, milady."

She glanced at the gift he'd pressed into her hand—a diamond-and-platinum cherub shining on the end of a glittering chain. Flint had bought her an angel.

* * *

Several hours later Flint weaved in and out of traffic. Gina sat next to him, fingering the pendant around her neck. It was foolish, she knew, to feel sentimental about his gift, but she couldn't help it.

What a complex man he was. Demanding, funny, aloof. Even romantic, she thought, clutching the cherub.

He checked the rearview mirror. "Guess who's behind us?"

She didn't need to guess. "The pesky photographer."

"The very one. Boy, is that guy persistent."

"Did you know it would be like this?" she asked. "Did you know the press would be so relentless?"

"Pretty much. I've been through this before."

"Of course. With Tara." The actress who'd been troubling her for most of the day. "They keep comparing me to her."

He glanced at his mirror again. "I know. Do you want me to try to lose this guy?"

Gina crossed her arms. How easily he'd dodged the Tara issue. "This is really bothering me."

"Me, too. He's been nipping at our heels for days."

"I was talking about Tara."

Flint frowned and shifted gears. "She's a movie star. She fascinates the press."

"What does that mean? That you knew they would drag her into our affair?"

"Not to this degree, but I knew her name would surface."

Gina studied his profile. He stared out the windshield, eyes fixed on the road. "Have you heard from her?" she asked.

"No."

"Do you expect to?"

"No," he said again.

Trying to get information from him was like pulling teeth

from a dinosaur. "Do you think she's upset? After all, they're saying that she and I will eventually end up fighting over you."

"I doubt the rumors bother her. Tara thrives on publicity."

"She's a married woman, Flint."

"So? Her husband is a celebrity, too. And his career is floundering right now. Sometimes in that business ignominious press is better than none at all."

Gina didn't think so, but what did she know of Hollywood? Or the type of man Tara had married?

"What about you?" she asked.

"What about me?" Flint countered.

"Do you thrive on publicity?"

He turned and shot her a frustrated look. "Of course not. I came up with this scandal because I knew it would work. And that's part of my job, Gina. Making scandals happen, diverting the press."

She sighed, and he blew a windy breath. They sat in silence for a while. Flint kept checking his mirror, and Gina knew the photographer was still on their trail.

Finally, he said, "Are you mad at me?"

"Dogs get mad," she quipped, recalling the line he'd tossed at her last week. "People get angry."

He broke into a grin. "Touché, milady. Touché."

Damn that smile of his. It drove her mad. Not angry.

"I'm really attracted to you, Gina. That part of our affair is real."

She touched the angel again. "I know. For me, too."

"Then why are we always fighting?"

"Because you're a pain in the rear," she told him.

"Oh, yeah?" He was still smiling. "Well, so are you."

Gina wanted to kiss him, to put her mouth against that cocky smile, those curved lips.

He turned onto a tree-lined street where multistoried houses loomed through an abundance of foliage. Most of the structures were brick, with large, manicured lawns. The neighborhood held an affluent air, but she sensed warmth, as well.

"I'm leading that cameraman right to my front door," he said. "I must be crazy."

And she must be crazy for wanting to kiss Flint.

He entered the driveway of an impressive home. The windows were stained glass, and the slates and stones that made up the two-story building embodied an alluring passage of time. The historic estate had been remodeled to reflect an artistic yet traditional style.

He parked the Corvette at a careless angle. "Maybe we should give the guy a photo op. You know, something juicy."

She checked the side mirror. A blue SUV pulled to a stop on the curbless street, but not in a blatant position. She assumed the driver tried to mask his appearance, shadowing part of the vehicle beneath an enormous tree. Apparently he didn't think he'd been found out. "We're going to accommodate that jerk?"

"Why not? He's fueling our scandal. Do you realize the newspapers have barely mentioned the pepper fiasco? No one seems to care about who spiced the gelato anymore. They care more about who's spicing the sheets." He sent her his signature grin. "And that's us, babe. You and me."

"So what do we do? Make out in the car?"

"No. On the porch. That'll give him a better view."

Gina's heart raced. "Sounds like a plan."

They ascended the porch, teasing each other with playful little nudges. Deep down, Gina knew this was more than a photo op. She wanted to touch Flint, and he wanted to touch her.

He jammed his keys into his front pocket. "I'll bet you can't take the keys away from me."

She glanced at his jeans. "I'll bet I can."

"Then go for it."

She reached down, but he caught her wrist. They wrestled like kids, bumping the porch rail and laughing. She managed to free herself and dig into his pocket. And when she latched onto the keys, he grabbed her other hand and pressed it against his fly.

Her heartbeat went haywire.

She toyed with his zipper, and he unbuttoned the top of her blouse just a little, just enough to send the brisk March air racing over her skin.

Suddenly he kissed her—in fury, in power, in a need neither of them could deny.

The wind kicked up, disheveling her hair and rippling his shirt. He moved his mouth lower, but not low enough. She wanted him to lick the tip of her breasts, to ease the ache, but her clothes hindered him.

And his clothes hindered her.

She popped the button on his jeans, then realized what she was doing. A photographer was out there, framing their foreplay.

"We have to stop."

"Just one more kiss," he said.

She clung to his belt loops. Yes, just one more kiss.

His beard stubble scraped her jaw. His breath warmed her cheek. One kiss turned into two, and she rocked against him, too dizzy to speak.

He fisted his keys and fumbled with the lock. Finally he made a clumsy connection, and the door opened.

Together, they stumbled into the entryway, still wrapped in each other's arms. He kicked the door shut.

And then a moment of clarity hit. The jig was up. No one could see them now.

He pulled back and dragged a shaky hand through his hair. She tried to focus on his house, but all she saw was a blur of antiques and a maze of color.

Blinking, she stared at a stained-glass window, but she wasn't able to discern the design. A few minutes later, she shifted her gaze to find Flint watching her with a look so intense he took her breath away.

"Tell me you want what I want, Gina. Tell me I'm not alone."

A chill streaked through her.

"Tell me," he implored, his voice edged with need.

"You're not alone, Flint. I want what you want." Desperately. So badly, she hurt.

He moved closer, then stopped when they were inches apart. "Now tell me that it won't matter afterward. That you won't hold it against me."

"It won't matter," she said, praying that she wouldn't get attached, that she wouldn't long to keep him later. "I promise not to hold it against you."

He reached for her, and she fell into his arms. For a silent moment he held her, then they looked into each other's eyes and lost control.

He pulled her blouse open, sending buttons flying. She yanked his shirt out of his pants and worked his zipper. He unhooked her bra; she shoved his jeans down his hips.

Next, they kicked off their shoes and nearly stumbled in their haste. And somehow, they kissed through it all, their mouths fusing, their tongues dancing, their lungs gasping for air.

When she was naked, he lowered his head and teased her nipples, taking one and then the other into his mouth. He suckled, filling her with warmth and pleasure.

And then he slid lower. And lower still.

Finally he dropped to his knees and looked at her. She gazed at him, struck by his beauty, by the flash of gold she saw in his eyes.

She touched his cheek, the roughness of his whiskers. Shadows washed over his face, giving an air of mystery to each dark, stunning feature.

Gina traced his mouth, the masculine line of his lips. But

when he nipped her finger, she got a sudden sense of danger.

Their affair wasn't supposed to be real. This wasn't supposed to be happening.

"It's too late," he said, as if he'd read her mind.

"I know." She slid her hands into his hair and combed through the thickness. She craved him. Urgently.

He licked between her legs, and she went hot. And wet. And gloriously feral.

Grasping her hips, he held her still. But she fought the stillness and bucked against her lover's mouth.

Her lover's mouth. Just the thought thrilled her.

His kisses were slick and sinful, wild and aggressive. He continued to taste her, and she knew he was as aroused as she was.

He wanted her to climax as badly as she welcomed the sensations he incited—the sensual chill tingling her spine, the flutter in her stomach, the wondrous pressure between her thighs.

"Flint." She whispered his name, and he deepened each intimate kiss, heightening the pressure. The excitement. The sexual power he wielded over her.

He would be her undoing, she thought. He would steal her resolve, making her crave more and more of his touch.

She said a fearful prayer, begging the heavens to keep her sane. But a second later an orgasm ripped through her, shattering the last of her control.

When it ended, she nearly melted in pool of silk.

Blinking through the daze that followed, she looked at a stained-glass window, the same one that had baffled her earlier. But this time, the design took shape, and she saw a naked woman, her hair fanned like a swirling rainbow, her body arched like a bow. Kneeling before her was a man. A beautiful, dangerous man.

Flint came to his feet. All he wanted was Gina—the woman who confused his emotions, clashed with his temper and made him hunger like a predator that needed to feed its soul.

"This might happen fast," he said. "I might not be able to hold on."

She leaned into him. "Just don't stop touching me. Please, don't stop."

"I won't." *Not ever,* he thought, realizing how insane the notion was. When their public affair ended, he would let her go.

He slid his hands down her waist and over her hips, then brought her flush against him. She was so damn beautiful, slim yet lush with curves. The angel he'd given her dangled between her breasts, the diamonds shimmering against golden skin. And her nipples, he noticed, pink and aroused from his touch, beaded like pearls.

He kissed her, daring her to taste herself. Their tongues met and then mated, and she made a sigh of surrender. She looked dazed, bathed in the afterglow of a skyrocketing orgasm.

Flint smiled, pleased he'd done that to her.

"Is that masculine pride I see on your face?" she asked.

"You bet it is." He backed her against a table in the foyer. Straddling her on the hardwood floor was out of the question, but he didn't think he could make it upstairs to the bedroom. Or even to the living room, where an area rug would provide a small measure of comfort.

He lifted her onto the table and pushed her legs open. The freshly polished antique held a vase of flowers his cleaning lady insisted on replenishing every week, and the heady scent filled his nostrils like an aphrodisiac.

Guilt clawed its way to his chest. Women liked soft, fluffy beds. They liked romance—candles, chocolates and heartfelt bouquets. And he knew a vase of decorative flowers didn't count.

Gina bit her lower lip and watched him. Daylight spilled

in from the window, illuminating her in a color-enhanced glow.

He entered her, and she clamped around him, warm and wet. He groaned, then froze, cursing his stupidity. He'd never forgotten about protection before, but the condoms he kept in his bedroom weren't exactly accessible right now.

"Gina, please tell me you're using something."

Her nipples, those pearl-pink nipples, teased his chest, and he shivered, aching to move.

"I'm still on the pill," she said.

Relieved, he let out the breath he'd been holding. "Still? Does that mean you haven't done this in a while?"

She nodded, and a rush of excitement washed over him. It had been awhile for him, too.

In the next instant he thrust so hard he made her gasp. But he sensed that she didn't want him to slow down, to ease the rhythm. She wrapped her legs around him and held on for dear life. When she tipped her head back, her hair tangled around his hands, as seductive as wild-seeded vines.

He got an image of Eve luring Adam with the apple, of a woman bringing a man to his knees.

But I've already been on my knees, Flint thought. He'd given her selfless pleasure. Now it was his turn to take what she so willingly offered.

Danger. Temptation.

Hot, hard, hip-grinding sex.

She touched him while he moved, while he pumped his raging body into hers. She roamed his shoulders and then flattened her palms over his chest. Her fingers danced across the muscles that rippled his stomach.

Her eyes locked onto his, and he battled the urge to spill into her. He wanted a few more minutes, a few more seconds to claim his mate.

The table shook under the pressure of their joining. The

vase of flowers rattled. Sensation slid over sensation, blinding him to everything. Everything but need.

She bit her nails into his back, and he welcomed the sting of lust, the draw of blood. Somehow, he knew she'd never done that to another man before. She'd never been this unbridled, this free.

He pushed harder and deeper, until his body went taut and he convulsed in her arms. She buried her face against his neck and made a sexy little sound, but he was too far gone to know if she'd fallen over the edge with him.

All he felt was his seed pouring into her, as warm and fluid as the climax flowing through his veins.

Eight

As Flint withdrew his body from hers, Gina became acutely aware of missing him, of wanting to keep him there.

"Are you okay?" he asked.

Did she look as confused as she felt? She'd never understood women who clung to a man after sex, and now she struggled with that emotion. "I'm just fine."

He skimmed her cheek. "So, I didn't hurt you?"

"No." Gina rose, then put her arms around him, succumbing to her emotions. She needed to cuddle, to burrow against him. "You didn't hurt me."

He nuzzled her neck, and she caressed his sweat-slicked back. He was strong and muscular, and the power he emitted made her heart beat much too fast.

Don't fall for him, she warned. *Don't get attached.*

Gina took a deep breath and glanced at the stained-glass window. While she held Flint, she searched for the naked woman and her lover, but the images didn't appear.

How could that be?

"I could have sworn…"

Flint lifted his head. "What?"

"I thought I saw a picture of a woman on that window, but now she's gone." And so was the man, she realized.

"Really?" He turned, and together they studied the translucent panels. "It was just an illusion," he said. "Stained glass has a way of creating magic."

"It seemed so real." She tried to bring the woman back to life, but all she saw were abstract shapes.

The lady and her lover had disappeared, reminding Gina that her affair with Flint would soon seem like an illusion, as well. Magic that wasn't meant to be.

She picked up her panties off the floor and slipped them on, then went after her bra.

He followed suit and reached for his boxers, but that was as far as they got. Before she could don her blouse, he took her hand.

"Are you hungry?" he asked. "We can fix a snack and climb into bed for a while."

She couldn't refuse, not his charming smile or his cozy suggestion. "That sounds perfect."

Dressed in their underwear, they rummaged through his kitchen and prepared a tray of whatever they could find. Flint produced a loaf of French bread, and Gina sliced a block of Cheddar cheese into thick, sandwich-size squares. He poured her an ice-cold soda and grabbed a beer for himself. She opened a can of fruit cocktail and spooned the contents into two bowls.

After they ascended the spiral staircase and entered the master bedroom, goose bumps raced up her arms. His room was nearly identical to hers. And even though she'd been forewarned, the impact of seeing it overwhelmed her.

But just momentarily. He set the tray on a nightstand and coaxed her into bed, where she slipped into the gentle, post-sex comfort he provided.

He handed her a slice of bread and a hunk of cheese,

and she spilled crumbs onto the quilt, realizing they'd both forgotten napkins.

"We should probably work out the details of our final fight," he said.

"Our final fight?"

"The public breakup."

A sharp pain lanced her chest. Had he done that deliberately? Had he meant to spoil the intimacy? To remind her that none of this was real? "That's your area of expertise," she said, hoping she sounded more unaffected than she felt. "You're the spin doctor."

"I guess it could happen at the Gatsby party my stepmother hosts every year. I'll make sure some reporters are on hand." He studied his beer. "Better yet, I'll start a rumor that Tara might show up. That'll have the press clamoring for an invite."

Stunned, Gina could only stare. "Won't that ruin your stepmother's party?"

"Are you kidding? It'll make it the place to be. The event of the season."

Jealousy gripped her hard and quick. Why didn't he just invite Tara and make the rumor come true?

"We'll stage a fight at the party," he said. "Then you can break up with me. I'm sure you'll be able to come up with a few legitimate gripes. Some reasons to dump me."

"Yes," she agreed. "I'm sure I can."

For a moment he fell silent. Then he took a swig of his beer. "Do you want to rehearse what you're going to say?"

"What's to rehearse? You're a shallow jerk who refuses to settle down. That ought to be enough."

He had the gall to look wounded. "I'm not shallow. And I plan on settling down. Just not with someone like you."

She narrowed her eyes. "Someone like me?"

"A woman focused on her career."

If the bed had opened up and swallowed her whole, she wouldn't have been more surprised. "That's the most chauvinistic remark I've ever heard.'' And she couldn't believe it had come out of his mouth. ''I intend to get married and have children someday,'' she told him. ''But that doesn't mean I should sacrifice my career in the process.''

''That's a pretty selfish attitude, don't you think?''

No. Gina thought it was progress, the way of the modern world. ''Get a grip on reality, Flint. Wake up and smell the century.''

He rolled his eyes, and she dropped her food onto the tray. She didn't intend to spend another minute in his company. But when she attempted to leave, he grabbed her arm.

''Where in the hell do you think you're going?''

She struggled to pull free. ''Home.''

''Oh, no, you're not.'' He yanked her onto the bed and she landed on top of him with a thud.

Face to face, chest to breast, they stared at each other. And then he flashed his spin-doctor smile.

She wanted to thrash him with her fists, to pound that damn smile right out of him. ''What are you grinning at, you big ape?''

''You, you little ape.''

He tapped her chin in a playful gesture, and she knew both of them were losing the battle. She wanted to be in his arms as badly as he wanted her there.

He stroked a hand down her back, calming her, soothing her with affection. ''Stay with me, Gina.''

She closed her eyes, afraid of what he was doing to her, of the tug-of-war, of the hope and harrow he unleashed. ''We have such different ideals. We don't agree on anything. We're not right for each other.''

He traced a lazy hand down her spine. ''I know, but I'm not asking for forever.''

''You're asking for uncommitted sex. For as much of it as you can get.''

''I can't help it,'' he said, his voice going rough.

"You're like an addiction. A drug. An ache I can't control."

His admission slid over her, as hot as burning wax, as daring as candles melting over bare flesh.

She opened her eyes and breathed in his scent. She could feel his pulse beating against hers, a rhythm much too unsteady to ignore. "I'm going to break up with you at the party."

"I know." He rolled her onto the bed, so they lay side by side. "But what about the time in between?"

"I'll be with you. And then, when it's over, it's over. We won't let it linger."

He pressed a tender kiss to her forehead, but his voice was still rough. "I wish it could be different."

"It doesn't matter." She didn't want to dwell on impossible wishes. They both knew they weren't meant to be.

"Do you still think I'm shallow?" he asked.

"Do you still think I have a stiff nature?" she countered.

His lips twitched, and she knew he was going to smile. "I've been calling you an ice princess in my mind, but now I'm not so sure the term fits. I haven't quite figured you out."

"Me, neither. With you, I mean." She didn't understand why he wouldn't marry a career woman. He seemed like a modern man, but that wasn't the case. His outdated values confused her.

He reached for a lock of her hair. "I'm going to miss you, Gina."

She would miss him, too. Desperately. "We're not done with each other yet, Flint."

She slid her hand down the front of his body, then pressed her thumb to his navel. His breath rasped out, and his stomach muscles bunched and quivered.

"Are you going to make the ache go away?" he asked.

"Yes." She would feed his addiction, the hunger he claimed he couldn't control.

She looked into his eyes and saw them turn a glittering shade of gold. He touched her cheek, and she smiled.

Slats of sunlight streamed in from the window, sending shadows across the bed. The day was chilled yet warm, breezy yet calm.

She moved closer, and they kissed. He took her mouth, and she took his.

But that wasn't all they took. Somewhere deep inside, they stole each other's souls. Not for eternity, she thought. Just for the moment.

She toyed with the waistband on his boxers, skimming beneath the elastic with her nails. He made a rough sound, and she scratched his stomach.

"I'm so turned on," he said.

"I know. So am I." She tugged at his boxers, and he lifted his hips to help her remove them, to give her free reign.

Exploring his length, she encircled him, stroking from shaft to tip. And then she tasted the saltiness of his skin.

His entire body jolted, and she took him into her mouth, setting a warm, fluid rhythm.

She knew how her touch affected him. And she was powerless to stop. She took him deeper, and he shivered from the pain, from the pleasure, from the pressure building in his loins.

"Gina." He said her name on a prayer, on a plea.

With her hair tangling around her shoulders and her pulse beating wildly at her throat, she stripped off her panties and bra.

And then she straddled him.

He reared up to kiss her, and she feared he would devour her in one voracious bite.

He grabbed her, and they rolled over the bed. Her heartbeat tripped and stumbled while her breath came in short, edgy pants. He used his teeth, his tongue, his entire mouth to arouse her.

He left marks on her skin, sucking her neck and biting her shoulders. She could feel the circles of heat, the rings of fire.

They couldn't make love without going crazy, and she reveled in the madness, in the sheer and utter insanity.

Once again she straddled him. Only this time she impaled herself, taking him inside.

He clutched the bedposts while she rode him, while she moved up and down, stroking him, milking him.

He watched her, his eyes locked intimately with hers. He was so powerful, she thought. So dangerous.

His chest rose and fell, his stomach clenched, his hips lifted to meet her generous thrusts.

Then suddenly he released the bedposts so he could hold her, so they could climax in each other's arms.

When it happened, she let herself fall, knowing she was addicted to him, too.

Later that night, Flint drove Gina home. He couldn't bear to ask her to stay, to sleep beside him. Somehow that seemed too tender, too loving. Too committed.

But now that they were parked in front of the brownstone, he didn't want to let her go. And that scared the hell out of him.

He turned to look at her. "We should go out tomorrow night," he said, trying to focus on the scandal. "There's a charity auction at the country club that's bound to get some press."

"I already have other plans. I'm having dinner with some friends. At their house."

He frowned, suddenly hurt and envious that he'd been left out. She was supposed to be spending her free time with him. "Who are they?"

"Robert and Lena Marino."

He cocked his head. "The pepper people?"

Gina made a face. "They're not pepper people. They're my friends."

"If you say so." Flint knew that Robert Marino was the man who'd suffered an allergic reaction to the habanero-spiced gelato. The man who could have died.

"What's that's supposed to mean?" Gina asked. "That you don't believe they're my friends?"

"I don't know. I guess. I mean, you're trying to smooth things over, right? Keep them from filing a lawsuit."

She crossed her arms. "This has nothing to do with the gelato tasting. Or with Robert having that reaction. I've always socialized with the Marinos. I care about them. They're special to me."

He tapped on the steering wheel. "So what do they think about me?"

"They know our affair was fabricated for the press."

He gave her an incredulous look. "You told them? You trust them that much?"

"Yes, I do. They're good people. And I need to get away, to spend some quality time out of the limelight." She brushed his hand. "Why don't you come with me?"

"You don't think they'll mind?"

"No, not at all."

"Okay, then I'll go," he said, satisfied that she'd included him in her plans.

A moment later he told himself to get a grip. He was behaving like a teenager with a crush. Hell, he was even jealous of her friends.

He took his keys out of the ignition. "Come on. I'll walk you to your door."

"Thanks. Do you want to come up for a nightcap?"

He stalled, unsure what to say. What if he ended up staying at her place? What then? The intimacy he'd been trying to avoid would jump right up and bite him in the butt.

"Flint?"

Tell her no, a sensible voice in his head cautioned.

"All right," he heard himself say. One drink wouldn't hurt, and he'd make it quick.

They reached the brownstone stoop, and she unlocked the front door. "Thank goodness, the reporters are gone."

"Yeah. We've had enough of them for one day." Because he longed to put his arms around her, he jammed his hands in his coat pockets.

They entered the brownstone and took the stairs. Silence engulfed the building, and Flint assumed Gina's sisters were already tucked in for the night.

Her apartment was dark, and when she flipped on a light, he stood like a statue.

Suddenly he wanted to sleep in her bed, to awaken beside her in the morning, to climax at dawn and then linger over coffee and croissants before they made love again in the shower.

He could almost feel the warm, pulsating water, the rising stream, the—

"Beer?"

He glanced up. "I'm sorry. What?"

"Would you like a beer?"

"Do you have anything stronger?"

She removed the jacket he'd given her and placed it on the back of the sofa. "I've got a full bar."

"Then I'll take a shot of—" He paused, deciding what his mood demanded. "Tequila," he finally said.

"Lime? Salt?"

"Sure." He wanted something with a kick, something to take his mind off a warm bed. And an even warmer woman.

He watched her walk to the bar. Her jeans hugged her rear, and her hair swayed while she moved.

As she prepared his drink, he studied her face, those violet eyes and that luscious mouth.

She handed him the tequila, and he downed it in one

desperate second. Then he sucked the juice out of the lime, recalling how she'd sucked—

"I think I'll have a glass of milk," Gina said.

Flint set the lime on the bar and tried to clear his mind. His dirty, male mind. "Milk? Is your stomach acting up?"

"It's burning a little."

"I'm sorry."

"It's not your fault," she said. "I just didn't eat enough today."

"I should have fed you more." But he hadn't been focused on food earlier, and the bread and cheese they'd prepared had been a snack, not a meal. "Maybe you should eat something now."

"I suppose I should. Are you hungry?"

"No. I'll just have another drink." While she went into the kitchen, he topped his glass, then stared at the amber liquid.

What was he doing? Waiting around for an overnight invitation?

Yes, he thought. That was exactly what he was doing.

Flint shrugged off the guilt. So what? So he wanted to spend the night. That wasn't a crime. After all, they were lovers. And she'd agreed to keep their relationship going, at least until the party that would end it all.

To bide his time, he picked through her VHS and DVD collection. She favored the classics, movies that made Hollywood seem glamorous. He appreciated her taste, her fascination with dames, dolls, gangsters and G-men. But as he came across an unexpected tape, a low-budget western from the late sixties, his gut clenched.

He didn't need this. Not tonight.

Desperate to numb the rising pain, he finished his drink and stared at the cover of the movie. He knew this film intimately. At one time he'd even been proud of it. But these days it made him hurt.

Gina returned to the living room carrying a half-eaten

sandwich, a glass of milk and a napkin. She set her drink on an end table.

He looked up and faked a casual air. "I didn't know you had one of my mother's movies."

"I meant to tell you. I bought it awhile ago."

"Before we met?"

"No. Right after." She picked at her sandwich. "I was curious about her."

He shifted the tape in his hand, once again keeping his tone light. "Why?"

"Because she's your mother, and I wanted to compare the family resemblance." Gina sat on the sofa, but he remained standing. "You're a lot like her, Flint. Not just how you look, but your mannerisms, your smile."

He was nothing like Danielle Wolf, he thought. Nothing like the woman who'd given him life, then taken it away. When he thought about his mother, he felt dead inside.

"Your mom had incredible sex appeal. She should have been a big star."

He flinched, but luckily Gina didn't seem to notice his distress. Then again, she was still caught up in the supposed similarity she'd uncovered between mother and son.

He glanced at the tape. "Her movies weren't that great."

"No, but she was. I'm sorry you lost her, Flint."

He did his damnedest to mask his emotions. His pain. "I was just a baby."

"It's so sad." Gina reached for her milk and sipped slowly. "It must have been hard on your dad, losing his wife soon after their child was born."

For an instant, Flint wanted to tell Gina the truth. He wanted to confide in her, to reveal the whole sickening story. But the torment in his heart kept him from saying it, from admitting what his mother had done.

"Death is never easy," he said instead. "But my dad found someone else. He remarried."

"I know. But wasn't it ten years later? That's a long time to wait."

"He's happy now."

"I'm glad."

"Yeah, me, too." But as hard as he tried, he couldn't forget his family's deception, the way they'd all covered for his mom.

Gina met his gaze, and he knew she'd finally picked up on his discomfort. He glanced away, wondering if he should pour himself another drink.

"I upset you, didn't I?"

Yes, he thought. Her compassion hurt. "I was taught not to speak too freely of the dead. It's not the Cheyenne way."

"I'm sorry," she said. "I didn't know."

"That's okay," he responded, ashamed of the lie. Although his grandmother had always followed that practice, Flint never did. He used to talk openly about his mom before he'd discovered the truth.

Flint put the tape on the rack, and Gina rose to toss her napkin away behind the bar.

"Are you all right?" she asked. "You still seem upset."

"Honestly, it's no big deal. How about you? Is your stomach better?"

She nodded and gave him a sweet smile, and he resisted the urge to sweep her up and carry her to bed, to take comfort in her body. Sleeping with her just to ease his pain didn't seem right.

"I better go," he said.

"You're welcome to stay," she told him.

"That's probably not a good idea. It's getting late, and we both have to work in the morning."

She walked him to the door. "Are you sure, Flint?"

"Yes, I'm sure." He pressed a chaste kiss to her forehead and went home with a troubled heart.

Nine

Robert and Lena Marino lived in a modest suburban home. Flint had expected as much, but he hadn't thought too deeply about what kind of people they were or why Gina claimed to care about them so much.

But now he understood. Gina had met the Marinos many years before. They owned an Italian market and deli in her neighborhood, but their hospitality went beyond the boundaries of their store. They'd adopted Gina into their lives and into their hearts.

Robert was an animated man, short and paunchy, with a heavy accent and a ready smile. He called his wife Mama and bragged about her cooking. Lena, as charming as her husband, appeared to mother anyone who came within hugging distance, so the name fit.

Flint and Robert sat at the dining room table, sampling a relish tray, while Gina and Lena bustled around the kitchen, seasoning sauces and stuffing artichokes with garlic-seasoned bread crumbs. Both women wore aprons tied around their waists, but the practical garment managed to look sexy on Gina.

As Flint studied her long, slim frame, Robert popped an olive into his mouth and slanted him a pleased look.

"You like our girl, eh?"

"Yeah, I like."

"You're the first boyfriend she has ever introduced to us. The first special one we've met."

"I see." Apparently Robert had figured out that their affair was real even if he didn't have the facts straight. But out of respect to Gina, Flint wasn't going to explain that he was just a temporary lover, not a boyfriend.

He knew his emotions were all tangled up over Gina, but he also knew when to cut his losses, when to sever a tie that would only make him bleed.

The sound of a baby crying interrupted Flint's thoughts. He glanced around and realized that the noise had erupted from a monitor.

"Nonna," Robert called into the kitchen. "Our boy is awake."

Nonna, Flint assumed, meant grandmother in Italian. Robert and Lena were a bit too old to be producing *bambini* of their own.

Lena wiped her hands on her apron and darted down the hall. In no time, she returned with a round-faced child in her arms. The kid looked ruffled from sleep, with dark hair and big, curious eyes.

She carried the tyke into the kitchen, and the boy grinned at Gina.

"That's Danny," Robert explained, beaming with pride.

"Your grandson?"

"*Sì,* our youngest. We baby-sit him when his mama and papa go out."

"How old is he?" Flint asked, unable to determine the child's age.

"*Nove mesi.* Nine months."

"He's a nice-looking boy."

"*Sì*, he's very handsome. And if you're not careful, he might steal Gina away from you, eh?"

Flint couldn't help but smile. The little rascal, all warm and snuggly in his teddy-bear pajamas and with his wild, wispy hair, did appear to be flirting with her. When she reached for him, he went willingly into her arms.

"Our Gina, she'll make a good mama someday," Robert said.

Would she? Flint wondered. Or would her position at Baronessa get in the way? Her career mattered so much to her, she'd gotten an ulcer over it.

Lena handed Danny a bottle, and the kid gave his grandma a sappy grin before he grabbed it and snuggled closer to Gina. She boosted him up and came toward Flint and Robert.

"There's your *nonno*," she said, making the boy flash that sappy grin at Robert. "And that's Flint," she added, shifting the child in his direction. "He's my friend."

Danny studied him with a serious expression, tilting his head and burrowing against Gina's breast. Then he held out his bottle.

Unsure what to do, Flint stared at it.

"He's offering you a drink," Robert explained with a grandpa chuckle.

A drink? He looked to Gina for help.

"It's apple juice," she said.

"I can see that." But did she realize it was only accessible through a rubber nipple?

Danny waved the bottle and made a fussy noise. Apparently the little tyke didn't take no for an answer.

Robert chuckled again. "He's stubborn, that one."

No kidding. Flint was being forced to accept the offering. He took the bottle, then made a face at the nipple.

Gina laughed. "You don't really have to drink, Flint. Just pretend."

Well, hell. His inexperience was showing. He didn't have any nieces or nephews or friends with bottle-sharing babies. He wanted children of his own, but he didn't know a thing about them.

"Got it," he said, hoping to recover his dignity. Cupping his hand around the nipple, he made a suckling sound and pretended to enjoy the juice.

Danny clapped and squealed, and Flint's heart went soft. Gina caught his eye, and they stared at each other, lost in a tender moment.

"Go ahead and hold him," Robert coaxed. "See what a sturdy boy he is."

Flint broke eye contact. Was the older man trying to make a dad out of him? A father to Gina's future children?

"Maybe Danny doesn't want me to hold him."

"Sure he does." Robert gestured to Gina to hand over the child.

The transfer wasn't the least bit awkward. Danny bounced on Flint's lap, happy as a little clam.

"Do you like your new *zio?*" Gina asked the youngster.

Danny nodded, then leaned back and sucked on his bottle. Flint shifted the boy to a more comfortable position and gazed at Gina.

"*Zio* means uncle," she said.

"That's what I figured." He accepted the title with honor. "*Na khan* is uncle in Cheyenne, for a mother's brother," he explained. "A father's brother is *nē hyō*, the same thing a child would call their own father."

"Really? It's the same term?"

"Yeah." Someday he wanted to be called *nē hyō*.

"That's nice." She stepped forward to brush Danny's cheek, to make the little boy coo.

Flint told himself not to be swayed by Gina's fondness for children. She wouldn't give up her career to raise a family, to be a wife and mother.

But when she sent him a warm smile, he found himself

swayed nonetheless. She looked sweet and maternal, with her hair banded into a messy ponytail and her apron slightly askew.

Soon she returned to the kitchen, and within the hour, they were seated at the table, dining on homemade cuisine.

Danny wiggled in his high chair, eating the food his grandma had prepared for him.

Flint leaned over and pressed his mouth to Gina's ear. "Will you come home with me tonight?" he asked.

"Yes," she whispered back.

"Will you stay for the rest of the week?"

"Yes," she whispered again.

Craving her touch, Flint reached for her hand. The rest of the week was all they had left. On Saturday night, at a party his family hosted every year, his love affair with Gina Barone would end.

Flint drove Gina to the brownstone so she could pack her clothes and toiletries. A reporter lurking outside of the building questioned them about the sex tape they'd supposedly made, but they refused to comment.

Once they entered the brownstone, Flint started for the stairs, but Gina turned in the other direction.

"Let's take the elevator," she said.

"All right." He stood beside her while she pushed the button.

"So, did you start that rumor or not?" she asked.

He knew she referred to the sex tape the reporter had pestered them about. "I might have."

"Flint?"

"Okay, I did. Well, not me personally. But it came from my camp, so to speak."

She shot him a teasing smile. "You're such a dog."

"Hey, it's my job. I can't help it."

The gated door opened, and they stepped inside.

"There's a security camera in here," she said. "Gee, maybe we ought to make love."

He looked around but didn't see anything that resembled a camera lens. "Where is it?"

"I was just kidding."

"Now who's being a dog? You know how aroused I get in elevators."

They reached the fourth floor, but neither Flint nor Gina made a move to leave.

"How aroused?" she asked.

A shiver slid straight down his spine. "You have no idea."

"I know how wild you are, Flint."

"Do you?" he countered. Although she wore a fairly conservative dress and a camel-colored jacket, the knee-high boots were enough to spark his imagination. "Are you wearing hose, Gina?"

She shook her head, and his gaze roamed over every inch of her.

"So your legs are bare?"

"Yes."

"Are you wearing panties?"

She gnawed a little nervously on her lower lip, and the innocent gesture excited him even more.

"Yes," she said. "I'm wearing panties. Do you want to know what color they are?"

"No." He moved closer, backing her against the elevator wall. "I want you to take them off."

She watched him through anxious eyes, then she reached under her dress and removed a wisp of material.

He got a glimpse of white cotton and pink lace before the panties disappeared into her purse. How tidy she was, he thought. How provocatively proper.

Unable to wait another second, Flint kissed her. Her apartment was just a few feet away, but he no had intention of spoiling the fantasy.

As she moaned against his mouth, he unbuttoned her jacket so he could bring her closer, so he could feel her heart hammer against his.

Their gazes locked in a flash of gold, in a spark of blue violet. She unzipped his pants, and when she pushed his underwear down and stroked him, fire erupted in his veins, bursting like a sea of liquid heat.

Desperate, he bunched her dress to her hips.

And then they made love.

Hot, wicked love, with their clothes on.

Blinded by passion, he thrust into her over and over again. She felt warm and slick, so wet he nearly lost his mind.

The fantasy raged out of control. He knew this was more than just sex. This was need. And it burned all the way to his soul.

As she wrapped her legs around him, he battled with the fear of losing her, with the knowledge that he didn't have a choice but to let her go.

Reaching behind her, he released her ponytail. And when her hair spilled over her shoulders in a riot of curls, he tugged her head back and kissed her. So hard, he nearly swallowed her whole.

From there, they moved, viciously, violently, craving a release. They bumped into the elevator buttons, and the gated door opened and then closed, reminding them of where they were.

Gina's eyes, those stunning violet eyes, sought his just once, before she tore the front of his shirt and cried out in orgasmic bliss.

He fought to stay focused, to watch her, to make her

climax again, but he was too close. Too aroused. Too damn hungry for fulfillment.

With a rough, jagged curse, Flint damned his addiction and tumbled into the sweet, satisfying abyss of the woman he couldn't keep.

At Flint's house, Gina unpacked her toiletries. The master bathroom had double sinks with plenty of room for two people, but she couldn't resist placing her cleansing creams and cosmetics next to Flint's shaving gear. Seeing their personal items side by side almost made them seem married.

Married?

She gazed at her reflection. Was she crazy? Having fantasies about being married to Flint? He'd invited her to stay with him, but that hardly spelled commitment.

He came into the bathroom and she felt flustered, afraid he'd figure out what she'd been thinking.

"Are you almost done?" he asked.

She didn't turn. She could see him in the mirror, standing behind her. "Yes."

"So, you unpacked your clothes already?"

"Yes," she said again. He'd given her ample closet space. He'd even cleared a dresser drawer for her.

"Hey, look, we have the same toothbrush." He picked up the electric plaque remover she used.

"A lot of people have those," she said, telling herself he'd offered to share his quarters with her because the sex was so great, not because he craved emotional intimacy.

"Yeah, I guess they do." He slipped his arms around her. "I built a fire downstairs. Why don't you come down and have a cup of hot chocolate with me?"

She met his gaze in the mirror. She could hear the wind

howling outside. The calm day had turned into a dramatic night.

"Gina?"

She leaned against him. He felt so strong, so perfect. "I'll be down in a minute, okay?"

"Okay."

He gave her a quick peck on the cheek and left her alone with her thoughts.

She splashed water on her face, hoping to wake herself. She wasn't sleepy, but she drifted somewhere between a dream and reality.

Heaven help her, she thought, as she dried her face. Coming here, staying with him was a mistake. Yet she wanted to be with him, to sleep in the same bed, to share the same bathroom, to pretend they were truly a couple. Which was a foolish, impossible notion. Her relationship with Flint was scheduled to end in less than a week.

Then don't fall in love with him, she told herself. *Don't let it happen.*

With silent trepidation, she went downstairs, then managed a smile when she saw Flint's dog.

The white and tan pooch ran to greet her, twirling and hopping in an excited circle.

"Now, where has your master been keeping you?" she asked, kneeling beside him.

"For the most part, he lives outside," Flint said, rounding the corner. "But that's his choice. Russ likes to patrol the yard. He thinks he's a Doberman or a rottweiler or something."

Gina laughed. Anyone could see that Russ was a Jack Russell terrier that probably didn't weigh more than fifteen pounds.

"He thrives on action and adventure. Don't you, boy?"

Flint picked up his pet, and Russ barked and grinned at Gina.

Within no time, the wannabe guard dog departed through a doggie door in the kitchen, eager to return to his post.

Gina watched him go, then helped Flint prepare the hot chocolate.

They settled in the living room, where a fire blazed warm and bright. Gina curled up on one corner of the sofa, and Flint sat next to her.

"Doesn't Russ get cold outside?" she asked.

"He has a custom-built doghouse, and he seems satisfied with it. But if he gets cold, he comes in."

She sipped her drink and stared at the flames, at the sparks of red and gold. Was Flint that casual with all his companions? Were his lovers free to come and go, too?

"I was thinking of commissioning Lewis to paint that portrait," he said.

She turned away from the fire. "What portrait?"

"The one of us from the tabloid picture. I thought it would be cool to actually have a painting done."

Stunned, she blinked. "Why?"

He shrugged. "I don't know. I just did."

Instantly, her heart hurt. She didn't want to be a trophy. A conquest. An illicit memory for him to hang on the wall for everyone to see. "Do you have a painting of Tara around here somewhere? Is she part of your art collection, too?"

He set his drink on the table, nearly spilling it in his haste. "What the hell is that supposed to mean? That I commission portraits of all my lovers?"

She gave him a tight stare. "Don't you?"

He stared right back. "No."

"So, are you finally admitting that you and Tara were lovers?"

"Yeah, that's right, I am. But I don't see why it matters. I mean, who cares?"

Gina drew her knees up. She cared. She shouldn't, but damn it, she did. "Were you in love with her?"

When he didn't answer, they sat in silence, their gazes locked. The flickering firelight shadowed the sharp angle of his cheekbones, and she resisted the urge to touch him, to feel the warmth of his skin.

"Flint?" she pressed, as a woodsy aroma scented the air, making the romantic atmosphere seem like a lie.

Finally he said, "Yes, I loved her. But I try not to think about it. Especially now."

"Why? Did she hurt you?"

"Yes, but I haven't spoken to her in years. I was tempted to call her right after I met you, but I decided not to."

"Will you tell me about her?" She needed to understand who Flint Kingman was and what Tara Shaw really meant to him.

"I—" He paused to clear his throat, then started over. "After I graduated from college, Tara contacted my father's company, looking for a PR consultant to boost her image, to prove that a woman could still be a sex symbol in her forties. Dad was going to send another consultant, but I insisted on taking the job."

"Why?" Gina asked. "Because you were attracted to her?"

"No, that wasn't it. I thought she was pretty, of course, but I never envisioned sleeping with her. I took the job because Hollywood fascinated me, and I wanted to be part of that world."

Gina studied him for a moment. And then suddenly she understood. "Hollywood represented your mother. It was Danielle you were searching for."

Flint nodded, then blew a rough breath. "I wanted to

feel close to her, to experience what drew her to Hollywood.''

''And did you?''

''Yeah, I guess I did. But I ended up falling for Tara, and that was the last thing I expected to happen.''

Gina's heart clenched, but she told herself to ignore the pain. ''Did Tara love you?''

''She said she did. But after we were together for a while, she told me it wouldn't work. The age difference bothered her.'' He reached for his cup, took a drink and set it down. ''And now that I'm older, I realize she was right. We wouldn't have made it. It wouldn't have lasted.''

''I'm glad you told me,'' she said. ''That you were honest.''

''That's not all of it, Gina. There's more.''

She looked up. What else could there be? What was left? ''I'm listening.''

''Tara wasn't just my lover. She was my friend, the first woman I'd ever confided in. I used to talk to her about my mom and why Hollywood meant so much to me.''

''And what did she say? How did she respond?''

His voice shook a little. ''She told me that the movie industry could be superficial and cold and that I should be proud of the fact that my mom left it behind to get married and have a child.''

''And are you?''

''I used to be. But I'm not anymore.''

Gina looked into his eyes, and she knew he was going to reveal something that made him ache inside. ''What is it, Flint?''

''My mother's death wasn't an accident. She committed suicide.''

Oh, God. Dear God. Danielle Wolf, a beautiful young

woman with everything to live for, had taken her own life? "How can you be sure?"

"About a month ago I overheard my father and my stepmother talking about Danielle. It was the anniversary of her death, and I guess it triggered some emotion in my dad." He glanced at his hands, his expression tense. "I hadn't meant to eavesdrop, but I couldn't turn away. And that's when I learned the truth."

"But she died in a car accident. How can that be suicide?"

"She ran her car off the road on purpose."

Gina tried to search Flint's gaze, but he wouldn't look up. "How can your father be sure?"

"Danielle left one of those pathetic suicide notes, asking him to forgive her."

She blinked back her tears, knowing she couldn't let him see her cry. "Oh, Flint. I'm so sorry. Did you talk to your dad about this?"

He glanced up. "Yes. And he's making excuses about why he lied to me all these years. He said he was only trying to protect me, but that isn't fair. I had the right to know."

"I can understand why your father didn't tell you."

"Really? Well, do you know what Danielle's note said?" he countered. "That she killed herself because of me. She couldn't handle being a mother. She couldn't cope with the pressure of taking care of her own child. But when I was little, my dad told me that she adored me, that she loved me more than anything. He let me grow up believing a fairy tale."

Gina's eyes filled with tears, and this time she didn't blink them away. She knew Flint wanted to cry, too, but he kept himself rigid instead, his arms crossed protectively over his chest, his features guarded.

"My dad said that Danielle got really depressed after I was born. She even admitted that she was a better actress than a mother. Apparently she regretted leaving Hollywood to get married and have a child."

Everything inside Gina went still, including her heart. Suddenly she knew why Flint refused to marry a woman focused on her career.

Someone like me, she thought. Someone who claimed she could conquer a demanding job and still raise a family.

"I'm sorry," he said. "I shouldn't have burdened you with this. There's nothing you can do."

"Oh, Flint." Caught up in his pain, she reached for him. And when she stroked his hair, he put his head on her shoulder.

Later, much later, as the fire burned low and the wind raged against the windows, she tried to think of a way to truly comfort him, to help him feel whole, but she couldn't. So she simply held him, realizing she was deathly afraid of admitting that she loved a man who might reject her.

Ten
___

Flint and Gina had been coming home from work early every day this week, but Flint hoped Gina would be running late this afternoon. He didn't know how to tell her that he wasn't comfortable bringing her to the powwow, so slipping off and leaving a note seemed easier.

He opened the cedar chest at the foot of his bed and removed his regalia, then placed some of the components in a garment bag and divided the rest between a hard suitcase and a leather satchel. A few minutes later he unwrapped his bustle, set it on the bed and assembled it.

The large, U-shaped bustle, which emulated the tail of an eagle, was designed to break down for easy transportation and storage.

As he fitted the pieces together, he checked each feather. He'd acquired the golden eagle feathers from *Niĭsh'kĭ,* and he considered them a priceless family heirloom, the most prized belongings he owned.

Ready to get underway, Flint slipped on a pair of jeans

over his bike shorts, then turned to find Gina standing in the doorway. He hadn't heard her come in, nor had he sensed her presence.

"Hi," she said.

She wore a sleek black business suit and a feminine blouse. Her hair, twisted into a ladylike chignon, shone soft and pretty.

"Hi." he repeated her greeting, wondering how he was now going to pull off the great escape.

She looked at the bed. "Oh, my. What is that? It's beautiful."

"It's a bustle, part of my regalia."

"Your regalia?"

"I'm a powwow dancer. I've been dancing since I was a kid. But I don't compete, not anymore."

Her eyes searched his. "I've never been to a powwow. What are they like?"

That, he thought, was a loaded question. If he invited her to go with him tonight, he wouldn't have to answer it. She would be able to view the festivities firsthand.

"A powwow is an Indian gathering," he said.

"I know. But what goes on?"

"A lot of stuff."

"Stuff?" she repeated, clearly disappointed by his lame explanation.

"Yeah, you know. Dancing. Food. Crafts. Some of the bigger powwows are affiliated with rodeos, and the celebration will last for a week."

"That sounds fun."

"The one I'm going to tonight is just a one-day event. There won't be much fanfare," he added, playing it down. "It's sponsored by a small Native American church."

"Is the public welcome?" she asked. "Or is it a private gathering?"

"It's open to the public, but this event doesn't get a lot of guests. Mostly it's the churchgoers who attend."

"I didn't know you belonged to a church group."

He pulled a T-shirt over his head and then laced up a pair of tennis shoes. "I don't. My grandmother asked me to join her there."

Gina sat on the edge of the bed. Although she eyed his bustle with quiet longing, she didn't disrespect him by touching it.

"Do you want to come with me?" he asked, suddenly unable to exclude her.

"Really? Oh, I'd love to."

"Okay, then. Change into something casual, and we'll get going."

He could handle this, he told himself. Although he'd never brought any of his lovers to an Indian gathering, he'd danced in front of plenty of spectators. He wasn't making a commitment to Gina. He wasn't asking her to join his scared circle, to become a permanent part of his life.

"I'll load the Tahoe," he said.

She removed her jacket. "You have an SUV?"

He nodded, realizing she hadn't seen the Tahoe. The garages on his property were separated, so he didn't park his vehicles together. "I don't take the Corvette to powwows."

"Why not?"

"Because like most of the other dancers, I get ready in my car, and the Vette is a bit cramped."

"It didn't even occur to me how or where a dancer would change."

"It isn't very glamorous," he told her.

She removed her shoes, then unzipped her skirt and let it fall to the floor. "I think it sounds perfect. Sort of romantic and gypsylike."

Their eyes met, and suddenly Flint got an overwhelming urge to hold her. He moved forward, reached out and took her in his arms.

She responded in kind, latching on to him the way he clung to her.

He ran his hands down the sides of her body. All she wore was a silk blouse, lace panties and a pair of thigh-high hose, attached to one of those sultry little garter belts. "Will you make love with me?" he asked.

She brushed her mouth against his. "Right now?"

"No. Later. After we get back."

"Of course, I will. What made you think of it now?"

A desperate feeling, he thought. A need he couldn't seem to control. "We only have a few days left, and we haven't fulfilled all of our fantasies."

She snared his lips in a moist kiss. "What fantasy do you want fulfill tonight?"

"I don't know. Something wild, something sexy."

Something that would mask the sudden panic in his soul.

Flint parked his SUV in a dirt lot, and Gina looked around. She saw several Native American couples heading toward a community hall. She noticed their children, too. Adorable little kids wearing buckskin, beads, fringe and feathers.

She could hardly contain her excitement. And then reality hit.

"Aren't people going to recognize us from the tabloids?" she asked.

"Probably, but most of the churchgoers know me. And I doubt they'll say anything. This is a spiritual gathering. It wouldn't be right for them to approach us about something so personal."

Maybe not, she thought. But the scandal would still be on their minds. Who wouldn't be curious? "They'll probably just stare."

"No, they won't. At least not the traditional Indians. It's not proper to stare or point." He removed his shoes and took off his T-shirt and jeans, which left him bare-chested in a pair of shorts.

She watched as he climbed into the back seat and began to dress, explaining what the components of his outfit were.

The transformation amazed her, and so did the beauty of his regalia. By the time he stepped out of the vehicle to complete his ritual, he wore a colorful ribbon shirt, a bone breastplate, a beaded vest and a leather apron that was used in place of a breechclout. Along with a handful of other accessories, he donned a porcupine roach in his hair, a set of fringed kneebands and a pair of fully beaded moccasins.

He went to the back of the vehicle, opened the double doors and sat on the edge of the storage area. Silent, Gina joined him. He painted his face into a striking mask, using sticks of greasepaint, a small hand mirror and the natural light the descending sun still allowed.

She wanted to tell him how beautiful he was, but she couldn't seem to find the words. He took her breath away.

"I'm going to smudge," he said. "Do you want me to smudge you, too?"

She nodded as he lit the dried herb. She knew burning sage represented a spiritual cleansing in his culture. She'd seen him smudge every morning this week, but he hadn't invited her to be part of it until now.

He fanned the smoke over himself, then combed it over her, filling her with a sense of longing. She wanted to touch him so badly, she ached.

"I owe you a thanks," he said afterward.

"What for?"

"For letting me confide in you."

She knew he referred to the heart-wrenching information he'd shared about his mom. "I'm your friend, Flint. That's what I'm here for."

He smiled, but the painted mask made him look a bit wicked. "Thanks."

"Is it true that you were taught not to speak of the dead?" she asked.

"Yes, but I never followed that practice. I used to like

to talk about my mom. But that was before I found out about what she did.''

"I'm sorry," Gina said. "I'm aware of how difficult it was for you to tell me.''

"Now that you know, there's not much more to say about it.'' He slipped a leather satchel over his shoulder. "What's done is done. And I have to find a way to live with it.''

Yes, she thought. He would tackle his grief by marrying a woman who wouldn't regret giving up her career.

Gina glanced at her left hand and pictured a wedding ring there. Could she give up her career for a man? Quit her job? Ignore her education?

No, she realized. She couldn't. She needed a husband who respected her work, who valued her for it.

Yet there was a part of her that could almost imagine sacrificing everything for Flint Kingman.

Dear God, she thought, as she turned to look at him. What had he done to her?

While Flint guided her toward the community center, Gina struggled to steady her pulse, to take a deep breath and relax.

They passed a row of food vendors, and she inhaled the mouthwatering aroma.

"Are you hungry?" he asked.

"Sort of, but I'd rather wait until we get settled in.''

He studied her for a second. "Are you sure your stomach is okay? It's not burning, is it?''

"No, it's fine. I can eat later.'' As they reached the front door of the community center, she realized he hadn't attached his bustle. "When are you going to put that on?'' she asked.

"Right before I dance.'' He smiled, and once again, the painted mask transformed him into a leering warrior. A man a bit too dangerous for his own good.

A moment later they entered the building, and all of

Gina's senses came alive. The music, a pounding drumbeat and a rhythm of native chants, drew her attention to the center of the expansive room, where people were already dancing, spinning and stepping in time to an ancient song.

"We're a bit late, so we missed the Grand Entry. The procession that marks the official beginning of a pow-wow," Flint explained.

"What's going on now?" she asked.

"The Drum is singing an intertribal song. That means all styles of dance are welcome."

Gina gazed at the arena again. "How many styles are there?"

"As far as competition dances go, about four men's and four women's. Kids have their own categories."

She zeroed in on the tots in the arena. Some clung to an adult's hand, and others demonstrated the remarkable steps all on their own.

"Specialty and exhibition dances are part of the program, too," he added. "There's a lot to see."

Gina met his gaze. Flint's world was fascinating, she thought. Filled with honor and pride. History and tradition.

"I need to find my grandmother."

He led her past a maze of craft booths until he located the lady he called *Nĭsh'kĭ.*

She was surrounded by a group of other elderly women, and when she saw her grandson, she rose to embrace him.

They separated, and he introduced Gina.

The older woman took her hand. "I'm so glad he brought you. I've been anxious to meet you."

"Thank you." In spite of her age, Flint's grandmother was an attractive lady, with gray-streaked hair and exotically shaped eyes. Gina suspected she had been a beauty in her day.

Nĭsh'kĭ motioned to a folding chair. "Come. Sit with me."

Feeling warm and welcome, Gina took the proffered seat,

then she and *Nĭsh'kĭ* spent several hours watching Flint dance.

He was a Northern Traditional dancer, she learned, a style inspired by an elite society of warriors centuries before.

Nĭsh'kĭ explained that this powwow wasn't designed for competition. All the dancers, including Flint, danced for pleasure.

Gina studied him, thinking how regal he looked, moving to the Drum, to the heartbeat of his heritage. The mirrors on his sash glinted, and the fringe on his regalia fluttered, catching the beat. He carried a wing fan in one hand and a staff in the other. The articles gave him balance, she'd been told. And the staff, wrapped in fur and decorated with an eagle claw, represented a coup stick from days gone by.

"He's magnificent," she said.

"Yes," the older woman agreed. "He is."

A while later Flint left the arena and returned with several cartons of food. After Gina sampled the stew, she tasted the fry bread, then caught Flint watching her.

"Do you like it?" he asked.

She nodded. The bread was a flat, doughy disc, generously sweetened.

"I put extra honey on it," he said.

She met his gaze, and when he flashed that wicked smile, she recalled that he had a honey fetish.

Instantly her cheeks warmed.

Was he revealing the fantasy he hoped to fulfill? Or had her imagination run away with her?

Unable to stop herself, she brushed his hand, desperate to touch him, to feel his skin against hers. And at that innocently sensual moment, she finally accepted her fate, knowing it was time to admit the truth.

She was in love with Flint Kingman.

Gina awakened the following morning feeling warm and sticky. She opened her eyes and peered at Flint. He lay beside her, one arm flung over the pillow, the other clutched possessively around her waist. The sheet was tangled around his legs, the quilt shoved to the foot of the bed.

Good heavens, what they'd done last night. A residue still clung to Gina's skin.

She tried to move, but Flint tightened his grip.

"Where are you going?" he asked, his voice groggy.

"It's time to get ready for work."

"Not for me." He squinted at her. "I don't have any appointments until this afternoon."

"Lucky you." She kissed his mouth and tasted last night's treat. They'd poured honey all over each other, then licked and laved and made sweet, sweet love. "I have to take a shower."

He flashed a sleepy grin. "We got a little carried away, didn't we?"

Gina smiled. Boy, did they ever. "The least we could have done was bathed and changed the sheets."

"I don't know. I kind of like this." He pulled her tight against him, and their bodies nearly stuck together.

She smoothed a strand of honey-clumped hair from his forehead. Beautiful, crazy, wild Flint. God, how she loved him.

He nuzzled her neck. "Can't you ditch work and stay home with me for a while?"

"I wish I could, but I'm swamped this morning." Her brother had called a mandatory meeting, and she was expected to be there.

"Will you try to come home early?"

"Yes. I should be back by four."

"Good." He snuggled deeper into his pillow and closed his eyes. "I'll shower and change the sheets later."

She studied his features, the chiseled cheekbones, the determined jaw, the arch of his brows. Heaven help her, but she wanted to keep him. And she had to say what was on her mind. She had to take the chance. "Flint?"

He opened his eyes. "Hmm?"

She released the air in her lungs. "Would you ever consider marrying a career woman? I mean, do you think you'd ever change your mind about that?"

Instead of answering, he turned the tables, putting the pressure on her. "Would you ever consider giving up your career for a man?"

She had already debated that question in her mind, and she had to speak the truth. "No. My position at Baronessa is part of who I am."

He sat up and cleared his throat. "Even if it gives you ulcers?"

"I can't help it if I'm a nervous person."

"Are you working there for you or for your family?" he asked.

"Both. What about you?" she challenged. "Why are you working for your father's company?"

"For him and for me. I really like what I do, but I have family loyalties, as well."

Suddenly she saw the pain in his eyes, the knowledge that his family loyalty had been jeopardized by what his mother had done.

She reached out and touched his cheek, wishing she could make him stop hurting. And when he put his hand over hers, she wished she could stop herself from hurting, too.

"I have to get ready," she said.

"I know." He kissed the palm of her hand and let her go.

Two hours later Gina entered Baronessa Gelati's corporate headquarters. Flint's touch still lingered in her mind, but she did her best to face the day without looking back, without picturing him alone in that big, honeyed bed.

After checking in with her secretary, she proceeded to Nicholas's office. Her brother sat behind his desk, his expression troubled.

"What's wrong?" she asked.

"We'll discuss it when Dad arrives."

"What about the other board members?"

"This meeting is personal, Gina. It's between you, Dad and me." He stood and rolled his shoulders. "Would you like a cup of coffee?"

"No." That would only stir her ulcer to life. "When is Dad scheduled to get here?"

"Any minute."

Carlo Barone arrived precisely three minutes later, wearing a dark suit and a tense frown. Although he wasn't tall, he was a powerfully built man who carried himself with pride.

Nicholas sat on the edge of his desk, and Carlo gestured for Gina to take a chair. Her father, with his booming voice and masculine demeanor, never failed to intimidate her.

As instructed, she sat and waited for the ball to drop. Obviously she'd done something that displeased him. She glanced at Nicholas, but he didn't offer any brotherly signs of encouragement. Apparently she was on her own.

"I heard you moved in with Flint Kingman," her dad said. "But only for the week. What kind of shoddy arrangement is that?"

Momentarily stunned, she stared. "This meeting is about Flint?"

"No, it's about you, Gina. I want to know what's going on between you and that man."

She defended herself. "Flint and I are working together. We're creating a scandal to divert the press, to keep them from trashing Baronessa's image."

"What about your image?" Carlo retorted. "Your brother and I should have never trusted that spin doctor. He's too Hollywood."

"Too Hollywood? He's a Boston businessman, Dad, and he's very well respected."

"This scandal has gotten out of hand." Nicholas cut in.

"And you're caught in the middle of it," Carlo added.

Gina's emotions were tangled. Her father and brother had called this meeting to defend her honor, to offer their support. It was the last thing she'd expected.

"I appreciate what the two of you are trying to do. But this scandal is nearly over." She stood and faced her dad. "And I can handle what's left of it."

"Are you sure?" Carlo reached out to hold her, and she found herself falling willingly into his embrace.

God, how she needed this. Her daddy's strong arms. His strength. His concern.

She stepped back to look at him, at his short dark hair and graying temples, at the lines that marked his eyes. "Do you think I'm good at my job?"

"Of course, I do. You work harder than anyone I know. But you take too much on. You let the stress wear you down."

She glanced at Nicholas. "Is that how you feel, too?"

Her brother nodded. "We brought Flint into this so you wouldn't have to tackle the press on your own. And now you're involved with him."

"Yes, I am. But that's my choice."

Her father cupped her face. "Just be careful you don't get hurt."

Too late, she thought. She was already hurting. "I'll be fine, Daddy. I promise. I will."

Later that day Gina told herself not to dwell on losing Flint. Instead she would cherish every moment they had left.

Determined to prepare a home-cooked meal for the man she loved, she stopped by Marino's market and picked up the items she required. Afterward, as she balanced the grocery bag and walked to her car, she spotted Maria and a dark-haired man on the corner not far from Baronessa Gelateria, the ice-cream parlor her sister managed.

And then she did a double take. The man was Steven Conti. Tall, handsome, blue-eyed Steven. The traitor of all traitors. In Gina's opinion, his family was responsible for the trouble at Baronessa. She was certain they had sabotaged the passionfruit promotion, spiking the gelato with those hot peppers. Steven's great-aunt was the woman who'd put the Valentine curse on the Barone family, and the withered old crone was still alive and kicking.

Gina studied Steven's body language, the way he leaned toward Maria. Was he attracted to her sister?

She shifted her gaze to Maria. The petite brunette smiled at the Conti villain.

What in heaven's name was going on? Had they just happened to run into each other on the street? Or were they up to no good?

Gina unlocked her car and placed the groceries on the passenger seat. Was Maria having an affair with Steven? A secret liaison? After all, she had been sneaking off, disappearing without proper explanation.

As Steven and Maria parted company and her sister headed in the direction of the gelateria, Gina shook her head. Just because *she* was having an affair didn't mean Maria was doing the same thing.

Then again, she knew all too well how easily a strong-willed, levelheaded woman could fall for the wrong man.

Thirty minutes later Gina returned to Flint's house and found him in the kitchen. For a moment she stood watching him, thinking how handsome he was. He wore a white shirt, gray trousers and a pair of black loafers, but he'd flung his jacket and tie over a chair.

He turned and spotted her. "Hey, you went shopping."

She shifted her bag. "I'm making Italian."

He laughed and reached into the fridge, removing a cellophane-wrapped package. "I bought steaks. Filet mignon. I was going to cook for you tonight. I even picked up flowers and candles."

"Really?" She moved forward and set her groceries on the counter. "We both had the same idea." And she wanted to hug him for thinking of her, for planning a romantic meal.

"What did you get?" He poked through her bag. "This looks good. Do you think maybe we could combine our food? Pasta and steak go together, don't they?"

"Yes." She gave in to the need to hold him. And when she put her head on his shoulder, he stroked a gentle hand down her back.

"Are you okay, Gina?"

She nodded, even though her heart hurt. "Are you?"

"Yeah, I'm fine." Flint rested his chin on the top of her head, thinking he wasn't the least bit fine. Every day that passed brought him closer to the end, closer to losing her.

"Should we start dinner?" she asked.

"Sure." He released her and stepped back.

She looked tired, a little weary, and he wondered if she'd had a rough day.

She discarded her shoes and moved through the kitchen in her stocking feet. He leaned against the counter and watched her.

His Gina. His sweet, wild, proper Gina. She still confused him, but he didn't see the point in analyzing their relationship, in beating it to death. Once she was gone, he'd get a grip on his feelings. Eventually the panic would end, and he'd stop obsessing about her. Life as he knew it would go back to normal. Or as normal as it could get for a guy trying to shake a woman from his blood.

"I bought an imported sauce," she said. "It comes out of a jar, but it's really good."

"That sounds okay to me." Realizing how idle he was,

he removed a head of lettuce from the fridge. "I'll make the salad."

They worked in silence, lovers side by side. Finally he broached the subject of the party. "I told my parents that we'd be staging a fight."

She turned to look at him. "And what did they say?"

"Not much. Someone usually gets drunk and causes a scene. I guess the roaring twenties theme brings out that kind of behavior in people."

She set a pot of water on to boil, then stared at it. "You don't plan on getting drunk, do you?"

"No." He couldn't help but wonder how much alcohol it would take to ease the fear of waking up alone on the morning after the party, of reaching for her and grasping nothing but air.

"I haven't found a dress yet," she said. "But I plan on going shopping tomorrow."

"Do you want me to go with you?"

She shook her head. "I can find something on my own."

He frowned into the salad bowl. "I wasn't trying to dictate your wardrobe, Gina. I was just offering you some company."

"I know. But I think it would easier if I went alone."

"Yeah, I suppose it would." He reached for a tomato and gazed at the knife in his hand. He could see his reflection, a distorted version of himself, shimmering in the blade.

"Where are the flowers?" she asked.

He diced the tomato and set down the knife. "On the dining room table."

"And the candles?"

"I placed them on the table, too. They're scented, I think. Raspberry or something."

She gave him a sweet smile, and he suspected she was trying to make the best of the time they had left.

"I didn't know you were such a romantic, Flint."

"I'm not," he teased. "I'm just in it for the sex."

"Really?" She laughed, but the humor didn't quite reach her eyes. "So am I."

"Then we make a fetching pair. Don't we, milady?"

"Yes, we do."

"Indeed." He took a steady breath, insisting he would do just fine without her. And she, in turn, would do just fine without him. They'd only spent two and a half weeks together, which amounted to nothing in the scheme of things.

Yet as he proceeded to finish the salad, to concentrate on the meal they'd planned, the day of the party loomed darkly in his mind.

Like an ominous cloud preparing for a cold, brittle rain.

Eleven

On Saturday afternoon Gina went home to the brownstone. She needed some time alone, a few hours of solitude before she returned to Flint's house to get ready for the party—the roaring twenties gala that would end her relationship with the man she loved.

Like a zombie, she sat on the sofa and stared straight ahead. How was she supposed to walk into the Kingman estate and pretend that her heart wasn't shattering into a million painful pieces?

She blinked and caught sight of the entertainment center—the television, the stereo, the DVD player, the nearly outdated VCR.

Shifting her gaze, she studied her film collection and thought about Flint's mother, the beautiful starlet who'd committed a selfish, dramatic act.

Damn you, Danielle. Damn you for hurting your son, for making him so wary, for tainting his views on marriage and motherhood.

Flint deserved better. He deserved a mother who'd cared about him, who'd remained by his side to watch him grow.

A knock sounded, interrupting Gina's thoughts. She took a deep, emotional breath, realizing one of her sisters must be at the door.

What if it was Maria? She wasn't sure what to say to Maria considering her suspicions about Steven Conti.

Then again, why should she say anything? Gina wasn't a saint. She'd been sleeping with Flint, knowing full well he wasn't going to make a commitment. So why condemn her sister?

She answered the summons and found Rita, not Maria, at the door. The nurse gave her a weary smile.

"Rita? What's going on? You look beat."

"I received another gift from my secret admirer. And I just needed to talk to someone about it."

"Oh, honey. Come on in," Gina said. "Could it be a birthday present?" She hadn't forgotten her sister's birthday.

Rita shook her head as she entered the apartment, and they headed for the living room, where they sat side by side on the sofa. "No. Why wouldn't there be a card?"

"Are you worried this guy could be dangerous?" Gina asked, studying the other woman's fretful expression.

"I don't know. Maybe."

"Was the gift overly personal? Or sexual?"

"No." Rita smoothed her hair. It fell to her shoulders in a rich shade of brown. "There wasn't anything disturbing about the gift. In fact, he's never given me anything that doesn't seem well-intentioned, yet I can't seem to shake this edgy feeling."

"Women's intuition?" Gina asked.

"Maybe. Or it might be just good old-fashioned fear, my imagination running amok. There are a lot of wackos out there."

Gina frowned. "Have you considered calling the police?"

Rita sighed. "I don't think it would do any good. I don't have any proof that he's a...stalker. I don't even know who he is."

"Maybe you should file a report anyway," Gina suggested, wondering if the police would take the case seriously.

"I will, if he does anything that could be interpreted as threatening. But for now I just wanted to get it off my chest."

"What are they saying at the hospital? Does anyone have any theories?"

"The other nurses are convinced he's a young, handsome intern." Rita picked up a magazine from the coffee table, then set it down, giving her idle hands something to do. "They think the gifts are romantic. And in a way, I suppose they are."

"But in another way," Gina added, "the whole thing is creepy."

"Exactly." Rita fell silent for a moment, then she gave Gina a serious study. "So, how are you coping with your corner of the world? Are you holding up okay?"

Instantly, Gina's heart clenched. She hadn't told her sister that she had fantasies about becoming the spin doctor's wife, but her eyes probably mirrored the truth. "I'm hanging in there."

"That doesn't sound very promising."

"I know, but I'm doing my best." Gina glanced at her film collection, troubled once again by Flint's mother, by the devastation she'd caused. "Rita, what do you know about suicide? About what drives a person to it?"

"Oh, my. What brought that on? Are you sure you're okay?"

"I'm sorry. I should have explained." She looked at her sister, at the concern on Rita's face. "A friend of mine is struggling with his mother's suicide. It happened when he was baby, but he just found out about it recently.''

"Did she leave a note?"

"Yes. Apparently she became overly depressed after he was born, obsessing about the career she gave up and panicking about raising a child. Can you imagine a new mother being that desperate? That self-absorbed?"

"Actually, I can," Rita said, her voice taking on a professional, if not clinical tone. "Have you ever heard of postpartum depression? Or better yet, postpartum psychosis?"

Gina moved closer. "Are you talking about the baby blues?"

"In a sense, but to a much stronger degree. New mothers affected with these mood disorders experience a range of symptoms and sometimes exhibit bizarre or dangerous behavior. The mild cases disappear on their own, but if a severe case goes untreated, it can lead to disaster."

"Like suicide?" Gina asked.

"Yes. Of course, there's no way to know about your friend's mother, not without her medical records."

"I suppose you're right." But that didn't mean she couldn't mention it to Flint, that it wasn't worth discussing.

Gina returned to Flint's house hours later. Armed with information, she searched the estate and found him on the patio, his hair disturbed by the wind.

He sipped a cup of coffee and watched the setting sun. The air was cold and brisk, the sky a scatter of clouds.

He turned toward her. "You're back?"

She sat across from him, praying that she could ease his pain, that together they could uncover the truth behind Danielle's suicide. "I have something to tell you, Flint."

He frowned at the landscape, at the perfectly groomed yard, at the towering trees and stone planters. "I have something to tell you, too."

He looked worried, she thought. Edgy. Like a dark, brooding warrior. "What's wrong?" she asked, realizing her news could wait.

He met her gaze. "Tara's coming to the party."

Gina felt the blood drain from her face, the air in her lungs expand. His ex-lover was attending their breakup? "Did you invite her?"

"What? No. Her publicist called and said to expect her."

"Why?"

"I don't know. But he said that she wanted to talk to me. Privately. And that it was important."

How important? Gina wondered. Was Tara going to make a play for him? Was she going tell him that she missed him? That her marriage was falling apart? That she needed comfort? Love? Sex?

Gina wrapped her arms around her middle, pride keeping her voice steady, her outward appearance intact. How could she compete with Tara Shaw? With the one true love of Flint's life? "Are you nervous about seeing her?"

"Frantic. I can't believe this is happening. Especially tonight."

Yes, she thought. Tonight. When their staged fight would set him free. "How could she just invite herself? That isn't right."

Flint blew a windy breath. "Maybe not. But there were rumors in the tabloids about her attending this party."

Rumors that he'd started, Gina realized. Maybe deep down he'd wanted Tara to show. Maybe he had fantasies about seeing her just one more time.

"Will her husband be accompanying her?" she asked, hopeful.

"No. Her publicist said she'd be there alone. Or with her bodyguard, I suppose. Around nine."

Suddenly nine o'clock seemed like the bewitching hour, the hour Gina would lose the glass slipper her prince would never retrieve. Letting Flint go was almost more than she could bear, but turning him over to his ex-lover made every cell in her body weep.

"Should we stage the fight before or after Tara arrives?" she asked, praying he would opt to cancel.

"Damn it. I don't know." He dragged a hand through his wind-ravaged hair. "Before, after. Either way, the press is going to blame Tara for our breakup. And those gossip rags are going to spread more lies. This thing will never end."

This thing? Their affair? The nights they'd spent in each other's arms?

She turned to look at the sky and saw the dim gray light of dusk, the promise of rain.

"You never told me your news," Flint said, drawing her attention to him.

Good heavens. She'd forgotten all about his mother. Now she had to tell him. She had to bring up another emotional issue.

"Danielle might have been ill, Flint."

He gave her a blank stare. "Ill? What are you talking about?"

"There's a disorder some women are affected with after childbirth. It's called postpartum depression. And there's an even stronger degree of it that's considered a psychosis."

He stood and pushed away his chair. "Please, Gina, don't make excuses for my mother."

"I'm not." She rose and walked toward him. "These disorders can be quite severe."

"I've heard of them. I've seen things in the paper about women using postpartum psychosis as a defense in court because they freaked out and killed their kids."

"I'm not here to debate the cases you've read about. But I'm telling you, these disorders are real. Rita is the one who brought this up, and she's a nurse." Gina put her hands in her pockets to ward off the cold. "And after I talked to my sister, I spent hours on the Internet researching postpartum depression and the varying degrees of it. I even called some of the support groups to ask questions.''

"My mother was depressed about losing her career.''

"Yes, she was. But maybe those weren't feelings she could control. If we talked to your father, if we obtained Danielle's medical records, maybe we could find out the truth.''

"We? I'm not going to drag you into this mess. And to be quite honest, I'm not sure it matters.''

"Yes, it does.''

"Why?'' he asked. "She's been dead for thirty years. Why should I care?''

Because you're hurting, Gina thought. *And you need answers.* "Danielle could have been struggling with any number of symptoms. Some women lack interest in their babies, and others have fears of harming them.''

Flint frowned. "Do they have fears of harming themselves, too? Is that one of the symptoms?''

"Yes.''

He shook his head. "It's just so hard to fathom.''

"I know. But according to the experts, postpartum psychosis is considered a serious medical condition and should be treated immediately.''

"Do you honestly think that's what was wrong with my mom?''

"I can't say for sure. But it's a possibility.''

"And you're willing to help me find out?'' he asked.

She nodded.

"What if we find out that she wasn't ill? That she just hated her life. And me.''

"I don't see how anyone could hate you, Flint.''

He moved closer, and when they were just inches apart, he reached for her. His touch, his affection made her ache, but she accepted his embrace, holding him in the circle of her arms.

"You used to hate me," he said.

"That isn't true. I never did."

"Are you going to miss me as much as I'm going to miss you?" he asked.

More, she thought. He would have Tara waiting in the wings, an ex-lover all too willing to console him. "Yes."

He pulled her closer, so close their bodies were nearly one.

She drew a shaky breath. How could he torture her like this? How could he pretend that Tara wasn't there, like a ghost drifting between them?

"We should get ready," she said. "We're expected at your parents' house by seven."

"It doesn't matter. We can be late."

He held her a moment longer, and suddenly the wind shifted, making way for a quiet rain.

As water drizzled from the sky, Gina closed her eyes and wished that she could find a way to stop loving Flint. Yet as she inhaled the scent of his skin and felt the wonder of his body next to hers, she knew she would love him forever. This man she couldn't keep.

The Gatsby party was in full swing when Flint and Gina arrived. The Kingman estate had been transformed into the jazz age, where speakeasies, prohibition and It ruled supreme.

It, Flint knew, was the 1920s slang for sex appeal. And everyone at his stepmother's party clamored to show everyone else that they had It.

Women frolicked in flapper dresses or glided through the mansion in long elegant gowns or pajama-style smoking suits. The men in attendance did their best to embody screen stars like Douglas Fairbanks, Sr., and Rudolph Valentino. Of course, some chose a more humorous approach, going for the Charlie Chaplin or Buster Keaton vibe. And then there were the mobsters, the tough guys who dipped their hats like Al Capone.

Flint used to enjoy this soiree, but tonight he was too damn nervous to slip into the party mode.

He turned to look at Gina. She walked beside him, as breathtaking as the rain-shrouded night. Her vintage dress shimmered, streaming to the floor like a silver-lined waterfall. Her hair, secured in a fashionable bun, was adorned with a jeweled headband that complemented the long strand of pearls draped around her neck.

Why was she so quiet, so elegantly reserved? Was she playing a role for the reporters? The regal heiress. The Boston princess preparing to face the Hollywood movie star.

He knew that Tara's impending arrival troubled Gina. It troubled him, too. He had no idea what Tara wanted. Nor could he deal with any more stress, not tonight. Not on the night he was losing the woman he—

He—

He what? Lusted after? Craved?

No, he thought. No. It went much deeper than that. Somewhere along the way Gina had become more than an addiction, more than the equivalent of a sexual drug.

She'd become part of him, part of every breath he took, every word he spoke, every smile, every frown, every emotion that made him who he was.

Dear God. Flint's knees nearly buckled.

He loved her. He truly loved her.

All this time he'd been fighting the panic, the obsession, the seesaw of emotions. The desperate twists and turns of a captured heart.

Now it was too late. Gina had agreed to end their relationship.

And why wouldn't she? He'd never offered her anything but sex, anything but an erotic tangle between the sheets.

There was no reason for her to love him back. He'd done nothing to earn that. He'd accused her of being selfish for wanting to balance a family and a career. Yet she'd come to him today, as a friend, trying to ease his pain about his family. About the mother who'd abandoned him.

"What time is it?"

Flint turned to the sound of Gina's voice. He wanted to hold her, to press her against his heart, but instead he took a steadying breath and checked his watch. "A little after eight."

"It's raining harder now," she said.

"Yes." Suddenly he could hear it pounding on the roof, rising above the music, the voices, the party that would end his affair with the woman he'd never really gotten to love.

A tuxedoed waiter stopped with a tray of champagne, and Gina shook her head, refusing a drink. Flint declined, as well.

"Gina?" he said, after the waiter moved on.

"Yes?"

"Do you want to meet my parents?"

"Certainly."

He took her arm and led her into the drawing room, where James and Faith Kingman socialized with guests.

Flint introduced her, and she smiled graciously at his family. James shook her hand, and Faith kissed the side of her cheek. The three made small talk while Flint saw his miserable life flash before his eyes.

His life as a bachelor.

Would Gina marry someone else? Of course she would, he decided a second later. She wanted a home, a husband, children. And she wanted to keep her career. Something he should have supported long before now. But he'd let his mother's suicide blind him, confusing an issue that had never been problematic in the past.

"Is your grandmother here?" Gina asked him, interrupting his thoughts.

"Yes. I sent a car for her."

"Where do you think she is?"

"I don't know." The party spanned from room to room, and Flint wasn't sure where his grandmother had chosen to be. "Let's go find her."

After excusing themselves from his parents, Flint and Gina searched for *Nĭsh'kĭ*, combing the mansion together.

Finally they found her, perched on a Chippendale settee. She watched the festivities in a tan dress and an old-fashioned mink stole.

The older woman rose to hug Gina, who all but melted in his grandmother's arms.

"Flint insisted that I come to this party. Can you imagine, an old woman like me doing the Charleston?"

Gina laughed, still clutching both of *Nĭsh'kĭ's* hands. "It is a silly dance."

"To say the least," his grandmother agreed.

They both turned toward Flint, but he just shrugged. His grandmother preferred to avoid these high-society events, but tonight he needed to be surrounded by family, so he'd asked her to come.

"I've picked up all sorts of twenties terms," *Nĭsh'kĭ* said to Gina. "Did you know that a sheikh was a handsome young man? And that his flapper girlfriend was called a sheba?"

"Those terms were inspired by Valentino. Because of the sheikh films he made," Flint said. "Of course, you might remember him, *Nĭsh'kĭ*."

"Bite your tongue, young man. I'm not that old."

Both Gina and Flint laughed, and then a disturbance caught their attention. They turned simultaneously, and Flint cursed beneath his breath.

Tara had arrived.

Twelve

Tara Shaw entered the crowded mansion in a jeweled, knee-length dress and cloche hat, her eyes rimmed in kohl liner. She'd dressed appropriately for the occasion, right down to rolled stockings and a long, slim cigarette holder.

Ever the movie star, Flint thought. The reporters flocked around her like sheep.

"I think I'll sit this one out," *Nĭsh'kĭ* said, returning to the settee.

Flint looked at Gina. "I wish this wasn't happening. Do you know what the reporters are going to speculate about Tara and me?"

"That she came here to make a play for you?"

He nodded. "I know that's not the case. But how I am going to dispel those rumors when I go off alone with her?"

"How do you know that's not the case?" she asked, rendering him nearly speechless. "How do you know Tara isn't interested in you?"

Troubled by Gina's question, he reached for her hand. They stood close together, their conversation quiet. "Do you trust me?"

She sighed. "I don't trust Tara, Flint."

Which meant that she didn't trust him, either. She thought he would fall prey to his ex-lover's charms. And that made him feel sick inside.

Should he tell Gina how he felt? Should he admit that he loved her?

No, he thought. Not here. Not now. Not while she was accusing him of being a potential cheat.

"Your opinion of me hurts," he said.

She took her hand back. "I'm sorry, but I can't help the way I feel."

Flint's body went numb. He wanted her to respect him, to believe in him, but she didn't.

"It's humiliating to have Tara here," she said. "Even if our affair is almost officially over, it still feels like a slap in the face."

He didn't dare steal a glance at Tara. He could still hear the commotion coming from the other room, where his ex-lover waited for him to acknowledge her.

"Then we're even," he said. "Because your lack of trust is like a kick in the teeth."

"So, if I tested your loyalty and walked in on you and Tara, I wouldn't see anything incriminating?"

He squared his shoulders. "No, you wouldn't."

When they both fell silent, she smoothed her gown in a self-conscious gesture, and Flint realized the reporters were watching from across the room.

Outside, the storm took center stage, raging against the elements. Thunder grumbled in the sky, and rain slashed against the windows.

"You better go," she said.

"I'm not attracted to Tara anymore," he told her, determined to defend himself.

"She's one of the most beautiful women in the world, Flint. How could you not feel something for her, given your past?"

Because I love you, he thought. "I just don't. There's nothing there. Why won't you believe me?"

"I'm trying."

He reached out to stroke her cheek, but the gesture fell short. He dropped his hand, realizing it wasn't quite steady. "Then try harder. Test my loyalty. Do whatever you have to do."

"Maybe I will."

She met his gaze, her eyes cluttered with emotion. Dark and blue-violet, he thought. As perilous as the night sky.

Finally, she blinked then stepped out of reach. Too far for Flint to attempt to touch her again.

Five minutes later Flint and Tara were alone in the study, surrounded by rich, dark woods and rare books. The weather still raged, and the party still rang with merriment. Music played faintly in the background, melding with festive voices and laughter. Flint wondered what Gina was doing, if she remained isolated or if the reporters had swarmed her, attacking like killer bees.

God, he hoped not. Gina might not be strong enough to bat away the bees, to survive their vicious stings.

He glanced up to see Tara watching him. She lit the cigarette at the end of her fancy jeweled holder, then leaned against a mahogany desk, her gaze instantly riveted to his.

"So, what's going on?" he asked.

"What do you think is going on?"

"I have no idea."

"Don't you?" Her lips curved into a small, painted smile.

"No, I don't." Irritated by her evasive game, he removed his jacket and tossed it on a leather chair. He wore a dark, vintage-style suit, and the damned thing was stifling him. ''Just tell me what you're after. Tell me why you're here.''

She blew a stream of smoke into the air. ''Figure it out, Flint. Think it through for a minute. After all, you're a young, brilliant spin doctor. That shouldn't be too hard for you.''

He winced, realizing that he'd been caught. ''You know, don't you?''

''That your scandal is fake? You bet I do. And I'm also aware that you dragged me into it.''

''The tabloids created all that bull about you and Gina fighting over me. None of that was my idea.''

''Maybe not.'' She gave him a cool, even study. ''But you didn't do a damn thing to dispel the rumors. If anything, you added a few of your own.''

''That's my job, Tara.''

''To mess with people's lives?''

No, he thought. That wasn't his job at all. ''I didn't mean to cause you any discomfort.''

''But you did.'' She sat on the edge of the desk. ''Derrick and I are having some trouble holding our marriage together, and all that crap in the tabloids isn't helping. Can you imagine how he feels, being pitted against you? My former lover? A young man I once cared about?''

Yes, suddenly Flint could imagine exactly how Derrick felt, how being compared to Tara's ex-lover could make him insecure and distrustful. Weren't those the emotions Gina struggled with? The very ones she had tried to convey just minutes before?

''I'm sorry,'' he said, recalling how cavalier he'd been about Tara's faltering marriage. ''Sometimes I get so caught up in what I'm doing, I lose track of what's really important.'' He paused to loosen his tie, which seemed like a noose around his neck. ''I never meant to hurt anyone. It was strictly business.'' A sharp, calculating scheme that humbled him now. ''I am truly sorry.''

Tara toyed with a lock of hair that curled around her hat. She'd aged, but she was still beautiful, a woman of grace and substance. Flint had loved her once, but not in the way he loved Gina. Tara had been an icon, an introduction to the world he'd craved. Gina, with her hot temper and angelic heart, simply was his world.

"It's a hell of a scandal," Tara said. "If it hadn't turned my life inside out, I'd congratulate you for it."

"How did you know it was fake?" he asked, thinking it had turned his life inside out, as well. "I thought Gina and I put on a pretty good show."

"You did. But I know you, Flint. I know how you think. You would never get trapped in a public affair, not after what you went through when we were together. You're too clever for that."

He frowned. "I can't take it back. I can't tell the press that I manipulated a scandal for the Barones. That would hurt Gina's family. It would destroy their reputation."

"I don't expect you to take it back. But I came here to prompt you to conduct an interview with me, to convince the press that there's nothing going on between us."

"Why didn't you try to arrange this ahead of time?" he asked. "Why didn't you call me and discuss it first?"

She placed her cigarette and its sparkling holder in a crystal ashtray. "I wanted you to sweat it out. To fret about what I was up to. I assumed you knew that I'd figured out that your scandal was fake."

He frowned again. She'd played him. And she'd played him well. But he deserved it, he supposed.

"This fiasco has to end, Flint. As soon as possible."

"It will. I mean, it's supposed to. But things are a bit shaky right now."

She gave him a wary look. "What things?"

He tapped his chest. "The things going on inside me. I'm in love with her, Tara. I fell in love with Gina. And if she'd have me, I'd marry her in a minute."

"Oh, my. You mean this scandal turned real?"

"Gee, thanks. Rub it in. That's really comforting. Just what I need."

She snuffed out her cigarette. "Oh, darlin', it'll be all right. Being in love isn't so bad."

"It is if you're on a one-way street."

"How do you know you're on a one-way street? Did she rebuff your feelings?"

"Not exactly. But she hasn't come forward with any kind of confession, either."

Tara rolled her eyes. "Men are such idiots. Young, old, you're all a bunch of morons. For goodness sake, Flint. Tell her how you feel. Make the first move."

His pulse shot straight up his arm. Tara was right, of course. He needed to put his heart on the line, to ask Gina to become his wife, to bleed at her feet if that was what it took.

Anxious, he dragged a hand through his hair. Brave talk, he thought, for a moron. For an idiot male who didn't have the slightest idea if the woman he loved even wanted him.

God, he was scared. Petrified that she would refuse his proposal. "Will you cover for me, Tara? Will you handle the press?"

"You bet." She reached for his jacket and handed it to him. "I'll give the interview of a lifetime."

"Thank you." He smoothed his lapels, and Tara came forward to straighten his tie, to offer him a boost of encouragement.

And that was when the door opened.

They both turned, and Flint saw Gina. Tara dropped her hands, but it was too late. He was face to face with his ex-lover, and Gina assumed the worst.

He caught the devastation in her eyes before she raced back to a party filled with curious onlookers.

Gina pushed her way through the crowd, desperate for an escape. He'd lied. He'd insisted that he wasn't attracted to Tara anymore. But his actions spoke louder than his words.

Much louder.

Tears burned her eyes, but she refused to cry. Blinking back the pain, she kept pushing, kept shoving her way through partygoers and reporters who had been handpicked to attend this fraudulent occasion.

Someone grabbed her arm, and she tried to jerk free.

"Gina, wait!"

She heard Flint's voice and struggled even harder to get away. But his grip was too strong.

She turned to look at him and saw the pure and utter remorse on his face. What a fine actor he was. As usual, he played his role to perfection.

Nearly every guest gathered to watch, to view the trashy scene.

Gina caught sight of Tara from the corner of her eye, wondering how the actress could be so cold, so unfeeling.

Just like Flint.

He took a rough breath and released her arm. "It's not what you think. Tara was straightening my tie. I know that sounds stupid, but it's the truth."

It did sound stupid. A lame excuse. And she didn't understand why he bothered to say it.

She prayed for the strength to continue this public charade, to keep herself from collapsing. Their fight was no longer staged. It had become real. Only now she had to improvise, to deliver her lines and convince Flint that she didn't care.

"What happened doesn't matter," she said, each syllable laced with pride, with an ache she refused to reveal. "It's degrading, but I'll get over it."

"Nothing happened, Gina. I swear."

God, he was good, she thought. Even his voice—that smooth vodka-on-the-rocks voice—quavered with regret.

"I'm so sorry." He reached out to touch her, to brush her fingers with his. "I never meant to hurt you, to cause a misunderstanding."

She pulled her hand back. She couldn't bear the pain of his touch, the lies, the betrayal. "I told you it doesn't matter. And neither do you. You're not worth my time. Not anymore."

His breath hitched. "Do you really mean that? Is that honestly how you feel?"

No, she thought. No. But how could she reveal her heart just seconds after he'd crushed it? She would rather die.

He stood, riveted to the floor, gazing at her with pain in his eyes. Trumped-up pain, she reminded herself. He was only sorry that he got caught.

"I love you, Gina. That's what Tara and I were talking about when you walked in." He paused, his pain-filled eyes turning watery. "I was going to ask you to marry me. But I know now that you'd refuse."

The crowd still watched. Some guests whispered and others gasped. Gina feared she might faint. "You're not serious," she said.

"Yes, I am. I've never been more serious in my life. You've become everything to me. My heart, my soul, my friend, my lover. But you're right, it doesn't matter now. I can't make you feel the same way about me."

A flood of tears rushed her eyes. "But I do. I just couldn't bear to say it. Not after what I thought you were doing with Tara."

"Oh, baby." He drew her into his arms, and she felt his heart pounding just as erratically as hers.

"Can we go someplace quiet?" she asked. Where they weren't being watched, where the reporters weren't listening to every word they said.

Every beautiful, dizzying, emotional word.

He led her through the crowd, and as they passed Tara, the actress smiled. Gina smiled back. She had never expected the other woman to become her ally, but Tara was already addressing the press, distracting them while Gina and Flint slipped away.

He took her to a garden room, where hundreds of flowers bloomed all around them and rain fell against the glass roof and walls. Finally alone with her, he kissed her.

His body was hard and strong, his mouth gentle and warm. Gina closed her eyes and clung to him.

He stepped back to touch her cheek, to run his thumb along her jaw. She opened her eyes to look at him, to memorize every feature.

"When did you know, Flint? When did you know that you loved me?"

"I'm not sure, but I finally admitted it to myself tonight. I'd been panicking all week, dreading this party, dreading the moment I would lose you. So maybe I knew all along and I was just too afraid to face my feelings."

"I was fighting my feelings, too."

"Really? For how long?"

"Since I moved in with you."

He took both her hands in his. "Will you marry me, Gina? Will you be my wife?"

Her heart tugged. "I love you, and I want that more than anything, but I can't give up my career, Flint."

"I'm not asking you to."

"How can you just change your mind about marrying a career woman?" she asked, fear shattering the moment. "What if it becomes a problem later on?"

"It won't." He paused to explain. "In the past, it never mattered to me whether my future wife worked or not. I used to think the choice should be hers, since she would be the one bearing my children. But after I heard about my mother's suicide, I changed my mind. I forced the issue."

For a moment they both fell silent, and Gina knew Flint was thinking about his mother. She brushed his lips in a tender kiss, and he drew her into his arms and held her in a warm embrace.

"I can handle the truth about Danielle," he said. "Whatever her reasons for doing what she did, I can deal with it." He slid his hands down her back, drawing her closer. "But that's because of you. Because you're the link to my heart, the piece I was missing."

Her eyes misted. He, too, was the link to her heart.

Silent, they listened to the rain for a while, and then she thought about the party at which they'd met.

"I dreamed about you that first night. It was raining then, too." She laughed a little. "You ambushed me right from the start. But I'm glad you railroaded me into your scandal, Mr. Kingman."

"Oh, yeah?" He stepped back to grin at her. "Good thing. Because I intend to nose in on your job, Miss Barone."

"We're going to be working together again?"

"You bet. Remember that contest you wanted to launch? The new flavor for Baronessa? I'm going to help you with the campaign."

"Are you now?"

"Damn straight."

"And when did you decide all of this?" she asked.

"A few seconds ago."

He shot her another impulsive grin, and she leaped into his arms. When he spun her in a dizzying circle, she laughed again, knowing this man—this insistent, sensitive, stubborn man—was hers to keep.

Later that night Flint took Gina to his house, and as they entered the master bedroom, he smiled.

Everyone had congratulated them. Friends, family and reporters alike. Tara had remained at the party to show her support, and his grandmother had danced the Charleston, luring him and Gina into the festivities. He'd never had such ridiculous, mind-boggling, heart-soaring fun.

Now he was completely alone with the lady he intended to marry.

"Will you share this house with me?" he asked, discarding his jacket.

She looked around his room, the one that mirrored her own. "I already feel like I live here."

Flint suspected they'd been living in each other's hearts even before they'd met. "You can bring anything from the brownstone that you want to keep. We can blend our furnishings."

"I think I'll leave everything there. Except for my personal belongings, of course."

And her angel collection. He knew she wouldn't leave her angels behind.

He reached behind her to unzip her dress, and she leaned into him. Together, they removed the shimmering gown.

Beneath it, she wore a satin bra, matching panties and a pair of hose the same color as her flesh. She was too curvaceous for the flat, mannish style of the 1920s, but she'd pulled off the look with charm and grace.

He released the pins in her hair and watched the curls tumble around her face and onto her shoulders. Such pretty shoulders, he thought, pressing a kiss to one and then the other.

Her perfume rose like a veiled mist, and he lost himself in the alluring scent, in the knowledge that this woman belonged to him.

"How many babies do you want?" he asked.

"A lot," she said. "But I want to wait a few years."

"That's fine." He slipped her bra straps down, just to see them fall. "How many is a lot?"

"Ten."

Stunned, he lifted his gaze.

She smiled and removed his tie so she could unbutton his shirt. "Or maybe eleven. I haven't decided yet."

"How about two?" he suggested, hoping she was teasing him.

"Three," she challenged.

"Deal." He stole a quick kiss and let her untuck his shirt from his pants. "When do you want to get married?"

"As soon as possible."

"Me, too." He opened his zipper to make her task easier. "How about tomorrow? Or the next day?"

She laughed. "Are you serious?"

He grinned. "You better believe I am."

"Then let's do it. Let's get married just as soon as we can arrange a fitting ceremony."

Flint put his arms around her, and for a moment they just held each other.

"I love you," he said.

"I love you, too."

She stepped back to undress him, to finish what she'd started, and then she kissed a fiery trail down the center of his body, showing him how much she loved him, how much she wanted to please him.

When she dropped to her knees, Flint caught his breath. She'd done this to him before, but not in this position. Not on her knees, like a wanton, wild goddess.

Her touch aroused him beyond reason. As she stroked him, he watched, mesmerized by her beauty, by the erotic rhythm of her mouth.

He slid his hands into her hair and twined the silky strands around his fingers.

Oral sex, he thought. Sweet sin. Masculine ecstasy.

Flint's blood roared in his head and crashed in his ears. Suddenly he had the wicked urge to rock his hips, to push deeper, to encourage her to take more.

But a second later she did just that. She took him so deep, he nearly lost control.

"You have to stop," he rasped.

She didn't listen, so he pulled her up and dragged her against his body. And then he removed her underwear, warring with tiny hooks, battling elastic, struggling clumsily with a pair of hose he fought to peel down her legs. Those long, endless legs.

She laughed and nudged him onto the bed, where she landed on top of him.

"We have to slow down," he said.

"Why?"

He searched for a logical reason. "Because we always go crazy."

She nibbled the side of his neck. "But I like crazy, and so do you."

Well, hell, he thought. She was right. He wanted it hard and fast. He wanted to devour, to feast, to feed like the male animal he was.

But he wanted to love her, too. To show her that he could be tender. That he could bring her unhurried pleasure.

He rolled so that he was on top of her, so that he could take control. Holding her wrists, he gazed into her eyes. Eyes a man could drown in.

"We're going to go slow," he said. "We're going to make this last."

"And I don't have a choice?"

"No," he told her. "You don't."

She struggled a little, but he refused to release her. Instead he lowered his mouth to hers and kissed softly.

She sighed, and he caressed her, running his fingertips lightly over her body, around each pebbled nipple, down a flat, quivering stomach, across the ridges of jutting hipbones.

And then he kissed between her thighs.

She moved against his mouth, making catlike sounds. When he rose to enter her, she was more than ready.

He made love to her as slowly as they both could endure.

For the longest time they danced to a sweet, seductive rhythm, danced until their bodies peaked and they became one.

One mind, Flint thought, as he spilled into her. One heart. And one soul.

Epilogue

Gina stood in front of a full-length mirror in the bedroom she shared with Flint, her soon-to-be husband. He waited downstairs while the women in her family fussed over her.

She and Flint had chosen to get married at home, arranging the ceremony as quickly as possible. The state of Massachusetts required a three-day waiting period for a marriage license, which gave an eager bride and an anxious groom plenty of time to plan a simple yet special wedding, even though it meant sending scouts all over the continent to acquire what they needed.

"You look so beautiful." Moira Reardon Barone, Gina's emotional mother, adjusted the crown of flowers in Gina's hair, separating the ribbon streamers. Then she paused to wipe her watery eyes.

"Oh, Mama, don't cry."

"I can't help it."

Gina turned, and as they embraced, Moira's tears fell in earnest. Happy tears, Gina thought, blinking back her own.

When they separated, they stared at each other for a long, silent moment.

Colleen, Gina's oldest sister and the one who didn't live at the brownstone, came forward to take over for their mother, who was in desperate need of a handkerchief.

In all, Gina had three sisters and four brothers, and most of them were present today.

She met Colleen's gaze in the mirror. "This wouldn't have happened without you." In a sense, Colleen was indirectly responsible for bringing Flint into Gina's world, considering that Gavin, the love of Colleen's life, was also Flint's friend. And the man who'd suggested that the Barones hire the spin doctor to begin with.

"You weren't thanking me a month ago," Colleen teased.

That was true. Gina had avoided Colleen and Gavin purposely, infuriated by Gavin's suggestion. Now she would be forever grateful.

Rita and Maria smiled, and Gina suspected they were thinking about her angry fits, all the days and nights she'd cursed Flint Kingman.

The man she loved.

"Goodness." The mother of the bride wiped her eyes again. "It's almost time, girls. We better get downstairs." She looked at Gina. "I'm sure your father is waiting for you, darling. I'll tell him you'll be out in a minute."

"Thank you." The other women rushed out the door, leaving Gina alone.

She took a moment to study her appearance, to admire the Italian silk gown with its jeweled neckline and lace hem.

Ready to embrace her future, she left the room to meet her father at the top of the stairs. Carlo Barone gave her a dashing smile and took her arm. She clutched a bouquet of cascading orchids and waited for the music to begin.

"I already told that young man of yours that he better be good to you."

"And what did he say?" she asked, knowing Flint had sent her father some carefully selected gifts, explaining that Cheyenne war weapons were sometimes offered to a bride's family in exchange for her hand.

"He said that he would honor you with his life," Carlo told her, in a voice rough with emotion.

And approval.

Just as her eyes misted, the wedding march sounded. Father and daughter descended the spiral staircase and reached the living room, where hundreds of white candles flickered like a sea of stars.

There, in the center of all that mystical beauty, was the most breathtaking man she had ever seen.

Flint turned to her, and their eyes met. He wore a ribbon shirt and deerskin pants laced with accessories from his regalia. A beaded vest spanned his chest, and an otter sash reflected a shimmering display of mirrors.

They had chosen to blend their cultures to create a ceremony that represented who they were and who their children would become. At the reception a home-cooked Italian buffet would be served, and a Native American Drum would sing a round-dance song, bringing the guests together in a sacred circle.

The circle Flint and Gina would share for the rest of their lives.

* * * * *

TAMING THE BEASTLY MD
by
Elizabeth Bevarly

ELIZABETH BEVARLY

was born and raised in Louisville, Kentucky, and earned her degree in English from the University of Louisville in 1983. Although she never wanted to be anything but a novelist, her career side trips before making the leap to writing included stints working in cinemas, restaurants, boutiques and a major department store. When she's not writing, Elizabeth enjoys old films, old houses, good books, whimsical antiques, hot jazz and even hotter salsa (the music, not the sauce). She resides with her husband and young son in Kentucky.

Prologue

There was no disputing the fact that surly Boston winters tended to slow things down in the emergency rooms of the city's hospitals. But that only meant it wasn't standing room only, Rita Barone thought as she gazed at the still-bustling E.R. this bitter early February morning. There was plenty here to keep the staff busy. Certainly enough to make her wish she hadn't picked up the shift to help out one of the other nurses. Normally, she worked in the coronary care unit, which was a walk in the park compared to the E.R. Still, Rita had started in the E.R. at Boston General, so in a way, this was like coming home.

At home, though, she didn't have to treat overblown cold sores and ingrown toenails. No, when Rita went home—home to the big Beacon Hill townhouse where she'd grown up, and not the North End brownstone she shared with two of her sisters—her parents pampered her like a princess. In fact, she could be living the life of a princess at this very moment had she chosen, since each of the Barone siblings had collected a million-dollar trust upon turning twenty-one. But Rita, crazy as it might sound, had wanted to be a nurse instead of a princess. Now, after almost three years of employment at Boston General, she knew she had made the right choice. Princesses, she knew, hardly ever saved lives. Plus, they didn't have nearly as good a health plan as she did.

Cold sores and ingrown toenails, here I come, she thought wryly now as she leveled an espresso-colored gaze on the wretched refuse cluttering the E.R. waiting room. The people seemed not to have changed one bit since she had been a regular staff member here.

But then, she hadn't changed much herself, had she? she thought further. She still wore the slate-blue scrubs she preferred for work, and she still bound her dark-brown hair in a tidy braid. But then, why fix it if it wasn't broken, right?

"Excuse me, but I've been waiting for more than a half hour now," a young woman told Rita as she leaned over the counter of the nurses' station. She seemed to be checking the desk to make sure there were no extra doctors hiding there. "How much longer will it be until I can see someone?"

Rita offered up a halfhearted smile. "It shouldn't be too much longer, I wouldn't think," she said, knowing she was being optimistic, but feeling hopeful all the same. "This flu that's going around has hit everyone hard. We're even short a doctor this morning because of it."

Plus, they were understandably obligated to take the most serious cases first. With a slight fever and cough, and no family doctor, this woman was in for a wait.

Now, too, they were expecting an ambulance, whose arrival they had been alerted to only moments ago. A homeless man had gone into cardiac arrest not far from the hospital. Rita had already notified the coronary care unit, and they were sending down their best—Dr. Matthew Grayson, who was something of a legend around Boston General.

Truth be told, his legendary status wasn't due entirely to his talent as a heart surgeon. No, part of his status was less legend-like than it was fairy-tale-like. Dr. Grayson definitely resembled a certain fairy-tale character—the Beast from *Beauty and the Beast*. It wasn't just because of his attitude, either, though certainly that had been described as beastly by more than one CCU nurse. One would think that as a result of working in the unit herself, Rita would have more than a nodding acquaintance with Dr. Grayson. But she didn't think anyone in the CCU—or at Boston General for that matter—had any kind of acquaintance with the man.

Although Rita had never been put off by Dr. Grayson the way many were, she could see why others might find him difficult. At times he was gruff to the extreme. Even in his best mood, he was standoffish. His beastliness was only enhanced by the scars on the left side of his face and neck. She didn't know what had caused those scars—Dr. Grayson never mentioned them, and neither did anyone else if they knew what was good for them—but whatever it had been had done a thorough job in marking him. It was obvious that he'd had cosmetic surgery, but even plastic surgeons couldn't work miracles. Dr. Grayson, she was sure, would remain scarred for life.

But whether he truly was a beast, Rita couldn't say. Yes, he could be intimidating, but he was a dedicated professional who saved scores of lives. Rita admired and respected his skill as a surgeon, and she figured he probably had a reason for his gruffness. In any event, he'd never turned that attitude on her. Come to think of it, he pretty much steered clear of her, which was just fine with her.

Besides, it took a lot more than scars and a bad mood to intimidate Rita Barone. The second-youngest of eight children from a celebrated Boston family, she'd had no choice but to learn early on to take care of herself and not let things get to her. She'd grown up with four rough-and-tumble older brothers who'd suffered every manner of injury known to humankind, not to mention their own forms of beastly behavior, especially when puberty struck them.

As if conjured by the thought, Dr. Matthew Grayson himself appeared then, rushing toward the nurses' station. His white coat flapped behind him over dark trousers, a white shirt and a discreetly patterned necktie in varying shades of blue.

"Has our cardiac arrest arrived yet?" he demanded without so much as a hello as he came to a stop behind Rita.

"Any time now," she told him.

Really, she thought, considering him, if it weren't for the scars on his face, he'd be an extremely handsome man. Standing at about six-foot-three, he towered over Rita, something she wasn't accustomed to at five-eight herself. Add to that impressive height his solid, athletic build, his dreamy green eyes and his chestnut hair with its golden highlights, not to mention the perfectly tailored, very expensive dark suits he generally opted for, and you had the makings of a Hollywood movie star. Only the scars marred his perfection.

Then again, she thought further, in some ways those scars almost added to his allure. They kept his exquisite good looks from being *too* exquisite, and somehow made him seem more human.

Of course, at the moment, he seemed more godlike, as he towered over her. Rita fought the urge to stand up, though that scarcely would have made a difference, thanks to the disparity in their heights. Instead, she remained seated, as if she were completely unaffected by his nearness. And she was—except for the way her heart rate seemed to have quadrupled the moment she saw him striding toward her.

But then, what else was her heart supposed to do? she wondered. They were expecting a cardiac arrest any moment, and Dr. Grayson had already surged into action in anticipation. It was normal that she be surging, too, albeit in *other* ways. Ways that had nothing to do with the good doctor's presence. Especially once she heard the siren outside announcing the arrival of the ambulance. She leapt up from her chair and circled the nurses' station with Dr. Grayson right on her heels.

In a flurry of motion and clamor, the paramedics wheeled in an elderly man who was screaming and keening and flailing his arms about. He was filthy, Rita saw as she approached, hurrying her stride to match the paramedics' as she directed them to an examining room, and he was clearly terrified. As she strode alongside him, instinctively she reached for the man's hand and held it, then winced a bit when he squeezed tightly enough to hurt her. He was obviously much stronger than he looked.

"It's okay," she told him as they came to a halt in a small room. "You're going to be all right." She didn't know if that was true, but she wasn't about to cite heart-attack survival statistics for him right now. "You've got the best here to help you," she said further. "We'll take good care of you."

The man stopped trying to strike the paramedics then, and he stopped shouting. When he turned to look at Rita, he was breathing rapidly and raggedly, and his pale-blue eyes were filled with fear.

"Who—who're you?" he gasped. Then he grimaced in pain.

"My name is Rita," she said soothingly, stroking her other hand over the one he had wrapped so fiercely around hers. As discreetly as she could, she took his pulse, not wanting to alarm him again. It wasn't quite as erratic as she would have thought under the circumstances, but it was still thready.

"You—the—doc?" the man asked with some difficulty, his voice raspy, his breathing becoming more labored.

"No, I'm a nurse," Rita told him as she noted the activity surrounding them. It looked as if half the staff was in the tiny room, tending to the man, even though she knew it was only a fraction of those working this morning. "But there's a doctor here," she said further. "You're in the emergency room of Boston General, and you're having a heart attack. I'm going to take your blood pressure now," she then added. When he recoiled and opened his mouth to shout again, she hastily, but very calmly, added, "It won't hurt, I promise. But you need to let us check you out, to see how you're doing."

"We've stabilized him," one of the paramedics said from the other side of the gurney, "but he's not out of the woods yet. Not by a long shot."

Rita threw the man a censuring look. The last thing this guy needed to hear was that he was still in danger.

"Am I—" He grimaced again, groaning. "Am I—gonna—die?" he demanded.

"No," Rita said firmly, gritting her teeth at the paramedic, who just shrugged off her reproach. "You're going to be fine. What's your name?" she asked the old man.

He gazed at her warily for a moment, still clearly frightened, then, evidently deciding she was okay, he told her weakly, "Joe."

"Do you have any family, Joe?" she asked as the others were working to monitor him, hooking him up to oxygen and an EKG. He fought the mask at first, but Rita soothed him, promising him it was for his own good and that it would only be temporary. "Is there anyone we can call who might make you feel more comfortable?" she asked again.

He shook his head, took another indifferent swipe at the oxygen mask, then surrendered to it. "No. No family," he told her, sounding even weaker than he had before. After a small hesitation, he added, "But—but you kinda—" He expelled a sound of pain, then grabbed her hand again with a brutal grip. "You," he tried again, "you—make me feel—more comfortable."

Rita smiled again, flexing her fingers against the force of his grasp. "Well, then, Joe, I'll just stay right here with you. How will that be?"

He nodded faintly. "That'd be good. Don't—go nowhere."

"I won't," she promised him.

"And later," he said, his voice quavering as he spoke, "after—after they's—done with me, if I—if I make it through—don't—go nowhere then, neither."

Rita patted his hand gently. "This is where I work, Joe. And you know, sometimes I feel like I never leave."

That roused a brief, if feeble, grin from him in response, but he was clearly growing weaker now. She sent up a silent prayer that he would be all right. She knew nothing about him except that he had no home and no family and that his name was Joe. But he was obviously a fighter—and a survivor—and she had no choice but to admire that. Surely he'd survive this, too.

"This is Dr. Grayson," Rita told him, nodding her head toward the surgeon who now stood on the other side of the gurney. "He'll be looking at you here in a minute. He's very good. The absolute best."

When she looked up, she saw that Dr. Grayson was studying her with much consideration, as if he wanted to ask her something, and she opened her mouth to ask what. But Joe began thrashing and screaming then, and thinking he must be in pain, Rita glanced back down to tend to him. But it obviously wasn't pain that was causing his reaction. He was looking right at Dr. Grayson and had somehow managed to lift his hand to point at the scars on the other man's face.

"Don't let 'im—come near me," Joe said with much agitation. "He—he ain't—no man. He's a—monster."

Dr. Grayson simply ignored the comment and reached toward Joe. Joe, however, shoved his hand away before the doctor could touch him, and began to thrash even more.

"Git 'im—away from me! Git 'im away!"

"Joe, please," Rita tried again.

But the old man wouldn't be calmed. "His face!" he cried, pointing at Dr. Grayson. "He's like one a'them— one a'them gargoyles on—St. Michael's. They—come after me sometimes—in my—in my dreams. To take me—to hell. They's monsters! Git 'im away!"

"Joe, it's all right," Rita said firmly, grabbing his arms and holding them at his sides. "Dr. Grayson is here to help you. He's an excellent surgeon and a wonderful man. No one is going to hurt you," she said even more forcefully. "I won't let anyone hurt you, I promise. I'm right here, and I won't let anyone hurt you."

For whatever reason, her vows reassured him. Or maybe it was just that he was too weak and in too much pain to fight anymore. Rita gave up trying to be a nurse then and let the other RNs tend to Joe's medical needs. Instead, she picked up the man's hand once more and held it tightly, and murmured soothing words about how he was going to be just fine because he had Dr. Matthew Grayson to take care of him.

And he would be fine, Rita told herself, feeling strangely attached to the old man for some reason. Because he did have Dr. Matthew Grayson to look after him.

Who wouldn't be fine with someone like that to watch over him?

One

The coronary care unit at Boston General in the trendy North End was quiet for a Friday at dinnertime—no doubt the rowdy April weather outside was keeping many visitors at home—which meant that Rita Barone actually found five full minutes to steal away from the nurses' station for a cup of bad coffee from the vending machine in the CCU waiting room. Coffee—even bad coffee—was her only hope to get her through the evening shift, one she hadn't worked in months. After three years at Boston General, she had finally landed regular hours in the day shift, and only had to pull night hours now to cover for friends, like tonight, or to pick up extra Christmas money. Not that extra Christmas money was generally a big deal, since the Barones of Boston were *never* strapped for cash. But Rita was the kind of woman who liked to rest on her own laurels, and not the family's, so she rarely, if ever, took advantage of the Barone family's very fat coffers.

Three years, she reflected again as she watched the vending machine spit its dark-brown brew into a paper container that was in no way large enough to qualify for a respectable cup of coffee. In fact, it had been three years to the day today, she realized further. She had begun working at Boston General as a student nurse exactly two months before her June graduation from Boston University, and exactly one month following her twenty-second birthday. Now, at twenty-five, here she was celebrating her anniversary by being back on the evening shift.

She glanced down at her watch, then shook her head morosely. She'd only started two hours ago, and already she was hitting the caffeine. The six remaining hours had never seemed like such a long, looming stretch of time.

She kept a close eye on the too-full cup of coffee as she made her way back to the nurses' station, then returned to her seat and set the hot brew to the side to cool a bit. Absently, she tucked a stray strand of dark-brown hair back into the thick French braid that fell to the base of her neck, then brushed at a stain of indistinguishable origin on the pants of her slate-blue scrubs. It wasn't until she was reaching for a patient chart that she saw the small white package tucked sideways into her note slot on the desk.

And she battled a wave of apprehension that shimmied down her spine when she saw it.

It hadn't been there when she'd gone for her coffee, because she'd had to reach into her mail slot to grab some of the spare change she always left there for the vending machines. So whoever had left it had done so just now, while she was gone. It was a small square box wrapped in white glossy paper, tied with a gold ribbon, obviously a gift. But instead of being delighted by such a surprise, Rita went cold inside. This was the third time she'd found a gift in her note slot wrapped in exactly this way. As always, when she looked for a note to accompany the gift, she didn't find one. And, as always, that bothered her. A lot.

Okay, she admitted, she *had* been delighted the first time such a gift had shown up, on Valentine's Day, two months ago—for all of a few hours. When she'd returned from lunch that day and found a tiny present tucked into her note slot, she'd been reluctantly enchanted, especially when she found that there was no note accompanying the gift to explain its presence. She'd been even more enchanted when she'd opened the box to find a small pin inside. It was a pewter heart, not much bigger than a postage stamp, wrapped diagonally with a gold Band-Aid. She'd thought it an appropriate gift for a cardiology nurse, and had immediately pinned the heart to the breast pocket of her scrubs, just above her name tag. Then she'd waited for the giver to come forward and identify him- or herself, and his or her reason for the gesture.

Of course, since the occasion on that first gift's appearance was Valentine's Day, her co-workers had proposed that Rita must have a secret admirer. Rita, naturally, had considered such a suggestion ridiculous. Grown men didn't have secret crushes on grown women—not emotionally sound grown men, anyway. But her fellow nurses had insisted, and it hadn't been long before the rumor mill at Boston General—an astoundingly active one—was churning out a story about Rita Barone's secret admirer.

Who could it be? everyone wondered. One of the handsome new interns? A co-worker who was too shy to make his affections known? A former patient who felt his life had been saved by the lovely, dark-eyed, dark-haired cardiology nurse?

Although a number of people had remarked on the pin that day, none had claimed to be the one who gave it to Rita. Nor had any of her co-workers seen anyone put the gift in her note slot. So Rita began to wear the pin daily, certain that eventually someone would admit to having given it to her. Perhaps there was supposed to have been a card, but it had got lost somehow. Perhaps someone simply wanted to tease her a bit by leaving her curious for a few days before identifying himself as the giver. Perhaps the person was shy, in which case that shyness might be assuaged if the person saw her wearing the gift.

But in spite of Rita continually wearing the pin, and in spite of the number of comments she received about it, no one ever came forward.

The second gift had arrived in her note slot last month, on her birthday. Again, it had been wrapped in white, glossy paper with a gold ribbon, and again, it had appeared without a card or note. When Rita had opened that one, hoping perhaps it might offer some clue as to the identity of its giver, she had found inside an inexpensive silver charm bracelet with a dozen delicate little charms related to the nursing field. She'd been reluctantly pleased by it, too, but hadn't quite been able to halt the feeling of foreboding that had accompanied her pleasure.

She'd told herself her apprehension was silly, that obviously she *did* have a secret admirer—and hey, why was that such a bad thing? Then she'd donned the charm bracelet, as well, hoping again to "out" the giver.

But again, no one came forth to claim the identity of Rita Barone's secret admirer. No one came forth for any reason at all.

Now, as she eyed this latest gift with a mixture of hesitant pleasure and growing dread, she lifted her right hand to stroke the bandaged heart pin fastened, as it always was, on the pocket of her scrubs. When she did, the charm bracelet clinked merrily on her right wrist.

Now the mysterious giver had struck again, had left her

a third gift—on the third anniversary of her having started work at Boston General.

Whoever it was, she realized then, was commemorating special occasions and events—first Valentine's Day, then her birthday, and now the anniversary of her first day at work. It must be someone who worked at the hospital, she thought. And it must be a secret admirer—for lack of a better ID. There were too many romantic overtones for it not to be. Still, she couldn't begin to imagine who might be leaving her gifts like this. She'd noticed not one hint of interest from anyone of the opposite sex, absolutely no clue that there was a man out there who regarded her as anything more than another human being who inhabited the same planet. Not at work, and not anywhere else, either.

Not unless she was overlooking any hints and clues a man might be giving out, which she supposed was possible, since she'd really never been much interested in the opposite sex. Her sisters Gina and Maria often told her she was so focused on her work that she was missing out on everything else life had to offer, including romance.

Of course, Rita didn't necessarily disagree with that. Her work *was* very important to her. More important, she admitted, than anything else. Except for family, of course. The Barones were a close-knit bunch, and family would always come first for all of them. But Rita had never wanted to be anything but a nurse, ever since she was a child, and the job gave her more satisfaction and fulfillment than she could imagine receiving anywhere else. She helped save lives here at the hospital. What could possibly be more important than that?

Well, there was saving her own life, Gina would always argue when Rita pointed that out, seeing as how Rita didn't much have one outside work. And there was living her life, Maria would chime in, the one outside work, anyway.

Whenever her sisters offered their opinions in such a way, Rita would blithely remind them that her work *was* her life, and she enjoyed it very much, thanks. And she truly did believe it was enough. She had a full, and very satisfying, life without having to wade through all the politics and games of a romantic relationship—especially a workplace romance.

Still, she thought now as she gingerly fingered the third little white package, it would be nice to discover who was leaving the gifts for her. If nothing else, she could rest easy knowing there was nothing more to it than someone having a bit of fun. Because she just couldn't quite shake the sensation that there was something a bit sinister about all this anonymous gift-giving, even if the gifts in question had been totally benign.

Rita checked one more time to see if there was a card or note to accompany the gift but, not surprisingly, she found none. So, inhaling a deep breath, she tucked her finger under the gold ribbon and slowly slid it off. Then she carefully peeled back the white paper. Just as it had been with the previous two gifts, the box was plain and white, too, with no markings that might identify where the gift had been purchased. Placing it cautiously on the desk, Rita lifted the lid, then pushed aside a fold of tissue paper.

"Oh, my," she said softly, reverently, when she saw what was inside. A small, cut-crystal heart winked merrily at her from its cushion of tissue in the box, shattering the harsh fluorescent overhead light into a billion kaleidoscopic colors. It was meant, she supposed, to be a paperweight. Somehow, though, it was much too beautiful for so functional a purpose.

A crystal heart, she remarked again. Was it a symbol of what she did for a living, caring for a fragile organ? Or a symbol of the giver's fragile feelings for her? And how would she ever know if the giver never came forward? And why wouldn't he? It had been two months since that first gift had appeared. Surely, by now, he was ready to make himself known. Unless…

Unless his intentions were less than honorable.

"Have you nothing better to do with your time, Ms. Barone, than enjoy an extended coffee break?"

Rita jumped at the gruffly offered question, not so much because of the question itself—unfair as it was—but because the voice belonged to Dr. Matthew Grayson. In addition to his medical skills, he was renowned for his no-nonsense approach to his work.

And also because of his complete intolerance for anything bordering on fun.

Tall, dark and brooding, that was Dr. Grayson. All the nurses and other doctors thought so. And most steered clear of him whenever they could, because they didn't want to get caught in the storm swirling in the dark clouds that always seemed to surround him. Rita, though, had always thought him rather intriguing. Nobody was born grouchy and aloof, she reasoned. Something had to happen in a person's life to make him that way. And Rita couldn't help wondering what had happened in Matthew Grayson's.

She also couldn't help wondering if it had anything to do with the scars he bore on his left cheek and neck. The worst of them were a trio of nearly straight lines that ran from his cheekbone to his jaw—three parallel stripes, roughly a half inch apart and three inches in length.

Automatically she slammed the lid back down on the box she had just opened. For some reason, she didn't want Dr. Grayson to know about her secret admirer—if admiring was indeed what was behind the mysterious gifts. As discreetly as she could, she slid the box back into her note slot, tossed the white wrapping paper and gold ribbon into the wastebasket beneath her desk, and then turned in her chair to face him.

Big mistake, she realized immediately. Because being seated while he was standing left Rita gazing at a part of Dr. Grayson she really shouldn't be gazing at.

"Dr. Grayson," she said as she abruptly stood, telling herself she was only imagining the breathless quality her voice seemed to have suddenly adopted. "I didn't hear you coming."

"Obviously," he replied wryly.

"And I wasn't enjoying a coffee break," she assured him.

He gazed pointedly at the cup sitting before her chair.

"Okay, yes, I *was* having coffee," she conceded. "But I *wasn't* enjoying it. It's from the vending machine," she added meaningfully.

Dr. Grayson, however, evidently didn't catch her meaning, because he only continued to scowl at her. Granted, it was kind of a handsome scowl, what with those dreamy green eyes and that full, luscious-looking mouth, but it was a scowl nonetheless. So Rita countered with the most dazzling smile she could conjure from her ample arsenal. She knew it made him uncomfortable to be smiled at. Probably, she thought, because he didn't know how to smile back. In fact, she'd never seen him smile. And, true to her supposition—and his own personality—Dr. Grayson only deepened his scowl. So Rita smiled even more dazzlingly, this time batting her eyelashes playfully.

There, she thought triumphantly. Take *that,* Dr. Grayson.

But instead of being immobilized by her mischievous warfare, Dr. Grayson only looked more ferocious. So, with an imperceptible sigh, Rita surrendered.

Point to Dr. Grayson.

"Rita," he said in a tone of voice that indicated he

wanted to start all over again and pretend the last few moments hadn't happened, which was fine with her, "we've just admitted a new patient who will be arriving in CCU shortly, a Mr. Harold Asgaard. He's scheduled for surgery at seven in the morning, but I want him monitored closely throughout the evening and all through the night."

Somehow, Rita refrained from a salute. Still, she dutifully replied, "Yes, sir. I'll see to it."

"Good."

"Anything else?" she asked when he added nothing more. She found it odd that he'd sought her out just to tell her to closely monitor a patient who was scheduled for surgery in the morning. That was standard operating procedure in CCU.

Dr. Grayson dropped his gaze to the chart he held in one hand, began scanning it, then shook his head. "No, I think that's all for now. You're on evening shift tonight?" he asked, stating the obvious, still scanning the chart, as if he were uncomfortable meeting her gaze.

"Um, yes," Rita replied in light of the obvious.

"Covering for Nancy?"

"Rosemary, actually," Rita said. "Her great-grandmother's one-hundredth birthday party is tonight, so she and I traded off today. Nancy's left the unit. She transferred to pediatrics last week."

Dr. Grayson nodded, as if just now remembering, and continued to scan the chart. Continued to avoid Rita's gaze. "That's right," he said absently. "I'd forgotten."

Rita eyed him suspiciously. It wasn't like Matthew Grayson to forget things. And it wasn't like him to avoid anyone's gaze. What was up with him today? He seemed a little...off.

"Is everything okay, Dr. Grayson?" she asked before thinking. "You don't seem like yourself."

His gaze shot back up to meet hers, and only then did Rita realize how familiarly she had spoken to him. Boston General didn't have rules against such behavior, but Dr. Grayson *did*. And everyone knew it, because he'd made it clear over the years that he was *not* the kind of person who spoke about personal things. But Rita couldn't help it. It was in her nature. Family matters were a big deal with the Barones, and were generally discussed quite candidly.

Still, she should have known better with Dr. Grayson. She didn't know what she was thinking to have asked him such a question and offered such a remark about his well-being.

"And who do I seem like, Rita?" he asked coolly.

"Uh, no one in particular. Just…you know…not yourself."

"And how does myself usually seem?" he asked further.

"Uh… I, uh… What I meant was… It's just that…" Great. Now she'd done it. How did one get oneself out of a painted corner without messing up one's shoes? she wondered.

"Yes, Rita, everything is fine," Dr. Grayson finally interjected before she gave herself enough rope for a self-inflicted hanging. And in doing so, he simultaneously put her out of her misery, and put her back up in the process. "Not that that's any of your concern," he added sharply.

Another point to the beastly Dr. Grayson, Rita thought.

She bit her lower lip to keep in a tart retort. Instead, she nodded silently and glanced momentarily away. But when she looked his way again, she noticed his eyes weren't meeting hers, though his attention was lingering on her face. More specifically, on her mouth, she realized. He was noticing how she was anxiously biting her lip and…

…and probably thinking her the worst kind of neurotic.

Immediately, she ceased her fretting and forced herself

to attention. "I'm sorry," she said, though even she couldn't detect a trace of apology in her voice. "I didn't mean to pry."

"Didn't you?" he asked.

She shook her head, knowing she spoke the truth. Why would she want to pry into Matthew Grayson's life? Just because she found his seemingly inexplicable gruffness intriguing? Just because he had such dreamy green eyes? Just because he seemed to be as dedicated to his work as Rita was to hers? Just because he had such dreamy green eyes? Just because she'd been wondering since the day she started working in CCU what his story was? Just because he had such dreamy green eyes? Just because she wished she could work up the nerve to ask him about those scars on his face and neck?

And had she mentioned his dreamy green eyes?

Get a grip, Rita, she told herself. This was Matthew Grayson, MD, whose green eyes she found so dreamy. He was a distinguished cardiac surgeon and an eminent curmudgeon, probably almost ten years her senior and too serious by half. He wasn't the kind of man she should be wondering about in *any* way. He wasn't her type at all.

Not that she had a type, she quickly reminded herself. But if she did have a type, it wouldn't be Matthew Grayson, MD.

Even if he did have dreamy green eyes.

"No, I didn't," she said, recalling now that he had asked a question. "I didn't mean to pry. I was just a little concerned, that's all."

Dr. Grayson studied her for a moment more, long enough to make Rita think he was wondering something about her, too. Then, in a brisk, that-will-be-all kind of voice, he assured her, "You needn't be concerned about me." Before she had a chance to comment further, he spun on his heel and walked away.

Point three to the Beast.

Rita was a Barone, though, and Barones always got in the last word, no matter how many points behind they were. Always. So, quietly enough that he couldn't hear, and to his retreating back, she said, "Trust me, Dr. Grayson, when I say that I *won't* be concerned about you. Ever."

Point to the Barone. Finally.

Then Rita returned to both her chair and her work. Still not feeling as if that last word was quite enough, however, she glanced back up in time to see Dr. Grayson's imposing figure disappearing around the corner at the end of the corridor. And she fired off another last word to punctuate the others.

"Beast," she said.

For some reason, though, it didn't make her feel any better.

Matthew Grayson managed—barely—to make it back to his office in the medical towers adjoining Boston General before his knees finally collapsed beneath him. He staggered over to his desk and toppled into the leather chair behind it, then inhaled a deep, ragged breath in the hopes that it might quell the rapid-fire banging of his heart. Then he called himself every kind of fool.

Rita Barone had come *this* close to catching him this time. When he'd seen her leave the nurses' station, he'd thought she was taking a longer break than a few short minutes, so he hadn't been in any hurry to slip the little package from the pocket of his jacket into her mail slot. Plus, he'd had to wait for another nurse and a visitor to conclude their conversation near the nurses' station and walk off before he could even approach. He couldn't risk anyone seeing him anywhere near Rita's station when he did what he had to do.

He'd only just managed to leave the gift and steal away before she'd returned. Lucky for him she'd been entirely focused on not spilling her coffee as she'd walked down the corridor. Had she glanced up, even for a second, she would have seen him standing there, then would have found the gift after he left, and then would have had no trouble deducing who had been leaving her mysterious presents for the past two months.

And damned if Matthew didn't feel like the biggest buffoon on the planet for leaving those mysterious presents. Here he was, a thirty-three-year-old man, one of the most noted surgeons in New England, and a member of one of Boston's most illustrious families, and he was behaving like a goofy junior-high-school kid, leaving secret gifts in the locker of the girl he liked. What in God's name had reduced him to such behavior?

Well, of course, he knew that. And he felt like an even bigger buffoon admitting it. It was the simple presence of Rita Barone in the coronary care unit at Boston General. The "beastly" Dr. Grayson—yes, he knew quite well what his nickname was around the hospital; he had ears, after all—had a crush on one of the nurses. And not just any nurse, but a nurse who was young and pretty and vivacious. A nurse who would surely be shocked and repulsed if she ever found out the identity of her secret admirer.

Talk about your Beauty and the Beast scenarios. Without even meaning to, Matthew had reduced himself to a cliché.

Gingerly, he lifted his hand to his left cheek, tracing his index finger over the scars that even the most talented plastic surgeons and the most sophisticated cosmetic surgical techniques couldn't erase. The deepest of the wounds had gone straight down to the bone. Well, the deepest of the physical wounds, at any rate. Over the past twenty-three years, Matthew had undergone more surgery for his face than he cared to think about. Really, he supposed he looked pretty good, considering the viciousness of the attack and the depth of the damage. Physically, any scarring that was left was relatively superficial. Emotionally, however...

Well. Those injuries had gone straight down *into* the bone, and in many ways, had been even more damaging than the physical ones. Nor were they as repairable. Although he knew no one was perfect, Matthew was imperfect in ways that most people were not. He couldn't imagine someone like Rita Barone—someone who *was* very nearly perfect, at least in his eyes—ever wanting to get any closer to him than she had to.

He propped his elbows on his desk, closed his eyes, and buried his face in his hands, hoping that by doing so, he might be able to think about something else, visualize something other than Rita's dark, soulful eyes and her lush mouth. But he couldn't stop replaying the image of her nibbling her lip the way she had, and he couldn't halt the heat that swept through him when he remembered it. He could still hear the sound of her soft sigh and her reverently whispered "Oh, my" as she opened the box with the crystal heart, and that, too, filled him with a strange sort of warmth unlike anything he had ever felt before.

She had liked her gift, he realized, relief coursing through him like a slowly thawing springtime stream. And she had been wearing the bracelet and pin, too, just as she had worn them at work every day since he'd left them for her. Something about that gladdened Matthew, as if there was a little part of him she kept with her every day, even if she didn't realize it herself.

Surely, he thought further, there was something wrong

with him, finding a guilty sort of pleasure in a secret he was sharing with no one.

No, he immediately corrected himself, dropping his hands from his face to place them resolutely on his desk. He did *not* have a crush on Rita Barone. It wasn't that at all. He focused his gaze on the opposite wall of his office, the one hung with his degrees and awards and commendations. He wasn't the kind of man to have crushes. He was far too pragmatic and accomplished.

He admired Rita Barone, he told himself, that was all. Admired her on a professional level, and nothing more. Surely there was nothing wrong with admiring a co-worker. Nor was there anything wrong with being unable to verbally articulate that admiration. There were plenty of people who were uncomfortable expressing such sentiments. Matthew had never been one for the touchy-feely sharing of emotions—none of the Graysons were—and God knew he wasn't about to start now.

He admired Rita Barone, he told himself again, more adamantly this time. He respected her dedication to her work, and he appreciated her ability to relate to patients in a kind and caring fashion.

Take last February, with a homeless man named Joe. Rita had calmed the man's fears, and stayed by his side throughout his open-heart surgery. Because of her, the old man had made a total recovery.

Matthew had been amazed by her kindness and nurturing during that time. He'd envied her then—and still did—the gift she had for relating to and sympathizing with others, two things he'd never been able to master himself. Of course, there was a reason for that, but it didn't keep Matthew from feeling diminished in that regard. As he'd watched Rita interact with Joe, Matthew had been touched on a level where he'd never felt anything before.

Back in February, he'd wanted to do something to let Rita know how much he had appreciated her help with Joe. Since he was uncomfortable vocalizing such things, he'd decided to leave some small token of his gratitude in her mail slot instead. He'd seen the bandaged heart pin in the hospital gift shop, and he'd thought it would make an appropriate gift. He'd written a note of thanks to leave with it, but the day had been so hectic, he'd forgotten to include it. He'd also forgotten that the day in question was Valentine's Day.

It was only later, when he began to hear the rumors about Rita Barone's secret admirer that he realized what he had done. The last thing he'd wanted to do at that point was identify himself and risk being labeled Rita's secret admirer by the hospital grapevine. That would have only led to teasing, and Matthew *hated* to be teased. There was a reason for that, too, but no one would have cared. All he'd known then was that he couldn't let himself be fingered as Rita Barone's secret admirer. So he'd tossed the note in the garbage and kept his mouth shut.

Of course, that didn't explain why he'd felt compelled to leave her another gift last month, on her birthday, or a third gift this evening, on the anniversary of her start at Boston General. Hell, it didn't explain why he even knew those dates. And it certainly didn't explain why he'd deliberately made sure those gifts were given anonymously. What did explain that, Matthew thought now, was...

Ah, dammit. He didn't have an explanation for it.

Sure, you do, he told himself sarcastically. *You admire her. On a professional level. There's nothing more to it than that. Even if she does have the kind of dark, soulful eyes a man could get lost in forever and never find his way back.*

Oh, stop it, Matthew commanded himself. *You're getting maudlin in your old age.*

And old was often how he felt around Rita Barone. Old and scarred and beastly.

Enough! he shouted inwardly. He had plenty to occupy his mind at the moment other than thoughts of a certain dark-eyed, dark-haired nurse that made him feel foolish. He had surgery scheduled early tomorrow morning, and he had yet to make his final rounds. Rita Barone was the last thing he should be thinking about. She was his co-worker, nothing more. And she was too young and spirited and beautiful to be interested in someone old and scarred and beastly.

And even if there was the potential for something to develop between them—which was highly unlikely—her family was the nouveau riche Barone clan, while his own was old-money Bostonian. The Graysons had come over on the *Mayflower,* for God's sake, and they never let anyone forget it. The Barones, on the other hand, had come over in steerage. They came from humble beginnings and had only recently made their fortune, and in the Italian ice-cream business, of all things. Talk about your frivolous pursuits. The Graysons, by and large, were financiers. Much more respectable work—at least, as far as the elder Graysons were concerned.

No, there was no way his parents would ever approve of a Grayson–Barone merger, and they'd make things very difficult for Matthew—and for Rita, too. Especially after the sordid, scandalous stories that had been splashed across the tabloids last month about one of Rita's sisters. He vaguely remembered something about suggestive photos better suited to men's magazines than respectable newspapers. Not that the tabloids were in any way respectable. But they were read. Doubtless the photos had never been meant for public consumption, but consumed by the public they had been—rabidly. And although the old-money Bostonians might turn their noses up at scandal and gossip, it certainly didn't keep them from gossiping about scandal. There was no way Matthew's mother would let any of the Barones come near her family or her home.

Not that it mattered. There were just too many things that didn't mesh between Matthew and Rita for there to be anything to worry about, he told himself again. Therefore, he wouldn't worry about it.

And he wouldn't think about her dark, soulful eyes.

Two

Rita was absolutely beat when she finally got home just after midnight. Not surprisingly, the brownstone on Paul Revere Way looked dark and quiet as she climbed the handful of steps to the front door and unlocked it. Her older sister Gina had moved out last month, after marrying Flint Kingman, and Rita and Maria were still trying to find a suitable tenant for the empty top-floor apartment. And her younger sister Maria was doubtless just out, as she so often seemed to be these days.

In fact, Maria had been going out way more often than usual lately, Rita reflected as she locked the door behind herself. Which was surprising, because Maria didn't have a steady boyfriend, or much of a social life outside of her work managing the original Baronessa Gelateria on Hanover Street. She used to be home as often as Rita was. But for the past couple of months she'd been out quite a lot, something that suggested there might be someone special in her life. But Maria hadn't mentioned meeting anyone, and Rita certainly hadn't seen her with anyone out of the ordinary.

As she stepped into the foyer of the brownstone, she realized immediately that she was indeed alone. The first floor of the four-story brick building served as a kind of community living room for the sisters, and tended to be a place of congregation, regardless of the hour. With its hard-wood floors and leafy plants and beige furnishings and powder-blue accents in the form of pillows and such, the first floor of the brownstone was inviting in a comfy, ele-gant kind of way that made people want to linger. At the moment, though, it was empty, and not so much as a dis-carded jacket or pair of shoes indicated that anyone had been home anytime recently.

Rita had, as she always did in the afternoons following her shift, walked home tonight, unconcerned about her safety because the streets of Boston's North End were al-ways well populated on a Friday night, even in a light driz-zle, as there was tonight. Now she shrugged off her raincoat and ran her fingers through her damp, dark bangs, then forsook the elevator to make her way up the stairs to her third-floor apartment. Once inside, she hung her coat on the rack by the door and went straight to her kitchen to brew herself a cup of chamomile tea. She wasn't normally a night owl, but she was still too wound up from her shift to go to bed just yet. So, dipping her teabag in and out of her mug, she moved to the bathroom for a long, hot soak in a tub full of lavender-scented water.

It was going on one-thirty, and she was about to turn off her bedside lamp, when she heard Maria coming in down-stairs. Pushing back the covers, Rita climbed out of bed and padded barefoot to her front door, waiting until she knew for sure that her sister was alone before opening it.

It wasn't so much that she didn't want to interrupt anything Maria might be doing with the potential someone special in her life that she didn't seem to want to tell anyone about, but Rita didn't want anyone else to catch her in her neon-pink pajamas decorated with ice-cream desserts, which she'd fallen in love with at the store and thought appropriate for a Barone. But she detected no footsteps other than Maria's on the stairs, so she stepped out of her apartment, peeked over the stair rail and called down to her sister.

"Hey, you," she said. "Where have you been?"

At the summons, Maria looked up over the stair rail two floors below and smiled. Her dark hair fell just below her shoulders, and her dark eyes twinkled merrily, even in the scant stairwell light. "Hi," she called softly out of habit, even though there was no one else in the building to disturb anymore. But instead of answering Rita's question, she asked one of her own. "What are you doing up so late?"

Rita hesitated a moment before telling her sister, "I got another anonymous gift at work tonight."

Immediately Maria's smile fell. "That's what? Three now?"

Rita nodded.

"And you still have no idea who's leaving them?"

Now Rita shook her head. "And no idea why."

"Let me drop my purse and shoes in my apartment," Maria said, "and I'll be right up."

Rita murmured her thanks and returned to her own apartment, leaving her door open so that her sister could come inside. A few moments later Maria arrived, still dressed in her Friday-night outfit of black capri pants and sapphire-blue silk shirt. The combination was striking with her dark good looks, and Rita, who was hopelessly fashion-challenged, made a mental note to copy a similar outfit the next time she went out. Then she wondered why she was bothering to make such a mental note, seeing as she never went out anyway.

She sighed fitfully as Maria took her seat on the overstuffed chintz sofa opposite the overstuffed chintz chair Rita occupied herself. Her decorating sense was no better than her fashion sense, so she'd copied the room down to every detail from a photograph in a magazine. Between the chintz furniture and the lace curtains, and the hooked floral rugs on the hardwood floor, she'd managed to capture an English-country-cottage look fairly well, right down to the dried flower wreaths and watercolor landscapes on the cream-colored walls. Usually, this room soothed Rita. Tonight, though, she just felt edgy.

"You didn't see who left it?" Maria asked without preamble.

Again Rita shook her head. "And it's really starting to creep me out, Maria. I mean, why would he leave gifts without letting me know who he is?"

"What do your instincts tell you?" Maria asked.

Rita thought about that for a moment. "I don't know," she said honestly. "Part of me feels like whoever is doing it is doing it because he's shy and is afraid I might rebuff him."

"How does the other part of you feel?"

Rita met her sister's gaze levelly now. "Like maybe he's not shy. Like maybe he's a—" She couldn't even say the word aloud.

"A stalker?" Maria asked, voicing the very word Rita had hoped so much to avoid. Just like that, a cold shudder went scurrying right down her spine.

"Yeah," she said. "Like maybe he's…one of those."

Maria looked doubtful. "I don't know," she said. "Maybe I'm being naive, but I bet you do just have some kind of secret admirer at the hospital. I mean, don't stalkers usually strike closer to home? And don't they inspire terror? What was the gift this time? Unless it was a decapitated pet or a dismembered Barbie doll or something, you're probably fine.''

Rita rose from the sofa and went to retrieve the square white box from her purse, then took it to Maria and placed it in her palm.

"Too small to be a decapitated pet," her sister quipped. "Unless you've been keeping goldfish you haven't told me about. Just promise me there's not a severed Barbie hand in there.''

"Maria," Rita said pleadingly.

"All right, all right. Enough with the sick jokes. I was just trying to make you feel better.''

"Talk of headless animals and doll parts is *not* making me feel better," Rita told her.

"I apologize. It's late," her sister said by way of an explanation. Then Maria opened the box and moved aside the tissue, sighing with the same sort of delight Rita had exhibited herself upon seeing what was inside.

"Oh, it's beautiful," she said as she carefully withdrew the crystal heart from inside the box.

"Yeah, but does it refer to my job, or the guy's feelings for me?" Rita asked.

"And it's also Waterford," Maria added, not answering the question, as she held the heart up to the light. "Which means, A, this guy's got good taste, and B, this guy's got good money.''

"How can you tell it's Waterford?" Rita asked, moving to the sofa to sit beside her sister.

"The little seahorse etched on the side," Maria said, pointing to the logo in question. "See?''

Rita did see the logo. What she didn't see was why the purchaser had spent so much money this time. She'd seen the bandaged heart pin in the hospital gift shop for ten dollars, and even with her unpracticed eye, she knew the charm bracelet couldn't have cost much more than that. This, though, was clearly a costly little trinket. Why the sudden leap in price tag?

"Okay, so the first gift came on Valentine's Day," Maria was saying as she admired the crystal heart, "and the second—" She gasped suddenly. "Oh, wow. I just now made the connection. Valentine's Day. The family curse. No wonder you're concerned."

Rita expelled an errant breath and told herself her sister was being silly. Oh, sure, there were plenty of Barones who believed in the curse Lucia Conti had put on the family two generations ago, but Rita had never been one of them. She was too sensible to believe in curses. Well, pretty much. But she'd heard the story like everyone else in the family, and she could see why some of the Barones believed in it.

When Marco Barone, Rita's grandfather and the founder of Baronessa Gelati, had first come to the United States from Sicily in the thirties, he worked as a waiter at Conti's, a restaurant on Prince Street that was owned by friends of his parents, another Sicilian couple. The Contis had a daughter named Lucia, who, it was said, loved Marco very much, and it was always understood between the two families that Lucia and Marco would someday marry. But Marco met and fell in love with Angelica Salvo, who also worked at Conti's, and they married instead. On their wedding day—Valentine's Day—Lucia, it was also said, had put a curse on them and every future generation of Barones. "You got married on Valentine's Day," Lucia was reported to have said, "and may your anniversary day be cursed. A miserable Valentine's Day to both of you, from this day forward."

Of course, not every Valentine's Day had resulted in

misfortune for the Barones. But a number of tragedies, and a lot of things that had gone wrong for the family had happened on that date. On that first Valentine's Day after their wedding, Angelica miscarried her and Marco's first child. Some years later on Valentine's Day, another child of theirs, one of a pair of twin sons, was kidnapped from the hospital nursery when he was only two days old and was never seen again.

And more recently, there had been a professional debacle this past Valentine's Day, when Baronessa Gelati had thrown a huge gala to launch a new flavor, passionfruit. Someone had spiked the gelato prior to the event with habanero peppers, and everyone who tasted it suffered from a burning mouth. One man had even suffered from an attack of anaphylaxis, a serious allergic reaction. It had been a public-relations nightmare that not even PR whiz Gina had been able to handle. The Barones had been forced to hire an outside spin doctor to help get the company's image back on track. They were still seeing repercussions from the incident.

Not the least of which was Gina's marriage to said spin doctor, Flint Kingman, which, now that Rita thought about it, sort of negated the Valentine's Day curse.

But Rita could still see why Maria might bring up the Valentine's Day curse now, even if Rita didn't believe in it herself.

"So the first gift came on Valentine's Day," Maria began again. "And the second gift came on your birthday. Both special occasions," she noted. "But today isn't a—"

"Today is the third anniversary of my first day working at Boston General," Rita said morosely. "Another special occasion of sorts. Whoever's doing this even remembers the day I started working there."

"But that narrows it down," Maria said triumphantly.

"That means whoever's leaving these is definitely someone you work with, and he must have been there three years ago when you started."

Rita rolled her eyes. "Oh, fine. That narrows it down, all right. To about a couple hundred people."

"But it must be someone you work fairly closely with," Maria said. "It's probably someone in CCU."

"But I started in the E.R.," Rita reminded her sister. "And then I worked briefly in geriatrics before I moved to CCU."

"It still must be someone at work," Maria said. "That's where the gifts arrive, and with this anniversary thing, you know that must be it."

It still didn't help, Rita thought. There were scores of people who could be possibilities.

"I think it's kind of sweet, really," Maria said. "Kind of romantic."

"Romantic?" Rita echoed, thinking that was a strange word to be uttered by a Boston University MBA who spent most of her time working. "Since when did you become such a romantic?"

Maria blushed a little at the question, something else Rita thought odd. "I'm not a romantic," she said. But there was something in her tone that suggested otherwise. "I just don't think it's a stalker, that's all. I think it's someone who has a crush on you."

Rita frowned. "Maria, grown men don't have crushes."

"Sure they do," she objected. "And sometimes it's the big, strong, tough guys who are the most susceptible."

Oh, spoken like an idealistic, virginal twenty-three-year-old, Rita thought wryly. Not that Rita should throw stones, seeing as how she was a somewhat idealistic, though definitely virginal twenty-five-year-old. Still, she had seen more of the world than her younger sister had, mostly thanks to that time in the E.R. And she hadn't seen any big, strong, tough guys who would qualify for secret admirer status. Stalker status, surely, but—

Oh, dammit. She'd let that word out again. Somehow, though, deep down, she wasn't any more convinced of that possibility than Maria was. Her instincts were good, and although she couldn't rule out the sinister entirely, Rita still felt more strongly that whoever was leaving the gifts had no intention of hurting her.

But she couldn't be sure.

Of course, she'd been known to be wrong before.

"I don't know what to do," Rita said. "Whether this person is a crazy psycho or not, I don't like getting anonymous gifts. But I don't know how to out the person, either."

Maria nestled the crystal heart back into its tissue bed and replaced the top on the box. "I don't think it's anything to worry about," she said. "But if it makes you feel that uncomfortable, then maybe you should stop wearing the pin and the bracelet. Maybe if you did, your secret admirer would notice, and then maybe he'd say something about it and reveal his identity."

"I suppose it's worth a shot," Rita said absently.

"And if you want to find a new home for this heart…" her sister added with a smile, holding up the box meaningfully.

Rita smiled back as she retrieved the box from Maria's grasp. She wasn't sure why she wanted to keep it, but she did. She wasn't sure why she wore the pin and heart to work everyday, either. Maybe, deep down, she did know whoever was leaving the gifts was doing it because he admired her secretly.

And maybe, deep down, something about that made Rita feel nice. She'd never had anyone admire her before. Not for herself, anyway. She'd had the occasional date in high school and college, of course, but she'd always wondered if the guys in question had only asked her out because she was one of the wealthy Barones. Especially after her twenty-first birthday, when, like all her siblings, she'd come into a trust fund worth a million dollars.

Rita had yet to touch her own million, however, and had instead left it invested, thinking someday she'd need it for something. She didn't know what. She did know, however, that she wasn't suited to the social butterfly life, and she loved working as a nurse. Maybe someday, she thought, she'd have children, and she could use the money for them. But her secret admirer obviously didn't know or care about her wealth, otherwise, he would have revealed himself to her right off the bat, and would have tried to insinuate himself into her life. So maybe it was Rita herself, and not her money, that attracted him. In that respect, she couldn't help but like him.

"No, the heart is fine where it is," she said as she took the box from her sister and cradled it in her hand.

She just wished she could say the same for herself. Because in spite of Rita's instincts saying the contrary, Maria was right in that stalkers tended to target women at their homes, eventually. Rita wondered if her mystery man knew where she lived. If it was indeed someone she worked with, he'd certainly have no trouble locating her. Even if it wasn't a co-worker, if he'd found her at the hospital, all he would have to do was follow her home one day to find out where she lived. Of course, if he'd done that, he'd also know she walked home alone. And he'd probably know Gina had moved out. And he'd probably know Maria was often not at home these days, something Rita was going to have to ask her younger sister about soon. Which meant he also probably knew that left Rita home alone much of the time.

She exhaled a slow, unsteady breath and told herself she was overreacting. Maria was probably right, too, in that whoever was doing this was harmless. Rita reminded herself that her instincts were good, and that her instincts told her she probably had nothing to fear. But in reminding herself of that, she inescapably reminded herself of something else, too.

That she'd been known to be wrong before.

"Do you have a date for the party next weekend?" Maria asked as she rose to leave. "You did remember the party next weekend, didn't you, Rita?" she added, probably because she thought Rita didn't remember.

And she was right. Rita didn't. Until now.

"The one at the Baronessa business headquarters?" Maria went on. "The one to launch the family's new PR contest to counter all the bad press from the passionfruit disaster? The contest that was Gina's brilliant brainchild? The contest where the winner gets to name a new flavor of gelato? Remember that?"

"Oh, no," Rita groaned. "I forgot all about it. There's been so much going on at work lately."

Her sister frowned at her. "Rita," she said in the scolding tone of voice impatient mothers used with recalcitrant toddlers. "You *are* going, aren't you? All the Barones are expected to be there, to show our support for the family and the business. You have to go. You know you'll never hear the end of it if you don't."

"Yes, yes, I'm going," Rita assured her sister.

"And you *do* have a date for the party, don't you?" Maria asked further. "Because you know you'll never hear the end of it if you don't," she repeated with a smile.

Rita closed her eyes and bit back another groan. What

Maria said was certainly true. The older generation of Barones was crazy for grandchildren and grand-nieces and grand-nephews, and they weren't afraid to let anyone—especially the potential bearers of said grandchildren and grand-nieces and grand-nephews—know it. Whenever a Barone of marriageable age showed up at a family gathering without a date, they were set upon by the older generation, wanting to know how they expected to get married and have children if they remained alone.

With Rita, though, who never brought dates to such events, it was becoming a problem of epic proportions. Naturally, it wouldn't have been a problem had she entered the Sisters of Charity as her sister Colleen had. Religious conviction was the only acceptable excuse for such longstanding abstinence from a social life. And even trying to use Colleen as an excuse these days didn't wash, seeing as how she had left the Sisters of Charity not long ago and was now engaged to her college love.

"Um, actually..." Rita began. But she couldn't quite make herself finish the revelation.

"Rita," Maria said again in that same motherish tone, "you haven't even invited a date yet?"

"I forgot, all right?" Rita said.

"And you probably don't have anything to wear, either, do you?"

"Well..."

"Fine," Maria said in a voice of put-upon patience. "I'll take off early Monday and we can go shopping. I wouldn't mind picking up something new myself. The date, though..." she added, letting her voice trail off meaningfully.

"I know," Rita said. "I'll take care of it. I promise."

Though how she was going to keep that promise was beyond her. This event was going to be a stellar, five-star,

formal event. It called for someone suave, someone debonair, someone who was tall, dark and handsome, and sophisticated, distinguished and well-connected. Someone
like...

For some reason, an image of Dr. Matthew Grayson
popped into Rita's head just then. And just as quickly, she
shoved the image right back out again. No way was she
going to ask Dr. Grayson to this thing. Not only would the
two of them have nothing to talk about and feel awkward
around each other all evening, but the last thing she needed
was for her aunt Sandra to start asking him when he was
going to make an honest woman out of Rita.

Uh-uh. No way.

"I'll find someone," she promised her sister again. She
just hoped it was a promise she could keep.

Three

Matthew knew plenty of physicians who preferred to get in their rounds early in the day—some of them before the sun even came up—but he wasn't one of them. He'd never been a morning person by nature, and contrary to the desires of some doctors, he liked to see his patients when their family members might be visiting, to answer any questions or alleviate any concerns they might have. So he rarely began his own rounds before ten in the morning, which often meant he ate lunch late.

Monday was no exception, except that he never ate lunch at all. For some reason, his rounds took longer than usual—possibly because Mrs. Harold Asgaard had roughly a million more questions and concerns than the average patient's family members did—so it was after three o'clock before Matthew had a chance for lunch. By then it was so late, he decided he might as well hold off a bit longer and have an early dinner.

Until he went to the hospital cafeteria for a cup of coffee to tide him over and saw Rita Barone seated all alone at one of the far tables.

She wasn't eating, and was instead wrapped up in reading a fat paperback. She was still dressed in her blue scrubs, and still had her hair woven into one of those elaborate braids she favored for work. There were other times, Matthew recalled, when she wore her hair twisted up at the back of her head in a style that reminded him of Grace Kelly—though Rita Barone was much more exciting and exotic-looking than the pale, fragile Grace. Invariably, at work, she had her hair tightly bound in one way or another.

It occurred to him then, not for the first time, that he'd never seen her wear her hair loose. He'd never even seen her in street clothes. Because he'd never seen her anywhere other than work. He knew her hair must be long, because her braid fell past the base of her neck, and he knew it must be thick, because a wealth of the dark tresses fell over her forehead. But he didn't know if it was straight or wavy or curly. And for some reason, suddenly, he wanted very badly to know which it was.

But that wasn't the reason why he strode over to her table after buying his cup of coffee. No, the reason for that was...

Ah, hell. He didn't have a reason for that, he realized as he came to a stop beside her. Which posed a problem for him when she glanced up to see him standing there.

"Dr. Grayson," she said when she saw him, an unmistakable note of surprise lacing her voice.

"Rita," he replied in his usual terse way, wishing he knew of some other way to be besides terse. It made him uncomfortable that all the nurses addressed him as "Dr. Grayson" when he addressed all of them by their first names. But it made him even more uncomfortable to extend an invitation to them to address him less formally. He just wasn't sure how to go about being informal, as much as he might like to try it on occasion.

Like this occasion, for instance.

She waited for him to say something more but, God help him, his mind went completely blank. All he could do was gaze into her dark, soulful eyes and try not to lose himself completely in their bewitching depths. Rita continued to gaze at him expectantly, however, so when he was finally able to grasp some semblance of coherent thought again, he said the first thing that finally popped into his head.

"Is this seat taken?"

Immediately after uttering it, Matthew cursed himself inwardly. He had revealed way too much about himself in that one short question. That he was an idiot, because he'd just asked a question for which there was an obvious answer. That he was trite, because the question was such a cliché. And, worst of all, that he might potentially be hitting on Rita with that clichéd, idiotic question, because why else would a man ask to sit with a woman unless he was interested in her?

She arrowed her dark eyebrows down in confusion, then glanced over at the obviously empty chair he indicated, then around at the obviously empty cafeteria surrounding them before she finally returned her attention to him.

"Ah, no," she said. "No, it's not taken. Help yourself."

To walk away now would *really* make him look like an idiot. Not that he wanted to turn down her invitation, anyway. He just wished he was a more socially adept person. And he wished he could spend more than a few seconds in Rita Barone's presence without feeling as nervous as a teenager.

"Thank you," he managed to mutter, and with a surprising amount of dignity he seated himself across from her. But for the life of him, he could think of nothing else to say.

Rita closed her book, then looked at Matthew expectantly again.

"I, ah, I hate to eat alone," he said by way of an explanation for his inexplicable behavior.

Rita smiled at him, and something inside Matthew went *zing*. Honestly. *Zing*. How unmanly. If strangely pleasant.

"You're not eating," she pointed out, and suddenly the zinging stopped, only to be replaced by what felt like crashing and burning.

"I hate to drink alone, too," he quickly countered. Oh, score one for the surgeon, he thought wryly. Quite the quipper he was today.

Rita eyed him thoughtfully for a moment, as if she were trying to decide whether she should say what she was thinking. "Interesting you should say that," she finally said. "Because I rarely see you drinking or eating any way *but* alone."

Matthew was too busy digesting the implication of her statement to be bothered by the statement itself. Obviously she'd noticed that he generally spent his time alone. She'd noticed *him*. He couldn't imagine why a woman like her would pay attention to a man like him.

"Just because I drink and eat alone," he said, "doesn't mean I like it." He was surprised by both having spoken the words and by the discovery that they were true.

Rita dipped her chin forward in acknowledgment. "Then by all means, stay as long as you like. I'll be glad to keep you company."

That surprised him, too. But before he had a chance to ponder her statement further, she continued.

"I'm off the clock," she told him, "but I'm waiting for

my sister Maria. She's supposed to meet me here at three-thirty to take me shopping.''

She uttered the last word as if it were the cruelest punishment inflicted in the deepest circle of hell. Matthew couldn't help but smile in response. ''Don't like shopping?'' he asked.

She made a face. ''Well, let's just say there are other things I'd enjoy more. A lengthy discourse on the mating rituals of the common earthworm, perhaps. Or an in-depth introspective on the Monroe Doctrine. Or watching cheese age. That kind of thing.''

He chuckled in spite of himself, and was again surprised by how good it felt to do that. He really should do it more often, he thought. Problem was, he didn't often have the opportunity. ''I thought a love for shopping was encoded into that second X chromosome you women have,'' he said lightly.

''Ah, ah, ah, Dr. Grayson,'' she chided playfully, ''that narrow-minded assumption about women encoded into your Y chromosome is showing.''

''Touché,'' he said, grinning. And then he realized how strange it felt to be doing that, too, because he so rarely did.

What was even stranger was that Rita grinned back. Women hardly ever smiled at Matthew. Probably, he thought, because he rarely gave them a reason to. But Rita Barone was a woman he would like to have smiling at him more often. And not just because she had such a beautiful smile, either. But because of the astonishingly good way it made him feel to see it.

''Maria, though, is not only a good shopper,'' Rita continued conversationally, ''she has good fashion sense, which I utterly lack.''

''And you'd be needing fashion sense because...?''

She made another face, this one even more eloquent than the first. "I have a family thing," she said.

Funny, Matthew thought, his grin failing, but she sounded like she enjoyed family gatherings about as much as he did.

"Not into family values?" he asked, hoping his voice betrayed none of the sourness he felt.

"No, it's not that," she hastened to clarify. "I mean, I love getting together with my family. They're wonderful. It's just…"

"What?"

She sighed fitfully. "Well, the Barones are a *big* family," she began.

Which, of course, was something Matthew already knew. In fact, everyone in Boston knew that. The Barones were well-known even beyond Boston as the founders of Baronessa Gelati, an Italian ice-cream business they'd built up from a single ice-cream parlor in the North End to a chain of popular stores across the country. Baronessa Gelati was also available in all major grocery stores in dozens of flavors. Matthew's favorite, for instance, was double chocolate mocha raspberry mint.

They were well-known for other things, too, Matthew knew. Like their long-standing feud with the Conti family, another renowned Boston family. Matthew wasn't entirely sure what the source of the feud was, but he, like everyone else in the city, was aware of bad blood between the two families over something that had happened decades ago.

"…and anyway, I need a dress for it," Rita was saying, and only then did he realize that his mind had been wandering—probably because he'd been gazing so deeply into her soulful brown eyes—and he'd heard scarcely a word of what she'd said.

"I'm sorry," he said, "but what kind of function did you say it was?"

Rita smiled again. And again went the zinging of his insides. And somehow, it didn't feel quite so unmanly this time. On the contrary, this time, when Matthew noted Rita's smile, he felt very manly indeed.

"I guess I didn't say, did I?" Rita said. "I was so busy going off on trying to avoid all the family prying that goes on at any gathering of the Barone clan."

"Prying?" Matthew asked.

"You know, all the questions the older generation asks about when I'm going to get married and start a family because my biological clock is ticking and I won't be young forever, and there are so many handsome young doctors at Boston General, why haven't I caught one yet?"

Despite the fact that he himself wasn't one of those handsome, young doctors, Matthew stopped himself from asking Rita that very question himself, even if he wanted to know the answer to it. He did sometimes wonder why she wasn't married. A woman like her should at least be involved in a long-term relationship. But he knew she didn't have a boyfriend.

So instead, he found himself commiserating with her. "I have the same problem with my family," he told her. "Only I imagine it's even worse, since I've held out much longer than you have."

"Hey, I bet I can hold out as long as you," she said, smiling even more broadly.

Somehow, though, Matthew couldn't bring himself to smile back. Probably because her assertion didn't make him feel particularly happy for some reason. "I just meant that my family wouldn't mind marrying me off, too," he said.

What he didn't add was, provided it was to the right sort of woman. Well, what the Graysons considered right, at any rate, which meant old-moneyed, blue-blooded, upper-crusted, fair-haired and fine-boned. Someone at the completely opposite end of the spectrum from Rita Barone.

"I guess it's one of those things you just have to put up with once you get out of college," he added, nudging thoughts about his family from his brain, since there were other, infinitely more enjoyable things to think about. Like, say, Rita Barone. "The nosy questions from relatives, I mean."

Just as it occurred to Matthew that he'd spent several minutes making perfectly harmless, wholly comfortable conversation with another person—something he couldn't recall ever doing—he saw Rita glance over his shoulder and lift a hand in greeting to someone. When he turned around, he saw a young woman who looked very much like Rita striding toward them. Her sister, he presumed. Which meant Rita would be leaving now, and he'd be left on his own, alone again.

Normally, it would have made Matthew feel better, since solitude was what he craved most in his life. Suddenly, though, for some reason, he didn't want to be alone. Not unless Rita Barone was alone with him.

Rita's sister—Maria, he recalled her name now—was the epitome of the professional businesswoman, dressed in a smart gray suit and low-heeled pumps. She stopped at the side of the table, leveling first a curious gaze on Matthew, and then a meaningful one on Rita.

With what sounded like a much-put-upon sigh, Rita introduced the two of them. "Maria Barone, Dr. Matthew Grayson. Dr. Grayson, my sister Maria."

"Nice to meet you," Maria said cordially. Then, to her sister, she added pointedly, "Why don't you ask him?"

Rita's eyes widened in clear horror at the suggestion.

Whatever it was, Matthew thought, since he had no idea what Maria was talking about.

Rita, however, evidently did, because she colored furiously and hissed, "Maria!" with a note of unmistakable warning.

The second Barone, though, clearly unfazed by her sister's outburst, turned to Matthew. "Rita needs a date for a big shindig we Barones are putting together this weekend. Otherwise, the rest of the family is going to badger her mercilessly about coming alone. She always comes stag to these things, and I think the older generation is beginning to wonder if she'll ever have a date with anyone."

In response to this, Matthew noticed that Rita blushed even more furiously—at least, he noticed that before she covered her face with her hands. Then she hissed an even more vicious, "Maria!"

"Personally, I don't see anything wrong with a woman going stag to a party," Maria continued blithely, clearly oblivious to—or else totally unconcerned about—her sister's reaction. "But we Barones are very traditional. We're big on old-country values. Especially marriage. And children. Which, of course, is obvious, since Rita and I have six brothers and sisters, not to mention four cousins."

Instead of hissing her response this time, Matthew noticed Rita only groaned.

"Not that I expect you two to get married and have eight kids," Maria continued, "but since you are sitting here talking, I figure you must be friends, so why shouldn't Rita ask you to be her date, you know?"

Logically, it made sense, Matthew thought. Sort of. Socially, it was totally acceptable. In just about every other way, however, it was completely undoable. Because... because...

Well, just because, that was why. And it was a good reason, too, dammit.

"So what do you say, Rita?" Maria asked. "Why don't you ask Dr. Grayson to come to the party with you Friday? Provided he's not otherwise engaged, I mean."

This time Rita only shook her head—still buried in her hands—in response to her sister's question.

"Unless, of course," Maria went on, "you've asked someone else." She began to laugh, as if she'd just made a little joke. "I was being sarcastic," she told Matthew. "Rita never dates anyone."

Another grim sound came from Rita's general direction.

"So, Rita," Maria tried again, "what do you say?"

Finally, Rita dropped her hands from in front of her face and turned to look at Matthew full-on. She was still blushing, but she roused a halfway decent smile. "I hope you enjoyed getting to know my sister," she said. "You'll be reading about her in tomorrow's paper. In the obituaries," she clarified enthusiastically. "Just ignore her," she added before he had a chance to comment. "She didn't mean it."

"Of course I meant it," Maria said.

"I'd love to go with you," Matthew said at the same time.

And he was as astonished to realize he had said it as Rita obviously was to have heard it.

Maria, however, seemed completely unsurprised. "See there?" she told her sister. "I got you a date. Now I can get you an outfit. You can thank me for both later. You ready to go?"

But Rita clearly wasn't listening to her sister, Matthew realized. No, she was much too focused on him.

"Are you serious?" she asked. "You'd really go with me?"

Matthew was surprised by her response. What man

would turn down the invitation to accompany Rita Barone to the ends of the earth on bare feet, never mind to a high-profile, high-society party?

But truth be told, he was surprised, too, by his easy acceptance. Usually he didn't do parties, especially with people he didn't know. In fact, he avoided large groups of people whenever he could, never having felt comfortable among them as an adult because he'd never been welcomed into them as a youth. The scars on his face might be less horrific now than they had been when he was young, but there had been a time in his life—a critical time, and a time that didn't feel so far in his past, even though decades had gone by—when he'd been disfigured in a way that had made people instinctively turn away from him, and then deliberately exclude him. And those vivid memories had stayed with him too well.

Somehow, though, he couldn't bring himself to say no to Rita—or, rather, her sister.

"Of course I'm serious," he made himself say before he could chicken out. "It sounds like fun. After all, the Barones are something of a celebrity clan in Boston. There would be a certain air of distinction in attending."

That was true. The event would be high-profile, high-visibility and high-society. As much as his own family might object to the nouveau-riche, scandal-ridden Barones, the Graysons still traveled in the same social circles, and, financially, at any rate, they were equals. So maybe in attending this bash with Rita, Matthew could bridge some small gap between the two families.

He tried not to think about why that might be important.

"What time should I pick you up?" he asked when Rita only sat there staring at him incredulously.

Or maybe she was staring at him distractedly, he thought. No, that was only thinking wishfully. Maybe she was panicked at the thought of spending time with him and was scrambling for an excuse to get out of going with him. After all, it had been her sister who had made the suggestion. Technically, Rita hadn't invited him at all. So maybe she was just trying to think of a way to let him down gently.

Then she smiled. And only then did Matthew realize he had been holding his breath. He released it in a long, slow expulsion of relief.

"No, I'll pick you up," she told him, smiling a smile of genuine delight. "For an event this big, they always send a car for the family members. It'll swing by for me first, then we'll come by your place. At, say…seven?" she asked.

Matthew nodded. "Seven it is."

She smiled again, and he told himself not to get his hopes up. Strangely, though, he didn't listen to himself at all.

"Great," she said. "Friday at seven. Be there, or be square." With that, she rose from her chair and began to follow her sister out of the cafeteria.

He watched her go, mostly because he couldn't resist doing so, and as she reached the exit, she turned once more to look at him. She smiled one final time and lifted her hand in a quick wave.

Only then did he notice that her wrist was bare, and that she hadn't been wearing the pin either. The pin and bracelet from her secret admirer. Her secret admirer, Dr. Matthew Grayson.

He couldn't help wondering what that meant.

Four

For the rest of that week, Rita felt as if she were walking on eggshells—no, ice-cream cones, a much more appropriate Barone comparison. Whenever she saw Dr. Grayson, she tried to pretend there was nothing different about them just because he was going to be her date—or, rather, escort, she quickly corrected herself.

Except that, somehow, everything felt different.

Suddenly every time she saw him, a funny little burst of heat exploded in her belly, and her mind went blank. She never knew what to say to him after that first hello, so she'd manufacture some excuse to flee his presence before he began thinking her a complete dolt.

She also started noticing things about him that she hadn't noticed before. Like how he put more sugar into his coffee than any health professional should. Like how long and elegant his fingers were—which was hardly surprising for a surgeon. But she was never thinking about him perform-

ing surgery when she noticed his hands. Instead she thought
about those hands doing other things, things to *her,* things
she really shouldn't be thinking about in polite and mixed
company. She noticed, too, how broad his shoulders were
beneath his white coat. And how he smelled so clean and
earthy and masculine. And how his dreamy green eyes
seemed to have flecks of blue in them whenever the light
hit them just so.

Things like that.

So, by the time Friday evening arrived, Rita just wasn't
sure how she was supposed to act. Not around her family
when she showed up at Baronessa's executive headquarters
with Dr. Grayson at her side, and certainly not around Dr.
Grayson himself. As she stood before the mirror in her
bedroom at half past six, pondering her reflection, she realized the outfit she had allowed her sister to choose for
her was nothing like the kind of outfit she would have
chosen for herself.

Talk about your little black dresses…

This particular black dress was just about the littlest one
she'd ever seen. And somehow it seemed a lot littler now
than it had in the dressing room of Lord & Taylor. In spite
of her efforts, the hemline kept creeping several inches
above her knees, the neckline kept creeping several inches
below her neck, and the cap sleeves several inches away
from her collarbones. Granted, Maria had said the dress was
supposed to be ''off the shoulder,'' but Rita couldn't help
thinking this dress was going to be off way more than her
shoulders before the night was through.

Then, when she realized how that thought had come out,
she really began to panic. She told herself there was no
way her dress would be going off anywhere tonight. Dr.
Grayson was much too professional a man ever to try anything like that with a co-worker. And Rita had promised

herself a long time ago that when she gave herself to a man it would be because she was utterly and irrevocably in love with him. And she wasn't in love with Dr. Grayson. Not utterly, not irrevocably, not any way. Ergo, the only place her dress was going tonight was back in her own closet.

Besides, she thought further as she tried to tug down the hem again, the garment was so tight, it was bound to cling to her body like a second skin. Somehow, though, that realization wasn't particularly reassuring, either.

She had accessorized the dress with a pearl choker, bracelet and earrings that had belonged to her Nonna Barone. And then she had slipped on the smoky black stockings Maria had also made her buy during their shop-till-they-drop excursion—real stockings, too, the kind you had to wear with a garter belt, even though Rita had protested that such an ensemble was archaic and uncomfortable, and more than a little silly.

But Maria had laughed off her objections, had insisted that wearing such a garment would make Rita feel feminine and playful and even a little powerful—Maria had read all about it in *Cosmopolitan,* after all—and that feeling that way would help Rita battle the nervousness she felt around Matthew Grayson. When Rita had asked her sister what made her think she felt nervous around Matthew Grayson, Maria had only smiled a secret little smile and had pitched the garter belt and stockings—along with a matching black-lace, strapless demi-cup bra—onto the pile of Rita's other purchases.

Now, as nervous as she was—and as reluctant as she was to admit it—Rita did feel more feminine and playful than she normally did. And, oddly, she felt a little more powerful. Maria had told her that she shouldn't want to be practical tonight, not when she was taking ''that yummy Dr. Grayson'' to the party.

That yummy Dr. Grayson, Rita repeated to herself as she pulled a brush one last time through her hair, which she'd opted to wear loose. Funny, but she'd never thought of him as yummy before. Other things, certainly, including intense, intriguing and enigmatic. And, oh, all right, handsome, too, in an imperfect kind of way. And, yes, sexy, as well. She admitted that. But not yummy. That was too frivolous a word for Dr. Matthew Grayson. What he was was…

Delicious.

Rita closed her eyes and made herself turn away from the mirror. He was *not* delicious, she told herself. He wasn't. He was Dr. Matthew Grayson, gruff, distant co-worker. And why had that funny little heat exploded in her belly again all of a sudden, when he wasn't even around to cause it?

With one final, deep breath, she opened her eyes and straightened her shoulders and told herself there was no reason for her to be nervous. She would be surrounded tonight by family and friends she'd known forever, and they would be celebrating a new direction for the family business that was bound to put Baronessa Gelati back on its feet after the debacles and scandals of the last two months. She would be festive and happy and bright.

Even if there was a funny little heat exploding in her belly at every thought she had about Matthew Grayson.

The executive headquarters of Baronessa Gelati were located near the Prudential Center on Huntington Avenue, in a five-story glass-and-chrome building that was ultra-modern, ultra-elegant and ultra-sleek. To Matthew's way of thinking, the structure was reflective of the Barones themselves, fresh and brash and stylish. Rita gave him a brief history and overview of Baronessa Gelati as they took the elevator to the very top of the building, where she said the offices of the CEO, COO and CFO were located—and also where the party would be held. Marketing and PR, she told him as they passed it, were located on the fourth floor, while the actual manufacturing plant was located just west of Boston in Brookline. In addition to those two business locales, she told him, the Barones had a family compound in Harwichport, on Cape Cod, to which they retreated on a fairly regular basis for holidays and such.

"Of course, I don't visit as often as some of my brothers and sisters and cousins do," Rita said as they stepped off the elevator and into the world of Baronessa Gelati. "What with work and everything, it's hard to take off for any length of time. Still, it's a wonderful house and location. Maybe sometime—"

She halted mid-sentence, without completing the thought, even though Matthew was fairly sure she had been about to extend another invitation to him, one that included joining her and her family there sometime. Or had she halted because, deep down, she really didn't wanted to prolong their liaison, or because she was afraid he would say no? The possibilities, he thought, were fascinating.

As was Rita Barone.

He still couldn't get over how beautiful she looked. He'd thought her pretty since the first day he had seen her, but dressed as she was tonight, *pretty* was far too tame a word for her. His mental thesaurus could conjure some much more appropriate ones with fairly little effort. *Gorgeous. Stunning. Ravishing. Magnificent.*

Those were good for a start.

When he'd opened his front door to find her on the other side, he had been immediately glad that he'd opted for his best, most elegant dark suit, white dress shirt and silk tie. But after that, the only thing he'd been able to register was all that skin on Rita. And how soft and supple and darkly exotic it was. He'd never seen her in anything but her scrubs, and he hadn't been able to help himself as he'd skimmed his gaze over her from head to toe and back again, noting the soft swells of her breasts peeking out of the top of her dress, and the long, long legs beneath.

And her hair. Finally, he knew how long it was, shimmering with dark fire as it cascaded to the middle of her shoulder blades. Straight and thick and silky, it was the kind of hair that drew a man's hand, and Matthew had been battling the urge to reach out to her all evening. Not just to touch her hair, either. No, there were lots of places on Rita Barone he'd like to touch. But not here, he quickly amended. Not surrounded by members of her family. It would be much better to touch Rita later, when they were alone.

But he was getting ahead of himself there. Farther ahead than he'd actually ever be, no doubt. Because Rita had offered no sign that this evening was going to be anything other than a family gathering to which she had invited a co-worker, and only because she needed an escort to prevent her from being harassed by family members about her state of singleness. Unless, of course, he took as a sign that dress she was *almost* wearing.

The dress that her *sister* had picked out for her, a little voice in his head reminded him when he recalled their conversation of Monday. So even the dress couldn't be construed as a sign. He'd have to rely on Rita herself for those. And unless he could convince himself that meaningless small talk was a come-on, she'd offered no indication she wanted anything more from him tonight than his simple companionship.

So far.

Speaking of meaningless small talk, he remembered then that they were supposed to be engaged in that activity. So he leapt on her final statement, especially since she had voiced something about which he had always been curious anyway.

"Why didn't you go into the family business?" he asked. "After all, the name Barone is synonymous with Italian ice cream here in Boston. Why did you pursue a career in nursing instead?"

Rita shrugged as she thought about it. "I don't know," she told him. "I got a toy nurse kit for Christmas when I was five, and there was just no going back after that. I can't remember ever wanting to be anything but a nurse. I mean, I could have gone into the business, I guess, if I'd wanted to. But I'm not especially business-minded, and I really never had that much of an interest in it. Not like some of my brothers and sisters did. Nicholas is COO, Joe is CFO, Gina is the VP of marketing and PR, and Maria manages the original Baronessa Gelateria on Hanover Street. But there *are* eight of us," she reminded him. "And cousins, too. My cousins Derrick and Emily both work for the company. I don't think even Dad could have found a place for all of us. Fortunately, some of us did want to follow other courses. My brother Reese is a day trader. Alex joined the navy. Colleen is a social worker now. My cousin Claudia does volunteer work. And my cousin Daniel…" She smiled. "Well, Daniel is sort of a professional thrill-seeker and playboy."

"Nice work if you can get it," Matthew commented wryly.

"Isn't it, though?" Rita agreed with a chuckle. "Come on, Dr. Grayson. I'll stop talking about them, and you can meet them face-to-face. I'm pretty sure just about everyone will be here tonight, except Reese and Alex."

As she took a step away from him, Matthew remained rooted in place. But he reached out to circle her wrist with loose fingers and pull her back toward himself. She faltered at the unexpectedness of his gesture, then overshot her original position as she stumbled backward, coming to a halt when there was scarcely an inch of space to separate their bodies. Instinctively, she opened her hand against his chest to steady herself, and for one split second, Matthew's entire body went rigid under her touch. When his gaze met hers, he could see that she was startled, though whether it was by his action or by his reaction to her action, he couldn't have said. But she never moved her hand, only pressed it even more intimately against him, as if she were afraid she might fall if she didn't. And he never let go of her wrist, as if he were afraid of something, too.

"What's wrong?" she asked softly, breathlessly, and something about the low, throaty timbre of her voice did funny things to Matthew's insides.

"I'm not going anywhere with you, Rita," he said quietly, "until you promise to stop calling me Dr. Grayson and start calling me Matthew."

She hesitated for a moment, her lips parting slightly, her gaze still locked with his. Her eyes were so dark, so deep and so hypnotic, that he felt as if he were nearly drowning in their bittersweet chocolate depths. Her mouth, too, was so succulent and seductive, he wanted nothing more than to dip his head to hers and brush his lips lightly, once, twice, three times, over hers. So focused on the thought was he, in fact, that he actually began to lower his head to hers, until...

"O-okay," she said, "M-Matthew."

Just like that, the spell was broken and Matthew realized the insanity of his thoughts. He pulled his head back and released her wrist, and Rita, seeming nearly as dazed as he, dropped her hand from his chest and back to her side.

At least he had finally heard her speak his name, he

thought, trying to reassure himself. Even if she hadn't been able to say it without tripping over it. Still, he liked the way she said it. He liked it a lot. When she took a step forward this time—though with a bit less determination than she had shown the first time—he followed her.

As she led him down a long corridor past offices and utility rooms and meeting areas, Matthew heard the faint strains of music drawing nearer, music filled with saxophones, clarinets and the soft brush of drums. Cool jazz. Finally, they turned a corner and cleared another, shorter, corridor, and then found themselves in a massive, glass-enclosed banquet room that had clearly been designed for social functions such as this.

Even from the entry, Matthew could look to the other side of the room and see the lights of Boston twinkling against a dusky sky washed with the deep lavenders and golds of impending sunset. Wispy clouds smudged with purple stretched from one side of the panorama to the other, hinting at the darkness that would come soon. Inside, there were twinkling lights, too, tiny white ones in scores of potted trees situated throughout the room, and crisscrossing the ceiling overhead. In the far corner, he saw the source of the jazzy music, a small combo near which a few couples were dancing. Portable bars and tables of elegant-looking appetizers and finger foods were interspersed throughout, and the place was packed with people.

"Boy, your family certainly knows how to throw a party," Matthew said as he followed Rita inside.

"That they do," she agreed enthusiastically. "Oh, look, there are my parents. We can start at the top of the Barone hierarchy and work our way down," she told him. "Once I get the family introductions out of the way, we can enjoy ourselves without the gloom of nosy questions hanging over us."

Matthew eyed her cautiously. "First tell me who's at the bottom of that hierarchy," he said.

She smiled. "Those of us who have the least illustrious and most difficult jobs," she said. "Like me, for instance."

As ending-up places went, Matthew thought, Rita Barone wasn't such a bad deal. In fact, he thought further, she'd be very nice to end up with. In a variety of ways.

Upon meeting Rita's mother, Moira Reardon Barone, Matthew realized that he needn't be so worried about building a bridge between Rita's family and his own. He'd forgotten that the red-haired, green-eyed current matriarch of the clan was the daughter of a former Massachusetts governor. That ought to go over well with his parents—if indeed there was any need for it to go over well with his parents. Which there *wasn't,* he reminded himself, because there was nothing between him and Rita.

Moira Barone, he also discovered, was gracious and friendly and clearly very interested in her daughter's escort tonight, as was evident immediately after Rita made their introductions.

"A surgeon, you say?" she asked with much interest, leveling an approving smile on her daughter. "Well, well, well. We don't have any doctors in the family. Yet."

"Mother," Rita said with clear warning.

"Which is surprising, really," Moira Barone continued, unbothered by her daughter's admonition, "because there are so very many of us. Oh, yes. A doctor could definitely come in handy."

"And this is my father," Rita hastily interjected, "Carlo Barone. Dad, this is Dr. Matthew Grayson, who works with me at Boston General."

The Barone patriarch had dark hair and eyes like his daughter, but his hair was cut with military precision and was graying at the temples. He stood pretty much eye-to-eye with his daughter, but where Rita was trim and curvy, her father was stocky and powerful-looking. Matthew could easily see him as the driving force behind Baronessa Gelati. Even speaking for only a few minutes, the man came across as vigorous and straightforward.

"You seem to get along well with your parents," Matthew remarked as they parted with the elder Barones after Rita had kissed each on the cheek. He always found it interesting to observe the relationships his peers had with their families, having never had a close alliance with his own. He wasn't sure if that was due to nurture or nature, but the Graysons just weren't the type to get too close. Not physically, and certainly not emotionally.

"I think it helps that I was second to last to be born," she said. "With six kids ahead of me, my parents had a lot of practice. But you're right—we do get along well. They're good parents. Dad was always kind of stern when we were growing up, especially with my older brothers, but he was never overbearing. Well, maybe with Reese, for a while anyway. But he seems to have mellowed over the years. And he always doted on us younger girls. I always kind of thought Nicholas and Reese and Joe broke him in for Gina and Maria and me," she added with another one of those dazzling smiles.

After lifting two stems of white wine from a passing waiter, Rita led Matthew toward a bank of windows overlooking the heart of Boston. But she forsook the spectacular view and instead pointed out some of the other Barones as they passed.

"That's my cousin Derrick," she said in a conspiratorial whisper, pointing discreetly at a tall, thin, tuxedo-clad man with dark hair and hawk-like features who was wearing a dour expression. He was standing at a nearby table and seemed to be trying to make an earth-shattering decision between the shrimp puffs and the mini-quiches. "We've always joked that he's the evil twin. My cousin Daniel," she added, pointing to another man who was a bit fairer and more handsome and athletic-looking than the first, "is Derrick's twin. Fraternal, obviously. But then, Daniel's no angel, either," she continued with a laugh. "Still, the two are like night and day. Daniel's always excelled at sports, and just about everything he touches turns to gold. Derrick, well..." She made a little face. "He tries, but he just doesn't have the touch the way Daniel does. He's always been overshadowed by his brother. And I think he knows it."

"They compete a lot, do they?" Matthew asked.

"In some ways," Rita said. But she seemed to be distracted as she said it, and overly focused on watching her cousin. Her distraction lasted only a moment, however, before she turned to Matthew. "How about you?" she asked. "What's your family like?"

Oh, great, she would have to ask something like that, Matthew thought. Where to begin?

"Small and *very* old Bostonian," he said simply, hoping that would be all she needed to know.

He should have known better.

"Oh, listen to you," she said, chuckling. "You talk as if they came over on the *Mayflower*."

"Well, as a matter of fact..."

Her chuckles ceased and she studied him with frank amazement. "Are you serious?"

"'fraid so."

"The Graysons have been here that long?"

He nodded.

"And they were probably rich and blue-blooded when they got here, too, huh?"

He nodded again. "There are rumors that we can trace

our lineage back to minor royalty in the old country, but I've never pursued that.''

"Not the princely type, huh?''

"Let's just say I'm better suited to cardiology.''

"Wow, that's pretty amazing. I'm only a second-generation American myself. My grandfather came to the United States from Sicily in 1935 and he waited tables until he started up Baronessa. Rags to riches. Peasant to capitalist. Interesting,'' she added, "that you and I should come from such different backgrounds only to be standing in the very same place now.''

"It is,'' he agreed. "Very interesting.''

"So what about brothers and sisters and cousins and parents?'' Rita asked. "What are they like?''

He groped for some acceptable adjectives to describe his family, but the only ones that came to mind weren't particularly flattering. Cool. Distant. Proud. Pale. For all their social distinction, the Graysons had nothing on the warm, affectionate, vivacious Barones.

"I have one younger sister,'' he finally said, forsaking the adjectives for now.

"Ah-hah, firstborn child,'' she observed.

"You sound as if you think that's significant,'' Matthew said, eyeing her suspiciously.

She lifted one rather delectable shoulder in a half shrug. "Maybe it is. Maybe it isn't,'' she replied cryptically. "So what does this sister do? Do the Graysons have a family business, too?''

Matthew shook his head. "Not really, though I am something of a black sheep. My father is a merchant banker, my mother is a CPA, and my sister is a stockbroker. My cousins, uncles and aunts, too, are all financiers.''

Rita laughed. "A successful cardiologist is the black sheep? Boy, what a rogue you are.''

"I never said we were interesting," Matthew reminded her.

"Oh, I wouldn't say *that*," she murmured as she lifted her wine to her lips for an idle sip.

He was about to ask her what she'd meant by her comment, but Carlo Barone took to the podium vacated by the jazz combo then, citing his need to make an announcement about an upcoming contest for Baronessa Gelati. Then he introduced Gina Barone Kingman, who Matthew recalled was the VP of PR.

Gina didn't much resemble Rita, however, beyond sharing the same olive complexion. Rita's sister was taller, had light-brown hair that was curly instead of straight, and even from a short distance, Matthew could see that her eyes were light in color, and not the mesmerizing espresso of her younger sister's. Like nearly every woman at the party, she was dressed in a black cocktail dress, though hers covered more of her than Rita's did, as befitted one of the company's executives.

Gina spoke for a few minutes about the history of Baronessa, made a brief mention of having abandoned a recently tested passionfruit flavor, then held up a letter-sized sheet of paper for everyone to see.

"What I have in my hand," she said, "is a list of the rules and requirements for our new Name That Flavor contest. Tomorrow's newspaper will carry this in a full-page ad. We're challenging anyone in the Boston metro area who's inventive and culinarily inclined to develop a recipe for a new gelato flavor."

A smattering of enthusiastic applause went up at this, along with the nodding of several heads.

"All recipes entered," Gina continued as the clapping eased, "will be duplicated and produced in a small batch at the Baronessa factory in Brookline, and a panel of judges that includes the executives of Baronessa and the board of directors—and also Mom,'' she added with a smile, again to much applause, ''—will taste each entry and, among them, choose a winner.''

More applause met the announcement.

''The creator of the winning recipe,'' Gina went on, ''will not only see his or her flavor become a reality in Baronessa stores across the country—not to mention supermarkets everywhere—but will also win $1,000 for his or her efforts, which is some pretty nice pocket change.''

Amid more applause, Matthew leaned over toward Rita and murmured, ''Have they totally abandoned the passion-fruit flavor, then? That sounds like it would be pretty good.''

Rita turned to look at him as if she couldn't believe he'd asked her such a thing. ''I think that's a safe bet, after the debacle at the launch.''

''Have you discovered how the habanero peppers got into the gelato?'' Matthew asked.

Rita shook her head. ''We have no idea. The family's pretty well divided into two camps. Some think it's someone from a rival ice-cream company, and some think it's the work of the Contis. Do you know about that?'' she asked. ''The big family feud?''

''I've heard about it,'' Matthew told her. ''I think anyone who's lived in Boston any length of time has.''

She nodded. ''I don't know, though. I can't see the Contis doing something like that. Personally, I lean toward the corporate sabotage angle. Though even that's hard to believe. I just can't imagine some legitimate business doing something like that.''

''You'd be surprised what people are capable of,'' Matthew said.

And when he said it, his voice carried an edge that Rita

hadn't heard before. Something told her not to pursue it, though, so she changed the topic of conversation to something more innocuous, telling him she hoped that whoever won the contest came up with some variation on chocolate, since that was her own personal favorite.

Gina said a few more words about the contest, outlining the requirements and such, and then the excitement gradually began to settle. After a few more announcements, she encouraged everyone to go back to enjoying the party.

The champagne never stopped flowing for the rest of the night. And since the atmosphere was so festive, and since neither Rita nor Matthew would be responsible for driving home, they both partook freely.

That could be the only reason, Rita decided later, after she had led Matthew out to the terrace adjoining the party room on the top floor of the building to gaze out at the lights of Boston, why she would ask him the question she did once they were finally alone.

"How did you get those scars on your face?" she said before she had even realized she meant to say it.

Immediately, she clapped a hand over her mouth, regretting at once having put voice to the question. But the thought had been circling in her head all night, ever since she'd seen him looking so exquisitely handsome in his expensive suit. She just hadn't been able to stop thinking that if it weren't for those scars, he would be absolutely perfect. And then, suddenly, she was asking how those scars had originated, when she should have kept her mouth shut. Not just because the question had been so frightfully impolite but because Matthew went absolutely rigid when she asked it.

"I'm sorry," she immediately apologized from behind her hand. "I had no right to ask that. Please…forget I said anything."

And then she shivered, though she told herself it was because of the cold April breeze that whirled around the building just then, and not Matthew's glacial stare.

The glacial stare lasted only a moment, though, and then vanished as quickly as it had appeared. He must have noticed her trembling, because his expression softened, and his voice was gentle as he said, "You're cold. I never should have suggested we come out here."

Before she could say anything else, he whipped off his suit jacket and draped it around her shoulders. Rita was going to decline the gesture and suggest they go back inside, but the moment the soft fabric settled over her bare shoulders and arms it began to warm her, and she realized it was Matthew's warmth. And then she noticed that it smelled like Matthew, too, spicy and clean and male, and that having his jacket around her was almost—*almost*—like having his arms around her. Suddenly she didn't want to go back inside. Suddenly she wasn't cold anymore. In fact, heat was starting to seep into parts of her she hadn't even realized were cold until that moment.

"Thank you," she said softly as she pulled the jacket more tightly around herself, reveling in the sensation of having him so close, even if he wasn't standing very near her. Then, once again, she said, "I'm sorry, Matthew. I shouldn't have asked. It's none of my business."

"No, it isn't that," he said quickly. But his voice was still somber and a little distant, as if he were lost in thought. "I just..." He sighed heavily. "It happened so long ago, you'd think it wouldn't be a big deal anymore. That it wouldn't bother me to talk about it."

"But it does?"

"Sometimes."

"Look, honestly, you don't have to tell me if you don't—"

"I was mauled by a lion."

Rita stopped speaking the moment he started, but never quite closed her mouth. She continued to gape at him when he concluded his brief—if shocking—revelation. Frankly, she wasn't sure whether to believe him. Was he joking, trying to make light of what had really happened? Did people actually *get* mauled by lions? It sounded like something from a nineteenth-century novel.

"When I was ten years old," he continued. "My parents and I were on safari in Kenya at the time."

She realized then that he was indeed telling the truth, but she still shook her head in silent disbelief.

"I strayed away from camp one night," he said, his voice quiet, sober, as if he were deep in thought, "even though they'd warned me against doing that. I was looking at the sky," he told her by way of an explanation. Then he turned his head to do that now. He gazed out at the star-spattered darkness above them as if he'd never seen it before. "It was so beautiful that night," he continued, "so clear, and I guess I just didn't realize how far I'd walked. I was like the baby wildebeest who strays from the herd," he added with a halfhearted smile. "Easy prey." His smile fell suddenly and he turned to look at Rita again. "The lion came out of nowhere. A female. One minute everything was quiet and still and magical, and the next…" He met her gaze levelly. "The next minute, I was literally fighting for my life."

"Oh, Matthew," Rita said. She couldn't imagine the confusion and terror he must have felt.

"Someone in the camp must have heard the commotion, because a group came running and screaming and waving torches, and the lion, amazingly, let go of me and disappeared into the darkness. My shoulder and back bore the brunt of the attack," he told her. "You think the scars on my face are something, you should see the ones there.'' He seemed to realize then that what he'd said might have a double meaning, because he glanced anxiously away and quickly added, ''On second thought, no, you shouldn't. The plastic surgeons did what they could with my face, but the first wounds went so deep—''

He didn't finish whatever he'd intended to say. But then, Rita thought, he really didn't have to. She understood. She had no idea what to say to him, however. But when Matthew looked up at her, he seemed so anxious about her response to him that she made herself smile. Then, strangely, she realized that her smile felt like a perfectly natural response.

''I think the plastic surgeons did a wonderful job,'' she told him. ''Of course, they had a good foundation to start with. You could be a movie star.''

''I don't know about that,'' he said, dropping his gaze to the ground again like a bashful teenager. ''But the whole thing certainly sounds like something from a movie. I've spent most of my life wishing it were. It wasn't much fun growing up looking like a beast.''

He looked thoughtful for a moment, taking great care about whether or not he should say any more. And he gazed up at the sky again when he finally did begin to speak. ''I remember once,'' he said, ''when I was in eighth grade. I'd started a new school—again—because I'd gotten thrown out of the last one—again—for fighting so much. Not that I was ever the instigator, mind you,'' he added parenthetically, as if he needed for her to know that. ''But I was in a new school, and like an idiot, I was hoping maybe things would be different this time. And there was a girl in my semantics class—''

His voice drifted off, but had mellowed to the point where Rita knew he was recalling what must have been a pretty powerful crush. She smiled in spite of his somberness.

"She was so pretty," he said with a halfhearted smile. "Blond hair, blue eyes, tight sweaters, every adolescent boy's idea of the perfect girl. And she always turned around whenever I was looking at her, as if she could feel me watching her. But she never seemed to mind, you know? She'd always look at me back. My rational mind told me she looked at me for the same reason everyone looked at me. Because I was a freak—"

"Matthew—" Rita began. But he hurried on before she had a chance to say any more.

"But there was a part of me that wondered, that hoped—" He shrugged. "I don't know. She just seemed to be different from the others. Then, one day, her best friend came up to me at my locker and told me this girl wanted to meet me. That she liked me. That she wanted to talk to me. I couldn't believe it. I was so happy. So I went to meet her behind the gym, where her friend said she'd be waiting for me."

He paused again, inhaling deeply before letting the breath out in a slow, melancholy exhalation. "Long story short," he continued, "the girl was indeed there waiting for me. With her boyfriend. She told me to stop looking at her in class, because I made her sick to her stomach. And then she let her boyfriend do the rest of the talking. Unfortunately, there wasn't much talking after that. And I had to leave that school for another one a few weeks later."

"Oh, Matthew," Rita said again.

"So, there you have it," he concluded flatly. "The life and times of the beast."

Something inside of Rita turned over at that. He couldn't possibly think of himself that way, could he?

"You're not a beast," she said.

He laughed, but there was nothing happy in the sound. "Aren't I?" he asked. "Everyone at the hospital seems to think so."

"That's not because of your scars," Rita was quick to correct him. "It's because of your attitu—" She halted again before finishing, slapping a hand over her mouth again, appalled at what she had just revealed. "Matthew, that's not what I meant," she hastened to clarify, dropping her hand. "You're not a beast," she said again, with more conviction this time.

As if she wanted to prove that, she lifted her hand to his face and, after only a small hesitation, skimmed her fingertips lightly over the scars he seemed to think so repulsive. At first, he jerked his head back, as if he didn't want her to touch him. But she moved her hand forward again, laying her fingers gently over his injured flesh, and this time, for some reason, he let her.

"You're not a beast," she insisted. "You're..."

His eyes met hers again, and she realized that somehow, at some point, they'd moved closer together, and that scarcely a breath of air separated them now. Matthew turned his head just the merest bit, tilting it to the side so that he might enjoy her touch more fully.

"I'm what?" he asked softly, lifting his hand to cover hers.

Now Rita opened her hand completely, pressing her palm gently to his face, cupping his cheek and jaw more completely. She felt herself moving closer still, and didn't recall making the decision to advance. Her instincts seemed to have taken over by then, and all she could do was follow them.

"You're..." she tried again.

But no words came to her aid to describe him. Probably because at that point he was...indescribable. But also very,

very desirable. Something about the way he was looking at her then sent a shudder of emotion spiraling through the center of her. And when he covered her hand with his the way he did, that spiral coiled even tighter.

Not sure why she did it and still following her impulses, Rita pushed herself up on tiptoe and pressed her lips lightly to his. The moment their mouths made contact something inside her ruptured, spilling heat and fire throughout her body. The sensation was so immediate, so intense, so startling that she instinctively pulled away from him again.

A quick peck, she told herself when it was over and she was back on her feet—however precariously. A brief, chaste, perfectly innocuous little kiss. That was all it had been. She had wanted to show him he wasn't repulsive, as he seemed to think. So she had brushed her lips gingerly over his, and then she had pulled away again.

A quick peck, she repeated to herself more firmly. No harm, no foul. Nothing to it. Somehow, though, she felt as if the entire earth had slipped away beneath her feet.

"You're not a beast, Matthew," she said one last time. "Not in any way." And then, because she was afraid of what might happen if they stayed outside—alone—any longer, she stepped back and added, "We should probably go back inside. They'll be looking for us. And it really is colder out here than I thought."

She felt like a big, fat liar as she turned away from him without awaiting a reply and made her way back toward the terrace door. Not just because she knew the last thing the Barones would do was look for her if she'd disappeared with a handsome, distinguished doctor. But because she'd never felt hotter in her life.

Five

What little was left of the evening seemed to drag, as far as Rita was concerned. Well, except for those few occasions when she turned to look at Matthew and caught him studying her with a burning gaze that scorched her from her head to her toes and all points in between. Then again, how could anything so mundane as a glittering high-society party possibly be appealing after that single, perfect kiss she and Matthew had shared out on the terrace?

She could no longer tell herself it had been an innocent little peck to prove a point. Rita knew better. She had kissed Matthew because she had been attracted to him. More than attracted. She had been moved by him. Enchanted by him. And not just this evening, either, but for some time. Only now was she beginning to realize that she had been attracted to him probably since the day she'd begun working in CCU.

Yes, he had been gruff at times, and often standoffish.

But she had always detected something beneath his surface that was almost…vulnerable somehow. Now she knew she had been right to sense such a thing. And now she knew why. He had suffered a horrible experience when he was a child. The physical wounds alone must have been unbearable for him. How must it have felt to grow up looking the way he did, and harbor memories of such a harrowing encounter? It was no wonder he acted the way he did around other people. He'd probably never had the chance to interact with them on a normal, everyday sort of level.

Tonight, hearing him speak the way he had about what had happened to him, she had begun to understand that there was still a wounded little boy inside him who was motivated by fear. And she had wanted to show him that she wasn't scared of him. On the contrary, knowing what had happened to him had only drawn her to him that much more completely. And she'd wanted to show him, too, that he shouldn't be afraid of her.

By mutual and unspoken consent, neither of them mentioned the kiss once they returned to the party. Of course, neither seemed to feel comfortable with the other anymore, either, and neither seemed able to meet the other's gaze—well, except for those few accidental scorching ones Rita had caught from Matthew. And those, she decided, she'd just as soon not mention, either.

She tried to reassure herself that by the time the two of them returned to work Monday morning, the whole thing would be forgotten. They were both bound to spend the weekend convincing themselves that nothing had happened out on the terrace—nothing save a chaste, innocent little peck—and by Monday, surely, they would have succeeded. Because, really, she told herself nothing *had* happened out on the terrace save a chaste, innocent little peck…and an carth-shattering awareness of each other that Rita was certain wouldn't pass anytime soon.

They were doomed.

There was no way either of them would ever feel comfortable around the other at work again. Not that they'd ever felt comfortable around each other at work before, she reminded herself. But she quickly abandoned that train of thought. She was afraid she'd admit how she'd always been attracted to Matthew Grayson—she might even go so far as to say she'd had a crush on him since the day she'd met him. And how *that* was the real reason she'd kissed him tonight.

She knew better than to think her memories of a kiss like that would fizzle out and be forgotten. No, her memories were bound to multiply and intensify until she had no choice but to seek him out and relive the experience. Over and over and over again.

Oh, yeah. They were definitely doomed.

"We should probably go," Rita told him at midnight, when she realized everyone else seemed to be leaving, too. Well, everyone except her family, who would doubtless party until the wee hours. She scanned the room for Maria, but was surprised to see that her sister seemed to have already left. More surprising was the recollection that after badgering Rita so mercilessly about needing a date, Maria hadn't brought anyone to the party tonight.

"I can take a cab home," Matthew offered, obviously still uncomfortable with what had happened out on the terrace and wanting to be free of Rita as soon as was polite.

"No, no, that won't be necessary," she assured him anyway. Mostly, she supposed, because she didn't want him to think there was any reason for them to alter their plans. "The driver is paid for the night," she added, "and he's expecting to take us both home. We might as well take advantage of him.''

The moment that final sentence was out of her mouth, she wished she hadn't said it. It made her want to think about taking advantage of someone else, too.

Matthew seemed to be thinking the same thing, she realized when she braved a glance in his direction, because his cheeks had grown ruddy, and his eyes had darkened dangerously. But he said nothing, only swept his hand toward the exit in a silent indication that Rita should precede him. As she strode past him, he extended his arm to her, crooking his elbow, as if he wanted her to take it. Fearing he might think her a big chicken if she didn't—and also because she yearned to touch him, however superficially—Rita complied, threading her arm through his to walk side-by-side with him to the door.

Although they remained arm-in-arm, they spoke not a word as they descended in the elevator, both of them fixing their gazes on the illuminated, decreasing numbers above the doors. When they exited, they silently crossed the lobby and strode through the big glass front doors, then toward the bank of limos waiting for the various Barones they were to escort home. When they found theirs, the driver hustled out to open the back door for them, and Rita entered with Matthew right behind her. The moment their chauffeur closed the door behind them, however, she tensed.

For the first time since that kiss, she and Matthew were alone. Utterly and completely alone, thanks to a pane of smoked privacy glass that cut off their view of the driver and, Rita knew, the driver's view of them. They were in a much more isolated—and much more intimate—setting now than the public display on the top-floor terrace where anyone might have stumbled upon them at any time. This was a much quieter, much cozier—much darker—environment than the one they had shared before. And it immediately made Rita think about doing things that hadn't occurred to her on the way to the party earlier.

Well, okay, maybe doing those things had occurred to her then, back in some dark, recessed, feverish, sexually deprived part of her brain. Maybe, once or twice, during the drive to the party, she had entertained a quick fantasy of what it would be like to make love with Matthew Grayson on the wide back seat of this very car. He'd just looked so incredibly handsome and sexy in his dark suit, she hadn't been able to help herself. But she'd only thought about it once or twice, only for a few seconds, and certainly not realistically. Now, though, after their kiss, she thought about it for more than a few seconds—and in much more graphic terms.

Oh, good heavens, what was wrong with her? she wondered. This was Matthew Grayson she was fantasizing about. The Beast from Boston General. In spite of all her earlier softening toward him and romanticizing about him, she tried to make herself be realistic. Yes, there were reasons for why he acted the way he did around people. But the fact remained that he *did* act that way. For all she knew, he might not even be capable of falling in love with a woman.

Then again, she chastised herself, what did love have to do with anything? She certainly wasn't in love with him. How had she gotten from hot sex in the back of a limo to hearts and flowers and happily-ever-afters? The two weren't necessarily connected at all.

"Are you going to bring it up, or should I?"

Matthew's deep, resonant voice knifed through the darkness with all the finesse of a finely edged blade, but the question itself hit Rita with the hacking impact of a dull meat cleaver.

"Bring what up?" she asked innocently, hoping that if she pretended she had no idea what he was talking about, Matthew would go along with the ruse.

She should have known better.

"Guess I'll be the one to bring it up then," he said dryly.

"Bring what up?" she tried again. Futilely, she soon learned.

"What happened out on the terrace tonight," he said plainly. "You...kissing me."

Rita started to deny it, started to insist that they had both been the ones involved in that kiss, but she knew she would be lying. Because in spite of his having done nothing to stop it, it had been she who'd kissed him, and she who had ended it. She alone must take responsibility for what had happened. She had kissed Matthew. She only wished she could tell him why.

"I'm not sure what happened," she told him honestly. "I just..." She gave a halfhearted shrug. "It seemed like the thing to do at the time."

He said nothing in response to that, and when she looked at him, his face was cast in shadow, so she had no way to gauge what he might be thinking. Then the limo passed beneath a street lamp, and for one brief second, she caught a glimpse of his face, and she saw that he looked...

Puzzled.

Of all the things she might have expected him to be, puzzled was one that would never have occurred to her. Matthew Grayson had always struck her as someone who would have an answer for every question, an explanation for every mystery. Yet he looked puzzled by what had happened between the two of them earlier that evening.

The realization heartened Rita. It meant they were on equal footing.

Until he said, "So if I kissed *you* this time, what would happen?"

And then, suddenly, things were totally out of whack. A splash of heat spilled through Rita's midsection, not just because of the question itself, but because of the way he uttered it—as if he fully intended to find out.

She swallowed with some difficulty. "Why, um, why would you want to do that?"

Thanks to the darkness, she sensed more than saw him shrug. But even in the darkness, she could tell there was nothing casual in the gesture.

"It just seems like the right thing to do," he told her. She could sense him drawing nearer as he said it.

And then he was kissing her, and she was kissing him back, and a swirl of tempestuous hunger was eddying up inside her. He lifted a hand to the back of her neck and curved his fingers over her nape, his touch warm and insistent and absolute. Her stomach seared with heat at the way his fingers pressed into the tender flesh of her neck, her heart humming with anticipation of what would come next.

Oh, dear heaven, she thought. What was happening? And why couldn't she make it stop? Why didn't she *want* it to stop?

There was none of the tentativeness or uncertainty in Matthew's kiss that had been present in Rita's earlier. No, when Matthew covered her mouth with his, it was with confident determination. He kissed her the way a man must kiss a woman when he knows that he wants her, and when he knows that he can have her. Rita had never been kissed that way before. Not because no man had ever wanted her, but because *she* had never wanted any man enough to allow him to kiss her that way. With Matthew, though...

She wanted. Oh, how she wanted.

Instinctively, she tilted her head to the side a bit, a gesture he used to his advantage to deepen the kiss. The hand at her nape moved to her jaw, and he splayed his fingers wide over her cheek and chin, silently urging her to open her mouth for him. Rita complied willingly, groaning with desire at the surging entrance of his tongue as he tasted her. A wild heat exploded in her belly at the intimate invasion, spreading its fever outward, flooding into her breasts and between her legs. Impulsively, she pressed her hands to his chest, driving one beneath his jacket and up to clutch his shoulder. When she did, Matthew looped his other arm around her waist to pull her closer still.

Her body flush with his now, Rita felt his heat and his hardness permeating his clothing, joining with her own warmth and softness as she touched him. Something inside her went a little wild at the recognition of how their bodies' differences complemented each other so perfectly. She couldn't help wondering in what other ways their bodies could correlate. So she pushed herself against him more urgently, one hand moving now to his hair, her fingers threading through its silky thickness. He seemed to like it when she did that, because a low moan emerged from some dark place deep inside him in response.

The realization that she pleased him made Rita feel bolder, and she tilted her head to the side again. But she used the motion to her own advantage, slipping her tongue into his mouth this time. The sensation of damp heat surrounding her was like nothing she had ever experienced before. Matthew tasted of champagne and caviar, and something dark and masculine and bittersweet. And all Rita could think was that she wanted to experience more of him.

She wasn't sure whether she was responsible for what happened next, or Matthew. But somehow, she ended up sitting in his lap, her legs stretching out across the wide back seat of the limo. She lost a shoe, but she didn't care, and in fact kicked off the other in what she could only think in her agitated state was a wanton effort to free herself from her clothing. Because suddenly, she wanted very much to be free of her clothing. Even more than that, she wanted Matthew to be free of his. Then they would be able to explore each other more completely. And in that heady, feverish moment, as the two of them volleyed for possession of their kiss, Rita realized she wanted very badly to explore as much of Matthew as she could.

He seemed to share her desire, because just as the thought was forming in her brain, she felt his hand glide slowly from her waist, over her hip and along her thigh, to settle at the hem of her dress. As he continued to kiss her, he began to push the fabric higher, inch by subtle inch, over her thighs. Bit by bit, her little black dress grew smaller still, until his fingers cleared the smoky silk of her stockings and met bare flesh. The moment Matthew realized what his fingers had already discovered, he jerked his head back from hers and, panting, gazed down into her face.

"Are you actually wearing what I think you're wearing?" he gasped.

Not trusting herself to speak—or perhaps unable to— Rita could only nod her response.

He studied her in silence for a moment longer, then began stroking the pad of his thumb gently over the bare flesh of her thigh. Every mellow touch set off tiny explosions in its wake, until Rita feared she would spontaneously combust if he didn't stop it. When he skimmed a finger beneath one of the silky garters, she bit back a groan of need.

"It's always been my understanding," he said roughly as he gave the garter a gentle tug, "that women only wear these for a...sexual encounter."

Did they? Rita wondered feverishly. How very interesting. Maybe she should start doing more reading. Who knew what else she might learn? All she was able to manage by way of a response, though, was a breathless, honestly offered, "It's the first time I've worn one."

"Really?" he asked with much interest.

Now she was only able to nod in response.

"I've never known a woman who wore one," he said.

Somehow, that surprised Rita. In spite of his scarred face and distant disposition, he seemed like the kind of man who would be well versed in the ways of women. Then he kissed her again, in a way that let her know he was indeed. And then she ceased thinking at all when he began tasting her deeply once more, and the fingers at her thigh began strumming over her sensitive flesh again. All Rita could do then was cup his face in her hands, turn her head to the side and kiss him back for all she was worth.

As she kissed him, she registered the movement of his hand along her thigh again, pushing the fabric of her dress higher still, until his fingers made contact with the edge of her black lacy panties. He halted there for a moment, as if he weren't sure she would allow him any further liberties, so Rita shoved her fingers into his hair again and deepened their kiss, fairly devouring him this time. He seemed to understand her eagerness, because he pushed up her dress farther, until he could cup his whole hand possessively over the right side of her lace-covered derriere.

That was when he tore his mouth from hers and pressed his face into the juncture of her neck and shoulder, murmuring something incoherent against her hot flesh before nipping it lightly with his teeth. Rita did groan this time, needfully, brazenly, then turned herself on his lap to give him freer access to her. In doing so, she felt him surge to life beneath her, swelling hard and heavy and ready for her.

The hand on her bottom clenched tight at her movement, and she bit back another feral sound. Then she dipped her head to his again, ravaging his mouth this time in a kiss full of demand.

By now he had pushed her dress up around her waist, so Rita turned her entire body to straddle his lap. She was thankful for the smoky, one-way glass between them and their driver and the outside world. Still, the fact that they were cruising through downtown Boston as they lost control only made it that much more exciting for her. Now as she faced Matthew fully, as her eyes met his in the dim light, she realized he looked like a man who was about to come undone. So, to help him along, she leaned forward. Instead of taking his mouth in a hungry kiss this time, she only brushed her lips lightly over his, once, twice, three times. Then, having no idea what possessed her to do it, she pulled back again, reaching behind herself to slowly, so slowly, draw down the zipper on her dress.

At first, he seemed not to realize what she was doing. But when she tugged the dress down over her arms, pushing it down around her waist, he had no choice but to notice. Without a word, his gaze never leaving hers, he lifted both hands and covered each of her black-lace-covered breasts. With one deft move, he bared a breast so that he could fill his hand with her naked flesh. He palmed the soft globe first in slow, gentle circles, his hand warm on her skin, confident, almost courtly.

Rita closed her eyes as he touched her, to better enjoy the sensation. And when she felt his mouth open over the tumid peak, she sighed eloquently and tangled her fingers in his hair. For long moments he sucked at her, pushing her breast higher with his hand, pulling her deep into his mouth, the damp pressure tugging at something too-long buried inside her. He laved her with the flat of his tongue, then teased her with its tip, then sucked harder still. Never in her life had she felt such an extraordinary sensation. And the pleasure winding through her was something she never wanted to have end.

"Take me home with you tonight," she said breathlessly as he traced the lower curve of her breast with his tongue.

She had no idea what made her utter the command, nor, really, what she was asking him to do. She only knew that she couldn't leave him yet, not after the things he had just introduced her to. She only knew that she wanted, needed, to be with him. Needed to know what else he could make her feel.

"Please, Matthew," she said again, her fingers convulsing in his hair as he dragged his open mouth up over her breast again. "Please take me home with you tonight. I want..."

But truly, she wasn't sure what she wanted. She only knew that, in that moment, she could not leave him. Not feeling as unsatisfied as she did.

Matthew drew back at her breathlessly offered request, and when she opened her eyes, she saw that he was gazing at her. But she couldn't discern his reaction.

"Are you sure?" he asked softly.

She nodded eagerly, even though she felt anything but certain. She reminded herself ruthlessly of the promise she had made to herself, that the first time she made love with a man would be because he would be someone special. But then she realized she had never felt more special than she did at that moment. Matthew made her feel special. He was special, too. He was... Well, he was everything. Everything she had always wanted in a man. Handsome, smart, sexy and kind. And he made her feel things... Oh, how he made her feel.

He would be an attentive lover, she thought further, considering the ways he had touched and pleasured her so far. She tried not to think about how much practice he must have had over the years, and focused instead on how he was here with her now. He had been gentle with her so far, and she sensed he would be gentle throughout. And that was what she wanted—and needed—for her first time. Most of all, though, she cared for Matthew, maybe more than she was willing to admit.

Of course, she'd always sworn she would be in love with the man her first time. But she was twenty-five years old, she reflected, and had yet to fall in love. Maybe love, she thought, was asking too much. Maybe for her first time it would be enough to admire and respect and care for her partner.

Matthew, she told herself in that moment, would be perfect.

"If I take you home, Rita," he said, his voice still soft, but now steeled with intent, "there won't be any turning back. Do you understand?"

She nodded again.

He lifted a hand to her face, framing her jaw in his palm before moving his fingers to her hair and brushing it back from her face. "Once we're inside, I'm going to lock the door and spend the entire night making love to you. And once I make love to you…"

He said nothing more after that, only met her gaze levelly in the darkness, with an unmistakable intent. She wasn't sure if he was telling her that after they made love nothing would change between them, or if everything would change. Somehow, though, in that moment, Rita didn't care. She only knew she wanted Matthew. More than she had ever wanted anything in her life. And she knew, too, that she would have him.

"I understand," she said.

Deep down, though, she wasn't sure she understood at all.

Six

Rita saw Matthew nod slowly in response to her assertion that she understood. Then he ran his hand over the crown of her head one final time, leaned forward to give her breast one long, final, leisurely taste, then, with clear reluctance, tugged up her brassiere and helped her back into her dress. For now. Even though she was shaking almost uncontrollably, Rita moved from his lap to the seat beside him just as the limo rolled to a stop in front of his brick townhouse, and she only barely managed to pull her dress down over her thighs and scoot her feet back into her shoes before their driver opened the door on Matthew's side.

He exited the car with grace and style, and no one ever would have suspected that only a moment ago he had been pleasuring a woman with her breast in his mouth. Rita, on the other hand, exited the car with anything but grace and style, because her entire body was trembling with what had just transpired between the two of them, and her mind was scrambled with thoughts about what was to come.

Matthew seemed to understand her state of agitation, because he draped his arm over her shoulder and pulled her close the moment she stood. Rita made minimal small talk with their driver and sent him on his way with assurances from Matthew that he would take her home after the two of them shared a nightcap here. She had no idea if the driver believed them, and frankly, she didn't care. She had far more important things to think about at the moment. Especially when Matthew began to guide her up the walkway toward his house.

He unlocked the front door and pushed it open wide, then stood aside to let Rita enter first. He crossed the threshold immediately behind her, closed the door and locked it, then reached for her and hauled her back against him.

His kiss this time was hot and demanding, with absolutely no pretense of taking things slowly. He moved his hand to the zipper of her dress and pushed it down, down, down, past her waist and over her hips, until he could spread the fabric open wide. He made short work of her bra, as well, and then she felt his hands on her bare back, rushing over her naked flesh as if he wanted to learn every inch of her. As he explored her, Rita went to work on his clothing, jerking loose his tie and tossing it to the floor, then freeing the buttons on his shirt one by frantic one. She shoved it and his jacket off his shoulders together, both garments falling to the floor alongside his tie. Then he pushed her dress down over her hips and thighs, letting it fall to her ankles. Rita stepped out of it and kicked it aside, and then they both stood half-naked and panting in the foyer.

A slash of pale light spilled over them from a lamp he had left burning in the living room beyond, and in that pale light, Rita drank her fill of him. He had a magnificent physique, lean and athletic, his chest corded with solid muscle, his biceps and forearms salient beneath his bronzed skin. She had heard him speak of skiing in winter and tennis in summer, and it showed. She traced both of her index fingers along the lines of his muscular shoulders, down over his biceps, along the solid forearms to the hands he had settled at her waist. Then she traced the route back up again.

At his left shoulder, though, she halted, noting for the first time the pucker of a wide scar that ran to nearly the center of his chest. She recalled then that he had said his shoulder and back had suffered the brunt of his attack, and she closed her entire hand gingerly over the scarred flesh of his shoulder.

"Don't," he said softly, shrugging out from beneath her touch.

But Rita followed his movement, closing her hand over him again. "I want to see, Matthew," she said softly.

But he shook his head. "Women don't react well to the sight," he told her decisively.

She tried not to think about how many women, then told herself it didn't matter. All that mattered was that the two of them were here together now. Everything that had come before was immaterial. And she wasn't any of the women to whom he had made love before.

"I want to see," she said again.

And again, he shook his head.

She relented, but only because she didn't want to jeopardize the newfound intimacy they had discovered together. She told herself there would be other opportunities, that this night with Matthew would be the first of many. She wasn't the kind of woman to go for a one-night stand, and she assured herself that Matthew must realize that. If they made love tonight, it was because they were starting something new together.

There would be other times, she told herself again. Because she would prove to him tonight that she wasn't like other women.

Even so, she heard herself ask him, "How many other women have there been?"

She couldn't look him in the eye as she asked the question, and instead continued to gaze upon his wounded shoulder and her own fingers as they traced the edges of the scar. Matthew pulled her hand away. But where she feared he would return it to her side, instead he moved it to his mouth and pressed a gentle kiss to her palm.

"Not as many as you seem to think," he told her.

Rita did meet his gaze then, and she saw that he was telling her the truth. "I would have thought that a man like you..." she began.

But he halted her assessment by roping his arm around her waist and hauling her against him, covering her mouth with his once again. Rita went slack at the contact, so potent was the effect of his embrace. For long moments, she only stood limp in his arms, her hands pressed loosely against his shoulders, her legs tangled between his own. Her heart, though, pounded feverishly, rushing blood so quickly through her body that she almost grew dizzy. Then, suddenly, her body came alive, with need and demand and hunger. She wrapped her arms fiercely around Matthew's waist and returned his kiss with equal fire.

He groaned raggedly at her response, walking her backward, toward the living room she couldn't see. When they'd entered, she'd caught a glimpse of an elegantly appointed room with leather furniture and fine antiques surrounding a darkly colored Oriental rug. As she drew nearer, she noted a grandfather clock with its softly swaying pendulum, rows of books on built-in shelves, and forest-green walls deco-rated with the occasional oil-on-canvas landscape. Expen-sive, refined, tasteful furnishings. Obviously, since Mat-thew Grayson was an expensive, refined, tasteful man.

He kept walking her backward until her legs bumped against a leather-clad sofa the color of fine red wine. Rita glanced toward the windows long enough to make sure the curtains were closed, and reassured that they were, she low-ered her hands to the fastenings of Matthew's trousers. As she unzipped his fly, he opened his hands over her naked back, then she tucked her fingers inside his pants.

She found him easily, so long and hard and ready was he, and she covered the head of his shaft with her hand, rubbing her palm over it in an indolent circle. Moisture bloomed against her fingers as she touched him, making it easier for her to glide her hand down the length of him. He moaned against her mouth as she touched him, then moved his hand down over her lace-covered fanny.

"You pulled your panties on over your garters," he mur-mured against her neck as he dropped his head to place a series of soft, butterfly kisses there.

"I thought that was how you were supposed to do it," she murmured in reply, throwing her head back to makc herself more accessible to him.

"Only if you're planning to take the panties off and leave the garters and stockings on," he told her.

"And isn't that what I should do?" she asked breath-lessly.

He uttered another feral, erotic sound, then chuckled low. "Oh, baby," he said, "you really know how to turn a man on."

She did? Rita wondered. Well, that was certainly prom-ising.

"Keep the shoes on, too," he added with a quick glimpse at her spiky heels.

She was going to ask why—that seemed so impractical after all—but the fire burning in his eyes gave her all the answer she needed. Matthew Grayson might be an expensive, refined, tasteful man, but he clearly enjoyed earthy, naughty, wanton sex. And something about the combination of the two made Rita want him all the more.

He hooked his fingers in the waistband of her panties and, without waiting for permission—not that Rita would have denied it—pushed them down over her hips and thighs. She stepped out of them easily and toed them aside, then returned to Matthew's arms. As she moved her hand back into his trousers and closed her fingers over him again, he slipped his hands beneath the silky garters and splayed them open over the soft lower curves of her naked fanny. Then he pulled her toward himself, and Rita rubbed her breasts languidly against the dark hair of his chest.

"I can't wait any longer," he told her. "I want to be inside you. Now, Rita. Let me make love to you now. Next time, I promise we'll go slower."

She nodded, then began pushing at his trousers. Together, they removed them, and Matthew urged her backward, down onto the couch. The sensation of smooth leather against her bare bottom was quite exquisite. As was the sensation of Matthew's gentle fingers when he moved them between her legs. Rita started to object, wanted to tell him she was ready for him *now,* but he deftly parted the soft, damp pleats of her flesh, then buried his fingers amid them, and she found that she couldn't say anything at all.

Again and again, he steered his hand expertly over her, each time delving more deeply along the furrows of those gentle folds. Rita cried out at the rush of erotic pleasure that wound through her in response to his touch, then instinctively parted her legs wider to facilitate his exploration. As he drove his tongue into her mouth again, he pushed a finger inside her delicate chasm, and she arched her body against him in reply, an action that only drove his digit deeper still, down to its very base. When she lowered herself again, his finger exited her, but before she had a chance to react, he pushed it into her again, penetrating her as deeply as before.

Once more, she bucked against him, and Matthew answered her by inserting two fingers inside her, splaying them wide at her entry before instigating a gentle in-and-out movement that nearly drove her mad. Every time he entered, Rita pushed her body against his marauding fingers, until the heated friction of the movement nearly undid her.

"You're so small," he whispered against her neck as he fingered her. "So tight. You haven't done this sort of thing very often, have you, Rita?"

Nearly insensate now with wanting him, all she could manage in reply was a feeble shake of her head and a raggedly gasped, "No."

She saw him smile at her response, as if the knowledge of her inexperience made him feel better. Then he kissed her deeply again. And as he kissed her, he moved his hand to the inside of her thigh, flattening his palm over her fevered flesh, pushing to open her legs more. Rita complied on instinct, bending her leg and dropping her foot to the floor. Matthew pushed the other leg against the side of the couch, bending that knee, too, and rising up on his own knees between them. He reached behind himself for a pillow then lifted Rita's hips so that he could tuck it beneath her, bringing her body closer to his surging erection. Then, gripping her hips in both hands, he moved forward, pushing the plump head of his member into her damp, eager opening.

She tilted her head back as she felt him entering her, loving the sensation of his hard shaft slipping easily into her saturated entrance. When he moved forward again, he pulled her hips toward him, and more of him pushed inside her, filling her. She gasped at a pinch of slight pain as he stretched her wider, then exhaled on a sigh of pleasure when she felt his hand close gently over her breast.

"How do you like it, Rita?" he asked her. "Slow or fast? Hard or gentle?"

Somewhere in her frenetic brain, she managed to comprehend what he was asking her, but she had no idea how to reply. She didn't know how she liked it, having never done it before. She'd heard it could be painful for a woman the first time, and she was already feeling a bit of discomfort due to Matthew's size, even though he hadn't even entered her all the way yet. The thought of him doing this slowly and gently made her think the pain would last longer. So maybe fast and hard was the way to go. The pain would be over with more quickly and then she could enjoy herself.

"Fast," she said weakly. "Hard. I want it fast and hard," she told him.

He grinned at that, a devilish, knowing kind of grin. "That's the way I like it, too," he told her. "Though there's something to be said for slow and easy in the right circumstances."

Tonight, however, he must not have considered the circumstances right for that, because before Rita had a chance to respond, he gripped her hips fiercely again and buried himself completely in her tender, very inexperienced, flesh. But not before hesitating over one small barrier he had to break to get there.

Rita cried out at the intensity of the pain that knifed through her at his penetration, and tears sprang to her eyes. Never had she imagined it would be like that, a pain so intense it nearly paralyzed her. Matthew immediately seemed to realize what had happened, because he quickly withdrew from her and pulled her up to a sitting position, facing him. For one long moment, he didn't say a word, only gazed at Rita as if he were very, very angry about something. Then his expression softened, and he lifted a hand to her face. Very gently, he thumbed tears first from one cheek, and then the other.

He still sounded stern, however, when he said, "Tell me this isn't your first time."

Rita feared he would change his mind about making love to her now that he knew of her uninitiated status—well, *previously* uninitiated status, at any rate. She was afraid that if she told him this was her first time, he would stop and ask her to get dressed and leave. And in spite of her earlier discomfort and distress, leaving was the last thing she wanted to do. She'd had a taste of what it could be like between a man and a woman—between Matthew and herself—and she wanted to learn the rest of it. All of it. The worst of it was over now, she told herself. She hadn't been prepared for him before, but now that she knew what to expect, it would be better. She was sure of it.

Still breathing raggedly from the fierceness of his initial entry, she asked, "What...what makes you think I...haven't... done this before?"

"Rita," he began, his tone pleading.

And then he began to set her away from him.

"No," she objected breathlessly, looping her arms around his neck to stop him. "Please, Matthew, don't stop. I want this. I want you to make love to me."

"But—"

"Please," she said again, hoping she didn't sound as desperate as she was beginning to feel. "Ycs, it's my first time," she admitted. "But I don't want you to stop."

He studied her in silence for a moment longer, obviously torn over what he should do. Finally he said, "I don't want to hurt you."

She shook her head fiercely now. "You won't."

"I already have."

"The worst is over," she told him, certain that was true. "Just go slow this time. It'll be fine. Better than fine," she immediately corrected herself. "It'll be wonderful. Because you're wonderful. Please, Matthew," she pleaded one last time. "Make love to me."

He searched her face as if he were looking for the answer to some unanswerable question. Then, very slowly, he lifted his hand to her face again. Once more, he brushed away a tear, then he leaned forward and covered her mouth gently with his. As he kissed her, he moved her body toward his again, seating her in his lap, facing him. Then he looped her legs around his waist. She felt him at the heart of her womanhood, still hard and hot and ready for her. Once again he lifted her hips, then lowered her over his stiff shaft. But he went slowly this time, entering her with great care.

Rita gasped once at their first contact, but when she felt him tense, she relaxed her body and kissed him. "Keep going," she whispered against his mouth. "I'm all right."

"Are you sure?" he whispered back.

"Yes."

And she spoke the truth. Because never in her life had she felt more all right than she did in that moment.

Yes, there was still some discomfort, and yes, a little pain. But she was ready for it this time, and Matthew was holding her in a way that helped her better accommodate him. Little by little, he entered her more deeply, giving her time to adjust to him, time for her body to open more fully to receive him. By the time he was buried inside her again, as completely as he had been before, she felt full and happy and very aroused.

"Oh, that's better," she said as she circled one arm around his neck and the other around his shoulder. "So much better."

He, in turn, cupped his hands beneath her fanny, then lifted her slowly, withdrawing himself bit by bit. The slow friction of their bodies created a delicious heat, a heat that wound through Rita with an erotic sort of indolence. Again and again he moved their bodies that way, gradually accelerating the speed and the depth and the intensity. Soon, she forgot all about the initial pain she had experienced, because she was too busy feeling the exquisite pleasure of this new way of lovemaking.

A wild energy ignited in her midsection, spiraling outward into the rest of her body. And just when she thought it would circle into the cosmos, it shuddered and stuttered and halted, then exploded in a tumultuous commotion unlike anything she had ever felt before. Matthew's body went rigid at the same time hers did, and he spilled himself hotly inside her. For one long moment, they stilled, caught in each other's arms, and each other's climax. Then he slowly relaxed and fell backward against the sofa, pulling Rita down atop himself.

They lay entwined in silence for some moments, their bodies heated and slick with perspiration and their release. Rita pressed her cheek to Matthew's chest, loving the way he stroked his hands idly over her hair and the flesh of her back and shoulders. Beneath her ear, she could hear his heart pounding in a rapid, ragged rhythm that matched her own, and gently, she tented her hand over the place above it, as if wanting to protect it. She smiled when she realized how perfectly in sync the two of them were.

"Why didn't you tell me it was your first time?" she heard him say softly from above her.

She closed her eyes, not wanting to spoil this moment, but knowing he expected an answer. "Because I didn't think it would matter," she told him.

When he didn't reply to that, she lifted her head to look at him, and saw him gazing down at her in stunned disbelief. He stopped stroking her hair and fixed his gaze on hers. "You didn't think it would matter?" he echoed flatly.

Rita shook her head, then realized how what she had said might be misconstrued. She wanted to tell him it had mattered to *her,* of course, but that she hadn't thought it would be of any significance to *him.* She really hadn't thought it would make a difference to Matthew if this was her first time or her fourteenth.

He tilted his head back and expelled a soft sound of disappointment. "You didn't think it mattered," he echoed hollowly.

"No," she told him, still muzzy-headed and unable to articulate exactly what she wanted to say. "Not to you."

At that, his head snapped forward again, and he glared at her as if he couldn't believe what she had just said. "That's what kind of man you think I am?" he asked. "That something like this, with you, wouldn't matter to me?"

The vehemence in his voice surprised her. "Well, *did* it matter to you?" she asked, afraid to even hope.

He continued to study her with an expression she couldn't for the life of her identify. But instead of answering her question, he asked one of his own. "Do you actually have to ask me that?"

She eyed him curiously. "Well, I... Yes," she finally said. "I do."

He studied her in thoughtful silence for a long moment, then, very slowly, he began to nod. Somehow, Rita got the impression that he had drawn a conclusion of extreme importance, but she had no idea what that conclusion was.

"I see," was all he said.

"Matthew..." she began. But she honestly wasn't sure what she wanted to say to him.

Although, she thought further as she noted the way his eyes seemed to go hard and cold when he gazed back at her, maybe deep down she did know what she wanted to say to him. She was just afraid to say it. She didn't want to reveal that much of herself to him right now, not when she was feeling so vulnerable and so confused.

She still wasn't sure what had happened tonight, or why. She only knew she had experienced something she'd never experienced before, something profound and intimate and momentous and, yes, even life-changing. And she had shared it with a man for whom she had feelings, but they were feelings she wasn't able to identify or name. If she started trying to talk about this, she would make a mess of things, she knew. So she said nothing, only gazed back at him, hoping her uneasiness and bewilderment didn't show.

Hoping she was wrong about how he suddenly seemed to be growing more distant now than he had ever been before.

Matthew, however, seemed to know exactly what he was feeling and what he wanted to say, because he looked her squarely in the eye and told her, "I think you should go."

He might as well have thrown a glass of ice water in her face, so startled was Rita by the announcement. "But—" she began to object.

"Really, Rita," he continued as he disengaged himself

from her and stood, "I think it would probably be best if we called it a night." He didn't even bother to look for his briefs, only reached for his trousers and tugged them on, then switched all his focus on fastening them. "I guess we shouldn't have sent the driver off, after all. I can call you a cab, though."

By now Rita was so confused, she had no idea what to think. But she mimicked his movements as she spoke, rising from the couch to search for her dress, slipping it on over the garters and stockings she still wore, forsaking her bra and panties in her haste to simply get herself covered up.

"But…you said you would take me home," she said, knowing she sounded hurt and bewildered. But there was a good reason for that: She *was* hurt and bewildered. "Matthew, what are you talking about?" she continued. "What's going on?"

He crossed the living room to the foyer and picked up his shirt, shrugging it on, but leaving it unbuttoned. Not, however, before Rita got a look at the scars on the left side of his back. He was right—they were terrible. But she would have never, ever, found them repulsive. Because they were a part of Matthew. And he was beautiful to her. All of him.

When he spun around to look at her, he seemed to be suffering almost as much pain as she was herself. But how could that be possible, she wondered, when he was the one causing it?

"Get dressed," he said. "I'll call a cab." And then he spun on his heel and left her standing there alone.

More alone, in fact, than she had ever been in her life.

Rita had heard talk about the "wee, small hours of the morning," but she'd never really been a part of them before. Oh, she'd worked them for a while, when she'd been on third shift, but she'd always been so busy that she'd never had time to notice them. Certainly she'd never seen such hours from a social perspective. But as she gazed at the streets of Boston's North End from the back seat of her taxi, she realized that quite a few people were comfortable with this time of night. Plenty of bars and clubs were still going strong, and there were even a handful of people walking down the streets, presumably toward home. Or perhaps, she couldn't help thinking, toward a romantic, erotic tryst much like the one she had just enjoyed herself.

Until, of course, her lover had told her to leave.

Don't think about it, Rita, she told herself as she squeezed her eyes shut tight. *Just forget about what happened with Matthew.*

Heaven knew he'd probably already forgotten about it himself. He'd stayed wherever he'd gone until her cab arrived, then he'd returned to the living room long enough to show her the door. Literally. She still had no idea what she'd done wrong, but it must have been something terrible for him to have chilled toward her the way he had, so quickly and so completely. She'd hesitated at the front door before stepping through it, long enough to gaze up into his face one last time to see if she could understand what was going on inside his head. But he'd only looked back at her blankly, offering her not a single clue.

His shirt had still been hanging open, and, helpless to stop herself, Rita had lifted her hand toward his chest. Matthew had flinched and taken a step in retreat, then had offered her a crisp "Good night, Rita." She'd had no choice but to leave then. But she hadn't said a word in farewell.

She should just leave matters of sexual significance to the creatures of the night who knew how to handle them, she told herself now, gazing back out the window. It would be a long time before she ever ventured into something like that again.

When the cab pulled up in front of her brownstone, Rita reached for her purse to pay the driver. But he waved her off, assuring her his fee had been taken care of when the taxi was called. Then he drove off, leaving Rita standing on the curb, nonplussed. Matthew had paid for the cab that had taken her home after he'd thrown her out of his house, she reflected. She didn't know whether to be grateful or be even more offended. She settled on being even more confused.

All she wanted in that moment was to escape to her apartment and lock the door behind her—then maybe throw a few pieces of her heaviest furniture in front of it. Then she could cower like a wounded animal in the privacy of her home for the rest of the weekend and pretend she never had to go back to work again.

If she could just make it inside the brownstone without falling apart, she told herself, then she would be fine. The minute she cleared the front door, though, she intended to collapse into a quivering mass of self-doubt and self-recrimination.

Unfortunately, even that small consolation was going to have to wait, she realized once she was inside. Because there, in the receiving area of the brownstone—in the wee, small hours of the morning—sat her sister Maria and her cousin Emily. Maria was in her nightgown, a simple white cotton number, holding a cup of what was probably tea or cocoa. But Emily was still dressed in the same dress she had been wearing earlier at the party, a tailored, ivory-colored sheath. A matching jacket was slung over the arm of the chair where she sat. Her chin-length, dark-brown hair was pushed back from her face with a pearl-studded headband, and her brown eyes looked troubled. Her cup, Rita noted, sat neglected on the coffee table before her.

Immediately, alarm bells sounded in Rita's brain, and for a moment, anyway, she was able to put thoughts of Matthew Grayson and her colossal mistake out of her head. Something was obviously wrong. Both women wore expressions of concern, and they were both looking at Rita as if she had just interrupted a *very* serious conversation.

"What's wrong?" Rita demanded as she closed the door behind herself and strode quickly into the room. "What's happened?"

Maria quickly lifted a hand, palm out, in the halt position. "It's okay, Rita," she said quickly. "Everyone is fine."

Rita glanced at Emily, then back at her sister. "But…"

Emily expelled a soft sound of resignation. "I was out driving after the party, Rita, thinking about some things that have been bothering me, and I decided I needed to talk to someone. The brownstone was the closest Barone residence by then."

Plus, Rita knew, Emily and Maria had always been close.

"What's wrong?" she asked again as she covered the distance between herself and the other women, taking a seat on the opposite end of the sofa from Maria. "No one goes out driving in the middle of the night to think unless it's really, really important."

Emily sighed heavily, reached for the cup on the table before her, then changed her mind and leaned back into her chair again. "There's something going on at Baronessa," she said. "I can't put my finger on what, but something isn't right."

"What do you mean?" Rita asked.

But Emily only shook her head. "I probably shouldn't

have come here. I shouldn't have bothered you with this. It's silly. Just a feeling."

"What kind of feeling?"

"Just…" Emily gave much thought to whatever she was trying to say, then gave up. "I don't know," she said, sounding helpless. "There's just…*something*…going on at Baronessa. Derrick's been acting kind of strangely lately, and I think he knows something he's not telling me. I came over here to see if maybe Maria had heard anything."

Derrick, Emily's older brother, worked for Baronessa as the Vice President for Quality Assurance at the Brookline manufacturing plant. Emily was employed as his secretary. From all reports, the two made a good team, presumably because of their familiarity with each other and the rest of the Barones. Rita had never heard of there ever being a problem with either of them.

She turned to look at her sister, to see what Maria would say.

But Maria only shrugged. "I told Emily I can't think of anything. As far as I know, everything's business as usual. Well, as usual as it can be, considering recent events."

"Like I said," Emily muttered, "I shouldn't have bothered you. It's silly. Especially now that I try to put voice to it." She sighed heavily. "I shouldn't have come. I'm sorry to have woken you up, Maria."

Maria waved off her concern and enjoyed a generous sip from her mug. "Don't worry about it, Emily. I was awake anyway."

Emily eyed her cousin with much consideration. "I thought you seemed awfully awake when you answered the door in the middle of the night. What are *you* losing sleep over?"

Rita turned to look at her sister, too. "That reminds me. There's something I've been wanting to ask you."

Maria looked vaguely alarmed by the statement. "What?" she asked warily.

"You've been spending an awful lot of time away from home lately," Rita said. "Much more than you used to. And at night, too, when you always used to be home."

Now Maria looked *definitely* alarmed. "I, ah… I've, um… Well… It's just that…" She swallowed with some difficulty and darted her gaze away from Rita's.

This ought to be good, Rita thought. Maria was the worst liar on the planet. She could never look at someone straight on when she was about to tell a fib.

"There's just, um," Maria began again, "there's, ah…there's just been a lot of work lately. At the gelateria, I mean," she added hastily, "what with the botched launch of the passionfruit flavor and this new contest, I've been putting in a lot more hours than usual."

Rita nodded, not believing a word of it. "I think you've got a guy," she announced flatly.

Maria's olive complexion flushed. "I—I—I have no idea what you mean," her sister stammered.

Rita and Emily exchanged looks, then both began to laugh, something that surprised Rita. She wouldn't have thought she could manage such a thing after the evening she'd had. But maybe teasing her sister was what she needed to take her mind off her own troubles with Matthew.

"You do, don't you?" she charged Maria. "You have a guy you've been seeing. And you don't want the rest of us to know about it."

"No, it isn't that," Maria objected vehemently.

Too vehemently, Rita thought. "C'mon, Maria, you're the worst liar on the planet and you know it. What's his name?"

Her sister's gaze darted from Rita to Emily and back again. For a moment, she looked utterly miserable. Then, suddenly, she smiled. Instead of revealing the name of her guy, though, she only said, "He's really wonderful. You'd both like him."

"Then why don't you bring him around?" Emily asked. "We'd all love to meet him."

Now Maria's smile fell. "Oh, I can't. He's, um, shy," she finally finished. "Yeah, that's it. He's shy. And you know how overwhelming the Barones can be."

Boy, did Rita know that. She'd spent a good part of this evening wondering how she was going to make Matthew feel comfortable within the Barone fold.

Dammit, she thought. Was she *ever* going to be able to think about anything again without Matthew wandering into the equation?

"Shy, huh?" she said, not bothering to hide her doubt. "Something tells me there's a little more to it than that." She sighed. "But I won't press you for details. And I promise not to say a word to anyone else. Emily does, too," she added with a quick glance at her cousin for confirmation, a glance that Emily returned with an affirming nod. "I figure you'll bring him around when you're ready," Rita added. "Especially if he means enough to you that the mere mention of him makes you blush the way you do."

She smiled when her sister blushed again. But her smile fell when she heard Maria's question.

"So what about *your* guy?" her sister asked. "You and the yummy Dr. Grayson looked pretty chummy this evening." She turned a meaningful gaze to the clock on the mantel. "And it's awfully late for you to be getting in," she added. "And is that your bra I see peeking out of your purse?"

Panicked, Rita glanced down at her purse, only to find that it was perfectly fine.

"Gotcha!" Maria said with a laugh.

When Emily joined in, Rita had no choice but to chuckle, too.

"So you admit your bra is in your purse?" Maria asked, still laughing.

"I admit no such thing," Rita said. "It was just a reflex."

"Mmm-hmm," Maria murmured. "If you say so. I won't ask about any other reflexes you might have had tonight."

Good, Rita thought. Because her reflexes tonight were the last thing she wanted to think about. She dipped her head toward the cup her sister held. "Is there any more of whatever that is?" she asked, hoping it was cocoa, because as everyone knew, chocolate was the universal comfort food.

Maria glanced down into her mug. "Chianti? Sure. We're Italian, Rita, remember? There's always room for Chianti."

Rita laughed again, and somehow, in doing so, some of the tension in her body eased. Now if she could just do something about the tension in her mind, her spirit and her emotions, she'd be just fine. Chianti sounded like a very good idea. That, coupled with a long soak in the tub—and a weekend barricaded in her apartment with heavy furniture pushed against the door—sounded like just the thing she needed. Eventually, she knew, she'd have to start thinking about Monday morning and seeing Matthew Grayson again. But she'd think about that later, she promised herself.

Probably on Monday morning.

Seven

———

Monday morning, Matthew reflected morosely as he gazed out his office window at the hazy gray drizzle falling on the other side. A rainy Monday morning, at that. How appropriate, as the weather reflected his mood. Actually his feelings were much more turbulent than the patter of rain that softly pelted his window.

With a muttered oath, he turned his back on the rain and paced the entire length of his office. Then he spun around and paced back to the window again. He had promised himself that by Monday morning, he would have done one of two things: Either he would have written off what had happened with Rita Barone on Friday night as One of Those Things and then forgotten about it, or else he would have thought of some way to explain to her why he had behaved like such an ass, offered her an apology, and then forgotten about it.

Unfortunately his deadline was now upon him, and neither of those things had happened. There was no way Matthew could ever casually write off what had happened with Rita Barone, because he cared far too much about her. And his appalling behavior of Friday night defied explanation.

He had just been so stunned by her assessment of him, that he hadn't known how to react. She had honestly thought him an unfeeling enough cad not to even care that she—Rita Barone, the object of his secret admiration—had made him her first lover. Even after the explosive way the two of them had come together, she had thought him so devoid of emotion that he wouldn't consider what had happened important. She had thought him that heartless and uncaring.

Which meant that, in spite of her assertion to the contrary, she thought him a beast. Just like everyone else at Boston General. She hadn't thought he was capable of caring for another human being, when in fact what he felt for her was—

He didn't want to think about that now, hadn't allowed himself to think about it. Not long enough to understand what it meant, at any rate. All he'd been able to think about for the entire weekend, all he'd been able to hear in his head, again and again, was the question she'd asked him.

Well, did *it matter to you?*

She hadn't been able to tell, he thought now. Even after what the two of them had done, what the two of them had shared, she hadn't been able to sense how he felt about her. She hadn't realized he—

Maybe he really was a beast, after all, Matthew thought, interrupting his own thoughts before they could get carried away and venture into territory he'd just as soon not visit right now. He must be a beast, because why else would he have reacted the way he had that night? Only a beast would have behaved in such a way.

He shouldn't have told her to leave, and he shouldn't have called a cab to make her leaving easier. His stomach still clenched into a cold fist at the memory of how he had done that. Never in his life had he behaved like such a heel toward a woman. But he hadn't been thinking. He had acted out of anger and fear. He'd been angry that Rita had been so ready to believe him heartless, and he'd been afraid of what he might say—or, worse, what he might reveal—if he had allowed her to stay. And now…

He expelled another frustrated growl and drove both hands into his hair, then went back to pacing like a caged animal. Now Rita probably wouldn't let him come near her to explain, he thought, even if he had any idea what to say. And, frankly, he couldn't blame her.

He halted by the window again, gazing down into the dreary street below. From his office, he could see the employee entrance to the hospital, and he was watching, as he often did on rainy days, for the arrival of a bright yellow umbrella. Under that bright yellow umbrella would be Rita Barone, he knew. Everyone else favored black umbrellas, more suitable to the mood of the weather. Not Rita. Hers suited her own sunny nature. Within moments of beginning his search, Matthew found his quarry. Six fifty-five, he noted when he glanced down at his watch. As reliable as a finely tuned clock was Rita Barone.

He wished he could say the same about his emotions.

Either write off what happened, Grayson, or explain your behavior and apologize, he told himself again. *Which is it going to be?*

One way or another, he needed to send a signal to Rita Barone. He had to let her know where the two of them stood. He just wished he knew exactly where that was.

They worked together, he reminded himself. They would inevitably be seeing each other, regularly at that. How were they supposed to be comfortable doing that after what had happened Friday night?

They wouldn't be comfortable, he answered himself immediately, not unless they came to terms with it. But just what, he wondered, were those terms going to be?

Rita felt edgy and hyperaware of her surroundings as she took her seat at the nurses' station in CCU Monday morning. She felt dizzy and disoriented from a lack of sleep—a quick calculation told her she'd managed to achieve roughly six nanoseconds of shut-eye this weekend—and her head was pounding.

It had only been once she was safely ensconced in her own bed Friday night—or, rather, Saturday morning—with the covers pulled up to her chin, that she had realized something very, very important: She and Matthew had neglected to use any sort of birth control when they'd made love. They'd both been so carried away by what was happening—so stunned and unprepared—that neither had given a second thought to what should have been their primary concern.

Some health professional she was, Rita thought. Some fast figuring had reassured her—sort of—that the timing was all wrong for her to have gotten pregnant, but she was shaken by her carelessness. Yes, it had been her first time, but that wasn't any excuse for not taking precautions. Mother Nature didn't care how many times you copulated before conceiving, only that all the biological mechanics were intact and running on schedule.

Fortunately, Rita's biological mechanics ran like clockwork, which meant she wasn't in danger of getting pregnant. Unfortunately, though, her emotional mechanics weren't nearly so reliable. Which meant she was in danger of being hurt.

She told herself to forget about what had happened Friday night and put it down to one of those stupid mistakes all women are entitled to make once in their lives. Once, she repeated emphatically to herself. She had learned something in making that mistake, and she would use that knowledge in the future to make sure she didn't make other mistakes like it. She would guard her heart more carefully, and she would not fall so easily into a situation like that again. Especially not with a man like Matthew Grayson, who could, quite literally, be making love to a woman one minute and calling a cab for her the next.

Now, her head was really throbbing, and her stomach was upset, too, because her breakfast had consisted of nothing more than two cups of coffee and three buffered aspirins. Maybe when the dietary aides brought up breakfast for the patients, they'd have an extra tray.

"Rita."

At the sound of Matthew's voice uttering her name so quietly, she went liquid all over. She really wasn't ready to see him yet. She wouldn't be ready for at least another century or two. Or ten.

With much reluctance, she turned in her chair to face him, and remembering what had happened the last time she'd done that, she stood up before her thoughts could get carried away. Then she realized that, thanks to Friday night, her thoughts about Matthew Grayson were going to include sexually explicit images for some time now. She wondered how long it would be before they started to fade.

Then she gazed up into his dreamy green eyes, noted the fine chestnut hair she had twined so lovingly in her fingers, saw the scars on his face that she had touched with such care, and she knew there would never be a day when she didn't think about him with a heavy heart and wonder what might have been. He was dressed in another one of his dark, sexy power suits, but had forsaken his white doctor jacket today. All in all, he looked wonderful and irresistible and she wanted very much to kiss him.

Instead, she mustered a professional voice and replied, "Yes, Dr. Grayson?"

He flinched a little at her use of the formal title, but recovered quickly. "Do you have a moment?" he asked, clearly finding it as difficult as she to remain businesslike.

She scrambled for excuses. "Actually," she said, "I'm pretty strapped for time. It's always this way after the weekend. I have a lot of catching up to do."

"It will only take a moment," he told her.

She bit her lip to keep herself from retorting with something like, *Oh, you mean like Friday night did?* That would only serve to make them both even more uncomfortable than they already were. And it would let Matthew know how much she was still hurting. The last thing she wanted was for him to think she cared about him as much as she did. Especially when he didn't return the feeling.

"Really, I'm just swamped," she told him dispassionately. "Maybe another time."

He glanced down at the place where she had been sitting—the totally tidy, uncluttered place where she had been sitting. The place where nothing seemed even to be happening, let alone swamping her. Likewise incriminating was the fact that her mail slot only had what appeared to be one memo inside it.

Damn. Of all the weekends for the CCU to be uneventful, she thought.

She blew out a halfhearted sigh. "All right," she conceded without looking at him, pretending to smooth out a nonexistent wrinkle on the shirt of her blue scrubs. "You may have a moment."

"Thank you," he replied. But she could tell it was taking a lot for him to remain unaffected.

She hadn't really thought he would tell her whatever he wanted to tell her there at the nurses' station—shift changes meant twice as many people as usual milling about—but Rita still flinched when Matthew's arm skimmed her shoulder as he gestured her forward. Even that small physical contact with him made her feel as if he'd struck a spark against her.

Obediently, however, she made her way forward, pausing only long enough to let him catch up since he was the one who knew where they were going. He ducked his head into the CCU waiting room as they passed it, but there were two people in there sleeping, so he continued on his way, as did Rita. Finally, he tugged on the door to a supply closet and, ever the gentleman, stood aside for her to enter first. She shook her head as she did, flicking on the light switch as she went. Matthew followed, letting the door swing closed behind him. Then it was just the two of them. And a couple hundred rolls of gauze and toilet paper.

What a romantic interlude this was going to be, she thought wryly. Then again, considering the way she felt, gauze and toilet paper might both come in handy.

She lifted her wrist and eyed her watch meaningfully. "Your moment begins now," she said coolly.

"Rita," Matthew began.

But in spite of his assurance that he wouldn't waste her time, he said nothing more after that. When she glanced up from her watch, she saw him gazing at her with what looked like a mixture of anguish and longing, and the coldness toward him she had nurtured all weekend suddenly began to thaw. She told herself not to warm to him, to remember the way he had acted Friday and not focus on his reaction to her now. If he was anguished, it was probably only because he feared she was going to make his working life difficult. And if he was longing for something, it was doubtless for things to go back to the way they were a week ago. Before they had made such a colossal blunder.

Finally, though, he said, in a rush of words so fast she missed most of them, "I'm sorry about the way I acted Friday night."

She arched her brows in both surprise and query. "What?" she said. "You're what?"

He expelled an impatient breath, but his eyes never left hers as he repeated, more clearly, "I'm sorry. About the way I acted. Friday night," he concluded uneasily.

She really hadn't expected him to apologize. She had expected him to offer up some lame excuse, and then tell her they should both just try and forget about it and pretend nothing had happened. An apology, though...

Maybe, she thought, there was hope for him, for *them,* yet.

"But I think we probably should both just try and forget about it and pretend nothing happened," he added.

Her heart sank. So much for hope. So much for him. So much for *them.*

It really hadn't meant anything to him, she realized. After the way he had been acting this morning, she had begun to think maybe she had been wrong about what had happened Friday night, and that he wasn't like most men. She had thought that maybe it really had meant something to him, the fact that he had been her first. But now he wanted to brush it off and pretend it had never happened.

Obviously it *hadn't* mattered. Not to him.

"Fine," she said shortly. Even though *fine* was the last thing she was feeling. "Is that it?" She glanced down at her watch again. "Wow, it really did just take a moment. You're good, Dr. Grayson."

Immediately she wished she hadn't uttered that last sarcastic sentiment. One sarcastic sentiment would have been plenty, but no, she'd had to push too hard. That was Rita. Just like a Barone, always overdoing it.

"Now, if you'll excuse me," she said miserably.

Damn, she felt the sting of tears welling in her eyes. The last thing she needed was for Matthew Grayson to see her crying. So she spun quickly around and headed for the door. She realized too late that he stood between her and it, and as she tried to push him aside so that she could make her escape, he snaked out his hand and circled loose fingers around her wrist, effectively stopping her in her place.

"Rita," he said again.

"What?" she replied tersely without turning around.

"I really am sorry."

She jerked her wrist free and reached for the door and pulled it open. But he flattened his hand against it and pushed it closed again. She was afraid to turn around, afraid to look at him, because she feared she would start crying if she did. So she only stood still, gazing at the closed door, mentally willing him to move his hand so she could make her escape.

Instead, he moved closer to her, coming to a halt immediately behind her, close enough that she could smell the fresh, clean scent of him and feel the heat of his body mingling with her own. His breath stirred her hair, and if she closed her eyes, she fancied she could detect the beating of his heart in sync with her own.

"Do you accept my apology?" he asked softly.

She nodded slowly, trying to keep herself on kilter, but the world still felt as if it were spinning out of control beneath her feet. "Yes," she told him. "I accept your apology." And she did. Even if she couldn't accept much else.

He still had his hand pressed against the door, but she thought she saw his fingers relax some.

"Then you agree we should just forget about Friday night and pretend it never happened?" he asked her.

She nodded again, even though she knew she was lying when she agreed with him. So she continued to keep her back to him when she replied, "Yes, we should just forget about it. We're both adults, and we can be mature about this. It was one of those things. Too much champagne, too much partying. We got a little carried away. It could have happened to anyone."

Except that it hadn't happened to anyone, she thought further. It had happened to her. And things like that didn't happen to Rita Barone. Not unless there was a good reason for it. And not without repercussions. Now if she could only figure out what that good reason was, and what those repercussions might be. Then maybe she could start to make some sense of it all. And maybe she could move on with her life.

And maybe, she thought further, while she was sleeping tonight, leprechauns would come into her room and dance the merengue by the light of the moon.

"Excuse me," she said again. "But I have to go to work."

For a moment, she didn't think Matthew was going to move his hand. And for that same moment, she thought he was going to move his body closer to hers. She tensed as she waited to see what he would do, then was almost disappointed when he removed his hand from the door to let her leave. Deep down, she had been hoping he would touch her, she realized. But then, why would he do that, when all he wanted was to forget about her?

Without another word, Rita reached for the door and tugged it open. Somehow, she managed to keep her composure as she strode through it and back to the nurses' station. She maintained that composure as she collected patient files and studied their requirements for the day. In fact, once Matthew left the area, she was able to focus entirely on her work and complete her job in the same fashion she always did, caring for her patients.

It never ceased to amaze her, she thought as she treated the people in CCU that day, what the human heart was capable of surviving.

She had agreed with him.

Matthew retreated to his office at the end of his morning rounds, slumped into the chair behind his desk, spun it around to gaze out at the rain and felt more empty than he'd ever felt in his life. After seeing more than two dozen patients, some of them in critical condition, all he could think about was Rita Barone, and how she had gazed at him so coolly, then turned her back on him and agreed that they should just forget about what had happened Friday night.

But, then, what the hell had he expected? he demanded of himself. How else would a woman react to a man who had almost literally thrown her out of his house after making love to her, without explanation, without so much as a fare-thee-well? Matthew was lucky she was speaking to him at all. Had he thought she would fall to her knees and beg him to give their relationship a second chance? They didn't even have a relationship to give a second chance to, because he'd ruined the chance for one to start.

He leaned his head back against his chair. Oh, who was he kidding? A relationship? Between beautiful, bubbly Rita Barone and the Beast of Boston General? Yeah, right.

And now she wasn't even wearing the pin or bracelet

he'd given her. He couldn't even enjoy his private thrill of that secret closeness to her anymore.

He wished he knew why she'd ended what had been a tradition for months now. She'd liked the gifts. He knew that. So why had she stopped wearing them? And how could he find an answer when he dared not ask her himself, or risk revealing his identity as the giver?

Now more than ever before, such a discovery would prove disastrous. It was bad enough being Matthew Grayson, MD, the Beast of Boston General. If anyone found out he was Rita Barone's secret admirer, he'd become Matthew Grayson, MD, the laughingstock of Boston General. He'd been a laughingstock before. He hadn't liked it, and didn't want to be one again.

Forget about it, he told himself. Forget about all of it. Forget about Rita Barone. Forget that you ever left her a gift. Forget you ever had a crush on her at all.

If only it were that easy. But something told him he'd never be able to banish her from his thoughts completely. Because in making love to her, he had allowed her to become a part of himself. And he was beginning to suspect that it was a part, like his heart, that he wouldn't be able to live without.

In the two weeks that followed her official breakup with Matthew—even though, deep down, she had to acknowledge that one couldn't break up a relationship one never had to begin with—Rita did everything she could to avoid seeing him. She switched shifts with other nurses, gladly taking on the graveyard shift she had once been so grateful to leave behind. She traded off units with other nurses in an effort to remove herself from CCU, but that only landed her in spots she didn't much care to visit—like neonatal, surrounded by babies, and the all-too-real reminder of what could be waiting for her in her near future, thanks to her carelessness. Fortunately, barely a week passed before she discovered there was no danger of her being pregnant. Strangely, though, when her period did arrive, she experienced an odd sort of melancholy about it.

She told herself she was crazy to be disappointed she hadn't gotten pregnant from her one-night stand with the beastly Dr. Matthew Grayson. But for some reason, the thought of having his child wasn't nearly as off-putting as she might have thought it would be. Of course, it would have helped enormously if Matthew was around to share in the blessed event, she would then remind herself brutally. That wasn't likely, since he'd grown tired of her within moments of making love to her.

No, she was better off free of Matthew Grayson, she assured herself.

After two weeks of avoiding him, however, Rita had no choice but to accept the fact that she was only putting off the inevitable. Short of a permanent transfer to another unit, or another hospital, she wasn't going to be able to escape Matthew. She would simply have to make the best of working alongside him, in spite of what had happened. After all, what had happened *wasn't* going to happen again, she vowed steadfastly.

She would just have to face the fact that she had given herself—her heart—to a man who couldn't possibly appreciate what it meant to have it, and then she would have to move on with her life. And she would just have to be more careful the next time she fell in love.

Oh, dear, she thought when that realization sprang into her head one very snowy morning in late April. Was that really what had happened? she wondered. Was that what was at the root of all of this? Had she honestly fallen in love with the beastly Dr. Grayson?

She thought about that for a moment as she stood in the hospital cafeteria, sipping a cup of mid-morning coffee and watching a thick curtain of snow through the windows. She had barely managed to make it to work before the storm had become nearly impenetrable. The weather forecasters said the late-season nor'easter was only going to get worse before it got better. But, then, that was spring in New England. Mild and sunny one day, blustery and stormy the next. And always unpredictable.

Much like Matthew Grayson, she couldn't help thinking. *Had* she fallen in love with him?

As Rita sipped her coffee and stared out at the snow, she began to think that maybe, just maybe, she had.

She was in love with Matthew Grayson. She had given her heart to a man who didn't want it. A beast, she told herself. Everyone at the hospital had always said so.

Immediately, though, she took exception to her own assertion. Deep down, she knew Matthew wasn't a beast at all. She never would have fallen in love with him if he had been. During that one evening the two of them had spent together, he hadn't been beastly in any way. No, he'd been quite charming. Kind, attentive, passionate. Until the end anyway. So why had he reverted to his old beastly self then?

Rita turned her back on the weather that so reminded her of Matthew Grayson and decided not to think about it. Not to think about him or about what had happened. She needed to forget about it, move on. She only wished she knew where she would end up.

When she returned to the nurses' station, it was with a feeling of foreboding. She didn't know if it was due to the ferocious weather raging outside, or the tumultuous emotions roaring inside her. But when she glanced into her mail slot, as she habitually did when she'd been away from the nurses' station for any length of time, the feeling only multiplied. Because there, tied with a gold ribbon, lay, not a white package this time, but a perfect, apricot-colored sweetheart rose.

Rita's first instinct was to glance around the unit, to see if there were any dark, shadowy figures lurking about. Naturally, though, she saw no one. In fact, the unit was surprisingly deserted, something that only made her feel more apprehensive. Some of the nurses had taken an early lunch, she knew, and the others were doubtless checking on patients or conferring with doctors. Some hadn't made it in at all, thanks to the weather. But in that moment, as Rita gazed down at the rose, she'd never felt more alone in her life.

Reluctantly, she reached for the flower, pulling it out of her mail slot and holding it up to her nose. Closing her eyes, she inhaled deeply of its tangy fragrance, an almost narcotic scent that evoked too many pleasurable sensations for her to handle in her emotionally fragile state. So she opened her eyes again, lowering the rose some, tracing the perfect, silky petals one by one.

Because of the gold ribbon tied around the stem, she knew the rose was from her secret admirer. Or perhaps her stalker. She honestly didn't know for sure. But why today? she wondered. And why a rose? It wasn't something he could wrap in his traditional white paper. And it certainly wasn't a special occasion of any kind.

Well, not to her secret admirer, at any rate, Rita thought. Though it was the two-week anniversary of the night she had made love with Matthew. Not that she was counting or anything, and not that she was commemorating it.

She lifted a trembling hand to her forehead, rubbing at a headache that seemed to erupt out of nowhere. This was crazy, she told herself. She had to find out who was doing this. She wasn't going to be able to relax until she did. As much as she tried to reassure herself that there was nothing nefarious behind the gifts, she couldn't quite convince herself of their harmlessness. Until she knew the truth, she wasn't going to feel safe or content at work anymore.

She had to laugh derisively at that. It wasn't just her secret admirer preventing her from enjoying her work anymore. It was the presence of Matthew Grayson, too.

Expelling a soft sound of frustration, Rita set the rose down on the nurses' station and tried not to think about her admirer *or* Matthew. Somehow, though, she knew it was going to be a long time before either of them stopped being a concern.

Eight

By the time Rita's shift ended at three o'clock, the storm had picked up enough speed and strength that a weather advisory was in full effect. No one was supposed to attempt travel unless it was a medical emergency. But Rita didn't want to remain at the hospital when her friendly neighborhood stalker might be lurking about.

He's not a stalker, she tried to tell herself again as she pushed open the door to the changing room and made her way to her locker.

She gazed at the sweetheart rose again, then placed it gingerly on the bench. It was truly spectacular, a perfect blossom in every sense of the word, more beautiful than anything the human hand could ever hope to manufacture. And somehow, it was made even more poignant by the presence of the storm outside. It was a breath of spring, an image of hopefulness and renewal, in the midst of an icy, bitter tempest. For that reason, if no other, she wanted to take good care of it.

And hey, even if the bearer of the rose didn't realize it, it had arrived on a special day. Special to Rita, anyway. Even if Matthew had probably forgotten all about it by now.

Two weeks, she marveled as she tugged her scrubs shirt over her head and stuffed it into the duffel bag. Had it really only been that long? In many ways, it seemed as if she'd lived a lifetime since making love with Matthew. And in many ways, she felt like a completely different person. But it had only been two weeks. Two weeks of trying to avoid him when she could, and pretending everything was fine when she couldn't. Two weeks of seeing those dreamy green eyes, and smelling that spicy fragrance he wore, and occasionally—accidentally, of course—brushing up against him in the close confines of the nurses' station or one of the crowded rooms. Two weeks of remembering the ways he had touched her and kissed her and filled her. Two weeks of feeling lonelier and more empty than she'd ever felt in her life. But her stalker/admirer couldn't know that, she told herself, pushing her melancholy ruminations away.

Who could it be? she wondered again. Thanks to the weather, the hospital was fairly deserted today. There had been few visitors, and staff was short. Had she not just worked a double shift herself, she would have been drafted into staying for another one. But she was exhausted as it was, and would probably do more harm than good. It would be better if she went home. Not only to rest, but to put some distance between herself and whoever had left the rose for her.

Quickly, she finished changing out of the scrubs she'd been wearing for nearly eighteen hours, and reached for the heavy clothes that would keep her warm as she struggled to walk home through weather better suited to polar bears. Then she gathered up her duffel bag, leaving the rose sitting on the bench.

She should leave it for someone else to find, she thought. Someone who would appreciate it for its simple beauty and not consider it a symbol of something potentially sinister. Besides, it would probably never survive the storm outside.

She took a step away, then immediately changed her mind. She didn't know why, but she wanted to keep the rose with her. So she picked it up again and tucked it carefully inside her shearling jacket, patting the thick fabric gently as she strode toward the locker-room door.

She had exited the hospital through the employee entrance and was wrestling with her mittens when a tall, solid body came to a halt beside hers. She glanced up, squinting against the cold wind that whipped snow up even under the protective awning, only to find Matthew Grayson gazing down at her.

He was dressed for the elements, too, only much more fashionably than she. His camel-colored overcoat was obviously cashmere, as was the Stewart tartan scarf folded neatly around his neck and tucked tidily into his lapels. His brown leather gloves looked butter-soft and smooth, and, somehow, he even made a brown, cuffed knit cap look elegant. Try as she might, Rita couldn't take her eyes off him. Funnily enough, he didn't seem to be able to take his eyes off her, either.

For one long moment, they only stood there, gazing at each other in silence, neither moving so much as an inch, as if they'd been frozen in place by the elements. Snow swirled up around them from the sidewalk below, spiraling and sparkling around them like fine, enchanted fairy dust. Finally, though, Matthew spoke, breaking the spell, making

Rita feel as if she had tumbled into a dream and back out again, more disoriented than before.

"You're not planning to walk home in this," he said.

She shrugged uneasily as she squinted at the flying snow. "I don't have much choice."

"It's fifteen blocks," he pointed out unnecessarily.

Rita opened her mouth to tell him she'd be fine, then stopped, eyeing him narrowly. "How do you know it's fifteen blocks to my house?" she asked. "You don't know where I live."

He reared his head back at that, looking uncomfortable. But his reply was utterly innocent, and his tone of voice bland. "I have the addresses and phone numbers of everyone in CCU," he told her. "Just in case."

In case of what? she wanted to ask. Then she told herself she was being overly suspicious. It made perfect sense that Matthew would want to be able to contact anyone in the unit about a patient or some other hospital matter. This whole stalker/admirer business had her jumping at shadows.

"I'm sorry," she apologized. "I'm just a little edgy. The weather," she said lamely.

He nodded. "All the more reason for you not to try and make it home," he told her.

"Well, I can't stay here all night," she said, nodding toward the hospital behind her.

"Why not?" he asked. "There's food, coffee, beds, heat, TV," he concluded the list with a smile, "everything you need to battle the inclement weather."

"Oh, sure," she agreed wryly. "Cafeteria food, bad coffee, hospital beds and no premium channels. And the heat can be iffy," she added. "Plus, I might run into someone I don't want to run into."

His expression and posture changed drastically at her

comment, going from uneasy armistice to vague hostility. "No, you won't," he told her flatly. "In case you've forgotten, it's only a couple of blocks to my house. I'm going home. You'll be perfectly fine here."

Only then did Rita realize that Matthew thought she was talking about him. "No, I didn't mean that," she hastily corrected herself. She even went so far as to extend her hand toward him, cupping her mittened hand lightly over his forearm to reassure him. "I wasn't talking about you, Matthew. I was talking about my stalker."

Then she squeezed her eyes shut tight at what she'd revealed and how she must have sounded. She hoped he didn't think her a paranoid psychotic harboring delusions of persecution.

"Stalker?" he echoed incredulously. "What are you talking about?"

"Well, he may not be a stalker," she quickly backpedaled. "I don't know what he is. But he makes me... uncomfortable. And I don't want to risk running into him on a dark and stormy afternoon when the hospital is deserted and no one will be around to hear my impotent cries for help."

He gazed at her without comprehension. "I'm sorry, but I still have no idea what you're talking about."

Rita blew out a long, impatient breath, and told him, with profound understatement, "It's a long story."

He gazed back at her for some time without speaking, as if he were weighing a matter of grave consequence. Then, softly, and not a little uncertainly, he said, "Why don't you come to my place instead of going home?"

Rita's eyebrows shot up to the edge of her beret in surprise. "I—I—I—" she stammered. "I—I'm not sure that's such a good idea. Thanks, anyway."

He expelled a frustrated sound. "Look, I'm not expecting anything to happen, okay? I just meant it's closer than your place, and if you're not comfortable staying here at the hospital, it might be a better alternative. And then I wouldn't sit around worrying about whether you made it home in this storm.''

''Thanks,'' Rita said again, ''but I don't think—''

''Rita,'' he interjected, his tone of voice mild, but firm. ''Nothing will happen. I promise. I'm suggesting this as one friend to another. I hope we are, at least, still that.''

She said nothing in response to that, not sure she trusted her voice not to conceal her true feelings. Friends with Matthew Grayson? After what the two of them had shared? She'd never done that with any of her other friends, and something told her she wasn't likely to. He was much more to her than a friend, she knew. But there was no reason she had to reveal that to him.

''I have an extra bedroom,'' he continued in that same innocuous, matter-of-fact voice, ''and if you want to barricade yourself inside it and pretend I don't exist, that's fine. I'll slip you some lettuce leaves under the door so you won't starve,'' he added with a tentative smile.

It wasn't a good idea, Rita thought. It really, really wasn't a good idea. There were reports that the storm was only going to get worse, which meant she could be stranded at Matthew's place for a lot longer than just tonight. But when she turned her gaze again to the churning snow, she saw that it was nearly opaque past the steps leading down to the sidewalk.

Still, could she accept his suggestion? Being alone with Matthew, feeling the way she did about him, she would doubtless say or do something she shouldn't. And then she'd feel even worse than she already did.

''Besides,'' he added, his voice turning serious again, ''I want to hear about this stalker of yours.''

"Well, he may not be a stalker," she said. "He may just be a secret admirer."

Matthew's expression went completely slack at that, and his lips parted slightly, as if he wanted to say something, but didn't know what. "Secret admirer?" he finally echoed, his voice sounding hollow and cold.

"That's what most of the nurses think he is," Rita told him. "I mean, you've probably heard the rumors, right? They've been going around since Valentine's Day."

"Valentine's Day?" he echoed again, still sounding a little stunned.

Rita nodded. "That's when the first anonymous gift showed up in my mail slot at the nurses' station in CCU. That little bandaged heart pin I used to wear on my scrubs all the time. Maybe you noticed it?"

"Bandaged heart pin?" Matthew repeated like a parrot, his expression still devoid of any identifiable emotion.

She nodded again, more slowly this time, thinking his reaction was kind of odd. "Yeah," she said. "And then he left me another anonymous gift on my birthday. A charm bracelet that I also used to wear until recently."

"Charm bracelet?"

"Uh-huh. And then, a few weeks ago, on the anniversary of the day I started working at the hospital, he left me a third anonymous gift. A crystal heart paperweight."

"Crystal heart paperweight?"

"Yeah," Rita said. Matthew really was acting weird, repeating everything she said like a wind-up toy. "It was really beautiful, but it was much more expensive than the first gifts. And it made me feel kind of…creepy."

"Creepy?"

"Uh-huh. And then today, just a couple of hours ago, in fact, he left me a rose. At least, I think it was him who left it. But today isn't a special occasion. Well, not to my stalker, anyway,'' she quickly corrected herself before she could stop herself.

But not before Matthew caught her implication. Because suddenly, he was completely tuned into what she was saying, his eyes fixed on hers, his mouth set in a firm, tight line. He, too, realized the significance of the date. He was thinking about two Fridays ago, just as she was.

''Come home with me, Rita,'' he said again, with more conviction this time.

''Matthew, I'm not sure it's—''

''Come home with me.''

And there was something in his voice when he said it that time that made her reconsider. Maybe she should go home with him, she thought. Maybe now that they'd put a little distance between themselves and that night, they could talk about what had happened more reasonably, find some closure, and then go back to living their separate lives.

Or maybe she would just barricade herself in his spare room and let him slip lettuce leaves under the door until the weather cleared and she could go home.

''All right,'' Rita finally conceded.

A *stalker?*

The word circled in Matthew's brain the whole time he and Rita fought the elements to make it home. And because the fierce weather meant they had no opportunity to talk, the word went deeper into his psyche with every new rotation. It continued to tumble through his thoughts as, side-by-side, they put together an impromptu dinner. The word distracted him even as they ate their meal together. In fact, his attention was diverted from the word only once, when the power went out and he had to go in search of candles.

Eating by candlelight did finally manage to budge Matthew's thoughts from the stalker business, but not in a way that was necessarily good—for either of them, because eating by candlelight roused all sorts of romantic implications that he was sure Rita was no more comfortable considering than he was. Nevertheless, he was helpless *not* to think in romantic terms after that. And not just because of the candlelit ambiance, either, but because Rita just looked so beautiful and so warm and so sexy, and she was here in his house again, effectively stranded for the whole night. When Matthew began to think about that, he could think of little other than what it would be like to make love to her again.

He would do it better this time, he promised himself. He would take more time with her, more care with her, and he would make sure her needs were met. Not that she had seemed dissatisfied last time—on the contrary, her climax had been as shudderingly complete as his own. But it could have been even better for her, he knew. And he certainly wouldn't end it this time by throwing her out of his house and sending her home alone. No, if they made love again, after it was over, he would pull her close and wrap her in his arms and murmur soft words and—

And never let her go.

It hit Matthew then, as he gazed at her across the candlelit table in his poshly decorated, but normally very empty-feeling dining room, that he really didn't want Rita ever to leave. They had spent the afternoon doing the mundane, everyday sort of things that couples do together—chatting, cooking, eating dinner—and even with the awkwardness that had arced between them, he'd enjoyed the experience more than he'd enjoyed anything for a very long time. Well, except for making love to Rita. But having spent the afternoon here in his home with her, he realized now just how solitary, how lonely, his life was without someone to share it.

And he realized, too, that the only person he would consider sharing it with was Rita Barone. Something about her just made him feel…better. Better about himself, better about his life, better about everything. Even though he'd botched things between them, he still felt better when he was with her. All he could do now, he thought, was to try to…un-botch things. He very much wanted to give whatever had been generated between the two of them two weeks ago—and maybe even before then—another chance.

But after dinner, with the power still out, when they were comfortably ensconced in front of a roaring fire sipping instant coffee spiked with good Irish whiskey—thank goodness the gas stove still worked so they could at least boil water—the word *stalker* rose up to taunt Matthew again. All this time, Rita had been thinking there was something sinister, perhaps even dangerous, behind those gifts for her.

What was she going to say and do when she found out the truth? How would she feel about Matthew then? Not that she necessarily harbored such great intentions toward him at the moment, he couldn't help thinking. But how was he supposed to tell her now that he had been the one who'd been leaving the gifts? Would she cast an even more distrustful eye on him? Worse yet, would she start thinking him sinister, perhaps even dangerous, too?

But then, could he blame her for thinking what she had? he asked himself. A beautiful single woman living alone in the big, bad city couldn't be too careful. He should have realized how she might misconstrue gifts from an anonymous admirer. Had he for a moment suspected she felt threatened by them, he would have identified himself a long time ago, and explained his actions.

Well, he would have done that if he *could* have explained his actions. He still wasn't entirely clear on all that.

Oh, the hell you're not, he chastised himself as he gazed

into the dancing, crackling flames and tried to think of something to say to Rita that would end the cumbersome silence lumbering between them. He was, too, clear on all that, he told himself further. Over the past two weeks, everything had become crystal-clear to him. He'd been leaving the gifts for her because he had a thing for Rita Barone—a major thing—and he'd been too scared to tell her. He'd been scared of being rebuffed by her if she ever found out. Scared of how humiliated he would feel when she rejected his attentions. She was Beauty, and he was the Beast. He'd been certain there was no way a woman like her would want anything to do with a man like him.

But she didn't rebuff you, he reminded himself. *She came home with you, and she made love with you. You. And no one else.*

He still wasn't sure why she had chosen him to be her first lover. He would have thought she would save that honor for someone special, someone who meant something to her. Someone with whom she intended to share her life. The way he'd often found himself wishing he could share his life with her.

His gaze shifted to the left then, to where they had placed their boots, side by side, on the hearth to dry. Near that were a couple of ladder-back chairs he'd pulled from the kitchen earlier for them to drape their coats over, likewise drying in the fire's heat. He'd changed his clothes when they'd arrived home, and was now dressed much as Rita was, in blue jeans and a heavy, whiskey-colored sweater. They sat on the floor in their stocking feet—side by side, but not too close—their backs propped against the leather sofa upon which they had made love two weeks before.

Neither had mentioned that, but Matthew was sure they'd both thought about it since entering the room and taking their current positions. That night had been full of passion and hunger and need. This evening, in the same place, with the same person, all he felt was comfort and coziness and camaraderie.

Interesting, not just that he and Rita could experience such divergent events and emotions in identical surroundings, but that he did indeed seem to be sharing his life with her right now. And she was sharing hers with him. And it felt very, very good.

"So tell me more about this stalker," he said, feeling more able to discuss that now than he had before, because he'd had time to deal with his surprise and didn't feel quite so flummoxed anymore.

And he did want to talk about it. He needed Rita to realize that there had been nothing threatening to any of the gifts. He wanted to assuage her fears. How to do that without revealing himself remained a mystery.

Then again, maybe he should reveal himself. Maybe he should tell her the truth about all of it. But how to do that and have it make sense remained a mystery, too. How could he make sense of it to her when he could scarcely make sense of it himself? And what would he do if, when Rita found out it was he who had left the gifts, she reacted badly? What if she misunderstood his intentions and thought him…odd…for doing it? What if she looked at him as if he were a creep, a freak—a beast?

He was going to have to tell her anyway, he decided. That was the only way she would realize there had been nothing sinister behind the gifts. Hopefully, an opportunity would arise during their conversation. Because if it didn't…

Well, he'd just have to figure out a way to make sure that it did.

He sensed, more than saw, her shrug in response to his request, because the only light in the room came from the warm, golden glow of the fire that barely reached out to surround them. Not to mention the fact that both of them seemed to prefer gazing into the fire instead of at each other.

"I've told you most of it," she said. "There's some guy at the hospital who's been leaving me gifts on special occasions, and I don't know who he is or why he's doing it."

"You're sure it's a guy?" Matthew asked, testing the waters.

"Well, I assume so," she said. "I can't see a woman doing that. Women are usually much more straightforward."

"Yeah, like Glenn Close in *Fatal Attraction*," he quipped.

"Please don't joke about it," Rita said, sounding distressed.

Matthew did turn to look at her then. And she responded by turning to meet his gaze. She really was scared of the person who had left the gifts, he realized.

How had everything gotten so messed up? he wondered. All he'd ever wanted was to do something nice for Rita Barone.

"I'm sorry," he apologized. Not just for making light of her fear, he thought, but for causing it in the first place. For too many things to name.

"It's just really got me rattled," she said, cupping both hands over her opposite arms, as if warding off a chill.

"Maybe it's just someone who wants to do something nice for you because you did something nice for him," Matthew suggested. That was a logical line of thinking, wasn't it? And it wouldn't necessarily incriminate him. Having noted the fear in both her voice and her body language, he was beginning to have second thoughts about identifying himself. He still wasn't sure where he stood with Rita, and he still dreaded being ridiculed and reviled if she found out the truth. If not by her, then by other people at the hospital. He wasn't sure he'd be able to handle it any better as an adult than he had as a child.

Rita shook her head. "I don't think so. I haven't done any good deeds lately," she said. "Nothing I wouldn't ordinarily do."

"Maybe what you consider an ordinary deed was an extraordinary deed to someone else," Matthew told her, recalling the way she had been with the homeless man, Joe. He'd certainly considered her efforts that day extraordinary. He never would have been able to soothe another human being the way Rita had that day. "Maybe this person just wants to show you that he thinks you're extraordinary yourself."

She smiled at that, a little sadly. "I'm not extraordinary in any sense of the word," she said resolutely.

And it was with no small degree of shock that Matthew realized she meant exactly what she said. She thought she was ordinary. Thought she was just like everyone else. She couldn't see what was the most obvious thing in the world.

"Of course, you are," he said before he could stop himself. But then he decided, What the hell, in for a penny, in for a pound. He turned his body to fully face hers. When she looked at him, he lifted a hand to cup it lightly over her jaw. "Rita," he said softly, gazing into her amazing brown eyes and holding on for dear life when he felt himself going under, "you're the most extraordinary woman I know. And if you can't see that, then it's no wonder you don't realize the truth about this so-called stalker."

Nine

Rita gazed back at Matthew in the faintly flickering, orange-golden light of the fire, totally confused by what he had just said. "What are you talking about?" she asked softly, her voice sounding shallow as it creased the mellow darkness.

He hesitated for only a moment, then told her, "I meant exactly what I said. That you're an extraordinary woman, Rita Barone."

She started to shake her head in denial, but that only served to turn her face more completely into his hand, intensifying the gentle caress of his fingertips against her skin. Heat thrummed through her midsection when she registered the soft touch, then spread slowly throughout the rest of her.

"Do you really think that?" she asked quietly.

This time he didn't hesitate before responding. "Yes. I do."

And then, before she even realized what he intended, Matthew dipped his head to hers and covered her mouth with his.

It was a kiss quite unlike any she had ever received, at once confident and tentative, demanding and exploratory. Somehow, she felt as if he were trying to tell her something as he kissed her, but that his feelings were a mix of emotions even he didn't quite understand.

Good, Rita thought as she kissed him back in the same way. That was good, because it put them on equal ground. She wasn't sure where this was going to lead, but somehow it felt right. It felt good. And she had gone too long feeling bad. For now, kissing Matthew was exactly what she wanted to do.

For long moments they only kissed, touching just where Matthew's fingers continued to stroke along the line of Rita's jaw. Again and again he dipped his head to hers, turning it first one way, then the other, as if he wanted to taste her from every angle. Eventually, she lifted a hand to his hair, threading her fingers gingerly through the silky chestnut tresses, loving the way they curled around her fingertips as if trying to trap her there. Then, little by little, he began to edge his body closer to hers, until she felt his thigh pressing into her thigh, and his hip nudging hers, and his shoulder brushing hers. With each move forward, he intensified the kiss, until it built into a fiercely burning embrace, one that threatened to blaze out of control.

No, Rita thought when she realized what was happening. Not again. She would not make love with a man who had thrown her out the last time they had come together this way. She tore her mouth from his and pushed her body away from him, then stood and moved to the fireplace, turning her back on him so that she was gazing at the fire and not his handsome, yearning face. One fire was hot enough, she told herself. There was no reason why they should start another one. Especially since it would go out all too soon.

She heard Matthew breathing raggedly behind her, but he made no move to follow her. "Rita?" he asked softly. "What's wrong?"

She realized then that her own breathing was as rough as his was, and she inhaled deeply in an effort to steady both it and her rapid heart rate. She heard sounds of movement behind her, but didn't know if he was standing up or only shifting positions. She swallowed hard, knowing she had to have an explanation for why he had asked her to leave after making love to her the night of the party. But she didn't know how to ask for it without sounding desperate and confused. Especially since desperate and confused was exactly how she felt at the moment.

"Matthew, can I ask you a question?" she finally said.

"Of course," he told her.

"The night of the party," she began. But she found it difficult to say anything more.

"Yes?" he spurred her.

Just ask him, she told herself. "After we…" She inhaled another breath and released it slowly. "After we…made love."

"Yes?"

"Why did you…" Ask him! "Why did you…make me leave?"

She heard more sounds of movement, seeming closer this time, then felt his presence immediately behind her. The fire threw wildly dancing shadows about the floor at her feet, and she could just make out part of Matthew's silhouette blending with her own. When she inhaled this time, she smelled him, too, the clean, masculine fragrance that was distinctly his.

His voice was as quiet as her mood when he replied. "I'm sorry about that," he said. "I shouldn't have done it."

"But why did you?" she insisted.

He hesitated another moment before telling her, "Because you didn't think I appreciated what happened between us. You didn't think I *could* appreciate it."

She turned around to face him, narrowing her eyes in confusion, shaking her head. "I never said that."

He looked sad and weary as he told her, "Yes, you did."

She searched her mind in an effort to recall whatever he thought he was talking about, then gasped softly when she finally remembered. She shook her head more firmly. "No. What I said was that I didn't think the fact that it was my first time would matter to you."

"Exactly," he said. "You didn't think I could appreciate the honor you were bestowing upon me."

"But—"

"When in fact, Rita," he continued, ignoring her objection, "there was nothing that could have mattered to me more."

"But—"

"And when you said you thought it wouldn't matter to me, it made me feel like you agreed with everyone at the hospital about me."

Now her eyebrows arrowed downward in bewilderment. "What do you mean?"

He lifted one shoulder and let it drop. "That you thought I was a beast, too. That I wasn't capable of having feelings for you."

"Oh, Matthew…"

"In fact I felt…"

He didn't finish whatever he had intended to say, only gazed at her as if she were the answer to every prayer he had ever sent skyward. She told herself to say something, do something, to show him how much he had come to mean to her. Then she made herself stop thinking and only allowed herself to feel. And her feelings in that moment were… Oh, so strong. She cupped her hand gently over his jaw, stroking her thumb over the skin grown warm from the fire and rough from a day's growth of beard. Then she lifted her other hand to the scars on his face that he thought made him so beastly, brushing her fingers gently over them, as well. Finally she pushed herself up on tiptoe and pressed her lips to his.

She kissed him in a way that she hoped he would understand meant she loved him. Because she was afraid to say the words out loud just yet. The feeling was still too new for her to understand it, still too fragile for her to share. But she wanted him to know how she felt. Kissing him the way she did was the only way she could think to do that right now.

He seemed to understand, though, at least some of it, because after a moment, he roped his arms around her waist and pulled her close and kissed her back with just as much feeling, just as much need, just as much promise. Rita's heart began to pound at the fierceness of the emotions racing through her. Never before had she felt like this. Not even that first night with Matthew. This was new, this was visceral, this was extraordinary.

Extraordinary, she thought again as she kissed him more deeply. That was what he had said she was. Extraordinary. That could only mean that he cared for her. But did he care for her as much as she cared for him? And did he want this feeling to last forever, as she did? Because Rita knew in that moment she never wanted to be apart from Matthew again.

Her thoughts drifted off into nothingness when he began

to tug at her sweater, and all she could do was eagerly lift her arms so that he could skim it up over her torso and shoulders and head. He tossed it carelessly to the ground when he did, then repeated the action for her thermal shirt. Then he unhooked her brassiere and slipped it down her arms and discarded it, as well. She wanted to cross her arms over her breasts, to hide herself, because she suddenly felt so vulnerable before him. But something in his eyes stopped her, something hot and hungry and needy. His gaze was fixed on her naked breasts, and she watched as, with aching slowness, he lifted one hand toward her again.

"You are so beautiful," he whispered roughly as he reached for her.

Gently, carefully, he traced the pad of his middle finger along the lower curve of her breast, then up the side, across the top, around again. With each new circle, he moved inward a little more, and with each new circle, Rita's heart pounded more rapidly. All she could do was stand there as he drew his invisible rings, and try, with little success, to keep her breathing under control. Eventually, he reached the center of her breast, hesitating only a moment before pushing the pad of his finger around her dark areola. Rita sighed with longing as he touched her, and he must have understood, because he closed his entire hand over her then, and dipped his head to hers for another eager kiss.

As he kissed her, Rita tugged at his sweater, too, jerking her mouth from his only long enough to yank the garment up over his lean abdomen and shoulders, then pull it completely over his head. As she discarded it to the floor, Matthew kissed her again, more passionately this time, tasting her deeply with his tongue. Blindly, she opened her hands over his naked shoulders, and then he was pulling her roughly against him, splaying his hands open over her bare back, rubbing his rough chest against her softer one.

The friction produced an almost unbearable heat, making Rita wonder if she might spontaneously combust. Instead of exploding, her fever only continued to intensify, and magnify, and multiply. Matthew, she could tell by the way he was touching her so needfully, hungrily, frantically, was experiencing the same sensations.

"I want you, Rita," he panted between kisses. "I want to make love to you again. I've missed you so much the past two weeks. Every night I dream about you. Dream about that one time we were together. I remember how you felt and tasted and smelled, and I remember what it was like to be buried deep inside you. And then I start wanting you again. Because I know that one time will never be enough. That I'll never have enough of you."

She told herself not to think about what he said, about what he meant. He wasn't telling her he wanted to be with her forever, she assured herself. He was only telling her he wanted to be with her again. She'd promised herself that the next time she made love to a man, it would be with one she intended to keep—and who intended to keep her— forever.

Then he kissed her again, long and hard and deep, and she could scarcely remember her own name, let alone any promises she had made to herself. When he kissed her like that, all she could remember was the way he had made her feel the night the two of them had come together in such a burst of urgency and conflagration. This time it was even more urgent, even more inflamed. She needed him even more now than she had before. Before, she hadn't known what she was missing, hadn't known how good it could be. Now, though, she did know that. She did remember, and she wanted to feel that way again. Oh, how she wanted it.

"I want you, too," she told him, not sure when she'd

decided to admit that, only knowing it was true. "Oh, Matthew, I want you so bad."

One corner of his mouth crooked up in something of a sly grin. "You want me bad, huh?" he echoed.

She could only nod in response to the fire she saw reflected in his eyes. Nod and feel as hot and wanton as he seemed to feel himself.

"Well, then, Rita," he murmured, "I'll do my best to be bad for you."

Oh, my, she thought.

And then he kissed her again, in a way that made it impossible for her to think at all. As he kissed her, he ran his hands over her back, cupping her shoulder blades, sketching her spine, tripping along her ribs one by one. Everywhere he touched her, he set off little fires of wanting. Rita explored him, too, loving the sensation of each rigid muscle her fingertips encountered on his broad back. His shoulders and arms were masses of solid sinew, too, and she marveled at how their bodies were so different, yet so complementary. Where he was hard, she was soft. Where he was rough, she was smooth. And where he was hot... Well, she was hot, too.

Now, she thought as she pulled her mouth reluctantly away from his. She wanted him now. Right now. Right here, in front of the fireplace, where the heat of the flames mirrored their own reaction to each other. But for some reason, she felt shy about undressing while he was watching her, so she turned her back as she reached for the button at her waistband of her jeans. Before she had the chance to unfasten it, though, Matthew stepped up behind her, pushing his body flush against hers, the coarse hair on his chest grazing her bare shoulder blades and sending a shiver of excitement rushing through her. The shiver turned to electricity, however, when he covered her hands with his and drew them away from her jeans.

"Let me do that," he whispered roughly near her ear as he moved his own hands to the place where hers had been.

Before she could answer, he dipped his head to the soft curve where her neck and shoulder joined, brushing his open mouth hotly over the tender skin there. Rita's eyes fluttered closed at the contact, and she was so wrapped up in enjoying the skim of his lips over her flesh that she barely noticed him slipping the metal button of her jeans through its denim hole. She reached one hand behind herself to tangle her fingers in his hair, and tilted her head to the side to facilitate the erotic exploration of his mouth. He uttered a soft, masculine sound, then slowly, oh so slowly, began pushing down the zipper of her jeans and spreading the fabric open wide.

Beneath, she wore brief cotton panties, but Matthew wasn't deterred for a moment. As he filled one hand with her breast again, he slipped the other beneath the supple cotton, pressing his palm against her flat belly, pointing his fingers downward, toward the heart of her femininity. Then, millimeter by leisurely millimeter, his fingers began a downward advance, halting momentarily at the edge of the downy curls between her legs. Rita gasped when she realized his intention, but Matthew was undeterred, moving his hand downward, pushing harder when the position of her blue jeans threatened to hinder his progress.

Instinctively, Rita took a small step to the side, widening her stance, giving him freer access to the prize he so clearly sought. When she did, he drove his fingers deeper, until he found his way to the damp folds of flesh and began to explore.

"Oh," Rita gasped when he touched her so intimately. "Oh, Matthew. That's so…"

"Do you like that?" he asked softly, his voice a damp caress against her ear.

"Oh, yes," she managed to pant. "Please... I want..."

"What?" he asked.

But all Rita could tell him was, "More..."

She wasn't sure, but she thought she heard him chuckle with much satisfaction as he drove his hand farther between her legs, fingering her gently, drawing erotic circles on her sensitive flesh and then tilling the tender folds with confident strokes. Her fingers tightened in his hair with each move he made, and she dropped her free hand to circle her fingers around his strong forearm, silently urging him to continue his erotic foray. So he did. Again and again he stroked his fingers over and along and between her, finally slipping one long digit inside her.

Rita gasped again at his scant penetration, then told him breathlessly, "I want you there. All of you, Matthew. I want you inside me again. Please, make love to me."

It was all the invitation he needed. After one final stroke, he removed his hand from her panties, dragging his damp fingertips up over her belly, and out to her hips. Then, without warning, he jerked her blue jeans and panties down over her hips, her thighs, her knees, baring her bottom and legs. Rita started to turn around to face him, but Matthew caught her hands in his and moved them to grip the mantelpiece instead. Reflexively, she clung to it, but looked over her shoulder to see him struggling with his own jeans. Quickly, but none too gracefully, he loosed the buttons of his fly and yanked down his pants. Then he stepped behind Rita and, gripping her hips in his hands, entered her from behind.

In spite of her position and the front-to-back love play in which they'd just indulged, she hadn't been expecting him to do that. Now to feel him push himself inside her the way he had, she was overcome with passion. Wanting. Heat. Need. He filled her so confidently, so adamantly, so completely, as if he and he alone had a right to be there. As if he belonged there. As if he were a part of her too long separated from her.

She knew then that he *was* a part of her. That he'd become a part of her that first night they'd made love. Because she had fallen in love with him that night. Totally, irrevocably in love. Maybe even before then, she thought vaguely as he withdrew himself and then pushed more deeply into her. Maybe that was why she had made love with him that night in the first place. Because on some deep, unconscious level, she had been in love with him all along.

He pulled out of her again, then entered her once more, and Rita pushed herself backward against him, until she felt as if he penetrated her to her very core. For some reason then, she vaguely recalled some misgiving she'd had after they'd made love the first time. Something about primary concerns and second thoughts. Something about precautions. Something about...

Pregnancy.

"Matthew," she managed to gasp. But she couldn't loose her hold on the mantelpiece, didn't want him to stop what he was doing, because it just felt so good. "We...we have to stop this. Now."

"What are you talking about?" he asked breathlessly against her neck. "We can't stop now."

She really didn't want to stop, either. Not when she was so close to... Not when they were so close to...

To maybe making a baby, she reminded herself brutally.

She made herself say what she had to say. "I could get pregnant," she told him softly.

He went still behind her, but didn't withdraw.

"We don't have any protection," she told him.

"We didn't have any last time, either," he said, his voice flat and even, belying nothing of what he might be thinking or feeling. And because she couldn't see him, she had no idea what his expression might tell her. "You could already be pregnant," he added with a surprising calmness in his tone.

She shook her head. "No. I've had my— Since then I've had evidence that I'm not. We were lucky."

"Were we?"

Weren't they? she wanted to ask him. But she was too muzzy-headed to figure it all out. "I don't want to take a chance again," she told him.

He hesitated, then she felt him nod. Carefully, he pulled out of her, then kissed her softly on her shoulder. "Upstairs," he said, "in the bathroom. I have some condoms. Meet me in my bedroom," he told her.

And then he was gone, melting into the darkness of the house as if he'd magically disappeared into the black beyond. Rita took a few deep breaths, telling herself she was too addle-brained from their loving to know what was going on. Nevertheless, she pushed her blue jeans and panties down around her ankles and stepped out of them, then pulled a ruby-red throw from the sofa and wrapped herself up in it. She had no idea where Matthew's bedroom was, but it was a safe bet that it was upstairs.

She made her way to the stairs, the fire offering her just enough light to find her way to the top. She looked left, then right. At the end of the hallway, a faint light glowed in one of the rooms, so she went toward it. The room was dark and masculinely furnished, a single candle burning on a mahogany antique dresser and the bedclothes on the massive sleigh bed turned back in invitation.

As she stepped in, Matthew slipped up behind her again,

wrapping his arms around her waist and burying his face at her nape to kiss her neck. "I thought you'd never get here," he murmured against her heated flesh.

She smiled as she reached behind herself to tangle her fingers in his hair. "It's only been a few minutes," she told him.

"It's been forever," he countered.

Slowly, he turned her around to face him, then urged the throw off her shoulders so that it pooled on the floor around her feet. Then he pulled her into his arms and kissed her deeply again, slowly walking her backward, toward the bed. She felt the mattress bump against the backs of her legs, then she was falling backward in the candlelit darkness, her feet still on the floor, with Matthew lying alongside her. Immediately, he rolled over onto his back, his feet still firmly planted on the floor, pulling Rita over with him until she lay atop him. After one final kiss, he cupped her shoulders with his hands and pushed her up, until she was kneeling over him, her legs on each side of his torso.

"You set the pace this time," he said. And then he covered her hips with his hands and smiled, a wicked, seductive little smile. He pushed her backward until her bottom made contact with his heavy, condom-encased shaft, then urged her up on her knees, positioning her over it. Inch by inch he brought her back down again, entering her slowly and deeply as he did. "You set the pace," he said again. "Fast or slow, deep or shallow, however you want it. Ride me, Rita."

Oh, merciful heavens, she thought. And then she realized she had no idea what to do.

She remembered that first time when he'd said he liked it fast and hard. But she wasn't sure she was ready for that. So, slowly, she pushed herself up on her knees again, then brought herself back down over him. Oh, that was so nice, she thought as she relished the slick friction of their bodies. Yes, slow and easy was definitely the way to go. For now.

Matthew didn't seem to mind, because he closed his eyes and lifted his hands to her breasts, filling his fingers with her. Rita opened her hands over his hard, muscular chest and lifted herself up again. She repeated the motion until both of them were breathing raggedly, their bodies glossy with sweat. Little by little, she increased the pace, gradually moving faster and harder over him.

Oh, yeah, she thought, there was definitely something to be said for doing it fast and hard, too.

Matthew moved his hands to her hips again, catching her rhythm, helping her pump against him more fiercely. Again and again he plunged into her, until she thought they would both explode from the heat their bodies were generating. A hot coil of pleasure began to tighten inside her, then, in a burst of fever, it began to consume her. As it did, he shifted their bodies again until Rita lay beneath him, and he hooked her legs around his waist. He took control of their coupling then, driving himself deep, deep inside her. Finally, with one last, fierce penetration, he cried out, going rigid and still above her. Rita, too, edged over the precipice then, her own climax culminating with his.

Then he collapsed alongside her, his breathing as labored and uneven as hers. For long moments they only lay there, their damp bodies entwined, their heat mingling, their thoughts scrambled. Then, weakly, Matthew began to push himself away. Instinctively, Rita reached for him, afraid he was about to do what he'd done before and tell her it was time for her to leave. He seemed to understand her fear, because he cupped his hand gently on her cheek and smiled, albeit a bit sadly.

"I'm not going to tell you to go," he said. "I just have to take care of our...precautions."

She closed her eyes, feeling stupid. Of course. But then, how was she supposed to know that? She wasn't exactly knowledgeable about this sort of thing. She lay quietly while Matthew was gone, marveling at what the two of them had just done, amazed that it could have been even better this time. And then he was with her again, lying beside her in the darkness, his body smooth and warm and hard, making her feel safe and pleasant and cherished. He lay on his side, one arm draped over Rita's waist, his hand gently cupping her breast. He stroked his thumb lightly over her nipple, and she shivered at the exquisite pleasure that shot through her in response.

"Cold?" he asked.

She shook her head. "Not at all," she told him.

"I can pull up the covers."

"No," she repeated. "I like being here with you like this." She turned on her side to look at him. "You have an amazing body, Dr. Grayson."

"In the dark," he qualified with a glance to the scant candlelight enveloping them. "In good light, it's not exactly a work of art."

She knew he was talking about his scars, and needing to prove to him that they didn't matter to her, she moved her hand to his shoulder, brushing her fingers over the puckered skin there with an affectionate caress.

"You're beautiful to me," she told him unequivocally.

He gazed at her silently for a moment, then reached for the hand she had opened over his scar. He withdrew it long enough to place a gentle kiss on her palm, then put it back where she had placed it before. But he offered nothing in response to her comment, only continued to gaze at her as if he couldn't quite believe she was real. Then he cupped his hand behind her head and pulled her toward him, kissing her again.

The kiss this time, though, was one of simple pleasure, a gesture meant to tell her how very happy he was that she was here with him.

"Stay the weekend with me," he said when he pulled away. "Stay until the storm is over."

Something twisted tight inside Rita at his words. Because although they were filled with longing and invitation, there was also an impermanence to them. He wanted her here until the storm passed, she told herself, but then what would happen?

"All right," she said, forcing a smile. "I will."

Inside, though, she was a mix of happiness and turmoil. She did indeed want to stay with Matthew until the storm was over. But that was because she knew the storm of her emotions was never going to end.

Ten

Rita stayed at Matthew's house until late Sunday evening, long after the great nor'easter ended, and long after the snowplows had cleared the streets. She wanted to stay even longer, but made herself return home for two reasons. One, so that she could sort through her feelings before going back to work. And two, because he hadn't invited her to stay any longer than the weekend.

Mostly, though, she did need to figure out what she felt for him. And she knew he needed time to himself, too, to try and make sense of his own emotions. Their weekend together had been an escape from reality in so many ways. On Monday morning, they would return to the real world of working with each other again, and she, at least, needed to be prepared, just in case Matthew decided to revert to his old beastly ways again.

She told herself that wasn't going to happen, especially after the way he kissed her good-night on the doorstep of

her brownstone after driving her home, then placed the
crystal bud vase holding her rose so carefully into her hand.
Strangely, he hadn't asked her about the rose once over the
weekend. But he had tended to it as carefully as she, making sure it had water and was placed in a sunny window.
It had been just another enchanting aspect of their time
together. There had been something magical about the
snowstorm, something unearthly and illusory about the entire weekend. The real test, she knew, would come in the
morning, when the two of them were thrust back into the
workday world. She just hoped they both still felt the same
way Monday morning.

But the first thing Rita saw on Monday morning was a
note from Matthew that he had tucked into her mail slot. *I
won't be in today,* the note read, *but meet me this evening
for dinner, 7:00 at Darian's. We have to talk. Matthew.*

It was that last sentence that caused Rita the most concern. What did they have to talk about? she wondered. She
folded the note and tucked it into the pocket of her scrubs
with some trepidation.

Tonight, she supposed, she was going to find out.

The restaurant Matthew had chosen for dinner was one
Rita had never visited before. Darian's was considered to
be one of Boston's finer venues, but its prices were hard
to manage on a nurse's salary. Yes, she was a member of
the wealthy Barone family but she was unwilling to dip
into her trust fund for something like dinner out.

Still, in light of the restaurant's reputation, she had
dressed in her only outfit appropriate for such an establish-
ment, the little black dress she'd worn to the party at Baronessa headquarters the night she and Matthew had made
love for the first time. And if a not-so-little part of her was
rather hoping this evening might have the same outcome

as that one, well, that was just something she'd have to deal with. And she had. In fact, she'd dealt with it by wearing the same naughty lingerie she'd worn that night, too.

Well, a girl could dream, couldn't she?

Until the night of the blizzard, Rita had been so certain things with Matthew weren't going to work out, that the two of them had been finished before they could even get started. And after that night, she began to realize how very badly she did want them to work out. Before the party at Baronessa headquarters, she'd liked and admired him. Yes, he was gruff and standoffish, but she'd always sensed that there was a reason for that, something in his past that had wounded him and kept him from getting too close to anyone else. At the party, of course, she'd learned what that something was. And when she had realized the depth of the wounds from which he had had to recover—both physically and emotionally—she'd experienced a new kind of admiration for him. And she had begun to feel a sort of affection for him, too. Affection that had gradually grown into love.

There were many things the two of them had in common. They both took their work seriously, and were dedicated to their callings. He had a wry sense of humor, when he showed it, and he'd always seemed confident and reasonably content with his life. Rita had simply responded to him on a level she didn't with most people. She'd always felt comfortable around him, in spite of his seeming distance, and always felt better whenever he was around.

She remembered once, back before Christmas, when the nurses in CCU were passing a boring shift by taking turns answering the question "If you had to be stranded on a deserted island with someone from the hospital, who would you choose?" Most of the nurses had chosen a notoriously handsome intern, but when her turn had come, Rita had thought for a moment, then had said she thought Dr. Grayson would be a likely choice. The others hadn't bothered to hide their surprise that she would choose the beastly MD, and a few had outright called her nuts. But Rita had defended her choice, had told the other nurses she thought he would be good to have around because he was smart and self-sufficient and wouldn't panic.

What she hadn't told them that day was that she thought he was kind of attractive, sexy even, in his gruff, standoffish way.

Even back then, she realized now, she had been attracted to him. And the more she got to know him, the more appealing he'd become. Making love with him had finally made her understand how very much she *did* care for him. How much she had come to love him. The reason she had made him her first lover, she understood now, was because she had known on some subconscious level that he was indeed special. That he was someone she wanted to share her life with. That he was someone she wanted to share herself with. Because she had loved him. Even then.

All she could do at this point was hope that Matthew shared at least some of her feelings. She wasn't sure what she would do if he saw this as little more than a passing fling. She didn't think he did. He didn't seem the kind of man who would indulge in something so frivolous and superficial. But she wouldn't know for sure unless he offered her some kind of sign that what was happening between them meant as much to him as it did to her.

Of course, inviting a woman to the most expensive restaurant in town was certainly a good start, Rita thought as she pushed open the door to Darian's and entered. She saw Matthew immediately, waiting by the hostess stand, his gaze fixed on the door as if he hadn't wanted to take his eyes off it, lest he miss her entrance. He was wearing another one of his dark power suits with a white dress shirt and a conservative, berry-colored necktie, and although she had decided the other day that she preferred him in his more casual attire of jeans and sweater—or, better still, his even more casual attire of nothing at all—she went a little weak in the knees at the sight of him.

He was so incredibly handsome. And so charmingly unaware of the fact. And he was so gentle. And so sweet. How anyone could ever think him beastly was beyond her. She smiled a bit tentatively, feeling nervous for no good reason she could name.

"Hi," she said softly.

He smiled in response to her salutation, a slow, easy, very confident, very sexy smile. A small bubble of heat burst inside her, sending a warm sensation reeling throughout her entire system. After exhaling a small, soft sigh that felt very much like contentment, she strode forward and stopped beside him.

"You look beautiful," he said by way of a greeting.

She grinned. "You don't look so bad yourself," she replied.

Then he surprised her by leaning forward and covering her mouth with his. It was a brief, spontaneous show of affection, and she felt as if she would melt right there on the spot. It wasn't a lingering kiss, but it was a public kiss, a public avowal that she was important to him. Somehow, that pleased Rita down to the very depths of her soul.

He pulled back with obvious reluctance, but by then the hostess had returned and was telling them their table was ready, if they'd please just follow her. Matthew held Rita's chair for her as she took her seat, then, instead of moving to the other side of the table equipped for four, he sat down immediately to her right, as if he didn't want even the scant distance of a table separating them. That sensation of heat spread through Rita again. A server appeared immediately to take their drink orders, and after a quick glance at the wine list, Matthew ordered something red and full-bodied.

He seemed impatient about something, Rita thought as she watched him make the decision and place the order. Though not in any sort of negative way. She got the feeling there was something he wanted to discuss with her—but then, he'd said as much in his note—something she now realized must be very important. But he didn't seem to know how to go about approaching it.

"What?" she said, hoping to spur him. "What's wrong?"

He looked surprised by her question. "Wrong?" he echoed. "Nothing's wrong. Why would you ask that?"

She shrugged lightly, even though she didn't much feel light. "In your note, you said we needed to talk," she reminded him. "You must have something on your mind."

In response to her remark, Matthew only gazed at her in silence. And suddenly, Rita began to feel doubtful about what she had felt so certain of only moments ago. Could she have been wrong about the mood of the evening? she wondered. What if he really did see this as nothing more than a fling? What if, instead of an effort to cement their relationship, he intended tonight to be the big kiss-off?

"It's not that I have something on my mind," he finally said "It's that I have something in my pocket."

"What?" she asked warily.

He studied her in silence for a moment longer, then sat back in his chair and reached into the breast pocket of his jacket. Just as he was beginning to withdraw whatever was in there, however, their waiter returned with their wine and Matthew set his empty hand back on the table between himself and Rita. Their server went about placing their glasses meticulously on the table, taking such great care and time to do it just so, that Rita nearly jumped out of her chair to throttle him. Finally, however, he seemed to reach the proper level of feng shui because he smiled and nodded at both of them, offered a quiet, "I'll just give you a few more minutes to study the menu," then pivoted and walked away.

Rita turned her attention to Matthew, but he was diligently perusing his dinner choices. "The veal looks good," he said blandly.

Rita mentally gritted her teeth at him. Whatever he had been about to remove from his pocket, he was clearly planning to wait to show her now. So she, too, turned her attention to the menu, choosing the first item upon which her gaze fell.

"Rosemary-encrusted lamb chops," she muttered, looking back up at Matthew. "I'll have that. Now then, what was it you were saying?"

He glanced back up at her, seeming confused about something. Then his expression cleared. "Oh. The veal. I was saying it looks good."

Argh, Rita thought. "No, before that," she said. "We were talking about something else."

"Were we?"

"Yes, we were," she assured him, biting back her impatience. "You—"

But she never got to finish her thought, as their server returned again to take their orders.

She placed her order, then listened impatiently as Matthew wavered between the veal and the New York strip. Finally, he opted for, of all things, the beef medallions, something that sent their server scurrying off to do whatever it was servers did when they weren't annoying their patrons by interrupting their dialogues at the most inopportune moments. Rita took advantage of his absence to fold her elbows over the table and lean forward, blatantly invading Matthew's space.

"Before the veal," she said, striving for a patient tone, "you were about to say something else."

Matthew opened his mouth with the obvious intention of telling her that he couldn't remember, but Rita cut him off by lifting one hand, index finger extended.

"You said you had something in your pocket," she reminded him stoically. "Something you were about to take out and show me," she added, just in case he'd forgotten that part, too.

He made a soft tsk and nodded. "That's right," he concurred. "I remember now."

Finally, Rita thought.

"But maybe I should wait for dessert," he said.

She squeezed her eyes shut tight and silently counted to ten. "No," she said slowly and calmly when she opened them again, "you should tell me now."

When her gaze met his, she saw that his dreamy green eyes were fairly twinkling with mischief, and she realized he'd been deliberately stringing her along all this time.

She smiled knowingly. "C'mon," she said, turning her hand palm up now, and wiggling her fingers. "Let's have it," she said.

He continued to gaze at her for a moment longer, then leaned back in his chair again and reached into his jacket pocket once more. But he still hesitated a moment before withdrawing whatever was inside, and he suddenly seemed to be a little anxious about what he was doing. Slowly, though, he pulled his hand back out, cupping it over whatever he held so that Rita couldn't see it. Then he halted completely before showing her what it was.

"Close your eyes," he said.

She expelled a mildly exasperated sound. "Why?"

"Just do it," he told her.

She obeyed his edict, sitting back in her chair and folding her hands in her lap, then closing her eyes. She heard the soft shuffle of movement, then nothing.

"Okay," he said, his voice still laced with something akin to apprehension. "You can open them now."

When Rita did, she saw first Matthew's handsome face gazing back at her with what was clearly trepidation. Then, more curious than ever, she lowered her gaze to the table. There, sitting before her on the white china plate atop the white linen tablecloth was a small white box. A small white box tied up with gold ribbon.

Just exactly like the small white boxes tied with gold ribbon that her secret admirer/stalker had left for her in her mail slot at the hospital.

"What…?" And then she understood. It had been Matthew all along. He had been the one leaving her the anonymous gifts.

She jerked her head up to look at him, and understood then why he looked so worried. Because he was the one she had been concerned might be stalking her. Even after she had voiced that concern to him, even after she had told him how uneasy, even frightened, she was about the anonymous gifts, he hadn't told her the truth. And he was uncertain what her reaction would be, now that she did know the truth.

In all honesty, in that moment, Rita wasn't sure what her reaction was.

"It's been you all along?" she asked.

He nodded. "Yes." When she only continued to stare at him in silence, he blew out an impatient breath and tried to explain. "That first time," he began, "all I really wanted to do was to somehow say thank you for your help in the

E.R. that day with Joe, the homeless man. Do you remember that?''

Rita nodded. "Yes," she said. "But, Matthew, I was only doing my job that day. You didn't owe me any thanks.''

"I owed you more than you realize," he told her. "You calmed the man down, and you made it possible for me to do *my* job. You also told him I was an excellent surgeon. The absolute best." He hesitated a moment before adding, "And you told him I was a wonderful man. And when you said that, you sounded like you really meant it."

"I did mean it," she told him.

He nodded. "I know. That's why I felt like I needed to thank you. Because no one had ever said anything like that about me before. Certainly no one had ever meant it."

"Oh, Matthew," she said, her heart turning over in spite of her dismay.

"When I left that first gift," he continued, "I thought I left a note with it, explaining why it was there, telling you thanks for your help in the E.R. It wasn't until later, when I heard the rumors of your secret admirer, that I realized I had inadvertently forgotten to leave the note. It didn't even occur to me until later that it was Valentine's Day. And once everyone started talking about Rita Barone's secret admirer, I was too embarrassed to make myself known.''

"Because you weren't an admirer," she concluded.

He shook his head. "No. Because I *was*."

She eyed him curiously. "But—"

"Looking back, I think maybe, subconsciously, I wasn't leaving you a gift to say thank you. I was leaving a gift to say I care about you. Because I did care about you then. I still do. That's why I left the other gifts, too."

"On my birthday?" she asked, even though she already knew the answer.

"Yes," he said.

"And the anniversary of my first day at the hospital?"

"Yes."

"And the rose, too," she said, making it a statement this time, not a question.

He nodded. "I wasn't sure you'd even make the connection with the date on that one, it having been two weeks since we made love. But you did," he added. "You were thinking about it that day, too."

"I've thought about it every day since it happened," she told him.

"Me, too."

She shook her head slowly, scarcely believing what he was telling her. "But how did you even know the anniversary of my first day working at Boston General?" she asked.

He inhaled deeply as he fixed his gaze on hers. "Because I remember that day very well," he said evenly. "I was in the E.R. when you reported for your first shift, and I remember how the first time you walked behind the nurses' station, the whole place just seemed to…light up, in reaction to your presence. And I remember every day that's passed since then, Rita. The day you came to Boston General was one of the most important days of my life."

She didn't know what to say, so she only asked, "Why?"

He leaned forward again, dropping his hands to the table, skimming one across the linen to cover one of hers. "Because that was the day that, for the first time since I was a child, I felt good inside."

She gaped softly at him. "What?"

He nodded. "It took me a while to figure it out, but there was just something about you that, from the first time I laid eyes on you, made me feel good again. And then, when you didn't shy away from me that first time we were introduced, when you didn't even seem to notice my scars, I knew you were someone special."

"Why would that make me special? And why would I shy away from you in the first place?" she asked. "I remember thinking how handsome you were the first time I met you."

He eyed her dubiously. "Don't tell me you didn't notice the scars."

"Of course I noticed them," she said. "But they didn't matter to me."

He nodded. "And that's why you're so special," he said. "Thinking back, I realize now that that was the moment I began to fall in love with you."

For a moment, Rita was sure she had misheard what he'd said. Or else, she had misunderstood. "But..." she began, not daring to hope.

"Open the box," he said before she could finish, as if he were afraid of hearing her answer.

"But—"

"Please, Rita," he said, a little more desperately. "Open it. It will be the last one, I promise." His expression turned a little grim. "One way or another. It will be the last."

She started to object again, but something in his expression halted her. She wanted to tell him she loved him, too, but again, something made her stop. It seemed very important to him that she see what was in the little package before she replied, so she turned her attention to it again. It was a perfect cube, roughly two inches. Gingerly, she picked it up, then carefully slipped off the gold ribbon. As the white paper fell away, she saw a black velvet box beneath.

A jeweler's box, she couldn't help thinking.

She looked up at Matthew, and once again she opened

her mouth to say something. But he stopped her with a gesture, pointing at the box.

With trembling fingers, Rita did as he requested, folding back the top to see what was hidden beneath. Then she caught her breath at the ring inside. A perfect, heart-shaped diamond solitaire on a platinum band.

Holding the box in one shaky hand, Rita lifted her other to cover her mouth. And when she glanced up to look at Matthew, she felt two fat tears spill from her eyes to stream down her cheeks.

"Are you, um, proposing?" she asked weakly.

He smiled, expelling a single, hopeful chuckle. Instead of answering her question, though, he asked one of his own. "Are you accepting?"

"That depends," she told him.

His smile fell some. "On what?"

"On whether or not you actually said what I think you said a minute ago."

He looked confused. "About what?"

She sucked up all the nerve she had and said, "About falling in love with me."

Now he looked stunned. "Did I say something about that?" he asked.

She nodded, but her heart began to sink. "I thought you did. You said that when we first met and I didn't seem to notice your scars, that that was the moment you began to fall in love with me."

"Oh," he said, clearly bothered by the reminder. "I, um, I really shouldn't have said that."

Something went cold inside Rita at his response. And all she was able to manage in reply was a fragile-sounding, "Oh."

"I misspoke when I said that then," Matthew told her. "I'm sorry."

She nodded dispassionately, but inside, she was wondering if she could make it to the restaurant exit without falling apart. "I see," she said softly.

And just as softly, Matthew told her, "Because I meant to wait until now to say it."

A small flicker of heat sparked in Rita's midsection, and she snapped her gaze to meet his once again. "Say what?" she asked faintly.

He smiled. "That I love you. That I've loved you for years, even if I didn't realize it, and that I will continue to love you until I take my last breath. And that I want you to be there when that last breath leaves me." He held her gaze intently as he added, "So what do you say? Will you marry me, Rita Barone?"

She looked at him for a long time in silence, then, unable to help herself, she smiled back. "And here I've always thought you were so serious about everything."

He sobered some at that. "I am serious. About loving you, anyway. Rita, I—"

"Matthew, I—" she interjected at the same time.

He smiled again, though he still seemed uncertain. "You go first," he said.

She swiped a bent knuckle under first one eye, and then the other. "Oh, it was nothing," she told him. "I was just going to say I accept your proposal, that's all."

His smile then went supernova. "Oh, is that all?"

She nodded.

"And here I thought you were always so serious," he countered.

"I am," she readily assured him. "About wanting to marry you. You see, it seems I've fallen in love with you, too, somewhere along the way. Maybe I've loved you since that first moment, too. And I want to be with you for all the moments we have left."

It seemed all Matthew needed to hear, because without another word, he took the jeweler's box from her hand and plucked the ring from its velvet housing. Then he lifted her left hand to slip the ring down over her third finger.

"A perfect fit," he said as he completed the action.

"Yes, we are," she agreed.

He lifted her hand to his lips then, placing a chaste kiss first on the back, then in the center of her palm, a gesture that sent a shiver of heat shimmying through her. Then he lowered their hands back to the table, his palm up, and hers palm down against it. The ring caught the candlelight from the table and reflected it back in a dozen dazzling shades of orange and gold and blue, and Rita couldn't help thinking it was a sign of just how bright the future was for both of them.

"Oh, my brother Nicholas is going to be so happy," she said as she turned her hand first one way and then the other atop Matthew's, admiring the way the gemstone sparkled. "He always wanted me to marry a doctor."

Matthew chuckled. "Isn't it usually the mother who's pleased about that?"

"Oh, Mom will be thrilled, too," Rita promised him. "In fact, all the Barones will be thrilled." She looked up at Matthew then. "How about the Graysons?" she asked. "How are they going to feel about their venerable blue blood mixing with the new-American Barone blood?"

Matthew looked grave at that. "When I told my parents my intentions," he said in a very serious voice, "they were so upset about it, they broke a long-standing Grayson code."

"Uh-oh," Rita said. "That doesn't sound good."

Matthew nodded. "They broke down and they..." He inhaled a deep breath and released it slowly. "They smiled,'' he finished. ''And then they did something really shocking.''

Rita grinned. ''What's that?''

Matthew shook his head in mock solemnity. ''They hugged each other,'' he confessed. ''And then they hugged *me*. It was quite a scene,'' he added. ''But I'm the first to marry, see, and they've been wanting grandchildren for some time now.''

Rita laughed. ''Gee, I guess we'll just have to accommodate them there. Eventually,'' she added meaningfully. ''I think I want you to myself for a while first.''

''Sounds good to me, Ms. Barone.''

''Soon to be Ms. Barone-Grayson,'' she said with a smile, entwining her fingers with his.

He nodded in approval. ''That has a nice ring to it.''

''Yes, it does,'' she agreed. And then she realized something that made her smile grow broader. ''Oh, wow. It just now occurred to me, I'm the fourth Barone to get engaged this year. I think it's becoming a new family tradition. And you know, we Barones take family traditions very seriously. I wonder who'll be next?''

Matthew squeezed her hand gently in his. ''I don't know,'' he said. ''All I know is I love you and I can't wait to start our lives together.''

''I love you, too,'' she vowed, dropping her gaze to their joined hands. ''And I think, for dessert, we should go back to your place and have something very special.''

''But they serve Baronessa Gelati here,'' he objected mildly. ''Didn't you see it on the menu?''

She nodded. ''But as much as I like Baronessa, there's something else I think we'd both rather have for dessert tonight.''

He grinned. ''What's that?''

She grinned back. ''Each other.''

"Well, gosh, why wait for dessert to have that?" he asked.

"Because I don't want to send our server into psychotherapy," she told him. "I don't think the poor guy could handle it if we just took off. He seems to take his job very seriously."

"If he has a good medical plan," Matthew said, "maybe his insurance will cover the cost of counseling."

Rita laughed. "Hey, I've got a good medical plan," she said. "One that involves a cardiologist and a nurse and some very naughty lingerie."

Before she could say another word, Matthew stood and reached back into his jacket, withdrawing his wallet this time. Then he tossed enough cash onto the table to cover their dinner and a tip. "Say no more," he told her.

"But don't you want to have dinner?" Rita asked as he moved behind her chair and pulled it—and her—out from the table.

"I'd rather have dessert first," he told her. "Lots and lots of dessert."

How could Rita possibly turn down an offer like that? She was, after all, a Barone. Dessert, she had always felt, was without question the best part of life. So, arm-in-arm, she and Matthew went home. To start the best part of their life together.

*   *   *   *   *

DYNASTIES: THE BARONES
continues…

*Turn the page for a bonus look
at what's in store for you in
the next Barones book—
only from Silhouette Desire!*

Where There's Smoke…

by Barbara McCauley

is on sale in May 2004.

Where There's Smoke...

by

Barbara McCauley

Emily Barone stood in the small, back office of Baronessa Gelati and watched the single white piece of paper slowly roll into the copy machine tray, then lie flatly on top of the three other copies she'd already made. Light flickered on the dimly lit walls; the machine shuddered, then clicked to a stop.

It's not true, she told herself for the hundredth time. It can't be.

But Emily knew in her heart that the evidence she'd found against Derrick *was* true. There was no other explanation, nothing that could absolve, or forgive, what her brother had already done.

Or what he still planned to do.

Her hand shook as she reached for the incriminating piece of paper that proved Derrick's crime: he intended to sell secret recipes from the family gelato business to a rival company.

He'd been careful not to raise suspicion, Emily knew. Even as Derrick's secretary, Emily might not have ever noticed anything amiss if earlier today she hadn't accidentally overheard a few whispered words of a phone call on his private line, words that had made her uneasy. When he'd left his office a few minutes later, she'd gone in and pushed redial, only to hear a receptionist for Snowcream, Inc., Baronessa Gelati's biggest competitor, answer the phone.

She'd had to wait until the plant had closed this evening and everyone had left before she could search for evidence to confirm Derrick's betrayal. It had taken her nearly an hour to jimmy the lock on his desk, another fifteen minutes to find the file containing detailed notes from his conversation with Grant Summers, CEO of Snowcream. The files also contained dates and times Derrick had met with Summers, listed the amount of money to be exchanged for the information and the Swiss bank account the money would be transferred into.

Emily swallowed the lump in her throat and blinked back her tears. She knew she was naive. At twenty-four, she still tried to see the good in people, still hoped that in the end a person would do the right thing. She'd prayed she'd been wrong about Derrick, hadn't wanted to believe that her own brother would steal from anyone, let alone Baronessa Gelati.

At the sound of a door closing in an outer office, Emily froze. Quickly she reached across to the single table lamp she'd turned on when she came in. She stood in the dark, listening, heard a quiet, shuffling sound, then nothing. Slowly she moved toward the closed blinds over the small copy room window and peeked out through the side. She'd left the outer lights off, but she could see the outline of a tall, thin man at one of the desks.

She gasped as the man turned. Dear God! It was Derrick.

When he glanced in her direction, Emily jumped back. She'd never been a good liar. If he found her here, she knew she'd never be able to talk her way out. He'd only have to look at her face to know what she'd discovered, and he'd be furious. She couldn't confront him yet, not until she talked to Uncle Carlo.

Pressing her back to the wall, she waited until she finally heard the outer door close. Slowly she released the breath she'd been holding. To be sure he'd left the plant, she'd wait a while before she came out. She could take no chances that he might return and find her putting the file back in his desk, or discover her on her way out with the copies she'd made.

After several minutes, there were still no sounds, except for the soft ticking of the copy room wall clock and the beating of her own heart. The office was quiet. Thank goodness. She breathed a sigh of relief. She'd wait two more minutes and—

Once again she froze. And sniffed.

Smoke.

She flipped on the lamp again and glanced down. Thin ribbons of wispy gray smoke curled up from underneath the door.

Oh God, no—

She shoved the blinds apart and looked out. Flames shot up from the middle of the office and were spreading quickly across the room.

Why hadn't the alarm gone off? And why hadn't the sprinklers come on? Unless Derrick—

No! She couldn't believe that he would do such a terrible thing. Selling secret formulas was one thing, but arson was another. He couldn't—*wouldn't*—commit such a heinous crime.

She grabbed her purse and both files. There'd be no time to replace the original back into Derrick's desk, but she couldn't think about that now. She had to get out quickly, before the fire completely engulfed the office. Since there was no window to the outside from the copy room, she had no choice but to make a dash across the outer office and hopefully skirt the flames. If she could get to the windows overlooking the street two stories below, she could attract someone's attention. If worse came to worst—and she prayed it wouldn't—she would have to jump.

She gulped in air, then threw open the door and ran. A blast of heat made her stumble, but she recovered and kept going. In the distance she heard the wail of sirens and the sound gave her hope. They're coming, she thought as the wail and the deep sound of horns grew louder. They're almost here.

The fire crackled around her, sparks flew, singeing her face and bare legs. The smoke burned her throat and her eyes. But she made it to the window, and was reaching for the handle when the sound of a loud crack from behind her made her whip her head around. She watched in horror as the heavy steel bindings that supported the dropped ceiling gave way. Like a giant zipper opening, the ceiling ripped apart, raining metal and plaster tiles. Frantic, Emily turned back to the window, but the crack overhead rushed toward her like a hideous, furious monster.

Helpless to stop it, she went down.

Also, look out for the next story from

DYNASTIES: THE BARONES.

Beauty & the Blue Angel

by Maureen Child

*is on sale in May 2004 in a two-in-one volume
with* Where There's Smoke…
by Barbara McCauley.

Beauty & the Blue Angel

by

Maureen Child

Daisy Cusak ignored the ribbon of pain snaking through her. "Just a twinge," she whispered, then ran the flat of her hand across her swollen belly. "Come on, sweetie, don't do this to Mommy, okay?"

The pains had been intermittent all day, but she'd brushed them off. All of the books said there was nothing to worry about until contractions were steady and just a few minutes apart. Well heck. One every hour and a half or so wasn't anything to worry about, right?

Besides, on a busy Friday night, she could make a lot of tip money serving dinner at Antonio's Italian restaurant. And right now, those tips would mean a lot.

All around her, the noise of the kitchen rattled. Pans clashing, chefs cursing, expensive china plates clicking together. It was music of a sort. And the waiters and waitresses were the dancers.

She'd been doing this for four years and she was darn good at it. Okay, so some people wouldn't exactly consider being a waitress a "career." But Daisy didn't have a problem with that. She loved her job. She met new people every night, had a few regulars who would wait an extra half hour just to get seated in her station, and her bosses, the Contis, were just so darn nice to work for.

Rather than fire her for being pregnant, the Conti family was continually urging her to sit down, get off her feet. Someone was always near to help her with the heavier trays and she'd already been assured that her job would be waiting for her after she took some time off with the baby.

"You'll see," she said, smiling down at the mound of her child. "It's going to be great. *We're* going to be great."

"Everything all right, Daisy?"

She turned abruptly and grinned at Joan, one of the other waitresses. "Sure. I'm good."

The other woman looked as though she didn't believe her, and Daisy silently wished she was just a little bit better at lying.

"Why don't you take a break?" Joan said. "I'll cover your tables for you."

"It's okay," Daisy answered firmly, willing not only Joan, but herself, to believe it. "I'm fine. Honest."

Her friend gave her a worried frown, then stacked

two plates of veal parmigiana on her serving tray. "Okay, but I've got my eye on you."

Along with everyone else at Antonio's, Daisy thought. She picked up a pot of coffee, pushed through the Out door and walked into the main dining room. Casual elegance flavored the room. Snowy white linens draped the tables, candles flickered wildly within the crystal hurricane globes and the soft strains of weeping violin music drifted from the overhead speakers.

Above the music came the comfortable murmur of voices, punctuated every once in a while by someone's laughter. Wineglasses clinked, forks and knives clattered against the china, and men and women dressed in starched white shirts and creased black trousers moved through the crowd with choreographed precision.

Daisy smiled at her customers as she offered more coffee and took orders. She bent to grin at a toddler, strapped into his high chair and laughing over the spaghetti he'd rubbed into his hair. Most of the wait staff hated having kids at their stations. It usually meant lost time when the customers left, because the mess left behind had to be totally cleaned before anyone else could be seated. And lost time meant lost money.

But Daisy had always loved kids. Even the messy, cranky ones. Which, Joan had told her too many times to count, made Daisy nuts.

A group of men in their thirties followed the hostess and began to thread their way through the maze of tables to the huge, dark maroon leather booth at the back of Daisy's station. As they passed, she caught a look of apology from the hostess seating them. Four men would be big eaters and probably end up running Daisy's legs off. On the bright side though, they might turn out to be good tippers, too. And she was always trying to beef up the nest egg building ever so slowly in the bank.

Another pain twisted inside her, this time sharply, briefly, in the middle of her back, and Daisy stiffened up in reaction. *Oh, no, honey. Not now.*

As if her baby heard that silent plea, the pain drifted away into nothing more than a slow, nagging ache. And that she could handle.

All she had to do was get through the next couple of hours and she'd be home free.

All he had to do was get through the next couple of hours and he'd be home free. At least, that's what Alex Barone kept telling himself.

He was the last to be seated and caught himself damn near perched on the edge of the leather banquette—as if ready to hit the floor running. When that thought flashed through his mind, he gritted his teeth and eased back on the bench seat. Damned if he'd feel guilty for coming into a restaurant.

Damned if he'd worry about the ramifications.

Although, if he'd known his friends were going to choose Antonio's restaurant, he might have bowed out. No point in going out of his way to antagonize an old family enemy. He glanced around at the place and smiled to himself.

As a Barone, he'd been raised with stories that

made the Conti family sound like demons. But if this was their hell, they'd made a nice place of it. Dim lighting, soft music and scents coming out of the kitchen that nearly made him groan in anticipation.

Nearly every table was full and the wait staff looked busy as ground troops settling in for a big campaign. That thought brought a smile. He'd been in the military too long.

While his friends laughed and talked, Alex let his gaze drift around the room again, keeping a watchful eye out for any loose Contis. But none of them knew Alex personally, and what were the chances he'd be recognized as a Barone? Slim to none.

So he was just going to relax, have dinner, then leave with no one the wiser.

And then in the next instant, all thoughts of leaving raced from his brain.

"Hello, my name is Daisy and I'll be your server tonight."

A gorgeous woman seemed to appear out of nowhere, standing right beside Alex as she gave the whole table a smile wide and bright enough to light up all the shadows in the room.

A purely male instinct had Alex straightening up in his seat for a closer, more thorough look. Her long, curly chestnut hair was caught at the nape of her neck with a slightly tarnished silver barrette. Her eyes weren't quite blue or green, but a tantalizing combination of both. Her pale skin looked satin smooth and soft, her voice held just a hint of humor, and Alex's interest was piqued—until her enormous belly nearly bumped him as she shifted position on what had to be tired feet.

Pregnant.

Taken.

Well, damn. Disappointment shot through him. His gaze dropped automatically to her ring finger, but she wasn't wearing a ring. There wasn't even a white mark to indicate there might have been one there at some point.

He frowned at himself. Not married? What kind of moron would walk away from a woman like this? Especially if she was carrying his child?

"Hello-o-o, Daisy," one of the guys, Mike Hannigan, said on a slow whistle of approval.

Alex shot him a disgusted look, but apparently it didn't bother the woman at all.

"Can I start you out with some drinks? Appetizers?" she asked as she handed around several long menus.

"Beers all around," Nick Santee ordered, and she nodded as she made a note on her order tablet.

"Your phone number?" Tim Hawkins ventured.

She grinned, and the full, megawatt force of that smile hit Alex like a fist to the gut. Damn, this was one potent female, even in her condition.

"Sure," she said, rubbing one hand along her belly. "It's 1-800-*way*-too-pregnant."

Then she turned and walked off to get their drinks. While the guys laughed and kidded Tim about his lousy pickup skills, Alex half turned in his seat to follow her progress through the restaurant. She had a bounce in her step that he liked. The smile on her face wavered only once, when she grimaced, dropped one hand to her belly and seemed almost as if she were comforting the child within.

And who, he wondered, comforted *her?*

As the evening wore on, his interest in her only sharpened. When she brought the pitcher of beer and four glasses, he slid out of the booth to take the heavy tray from her.

"Oh. I'm okay, really."

"Never said you weren't, ma'am."

She looked up at him and he decided that her eyes were more blue than green.

"It's Daisy. Just Daisy."

He nodded, standing there, holding a tray full of drinks and looking down into fathomless eyes that seemed to draw him deeper with every passing second. "I'm Alex."

She licked her lips, pulled in a shuddering breath and let it go again. "Well, thanks for the help...Alex."

"No problem."

He unloaded the beers, handed her back the empty tray and then stood in the aisle watching her walk away.

"Hey, Barone," Nick called, and Alex flinched, hoping no one else had heard his last name.

"What?"

One of the guys laughed.

Nick said, "You gonna sit down and have a beer, or do you want to go on back to the kitchen and help her out there, too?"

Embarrassed to be caught fantasizing about a

pregnant woman, Alex grinned and took his seat. Reaching for his beer, he took a long drink, hoping the icy-cold brew would help stamp out the fires within.

But still, he couldn't help watching her. She should be tired. Yet her energy never seemed to flag. And she was stronger than her fragile build indicated. She lifted heavy trays with ease and kept to such a fast pace, he was pretty sure if she'd been walking in a straight line, she'd have made it to Cleveland by now.

"Geez, Barone," Nick muttered as he leaned in. "Get a grip. There're lots of pretty women in Boston. Do you have to home in on one who's obviously taken?"

"Who's homing in?" Alex countered, but silently reminded himself that she wasn't "taken." At least not by a man who appreciated her enough to marry her. "I'm just—"

"Window-shopping?" Tim asked.

"Close your hole," Mike told him.

Alex glanced around at the men gathered at the table. Men he'd known for years. Like him, navy pilots, they were the guys he'd trained with, studied with and flown with. There was a bond between them that even family couldn't match.

And yet...right now, he wished them all to the Antarctic.

Stupid, but he wanted their waitress to himself.

When she set their check on the edge of the table, Alex picked it up quickly, his fingertips brushing across hers. She drew back fast, almost as if she'd felt the same snap of electricity he had. Which was some kind of weird. She was pregnant, for Pete's sake. Very pregnant. Which should have put her off-limits.

"So, are you guys shipping out now?" Daisy asked, trying to keep her gaze from drifting toward the man sitting so close to her.

His friends were easier to deal with. They were friendly, charming, casually flirtatious. Like most of the navy men she'd waited on at Antonio's. And she'd treated them as she did all of her customers. With polite friendliness and nothing more.

Since the day Jeff had called her a man-trap and walked out the door, leaving behind not only her, but his unborn child, Daisy hadn't given any man a second look. Until tonight. This one man—Alex— with the dark brown eyes and sharp-as-a-razor cheekbones was different. She'd known it the minute he looked at her. And the feeling had only grown over the last hour and a half.

She'd felt his gaze on her most of the night and didn't even want to think about the feelings that dark, steady stare engendered.

Hormones.

That had to be the reason.

Her hormones were out of whack because of the baby.

"No," Alex said, and she steeled herself to meet that gaze head-on. "We're on leave, actually."

"Are you from Boston?" she asked, and told herself she was only being friendly. Just as she would with any other customer. But even she didn't believe it.

There was just something about this man that—

"I was raised here," he was saying.

One of the other men spoke up, but his voice was like a buzz in her ears. All she heard, all she could see was the man watching her through the darkest, warmest eyes she'd ever seen.

"You have...*family* here?"

A slow, wicked smile curved one side of his mouth and her stomach jittered. "Yeah, I come from a big family. I'm the fifth of eight kids."

She dropped one hand to the mound of her belly. "Eight. That must be nice."

"Not when I was a kid," he admitted. "Too many people fighting over the TV and cookies."

Daisy smiled at the mental image of a houseful of children, laughing, happy. Then sadly, she let it go. It was something she'd never known and now her baby, too, would grow up alone.

No. Not alone. Her baby would always have *her*.

His friends eased out of the booth and headed for the front of the restaurant. Alex watched them go, nodded, then reached into his wallet for a few bills. He handed her the money and the check and said, "Keep the change."

"Thanks. I mean—" He was leaving. Probably just as well, she told herself. And yet, she felt oddly reluctant to let him walk away.

"What are you doing in my restaurant?"

Daisy spun around to watch in amazement as Salvatore Conti, her boss, came rushing out of the kitchen, flapping a pristine white dish towel, like some crazed matador looking for a bull.

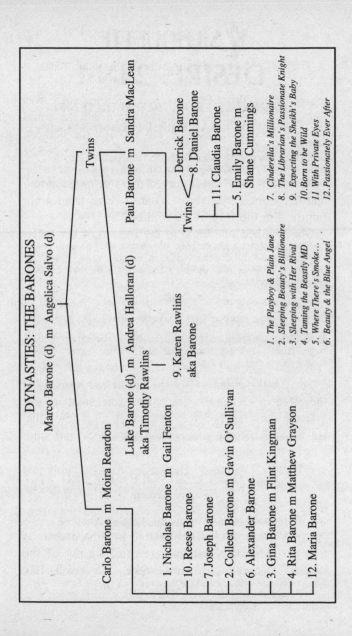

DYNASTIES: THE BARONES

Marco Barone (d) m Angelica Salvo (d)

Carlo Barone m Moira Reardon

Luke Barone (d) m Andrea Halloran (d)
aka Timothy Rawlins

9. Karen Rawlins
aka Barone

Paul Barone m Sandra MacLean

Twins

Twins ⎰ Derrick Barone
       ⎱ 8. Daniel Barone

11. Claudia Barone

5. Emily Barone m
Shane Cummings

1. Nicholas Barone m Gail Fenton
10. Reese Barone
7. Joseph Barone
2. Colleen Barone m Gavin O'Sullivan
6. Alexander Barone
3. Gina Barone m Flint Kingman
4. Rita Barone m Matthew Grayson
12. Maria Barone

1. *The Playboy & Plain Jane*
2. *Sleeping Beauty's Billionaire*
3. *Sleeping with Her Rival*
4. *Taming the Beastly MD*
5. *Where There's Smoke…*
6. *Beauty & the Blue Angel*
7. *Cinderella's Millionaire*
8. *The Librarian's Passionate Knight*
9. *Expecting the Sheikh's Baby*
10. *Born to be Wild*
11. *With Private Eyes*
12. *Passionately Ever After*

♥ SILHOUETTE®
DESIRE™ 2-IN-1

0304/51a

AVAILABLE FROM 19TH MARCH 2004

THAT BLACKHAWK BRIDE Barbara McCauley

Secrets

Clair Beauchamp was handed the perfect escape from a loveless marriage by PI Jacob Carver, and on the journey together to find her family they gave way to mindless passion. Was this taste of heaven theirs to keep...?

BILLIONAIRE BACHELORS: GRAY
Anne Marie Winston

Catherine Thorne couldn't explain why she felt so at home in Gray MacInnes's powerful embrace—after all, he was a stranger, wasn't he? Gray had the heart of another man beating in his chest... Did he have his memories, too?

RENEGADE MILLIONAIRE Kristi Gold

Dr Rio Madrid's kisses had left Joanna Blake swooning, and when they started to work together she was on the verge of accepting his dangerously tempting invitation...

THE GENTRYS: CINCO Linda Conrad

The Gentrys

When Air Force captain Meredith Powell was forced to stay at Cinco Gentry's ranch for her own safety, she had to resist him at every turn, until danger forced her into his passionate embrace.

MAIL ORDER PRINCE IN HER BED
Kathryn Jensen

Maria McPherson's birthday present from her colleagues was supposed to be a fake—but handsome Prince Antonio Boniface was the real thing—and he was more than willing to teach her all about love...

HEARTS ARE WILD Laura Wright

Maggie O'Connor might have had no experience with men, but that didn't mean she couldn't find the right matches for her female clients...until she met dangerous Nick Kaplan, who was no one's perfect man—let alone hers!

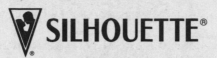

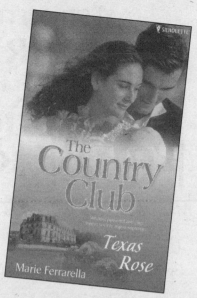

SILHOUETTE®
DESIRE™

are proud to introduce

DYNASTIES:
THE BARONES

Meet the wealthy Barones—caught in a web of danger, deceit and...desire!

Twelve exciting stories in six 2-in-1 volumes:

SILHOUETTE®
SPECIAL EDITION™

proudly presents

a brand-new five-book series from
bestselling author

SHERRYL WOODS

The Devaneys

Five brothers torn apart in childhood,
reunited by love!

RYAN'S PLACE
December 2003

SEAN'S RECKONING
January 2004

MICHAEL'S DISCOVERY
February 2004

PATRICK'S DESTINY
March 2004

DANIEL'S DESIRE
April 2004

1203/SH/LC75

SHERRYL WOODS

along came trouble

In Trinity Harbour, a little trouble breathes new life into an old love. . .

On sale 16th April 2004

Available at most branches of WH Smith, Tesco, Martins, Borders, Eason, Sainsbury's and all good paperback bookshops.

0504/047/SH74

FREE

2 BOOKS
AND A SURPRISE GIFT!

We would like to take this opportunity to thank you for reading this Silhouette® book by offering you the chance to take two more specially selected titles from the Desire™ series absolutely FREE! We're also making this offer to introduce you to the benefits of the Reader Service™—

★ FREE home delivery   ★ FREE gifts and competitions
★ FREE monthly Newsletter   ★ Exclusive Reader Service discount
★ Books available before they're in the shops

Accepting these FREE books and gift places you under no obligation to buy; you may cancel at any time, even after receiving your free shipment. Simply complete your details below and return the entire page to the address below. *You don't even need a stamp!*

YES! Please send me 2 free Desire books and a surprise gift. I understand that unless you hear from me, I will receive 3 superb new titles every month for just £4.99 each, postage and packing free. I am under no obligation to purchase any books and may cancel my subscription at any time. The free books and gift will be mine to keep in any case.

D4ZEF

Ms/Mrs/Miss/Mr ....Initials.................................
BLOCK CAPITALS PLEASE

Surname...

Address..

....

....Postcode ....

Send this whole page to:
UK: FREEPOST CN81, Croydon, CR9 3WZ
EIRE: PO Box 4546, Kilcock, County Kildare (stamp required)